C.20

Grand River and Joy

SWEETWATER FICTION: ORIGINALS

GRAND RIVER AND JOY

Susan Messer

The University of Michigan Press
Ann Arbor

Copyright © 2009 by Susan Messer
All rights reserved
Published in the United States of America by
The University of Michigan Press
Manufactured in the United States of America
⊗ Printed on acid-free paper

2012   2011   2010   2009   4 3 2 1

A CIP catalog record for this book is available from the British Library.

Library of Congress Cataloging-in-Publication Data

Messer, Susan, 1948–
Grand River and joy / Susan Messer.
    p.   cm. — (Sweetwater fiction: originals)
    ISBN-13: 978-0-472-11699-7 (cloth : alk. paper)
    ISBN-10: 0-472-11699-1 (cloth : alk. paper)
    I. Title.
PS3613.E7893G73   2009
813'.6—dc22   2009004568

ISBN 978-0-472-02210-6 (e-book)

For Shavey and Martin

ACKNOWLEDGMENTS

Among too many to thank, I must mention William Colburn, my guide and inspiration through all things Detroit; Jimmy Darley, for the bicycle giveaway; Russ Gibb, for his memories of the Grande Ballroom; Phil Herbst, for the *Color of Words: An Encyclopaedic Dictionary of Ethnic Bias in the United States;* early readers Stephen Huth and Rita Cashman (so sad that Rita couldn't be here to see that I followed her advice); William LeFevre, archivist extraordinaire at Wayne State University's Walter P. Reuther Library; Lilah Lohr, for canine and Doberman insights; the regulars at Molly Malone's open mic (second Monday of every month), for giving me a place to read my work all these years; Linda and James Moody for the zebra joke; Tim Stefl and the boiler pros at The Wall (heatinghelp.com) for expertise, counsel, and entertainment; walking partners Linda Bauer, for emotional support "through all kinds of weather," and Etta Worthington, for deciding to create a community of writers and knowing I needed to be part of it before even *I* knew I was a writer.

Gratitude to Colleen Mohyde, my agent, for embracing this project and finding it a meaningful home; Chris Hebert, my editor, for being so skillful a guide; Carol Sickman-Garner, my copyeditor, for the detail work that makes so much difference; Scott Griffith and Marcia LaBrenz at the Press, for their competence and kindness; Judy Budnitz, Nadine Epstein, the Karma Foundation, and *Moment* magazine for granting first prize to the short story from which this novel grew; the welcoming staff of Ragdale for providing a room of one's own (with a view); and finally, Jim and Selena, who are at the heart of the heart.

CONTENTS

BOYS

He was working with his sister at the time. So it was just the two of them. And he stopped to pick her up on the way down, which was how he described the trip. "I'm heading down," he would say to her, when he called before leaving the house. "Are you ready?"

All he meant by "down," or all he thought he meant, was that the route to the business took him more toward downtown than not. He drove his silvery-blue Dodge Dart, a new model, 1966, through the streets of his neighborhood, over to hers, the autumn elms and oaks and sugar maples arching over the streets, stopping in front of her house, her waiting on the porch when the weather was fine, as it was that day. A perfect golden day for Halloween—something you couldn't rely on in the Midwest.

They said their hellos, Harry and Ilo, not much new since yesterday. He'd come to feel that this was his life, and this was how it would be, from today until tomorrow and on and on. Not a bad life. With his wife. His daughters. Your basic comforts. Summer vacations at the Michigan lakes, the great and the small. Then he and Ilo were nearing the end of their well-worn route *down*, making the turn onto Grand River, crossing Joy Road.

It was Detroit, and by 1966, Grand River south of Joy was all concrete and brick, with barely a tree or shrub, barely a patch of grass.

Joy Road—now there was a misnomer. That stretch had broken windows and traffic snarls, and grown men with nothing to do during the day. Up and down these broad streets, buses belched clouds of black smoke as they roared past the metal-grated building faces. And as if inviting trouble, Levine's was the only business along the stretch that lacked one of those grates.

Whenever Harry talked about the place, his sisters-in-law and cousins, with their stiff beauty-parlor bouffants and manicures, held their faces and said *schwarze* this and *schwarze* that. Same for the big-bellied brothers-in-law with their ruby pinkie rings and slicked-back hair.

On Grand River, the un-grated Levine Wholesale Shoes stood beside the tiny White Castle hamburger building with its crude crenellated top. Across the street and down a few blocks was the magnificent, decaying Riviera Theatre, or "the Iviera," as his sister called it. The *R* in the towering vertical marquee had become a jagged hole; farther down, the upper bar of the *E* appeared gangrenous, and the final *R* and *A* were also festering.

In the alley behind the business, two small boys scuffed along, kicking the alley stones as they went on their way to school. Ilo checked the door locks. The boys switched to single file, so Harry's car could pass.

"No costumes," Harry said.

"Halloween's for people who've got something to give away," Ilo said. She shifted her purse from lap to floor.

Harry pulled into the parking space under the wooden fire escape that led to the upstairs apartment. Curtis, Harry's tenant, stood on the landing.

Harry waved to him as he got out of the car. It was a warm day, with a Technicolor blue sky, promising a smooth road, straight through to evening; a gift for the children, who could run through the leaves without blustery-cold wind or driving rain, without arguments about sweaters that would bulk out costumes, or stupid coats that would obscure them entirely.

"Morning, Mr. Levine," Curtis said. "Any work today?"

It was a gift, too, in a way, to have Curtis upstairs, available whenever Harry needed him. But also, in a way, a burden of responsibility whenever he didn't. "We'll see what we've got," Harry said.

Harry tended to the keys, the unlocking, and Ilo followed him into the whole familiar cloud of smells, old and new, musty and fusty: wood and brick and rubber, leather and canvas, cardboard and jute. The two did their morning chores: turning off the burglar alarm, closing the metal bars behind them, snapping the padlock, then closing the big wooden door, fastening the two dead bolts, straightening the rows of shoe boxes in the aisles of gray metal shelving that reached practically to the ceiling, and checking the thermostat near the bathroom door. Harry asking Ilo what she thought about having Sappho, his family's Doberman, for the evening so the barking wouldn't chase the trick-ortreaters away, Ilo saying "Oh, all right. Two old maids spending the night together." Harry saying thanks. Coming along, coming up the hall, doing this little job and that, arriving in the front.

The front of the building was composed of two rooms. In one, a simple window display: three pairs of old-fashioned lace-up boots in black and brown, mini-torture chambers, with their needle-point toes so narrow through the foot and up the ankle that they suggested severe structural damage. Harry's father—that was Joe—who had started the business, had found them in the cave-like basement of the building they'd owned on West Jefferson. He brought them along when they moved to this new address, left them behind when he moved to Florida and then died shortly after, willing the building and everything in it to Harry. Not that Harry had ever wanted it. Not that Harry was any kind of expert on what he wanted, mostly afraid to want anything.

Ilo had placed those old shoes in the window, on a wooden table below the dark-green arcing letters that said "J. Levine Wholesale Shoes." She dusted them once a week and polished them once a year, with brushes and buffing cloths, and fussed with the arrangement, adding seasonal accessories, as if she were a window decorator at J. L. Hudson's, Detroit's big downtown department store. Harry said nothing about her display, as he said nothing about much of what she did, in their long history of brother-sister silence. But he did like having the shoes there, as they seemed to elevate their business, along with the concept of shoe, into the sweep of history, one chapter in the world's march toward human comfort, toward understanding the health function of a foot in a shoe.

Because of the chores, the routine, on the way up the hall to the two front rooms, Harry didn't see, or notice, the front window until the Halloween-morning sun glinted off it full on. And because he'd never seen anything like this before on his own front window, but because he had seen pictures, and because a deep ancestral memory of facing something like this was stored in a brain region that science had not yet identified, he now had a conjunction of shock and recognition, a sense that he'd always expected it, but that it didn't hurt any less for the expecting.

And because Ilo always came up behind him, as if to say, let him be the first to face whatever happened during the night, let him be the scout, and because she had stopped in the ancient bathroom, where the door didn't close all the way because of the warping and the layer upon ageless layer of paint, to check her lipstick—lipstick of all things, in a place like this. And because she was about to see the same front window he'd seen, he moved quickly in front of it and fooled with the old-fashioned shoes, thinking he might cover what he'd seen or simply distract her so she wouldn't see, or distract himself so that he wouldn't see, wouldn't fully see. Of course, the letters were backwards, when viewed from the inside, but it was surprising how many of them worked either way.

Ilo said it out loud. It was written in soap in big block letters—the *honky* and the *Jew* in horizontal bands, one above the other, and the *boy* below in a vertical that dead ended at the store's name. Dead ended because the writer or soaper had used the Levine *v* to make the boy *y*, crudely artful, like on a Scrabble board—triple word score. *Honky Jew boy.*

And, too, it looked as though the *o* of the *boy* could drop into the open arms of the *v*, now a funnel *y*, and then lodge there in the throat if the passage was too narrow, or if not, perhaps slip right through and become impaled, skewered, on the second *l* in *Wholesale*, like a Greek letter or a marshmallow on a stick.

If you were Harry, you could Scrabble it any which way, turn it into a game, like they did with the children on long car trips—playing I spy, or telling the girls to find all the letters of the alphabet on the signs they passed, and the first one who found them all was the winner. "Do license plates count?" Joanna, the middle daughter, always asked, as if there were an official set of rules for these made-up distractor games.

"Honky Jew boy?" Ilo said again, in that reading-group-2 way, where each word is a separate entity rather than a meaningful link in a chain.

Harry remembered what Ruth, his wife, said: that the word *Jew*, by itself, could sound ugly, spit out. It was better when softened with the *ish* ending, as in short-ish or small-ish, suggesting not exactly short or small but somewhat.

"At least it wasn't a brick," he said.

They stood near the window. He thought about how they might go on with the day, how they might move on to business, like any other day. His instinct was to minimize, something he'd learned to do in a house full of females, a wife and three daughters, whose emotional responses to him more often than not seemed overwrought, unnecessary. He had learned to balance, to offset, as on a teeter totter, with Ruth and the girls massed at one far end, and him, maintaining the weight and the force to keep them in balance.

"If you'd put up a grate like all the other business owners, like I've been telling you," Ilo said. She was always scolding, always telling, always what she'd said before, who hadn't listened, who hadn't understood what she so long ago had grasped, told, instructed.

"Some kid on Devil's night. Don't make a big deal." Devil's night, what they called it in Detroit—the mischief-making before Halloween, when kids soaped windows, toilet-papered trees and bushes, slathered shaving cream on sidewalks, rung doorbells, and smashed eggs. Those were innocent days.

"Oh yeah," Ilo said. "Trick or treat." Her hands in fists, on hips, her head shaking.

"I'll get Curtis to clean it," Harry said. He went to his desk.

His desk was in the other front room, set off by a wood-and-glass partition. In it were the two desks, an adding machine and phone on each, a black Underwood on Ilo's, the big old safe that Joe bought when he first started in business and that he lugged with him from West Jefferson to Grand River, along with the old-fashioned shoes. Both Harry and Ilo knew the combination, and every night, they opened it to store their petty cash, their checkbooks, their bookkeeping ledgers. And every morning, they reopened it to take out what they needed for the daily business.

Harry opened the safe, his fingers on the cool metal dial, his focus on the whirs and clicks of a reliable old lock. He shuffled through the pink order forms, the ones he needed to fill and deliver today. Keeping busy. That was his way.

"You could get his son to clean it, seeing he's probably the one who did it." She meant Alvin, Curtis's son, with the heavy-lidded slit-eyes and unsmiling lips that said he'd already seen enough to know how much was wrong with the way things worked. Alvin, with his head so finely sculpted it might belong to a mannequin, his flat smudged eyebrows, as if thumbed on with finger paint. Alvin, with the beautiful voice that could go to falsetto. Harry heard him singing all around the building— upstairs through the floorboards, out in back when the windows were open.

He ran his knuckle over his mustache. He had a high forehead, and

5

significant, dark eyebrows, a roof over each dark eye, black wavy hair that made you think of Xavier Cugat, south of the border. "There's no way to know it was Alvin."

"No," she said. She fiddled with her window display—small gourds in oranges and greens, striped and mottled, with odd ridges and nose-like protrusions, each distinctive, lying on a bed of brown oak leaves she'd collected from her yard, with *Honky Jew Boy* as their backdrop. "Could be one of his friends." She joined Harry in the office.

"You think someone would do that to the place they live?" He shuffled through the papers on his desk. "Now tell me why someone would do that to their home."

She made the sound in the throat, a sarcastic cough, that declares the question ridiculous, undeserving of an answer. She sat at her desk. "What are you? Anne Frank?"

Foot traffic picked up on the sidewalk. Buses pulled up at the stop near Levine's front door, letting people on, off. People changed places, all around the city, a big game of musical chairs. People passing on the bus looked at Harry's window, people getting off the bus saw it, too, carrying the questions and private thoughts away with them, into their own days, perhaps telling the story to someone else, what they'd seen, what it meant.

"Soaped windows, okay, they're an annoyance," Ilo said. "But they're in the range." She went back to the window. "*This*," she said, "is not in the range." People at the bus stop, whose gazes were usually fixed down the street, as if the act of watching summoned the bus, stole glances at the defaced window. They emerged from the customary isolation to talk among themselves. Heads shaking, shoulders shrugging, embarrassed by what the words said, unsure how to respond, whether to be caught looking.

"If you won't do something," Ilo said, "I will. You have to show them."

"Show them what?" Harry asked. "Show who?"

"That you're not afraid."

"Who said I'm afraid?" Everywhere he went, from home to work to home, it was women, telling him what he felt, what he was, what he wasn't, what kind of mistakes he was making. "I told you I'll take care of it."

"What do you mean 'take care of it'?" It was a good question. Preserve? Coddle?

6

"Clean it off," he said. They spoke to each other this way—clipped, devoid of commiseration, not wanting to feel. He pushed his chair back from the desk.

"You don't want to know who did it?" she asked.

"And once we know?"

"When we call the police, that's for them to decide."

He was on his way to the storage closet. His back was turned to her. "We're not calling the police."

"Oh, you." The gesture she threw after him, a silent, empty over-hand pitch, was one of their mother's, imprinted early, meaning that an argument may have been lost but it wasn't over, that once again being overruled, censored, made powerless, left her wanting to fling something at the censor. "The cleaning stuff is in the storage closet," she called after him. "Or down in the basement." Curtis had used it last, when he washed the window the other day. She'd seen him working, making sure to catch every drip, checking for smudges both inside and out. She got up, as if she would follow Harry, to make sure he heard her, but the phone rang, a loud ring, echoing through the building.

"Hallo," she said, the accent on the first syllable, impatient, as if it were her hundredth of the morning. She pulled the order pad from the shelf, lifted a pencil from the gas-station jelly jar, settled into her chair and checked off boxes, filling numbers into columns. "Uh huh," she said. "Yup. Nope. Anything else?"

Oh, how she wanted to tell the customer what had happened, the window, the words, Harry's response versus hers, to tell on him, his dismissal of a weighty matter. But something stopped her. Loyalty. Obedience. Work ethic. "Twelve women's eights?" she said. "Navy or white?"

"Ilo," Harry yelled. He was in the storage closet. "Where's the bucket?" She didn't answer. He rifled, and finding nothing he wanted, backed out. And so, to the basement. There, Harry stored the extra shoe inventory. It was Curtis, mainly, who carried the shoe boxes down when a shipment came, sorting them by size, and arranging them on the shelves. The staircase was narrow, the steps uneven and worn, so balancing the stacks of eight or ten shoe boxes at a time, while watching one's footwork, was difficult, sweaty, and repetitive. Bringing them up again to restock the upstairs shelves was no picnic either. Still, Curtis did it without complaint, though Harry often apologized for it.

At the bottom of the stairs were two big inventory rooms, one on either side of the long hallway, and they were filled with long rows of high metal shelving, like the ones upstairs, and stacked with tan and white boxes, patiently waiting to be called to duty. Beyond those rooms was the furnace room, with the huge old boiler, its pipes reaching up and out through the basement ceiling.

Beyond the boiler were the rooms where he stored business records—some going back to the forties—and other mysterious detritus from the building on Jefferson that they had brought along but never looked at again. In those rooms, also, they stored the contents of Ruth's parents' house—moved here after both had died. Storage: the solution to the problem of not being able to part with something, but not being able to use it either. Upstairs, he could hear Ilo, the rollers of her chair on the wooden floor, the phone, her heels clicking as she moved from the desk to the file cabinet and back.

He pulled the light chains as he went deeper in, to one of the rooms behind the furnace, where Curtis perhaps had left the ladder and the buckets. As he moved from pull chain to pull chain, he felt like a chimpanzee, brachiating, as his Lena, the daughter studying anthropology, called it, and swatting away the cobwebs.

Light from bare bulbs revealed cartons stacked in corners, labeled with magic marker: Pesach dishes, linens, records 1950–1960, photos. And in the pile, a small dust-covered box, small enough for a bird you might find in the backyard. Harry's prototype. The baby shoes he had designed all those years ago.

And, beside it, cobwebby, was an item of high dispute among Ruth and her siblings: the pieces of Ruth's father's *sukkah*—the little house he constructed in the backyard every spring, where they ate their meals during the full-moon festival of Sukkos. None of the siblings put up a *sukkah* in their own yard, and as Harry had predicted, none ever would. So down it went, to the basement of J. Levine Wholesale Shoes—the bottomless repository of lost traditions and small, painful reminders.

He wound through the small windowless rooms, past the business and family history, and when he brachiated into the next room, pulling the chain on the next light bulb, he wasn't sure what he was seeing. He had to blink once, twice, like they did in cartoons. The room had been made into something, someone's notion of a clubhouse, or a living room. Carpet samples, a mix of colors and textures, were pieced together to cover the floor. Mismatched chairs were arranged in a ragged circle. Two were of the narrow wooden folding variety one saw in shul basements. In fact, they probably were from a shul—Ruth's father's old chairs, that he had carried back and forth to the shul when the congregation needed extras, and that had ended up in Harry's basement when no one knew what else to do with them.

Also in the circle was a fifties-style stuffed armchair with no legs, a dingy plaid couch with worn arms that had an old brocade curtain thrown over it. The circle included three metal lawn chairs with broad shell-shaped backs. Ruth's parents' coffee table, covered with books and papers in neat piles. An end table, and a carved onyx lamp with a torn lampshade, also from Ruth's parents' house. Ashtrays, overflowing. Marijuana cigarettes, whole ones and parts, lay in and around the ashtrays. Harry recognized them from the pictures in *Time* and *Newsweek*.

Above, again, Ilo's movements, her spike heels drumming against the wooden floor on her way to the bathroom. He followed her footsteps through the building to the basement stairs, tap-tapping.

"Harry," she called. "What are you doing?"

What he didn't want was for her to come down. Because down here, there were even more discoveries: A small red record player, set into a leatherette box with a handle, like a suitcase. Albums. On the top one, five Negro men, made to look as friendly and safe as possible, all dressed alike, in bright blue suit jackets with skinny velveteen lapels, velveteen bowties, and black pocket handkerchiefs to match the lapels and bowties. Their shirts had French cuffs and gold cufflinks, and they all had amazing sculpted hair. The Temptations.

"I'll be up in a minute," he called. He heard her hesitate, then the spike-heel tapping, back to her desk and her work, the bookkeeping, the columns of numbers entered in the little boxes on the ledger sheets. On the wall above her desk was the index card with the emergency phone numbers—police, fire department. It had been her idea, to hang one there, and one on the wall next to Harry's desk too.

On the basement floor, beside the couch, was a powder-blue phone—one of those new princess phones, the kind Joanna had begged for. As if talking into a phone like this one with its sleek lines would somehow make life different or better—more princess-like. The peculiar thing about this phone was that Curtis and Alvin didn't have phone service.

So what was this princess phone doing here? He bent, picked it up, heard the dial tone, the sign of life and connection, and put it down. "How the heck . . . ?" He followed the tangle of multicolored wires, reaching out to touch here and there, as if to assure himself they were real. At the end, on the far side of the room, the main wire hooked in with Harry's own phone box in a jumble that despite its wild appearance had generated a dial tone.

He returned to the coffee table, covered with books and papers. He sat. He perused. *The Autobiography of Malcolm X.* Harry, of course, knew the man's history, a self-educated man, a former thug, who'd become a leader, lived in Detroit at one time, then was assassinated, just last year. He'd seen the pictures in the paper, the stern eyes, the close-cropped hair, the black-topped glasses, always dressed in a suit and tie (but not the cheerful blue kind of the Temptations). Always the pointing finger, saying whatever he liked—that Kennedy's assassination was the chickens coming home to roost, that revolution was what the Negro needed, that revolution was always violent, and that locking arms and singing "We Shall Overcome" was no kind of revolution. Harry wouldn't go so far as to say, or even to think, he was glad Malcolm X had been assassinated, but the man had scared him.

On the coffee table that used to belong to his in-laws, where in the old days in their living room he'd find a bowl of walnuts and almonds with the old brass nutcracker, copies of the *Detroit Jewish News,* and a framed photo of some relative lost in the old country, he now found a clipping from the *South End,* Wayne State University's newspaper. The headline was "White Privilege and the Horatio Alger Myth," by John Watson. Lena was a student at Wayne State, and she often quoted the *South End,* as the paper had grown more radical, a good thing in her estimation. "It is nonsense," Watson had written and someone had underlined, "to say that anyone could pull himself up with hard work. Whites come into the world with a full array of resources and privileges—many of them flowing from the washed-out color of their skin, their built-in bootstraps."

"Harry." It was her again. Partway down the stairs now. "Don't leave me to handle this myself."

He tossed the *South End* on the couch and wound his way through the rooms to the staircase. He could see her on the third step from the top, first only the shoes, pumps, nice ones, then as he got closer, the thick ankles, the legs, the hem of the skirt, then all of her, bending over, holding onto the banister and looking sour. "I'll be right up," he said. "I'm looking." He was certainly doing that.

"I don't like being up here by myself," she said.

"You've been up there plenty of times by yourself."

"You know what I mean."

"Okay. I'm getting the stuff. I'll be right there." And he stood, watching until she backed up the stairs, and until he heard her returning to her desk.

Back in the room—Alvin's lounge was how he already thought of it—on the coffee table was a narrow pamphlet with big hand-lettered words. "Black Panther Party Platform: What We Want; What We Believe." *What we want*, Harry thought. He unfolded it. He rarely let himself want anything. Yet here was a whole numbered list.

1. *We want freedom. We want power to determine the destiny of our Black Community*. We believe that black people will not be free until we are able to determine our destiny.

2. *We want full employment for our people*. We believe that the federal government is responsible and obligated to give every man employment or a guaranteed income. We believe that if the white American businessmen will not give full employment, then the means of production should be taken from the businessmen and placed in the community so that the people of the community can organize and employ all of its people and give a high standard of living.

He folded the pamphlet and put it in his pocket. This was something he'd have to read later. He picked up another clipping. This one by Stokely Carmichael, another angry Negro, or black, as some of them now wanted to be called. Carmichael had been in Detroit recently, speaking downtown, at Cobo Hall. A sentence underlined in blue ink: *It was for example the exploitation of Jewish landlords and merchants which first created black resentment toward Jews*. This was Alvin's place, and these were his things, and this was what he read.

Stan, one of the other Grand River business owners, referred to Carmichael as that colored terror-monger. "You know what he said to his people that day at Cobo?" Stan reported to Harry. "'Don't let them send you off to Vietnam to fight and kill. Stay here and do it.'" Stan loved to quote that line, his face flaming up. "Stay here and do it," Stan said. "What grown man talks like that?" Stan and four other men were trying to form a Grand River business association to demand more police patrols along their stretch, and more police attention to the young people—a number of whom lived in apartments upstairs from their stores.

Stay here and do it. Harry didn't approve of those words, but an alliance with the other businessmen was not "his thing," an expression his daughters used—for example, when they said it was not "their thing" to help him clean up after Sappho in the yard. When one of these men called or stopped by, Harry always said he was too busy. He preferred to work, not kvetch about hard times, about potential dangers. He was sure they talked to Ilo when he was out, and she probably loved it. Some people loved to be scared.

"Harry," Ilo called again. He hadn't even noticed that the tap, tap, tap of her heels above him had returned. "What is going on down there?" Good question, he thought.

He walked through the maze of rooms, carrying the Carmichael piece with him. "I said I'll be there in a minute."

"It's already been a minute," she said.

"Let me be, Ilo. I'm almost done." He didn't hear it, but he could picture it—the arm fling, the huff of annoyance.

Harry returned to the lounge. Curtis and Alvin had access to the basement through the front of the building. It wasn't that. Not that he'd broken and entered. Nothing like that.

He picked up all the marijuana cigarettes from the ashtrays—the wholes and the halves and the quarters and the tiny ends, which left smudges on his fingers when they crumbled. He folded the Carmichael article, to make it into a small packet for the marijuana cigarettes, and he put the whole thing in his pocket beside the Black Panther wants and beliefs.

He left the room, pulling the light chains as he went, passing through the furnace room. He went into one of his inventory rooms, and walked up and down every aisle, looking at the stacks of boxes, all the sizes—men's work boots, police oxfords, baby shoes. He walked across the hall to the other inventory room, and there he did the same, walking up and down every aisle, looking up, at the boxes stacked almost to the ceiling, and down, the lowest shelf inches off the floor. He walked out into the hall, and just about to climb the stairs, he saw the stepladder, leaned against the wall, and on the wooden shelves beside the steps, the buckets and sponges and squeegee and scraping tool, rags and paper towels—all arranged carefully where Curtis had left them. He looked at his watch. He'd only been down here fifteen, twenty minutes. What was she complaining about?

He gathered what he needed, hung the stepladder over his shoulder, and climbed the stairs, ladder digging into his shoulder, pail knocking against his leg and then against the brick wall, keeping time like a metronome.

When he came rattling and banging into the front office, two policemen stood with Ilo on the sidewalk, one on either side of her, looking at the window, their car parked behind them, at the bus stop. One officer had a notepad, and he wrote, as Ilo looked over his shoulder, pointed to the page, likely instructing on her name, in the way she always did: Ilo, which rhymes with high-low, and Levine, which rhymes with the queen. As if the police cared about getting her name right.

Harry put down his bucket, removed the ladder from his shoulder, and leaned it against the wall, moving slowly, showing the police that not every Levine was so excitable. Halfway to the door, the phone rang, and he decided to get it, stall for time, for thoughts. He tried to imagine the headline in tonight's paper, some clever word trick that wove in the themes of anti-Semitic slurs, Halloween devilry, and the shady slumlord with the den of iniquity in his basement and the stash in his pocket.

On the phone, it was Al from Keene Shoes, and the mindless exchange began, the preliminaries, the how's business, how's the family, Harry looking at the neat papers on Ilo's desk, an order ready to be filled, for Jarousek's on the east side.

"Al," Harry said. "I'll get my sister to take your order. Just a minute." A minute here, a minute there; soon it would add up to a whole day.

Out on the sidewalk, weighing in with Ilo and the police were Bernie Segal from Formica City, the furniture store across the street, and Stan Fink, from Fink Hardware, two buildings down, who so loved to quote Stokely Carmichael. *Stay here and do it.*

"You, of all people?" Bernie said when Harry came out. "To get this treatment?" Ilo reluctantly went in to get the phone when Harry asked her.

13

Bernie. He was Jewish skinny—meaning he'd learned early how to break a woman's heart, starting with his mother, as she sat long into the night, pleading for him to take one more bite. Bernie wore a big thick mustache, well groomed, a handsome specimen, like a thatched roof compared with Harry's thin dark fringe. "We go back," Bernie said to the police. He did a back-and-forth gesture between himself and Harry.

It was true. They did go back, back to the old neighborhood—Linwood near Dexter and Davison—where Bernie had been a regular at Ruth's house, a friend of her younger brother Irv.

"Yeah," Harry said. "We go back." Which didn't mean Harry loved him, or even liked him. He hated the man's crude language and humor, the sex jokes. Someday, when Bernie was old and frail, or when he predeceased Harry and could no longer flirt with Ruth, the history would likely hit Harry in one big wet eye rush, but not right now, not with the actual physical person to contend with.

"What are we going to do about this, fellows?" Bernie asked the police, as if he'd been called in on special assignment.

Two ladies waited at the bus stop, and a third joined them. Harry nodded to the thin woman with the shopping bag, Mrs. Johnston, who had been his tenant before Curtis and Alvin. She nodded back, with the short, businesslike nod of a person whose main objective is to carry on unimpeded with her daily routine, but who recognizes that this congregation on the sidewalk could potentially derail it, and thus is struggling with conflicting feelings of concern, fear, and simple curiosity.

"It's not like we haven't asked for extra help," Stan told the police. His voice suggested a heavy, consistent infusion of cigarette smoke. "Oral," Ruth called him. A nail biter. "Licking his wounds," Ruth said of him, as she said of all nail biters. "What is this?" he asked, addressing the police officers. "Munich? We're supposed to put up with this?"

"Look," Harry said. "Why don't you let me talk to the officers?"

The bus pulled up behind the police car and rescued Mrs. Johnston and the other women. Harry could see them watching as the bus took them off, to their lives in other parts of the city, while he remained, sadly, behind, feeling as if he'd been up all night digging a trench or fighting a fire, something he had fortunately never had to do.

"Mr. Levine," the bigger officer said. His name was Pawlikowski, and he was the kind of big that was marginally contained within his clothes—the buttons, the belt, the laces on the shoes, all doing hero's work. He had a pasty complexion, pitted with acne remnants or chicken pox. Officer Pawlikowski stifled a burp, as big men sometimes do.

By comparison, his partner, named Dunn, was small, with eyes that pointed in two directions at once, making Harry wonder where he was looking, what he was seeing: Harry's face, the words on the front window, or something beyond what others could see? Harry slid his hands into his pockets, and for a moment he was surprised to find something beyond change and a handkerchief. He almost pulled the something out to see what it was.

Traffic slowed and clogged at the sight of the human drama whose meaning passersby could only guess—the police, the white men, the writing on the store window. *Gapers' block* they called it years later—the delay caused by people straining to know.

"Your sister's pretty upset about this," Pawlikowski said. "She flagged us down. Ran into traffic waving her arms . . . You would have thought it was a . . . You know."

"Yeah," Harry said. "I know." Harry understood that the order, or veneer of order, that prevailed around here depended, in part, on the police presence, the gun holster at the hip, the roaming squad car. But in a city like Detroit, created in large part by the vision of that rotten Henry Ford, anti-Semitism was practically official policy. Whatever Harry might be a victim of would likely be seen as something he had coming to him.

Harry read it this way: The police were inviting him to view the situation man to man, to join together in giving the hysterical woman the brush-off. Together, they could concoct a scenario that would be quickly concluded: a joke between men on the street. A beautiful fall day. Halloween mischief. An ugly sign on the window, to be sure. But one that could be washed off. It was only soap. Itself a cleansing product.

"She says she wants us to talk to the tenant," Officer P. said.

"You know women," Harry replied. He motioned in a general way toward the place where she sat at her desk. They could see her in there, phone to ear.

Bernie and Stan stood a few feet off, smoking. Bernie scratched at the soapy *w* on the window with the cover of his matchbook.

"You disagree, then? About talking to the tenant?" Officer Pawlikowksi looked like a man whose feet were tired, even this early in the morning, still swollen from the day before, throbbing inside his police oxfords, which Harry noted as Bates, Goodyear welt construction. He looked like he'd probably snuck a kielbasa for breakfast—against doctor's orders—and it was getting back at him now.

"She mentioned he has a kid," said Dunn. "A teenager." Of the two officers, he was the friskier, possibly the more dangerous. Harry looked at him. A pipsqueak with the confusing eyes, not all that much past teenager himself. This string of words they were using with each other, "women," "tenant," "teenager," was getting to Harry—as if one word was all you needed to know, as if it telegraphed everything, funneled whole populations down to a label, like the label on the window, like the *y* in *boy* with its narrow throat in which a whole huge history of meanings and individual variations could disappear. Women: foolish. Tenants: losers. Teenagers: delinquents.

"He's a youngster," Harry said. "That's all. A good kid." He kept his hands in his pockets. He was anxious for the police to leave, anxious for this incident to fade into a little nothing. Let the police completely forget it after they left. Maybe tell it as an amusing story to their wives when they got home, between the visits of the trick-or-treat kids. Or after the Dunn and Pawlikowski kids were in bed, as the parents rifled through the treats the kids left on the living room floor. This business could become an anecdote. A "those people" kind of story, where the "those people" could refer to Harry, to Alvin and his friends, to Curtis, to the whole neighborhood. It could be anyone but them. "Look," Harry said, "you can understand why my sister's upset. Just think, if it was your building. Your people. Polish, Irish. You know what it's like. Your people have been through it."

Bernie and Stan exchanged looks, checked watches, cleared throats, tossed cigarettes, toed them into the sidewalk. "Harry," Bernie said. "What are you, crazy?"

The police ignored the comment. "You're saying you've never had trouble with the boy?" Pawlikowski asked.

"Never," Harry said. "Alvin keeps to himself. He works for me sometimes. His father's a good man, too. He keeps a close eye."

Cars slowed and honked as they passed. A VW bus painted in dayglo colors slowed. It had the three-leafed marijuana symbol decaled on its side, and a man with bushy dark hair and a beard stuck his head and shoulders out the window. "Pigs," he screamed. The police barely looked.

"Harry," Bernie said. "You're going to let him get away with this?"

He rattled the coins in his pocket. Restless. Ready to get back to work if this scene was going nowhere.

Harry found the coin-rattling crude—advertising what you've got, weighing it. "Get away with what?"

As if beckoned by the fates, three teenaged boys rounded the corner, Alvin among them. The three friends were together often, out on the sidewalk in front of the building, or sitting on the wooden fire escape in the back, long legs hanging over railings, singing harmonies.

Bernie and Stan would stay for this. They'd complained to Harry about how these boys gathered with others, on the sidewalks, in front of stores, got rowdy, making it hard for people to pass. The business owners said it discouraged foot traffic, customers. But this was not a concern for Harry, tucked away behind his locked doors; a wholesaler didn't care about foot traffic.

Harry had met these friends, Wendell and Otis, Alvin's sidekicks, his back-up singers, who lived in the two-family flats on the nearby side streets. None of them looked to Harry like the Black Power types, with their numbered wants and beliefs, who wore their leather jackets and berets, dressed to kill. These three looked more like the Motown types, velveteen-lapelled and ready to croon their way into the stage lights.

These boys had hair pressed into small, tight waves, a conservative style in an era when hair broadcast far more radical messages. And they were dressed smartly: high-waisted pants, one pair in maroon, one in teal, one in black, all with a rayon sheen. Wendell, with the lightest skin of the three, wore a thin tie with a crisp white high-collared shirt; the other two wore sweaters.

As the boys came up the street, their arms swung, smooth and loose, a book, a notebook, resting in cupped hands. But they slowed, lowered their eyes, straightened their shoulders, as they approached Harry's group, conversation caught in mid-sentence.

"Alvin," Harry said by way of good morning. Alvin looked up briefly when Harry spoke to him. In his pocket, Harry touched the paper packet. Bernie, too, had his hands in his pockets, jingling his coins, his own stash.

"Alvin Evans?" Officer Pawlikowski said.

"Yes, sir," Alvin said. Still looking down, the looseness gone.

"Where you and your friends headed, Alvin?" the big officer asked.

"School," Alvin said. But he said it quietly, and the word might have been lost in the sounds of the cars passing. It might have bounced off the brick buildings, the pavement, and been muffled by the roar of the bus stopped behind the police car, as its driver prepared to pull out into traffic.

Alvin kept his eyes down, on his black, polished pointed-toe shoes, which, Harry noted, were not the ones he had given Alvin in September, offering them as back-to-school shoes, giving them to Curtis one day while they worked, a quick handover, trying to minimize embarrassment, saying, "Take these for Alvin. He could probably use a new pair."

Over the three or four years that Curtis and Alvin had lived upstairs, Harry had given them shoes each season—tennis shoes in spring and summer, work boots in winter, black leather oxfords with rubber soles in fall. Joanna said that only a spaz wore that style. Harry had never seen Alvin wear any of the shoes he had given.

The officer wanted Alvin to speak up, to look him in the eye, so he asked again where they were going, even though he knew what the answer had been.

"He said he's going to school," Harry answered.

"The boy can speak for himself," Pawlikowski said. He looked at his watch, making a show of it, as if telling time were a very, very complex matter, as if the calculation were a demanding one. "Didn't school start about a half-hour ago?"

"Help my dad out with some things first," Alvin said. His friends watched, as did Harry's fellow business owners—a symmetry of three and three.

The big officer turned to Harry. "That would be Curtis?" Pawlikowski asked. "The tenant your sister told us about?" By now, Ilo had finished her phone order. She stood in the door frame, watching. By now, another small group of people had gathered, too, waiting for the next bus to come. It was like this—wave after wave of people, gathering, waiting, moving along, off somewhere, into the city. One woman at the bus stop had a small child by the hand, and the child wore a cowboy costume, a little hat, a neckerchief, boots, and at his waist, a small holster and shiny gun. The first and only sign of Halloween in the neighborhood. The little boy turned to watch the events in front of Harry's store, but his mother turned him away, to look with her at the traffic on Grand River.

"Curtis is my tenant," Harry said. "He and his son were helping me this morning, unpack a load of shoes." Alvin looked at Harry, as did Ilo.

"I thought your sister said you just got in," the officer said. "That you found this . . . defaced window a short time ago."

Ilo began to speak, but Harry cut in. "Yeah," Harry said. "An hour or so."

It didn't have to happen this way, but the statement was suspiciously meaningless, the clock was ticking, and Dunn lost patience—the standing around, the need to show something, to accomplish something.

"Okay, boys," he said to Alvin and his friends, "turn and put your hands above your head, on the wall." The small cowboy at the bus stop pulled his hand free from his mother's and turned to see who had stolen his lines, whether his Halloween dream of the Wild West had come true.

The look on the faces of Alvin and his friends bore the same blank incredulity that Harry's face had when he first found the three soapy words on his front window. The look of someone for whom the thus-far-narrowly-avoided and the present-time-reality have narrowed down to one.

The three friends put their books on the ground, splaying their hands against the wall. "That's right," Dunn said.

He started with Alvin, patting him under the arms of his cream and tan sweater, then down his sides, down his legs to his ankles. Dunn looked nervous—imagine, him, the nervous one—reaching in, as if trying to move a sprinkler without getting hit by the spray. He frisked the other two in the same jumpy way while everyone watched: the little cowboy, his mother (who had momentarily forgotten to shelter her young son), Stan, Bernie, Ilo. People in buildings across the street; people no one could even see.

"Officer," Harry said. "Leave the boys alone." A bus pulled off, picking up the small cowboy, who departed with his face pressed against the window. "What do you think you're going to find? A bar of soap?"

Dunn looked at him, but he kept his hands where they were, on Otis's sides, on his bright blue sweater.

"I said leave the boys alone." Harry stepped closer. Even he was taller than Officer Dunn. "I've worked here a long time. I know these people. Let's not make it into a bigger deal than it needs to be."

The officers looked at each other, Dunn still leaning over Otis, his hands still on his body, not used to being told to stop what he was doing. The power to make others do what he said was one of the few benefits of risking his life daily, of being called pig because he did what he'd been hired to do.

Harry was the first to see Curtis. He stood at a distance, near the narrow door that opened onto the steep staircase that led to his apartment. He was a big man, with smooth dark skin, Maxwell House–coffee dark. But unlike Pawlikowski, Curtis had learned to scale himself back, to become the kind of person thought of as a "decent Negro." His eyeglasses helped, the way they teetered on the bridge of his nose, as did the navy blue workman pants and the clean white T-shirt, the clean handkerchief in his T-shirt pocket. Mostly, it was his downcast eyes, as if he'd gotten used to holding back his thoughts. Bernie and Stan knew him, felt comfortable enough with him to ask him over to do odd jobs sometimes. "My son causing trouble?" he asked. He saw the writing on Harry's window. "Did you write that?" he asked Alvin.

"No, sir," Alvin answered.

"And your friends?" Curtis asked.

"No, sir," Wendell and Otis answered.

"It's a misunderstanding," Harry said. Ilo shook her head and went back into the building. "Like I said before, I'm not too worried about the window. I'll wash it off. We've all got things to do. How about we call it a Halloween prank and be done with it?"

The cars streamed in both directions. Dunn dropped his hands and straightened, stepped back. The traffic lights at Joy Road cycled red, yellow, green, red. Mrs. Johnston by now might have arrived at the school lunchroom where she worked and put on her apron. The little cowboy would soon be inching through his school day, thinking mostly of the magical evening ahead. Ruth would be shopping for Halloween candy on the two-for-one table, then rushing off to a meeting she'd been preparing for over the past weeks. Sappho would be sleeping in her favorite spot by the heat register in the corner of the dining room, the golden autumn sun streaming in on her through the window.

All along Appoline, the street where Harry lived and Sappho slept, were the green lawns and the elms, the oaks, the sugar maples, making their way through this transitional season—some still green, others bare, and then the glorious variants of in-between: the translucent reds and oranges, purples even, glowing in the autumn sun, against the bluest blue sky. The leaves would be clinging and falling and twirling along Outer Drive, the big boulevard that crossed Harry's block, and adorning the grand houses, carpeting their lawns in colors so startling they had no names, unless you made them up—like raspberry parfait or Tropicana burnt orange, or translucent copper-pink.

Harry's daughter Lena would be settling into a front-row desk for her Communism, Fascism, and Democracy class at Wayne State, taught by a curly-haired charismatic professor with wire-rimmed glasses. Joanna would be shrinking down in her economics class at Mumford High School, hoping that the terrifying Mr. Bremen would not notice and call on her. And Franny, one of the few remaining white children in her class at MacDowell Elementary, might be passing a note to her friend Renee, another of the few remaining, making plans for the evening's trick-or-treating. But there on the sidewalk, the parties in the Honky Jew Boy incident were stalled. Not a tree, not a leaf, not a blade of grass on this stretch of Grand River, not a hint of the joys of autumn to soften the scene, and each participant waiting to see who would take charge, who would break the spell.

It was Pawlikowski: "We'll leave it at that, then," he said. He closed his notebook. The boys lowered their arms. They turned and straightened their clothes, Alvin first. Stan was high-blood-pressure red, the missed opportunity practically searing him, and Bernie threw down his cigarette.

"Gentlemen," Pawlikowski said, nodding to each member of the group in turn while he folded himself into the squad car. He saluted to Ilo, who had come back to the door.

Once Officer Dunn had started the engine, once the two cops had pulled off from the curb, once Ilo had gone inside with Curtis, who would get the window-cleaning things that Harry had dragged up from the basement, once the boys had gathered their books, getting ready to move on to school, now at least an hour late, Wendell, straightening his tie, looked at Harry, not into his face or his eyes, but generally, in his direction.

"We're not boys," he said.

WOMEN

It was a homemade card, all Harry, standing on the kitchen table in a beam of golden morning light, and waiting for Ruth when she came down for breakfast. On a piece of orange construction paper, he'd taped an old black-and-white of them, a little crooked, the one in which someone had caught them on a blanket in a field on Belle Isle when they were dating. The photo had always plagued her. Her hair looked like straw, her dress was tangled around her legs, halfway up her thighs, and her face looked completely blank, on the edge of hostile, a look she could not decipher. He looked like he'd been woken from a dream, his face puffy, his jacket thrown into the grass beside them, cast off, as if to say, this blanket is our raft, fling everything nonessential overboard. And inside the card, all it said was "Boo."

Just "boo." No acknowledgment of her meeting that afternoon. Nothing about the thing she had been wrestling with for months, the subject she had been taking to bed with her, that little matter that woke her, tossed and turned her. Where was the support, the encouragement, the assurance that he believed she could lead the meeting with confidence, that the report she'd prepared was sound, important? Nowhere. Just this card, harkening back to some incomprehensible moment from their past.

Just "boo." What did he mean by that?

One thing about Ruth, she was easily annoyed. The way Harry drank from a glass annoyed her, vacuuming in the last drops. The fact that he told her to wait until the last minute to buy the Halloween candy because you could get the best deals. The way he mispronounced certain words— *malk* instead of *milk, prid'ner* (like *prisoner*) instead of *pretty near,* which was something for some reason he said a lot. "I'm prid'ner done here," or "It's prid'ner dinner time." Like he was a country boy or something.

And not just Harry. Other things: The way people stuck their hands in the cereal box to guide the cereal out—as if it couldn't make it on its own. People who slurped spaghetti. People who said "you know" every other word. People who left their wadded Kleenex around. The way her daughters left the cap off the shampoo annoyed her, and the way hairs of every length cluttered the bathroom floor, sink, and tub, as if she lived with a house full of pets.

Her mother's lumbering pace had annoyed her. In fact, slowness in general annoyed her—slow speech, slow movements. When someone helping in the kitchen—Harry or a relative there for a party or holiday meal—cut vegetables too slowly or precisely, it annoyed her. When people hesitated too long before responding, or drew out a word too long—like *well* or *no*—it grated on her. When people made too big a deal about something (a cut on the finger, the fact that a child was about to get braces), it annoyed her—although one could say that by being annoyed by something as small as a way of eating or drinking, she was making a big deal.

It wasn't only the people in her immediate family who annoyed her. If she was out at a restaurant, for example, even in the grocery store, and heard someone say something too obvious—"His whole family died in the Holocaust; a real tragedy"; "the price of peaches!"—it annoyed her. In her opinion, if the price of peaches was too high, you either walked right past or you bought them. Who needed to talk about it? To talk about it was either boasting (that you could afford the peaches, even at that price) or complaining. Shut up and eat the peaches. That was her philosophy.

None of this was to suggest that she was against conversation. Conversation should be about books and ideas; it should have insights. Her daughters accused her of trying to make everything deep; they said that her favorite word was *probe*, as if it were a pointy instrument that gave them the creeps rather than a way of looking more deeply into something. So you could say that this quality in her annoyed them, that perhaps she had taught them to be annoyed.

You never knew with her, which was what Harry sometimes said to her. "I never know with you," he might say, "what sets you off." Like the card that morning, intended as a loving gesture.

The family had gotten used to it, or they appeared to, as much as a person could get used to something like that. What few of them understood was that for her, annoyance was a kind of power, a compensating force against uncertainty, a tool of the meek.

All in all, Harry felt, everyone was a little bit nuts, a little bit mean, some more, some less, and Ruth had good reason for her unpredictable temperament. Harry forgave her. He loved her. He left her little gifts, like that Halloween card that almost sent her into orbit.

Boo? Was he kidding?

Ruth was the third of seven children, the last of a trio of girls who (thank god, from the father's perspective, and then as a result, also from the mother's, because maybe then, he would leave her alone, and the endless pregnancies would stop) had given way to a trio of boys, and ended in the final punctuation mark: another girl. In her teens, the oldest sister in the family had contracted tuberculosis, and thus been sent off to a sanatorium, where her chest caved in and made her practically unmarriageable, and the youngest had managed to survive polio without spreading it to anyone else in her family, but was left with a shrunken leg and a club foot.

The second-oldest daughter, dark-eyed and plump, sat staring for hours into her upturned hands, as if she were a palm reader struggling to remember her trade, and eventually, as a young woman, had been lobotomized in an attempt to put her out of her misery, or help her discover her fortune, neither of which it accomplished. One of the younger boys roamed the streets shouting the *shema* as if it were a curse, waving his fist, his crossed eyes and swollen belly warning enough that something was seriously wrong, even if he hadn't shouted a word.

But the first boy born into the family, the golden, blessed child, was the skinny and undernourished Irving, sent to Maybee Open Air School, where everyone hoped he would grow stronger, the irony of the school name lost on the greenhorn parents. Ruth was consigned to accompany Irving, like a bodyguard, on the bus to his school and then back to pick him up at the end of the day.

The short, strong, bearded father, Avrum, was the *shammes,* or caretaker, of Detroit's Galitzianer shul, and for extra income, he worked as a *shochet,* or ritual chicken slaughterer, in a small and smelly poultry shop on Hastings Street, near where they lived. His wife, Rosa, helped out at the chicken business, and they both came home at the end of a long day of squawking and flying feathers, reeking of flesh and blood, sometimes a few feathers sticking to the hair, to more squawking and flying feathers from all those children.

This father, like so many other wrath-filled immigrants, had been thrust forth from his homeland, from everything familiar, and forced to make impossible choices, along the way losing loved ones in the pogroms and fiery furnaces of Europe. He had been unable to do anything about the losses and the loved ones from so far away. And from this powerlessness grew his great explosions of violent temper—some would say you could hardly blame him—and the children whispered among themselves of the dreaded airplane rides, when his rages boiled up from his chest, shot out through his arms into his hands, and he lifted one of the children up off their feet to swing them in the air in a way that was neither playful nor asked for.

Ruth developed her own version of the airplane ride, a weapon for keeping the younger siblings, especially the boys, in line—the so-called Ruthie punch, in which she made a fist and bent her middle finger so that the knuckle protruded—a poker, a probe driven into the soft flesh of the upper arm. When things looked like they were getting out of hand, she had only to display her weapon for the boys to shield their upper arms and comply.

That was one thing she was proud of—her power to keep those rascals in line. The other thing she was proud of was the family name: Bruchenhartz. No *man* or *son* or *stein* or *berg,* as in so many other Jewish names. No *silver* or *gold* or *baum* or *rosen.* Bruchenhartz, a name with a resonant meaning that suited them very well.

Just "boo." The man was in his own world. Let him have a wonderful day. She put down the card and got on with it, the breakfast dishes, the chicken out of the freezer to thaw for dinner, a glance out the window at the golden day, the leaves tossed about the yard like a messy room that hadn't yet been swept.

The subject of her meeting was white flight, which always made her think of a flock of birds, wings beating against each other in beautiful, frantic, and chaotic patterns as each white creature attempted to clear a space for itself among the many others, all rising at the same time, or trying to. In the past, men had made the decisions about when to take flight, but this was the sixties, and the Detroit Council of Jewish Women wanted a voice.

The topic was changing neighborhoods—a subject even the closest friends tiptoed around. She could be as sociological as she wanted, but the truth was, what everyone wanted to know was when you were moving,

and how they could find out without revealing their own plan. She and
Harry had no specific plan to move, though they had made the Sunday
drives to the northern suburbs, probably everyone had, to see the homes
and subdivisions and roads as they emerged from the wooded lots.

She'd thought about starting the meeting by asking, straight out.
She'd go around the circle and have people say what they were thinking, what they were planning.

Harry looked at her like she was nuts when she had mentioned that
idea two nights ago. They were in their bedroom. She stood in front of
her dresser mirror, dabbing night cream on her face and throat.

"You can't ask people questions like that," he said. "What if someone asked you?"

"I'd tell them the truth: We're talking about it. We drove around.
But we never got out of the car."

"Yeah?" he said. "What about at Green Trees, in Southfield? We got
out of the car there."

"No one has to know about that," she said. And before long, he was
snoring while she was pacing.

After Franny and Joanna left for school, Ruth went to the small desk in
the living room and laid out her note cards, going over the ideas, reorganizing them, putting them back the way they'd been. Sappho roused
herself from the sunbeam near the heat register in the dining room
and strolled in to survey the situation.

"Outside?" Ruth asked, not in a friendly way. And the dog scrambled over to the kitchen door, which meant yes, so Ruth held it open
while the black glossy streak of coat shot past her into the yard, into the
fallen leaves, and the liberated Sappho barked her way after a squirrel.

Back at her desk, she reviewed her themes: the Jewish and Negro
populations moving in tandem across the city, their attitudes about each
other, the injustices of the past, the challenges of the present, boiling it
down once again, reciting the opening sentences, reworking her closing.

Her idea was to get the group thinking about their own attitudes
and behavior, why they felt compelled to move. Did they really have to,
and if so, why? Why accept it as a given?

In the bedroom, she agonized over the outfit, the closet contents.
Flinging a dark green skirt onto the bed because it had a stain she
hadn't noticed when she put it away, remembering that her blue blouse

26

made her sweat, that it felt like a straitjacket, trying a black skirt but finding it tight around the waist when she straightened up to button it. After that tight waist, the enterprise seemed doomed. Everything was old, boring, too heavy. Couldn't a person expect at least a little cool weather by the end of October?

She tried on skirts, threw them on the bed. The white blouse, the dotted one, the silky jersey pullover, the boatneck knit. Try, toss, try, toss. She didn't have any flair, not like her older sister, who had somehow overcome the tuberculin chest and learned to dress—put swirls together with tweeds in a way that worked, tilt a hat over the eye just so, to look smart and rakish, coordinate the colors of her clothes with her hair and eyes and lipstick into a perfect dream. What was wrong with Ruth that she'd lived this long and still couldn't do that?

Finally, she settled. A nubby skirt, in shades of brown and black. It buttoned up the side, leaving a small slit at the bottom. She paired it with a plain black lightweight pullover. It was . . . adequate, perhaps even . . . handsome. A woman had once referred to her as handsome— a handsome woman—meaning not pretty, nothing frilly. Substantial. Okay. Not a bad thing.

Some of the Council women had fabulous homes in Detroit's Sherwood Forest and Palmer Woods. But this month's meeting was in the little apartment where Alva Portnoy had moved after she learned that her husband was cheating with a skinny blond shiksa he'd met at the Stone Burlesk on Woodward near Grand Circus Park. The apartment was in a brick building, in a complex of identical brick buildings on Shaffer. *This* had to be the place for Ruth's presentation? An apartment where you smelled the neighbors' cooking, where Alva slept on a foldout couch in the living room while her two teenaged daughters, one recently picked up for shoplifting, shared the tiny bedroom.

The buildings all clustered in a compound of weaving, looping streets with painted signs pointing to number ranges (19735–19995), which all dead-ended at a high brick wall that ran along Eight Mile Road, a buffer against incursion from the Negroes who lived on the other side in the city's northernmost attempt to stash them somewhere. The six-foot-high wall even had a name—the Birwood wall—and kids tried to climb it, as kids do. But it was no kid's game, that wall, built in the forties so that whites, and their mortgage lenders, would view their real estate investments to its south as protected.

Ruth had never once found Alva's place on the first try, and again today, she found herself coming up against the Birwood wall, in one dead end after another that didn't include any of the numbers in Alva's address. So she backed out and continued her roaming search, watching the time, seeing that she would miss the 12:30 lunch, even be a little late for the 1:00 meeting start time.

She reviewed her thoughts as she drove in the endless circles of identical buildings fronted by the same small patches of grass, the same miserable shrubs, the arrows with the painted number ranges. And she went over the phrasing, the ideas she wanted to be sure to include, like a tape loop she'd been over hundreds of times: How Detroiters had dealt with changing neighborhoods in the past—how the Jews had themselves been barred from many neighborhoods, how whites and Negroes had clashed repeatedly in Detroit over housing and jobs. The bloody race riot of 1943. The neighborhood associations and restrictive covenants. The possibility of a new approach. And that Birwood wall.

All the women in the group had witnessed the trends, not only witnessed but lived them. The for-sale signs, the worries over their children in the changing schools, new owners in the neighborhood businesses, their own fathers and husbands deciding whether to stay or go, seeing the institutions—the shuls, the Jewish Center—struggle with the hard choice about when and where to lay the cornerstone for the new building. No one wanted to be the last to go, but it was also hard to be the first. This meeting was a way of reviewing the past and thinking about the future. Let the women educate themselves and take a stand.

"Stay or go, it doesn't matter," she would say. "The important part is to give other humans a chance to be human." What a stupid argument. Face it. It mattered. Property values mattered. Safety mattered. Even if you were the most progressive, tolerant, enlightened person in the world, you still wanted to get a good price for your house.

Finally, without knowing exactly how, she ended up in the right loop, and there was Alva's building. So she moved forward with the inevitable: hitching the satchel with all her materials over her shoulder, locking the car, waiting to be buzzed in, walking the long stale hall, past the many closed doors, all the way to the end, where Alva stood waiting.

"What?" Alva asked. "You got lost?" It was a stupid way to greet someone, and it didn't merit a response. Ruth looked past her, into the apartment, at her audience, the backs of their heads—maybe twenty women—turning to look at her, seated around the small L-shaped living/dining room on folding chairs. The room smelled of coffee and perfumes, with an undertone of buttery pastry.

Alva gestured to the sofa, near the windows, where the middle cushion was reserved for Ruth, with the coffee table in front, "so you have someplace to put your papers," Alva said. On the couch, next to Ruth's empty cushion, was Mildred Lazar, the group's president, the one who'd pushed her into this assignment. She sat forward on the couch, a dessert plate on her lap.

"Sit, sit," Alva said to Ruth, motioning.

"Can I just . . ." she asked, pointing down the hall to the bathroom.

"Of course," Alva answered, and Ruth placed her satchel and purse near the door, hearing the conversation pick up again behind her.

Well, she couldn't put it off any longer, despite the disapproving look she'd gotten in the mirror in Alva's bathroom. The hair! She'd had it done yesterday, so it would look good for the meeting. Last night, she'd imagined that it had something of the Jean Seberg look. What a fiasco. She was never going back to that hairdresser.

In the living room, she wove toward her place on the couch. Alva asked her if she wanted anything to eat or drink, and showed with her hand what she had to offer. It was quite a spread—dark chocolates in their fluted papers, arranged on a pedestal china dish, a pecan coffee cake (scrumptious looking), rugelach (oy), small fruit tarts, silver bowls of salted nuts. Bagels and cream cheese left over from the lunch Ruth had missed. And, a nod to the holiday, a bowl of peanut-butter taffies, in their orange and black waxed wrappers, a bowl of candy corn, and a bowl of miniature Hershey bars.

"No," Ruth said. "Just water. Thanks." While Alva placed a glass of cloudy liquid on a coaster, Ruth settled on the couch and pulled her materials from her bag, a notebook, the stacks of 3×5 cards, and the handouts—a timeline of key historical events and statistics, so they could get the overview.

In the room, both familiar and unfamiliar faces. In the front row, Minnie Rappaport, a squirrel of a woman, in some little rumpled brown outfit, face, eyes, lips always twitching. In the row behind her was Ellie Glazer, founder of the Detroit Women's Center for Justice, with her daring slash of eyebrows and her hair pulled back in the low, tight bun. Her purple suit, stunning as it was, did nothing to change the fact that her older son, who had been in school with Lena all the way through, was the first to get arrested for drunk driving, as well as the first to be arrested for selling drugs. And that was before marijuana had even made it to the covers of *Time* and *Newsweek*.

Beside her, Selma Schneider, a well-known Detroit artist, with her long, thick black hair framing her face like curtains, the heavy black liner around her eyes, a beautiful silky shawl in autumn colors draped across her shoulders. And at the end of the row, Lynn Hochman, the pianist, who taught lessons to many of Detroit's privileged children, and whose husband was an oboist with the Detroit Symphony. Ruth had heard her play many times, on the concert pianos at Baldwin Hall, near the Art Institute, and during the music festivals at the Jewish Community Center.

Margo Solomon was there, in the same row with Ellie. She waved at Ruth, and Ruth nodded. The Solomons owned the big house on Ruth's street—a reddish stone Georgian with an ivy-covered stone wall enclosing the yard—the lord's manor compared with the modest colonials that lined the rest of the block. Margo wasn't a regular at Council meetings, though she had been at Ruth's Jewish humor program and stopped her afterward to say how much she'd enjoyed it and how much she'd like to get together with Ruth.

And oh god. There was Myrna Goldbloom—the crazed genius with the flashing eyes. No one could stand her, and especially, no one could understand how her husband could stand her, maybe he couldn't, with her unwashed hair, the wrinkled blouses with the yellow underarm stains, the teeth that looked as though they'd never met a brush.

Thelma Weisman was not there, though she had said she would come. Nor was Diana Goldstein. Ruth could imagine Diana's husband, the big-shot banker, hearing about the meeting and saying, "What do you need with that?" And maybe Diana hadn't had an answer.

Around the room, Ruth took time to see, a few unfamiliar faces mixed in. Not unusual. New women came, old ones didn't show; people brought friends, invited neighbors. One old lady wore a big green corduroy hat, what Ruth would call a newsboy hat, but huge, and she was making her way through a big plate of pastries, crumbs falling everywhere. Ruth had seen other women like her, at the shul, at the Jewish Center; having outlived their husbands by too many years and with their adult children too busy to look after them, they landed somewhere for the afternoon in whatever odd articles of clothing they happened to show up in. Down the row from the old lady sat three younger women, probably in their thirties, the next generation of Council women. The one in the middle wore cowboy boots with a ruffled skirt and was very pretty, with perfect skin and dark eyes. She might be the one Mildred was hoping to bring into a leadership position—social action chair or community service committee. Something like that.

Dark-haired Mildred with the short, matronly curls opened the meeting, calling for the group's attention ("Ladies," she said, clinking a teaspoon against her coffee cup), thanking them for coming, making the regulation announcements, then getting to the main program: Ruth.

"As you know from the newsletter announcement, the topic of today's meeting is Detroit's Changing Neighborhoods: Stay or Go? Our hope is that we can formulate a recommendation for the boards of our cornerstone institutions—the large synagogues, the JCC, Jewish Family Services, and so on. Many of you know Ruth Levine, who has been a member of our group since its beginning. Many of you enjoyed her presentation on Jewish humor last year. And many of you still laugh when you think of her jokes." Ruth looked down at her notes.

That was her big credential—the humor presentation, where she told the stories about her family, and especially her father, who screamed "anti-Semite" if a bus driver pulled away from the bus stop too soon, and who made her call everyone in the congregation to inform them that Mr. Schlussel had died, then found out that Mr. Schlussel really had not died, so he made her call all the congregants back again to explain—incidents you wouldn't necessarily think were funny but that became funny the way Ruth told them, with the right pauses and hand gestures and the hoarse tension of her voice.

"Although this subject is no laughing matter," Mildred continued, "we asked Ruth to take it on because she and her family are longtime residents of Detroit, and have seen neighborhoods change, have moved several times themselves." She turned to Ruth. "How many neighborhoods?"

"Four," she said. "First, Hastings."

Hastings was the street that ran through the east-side neighborhood where the immigrant Jews had originally settled. It was Detroit's *shtetle*, its Jewish ghetto, where the newcomers had packed themselves into dark little apartments, where Yiddish was the dominant language, and where men made their living from pushcarts until they had enough to move into little storefronts, like Harry's father had, with his dry goods. Hastings was the neighborhood that all their families had left as soon as they put enough money away to buy homes, farther north and west, across Woodward.

"When my family moved from Hastings Street, around 1924," Ruth said, "I was seven or eight, and my job was to carry a lamp and a couple of brothers on the bus from the old apartment to the new house on Highland, our second neighborhood, near Dexter and Davison." This part was easy for her, telling the personal history. "In the forties, when Harry and I came back from the service, we bought a little bungalow on Fairfield, near Livernois and Puritan. And in the fifties, we made our fourth move, to Appoline, near Outer Drive and Meyers, where we live now."

"Sounds like good credentials to me," said Mildred. "Many of us have followed that same pattern. Also, because Ruth's father was the *shammes* at Beth Abraham for many years, she knows from the inside how institutional leaders made their decisions about moving." Ruth wasn't sure about that second point. Her father wasn't the type to tell the family much of anything, and she wasn't even sure he had been let in on the big decisions.

Mildred adjusted her skirt over her knees. "Before Ruth gets started, let me say that these are important times for women. Many of us are ready to have a voice in the big global decisions, like where our troops, and sometimes our sons, may have to fight, as well as in the smaller domestic decisions, like where we're going to live and where our children will go to school. I know that Ruth has put a lot of effort into preparing for this meeting, so please give her a warm welcome."

Her mouth was dry, her shoulder muscles tight. A throb in the temple. Even with the applause. Even the word *warm*. Why didn't someone open a window? She took a breath. Hands folded in lap, to resist the nervous gestures. Her chance to be taken seriously. The sole reason she'd taken the assignment. A glutton for punishment. "How many of you know that Mary Cavanagh, the mayor's wife, recently refused to move into the donated mayor's mansion, even though everyone, including her husband, expected her to?" Cavanagh was a young, handsome man, like John Lindsay, the mayor of New York, and like JFK, who had been his friend.

"And do you know why Mary Cavanagh refused? Because she didn't want to leave the neighborhood where her friends were, where her children went to school. And she said the mansion didn't have enough bedrooms for her eight children. They were comfortable where they were."

"Eight children?" Alva said. She had gotten up from the couch and now stood near the kitchen counter.

"The point is," Ruth continued, "Mrs. Cavanagh is a woman of her time. No need to keep silent anymore, if there's something important to say."

"I for one am glad she's dropping that phony Jack and Jackie façade." That was Alva again, rearranging pastries on one of her platters.

"She's a brave woman," Ruth said, "to stand up to her husband, a powerful public figure."

"Agreed," Mildred said.

"A woman speaks up for herself, and we need to award a congressional medal of honor?" Myrna, the trouble-monger, said. "She's a spoiled, privileged woman. There's no political agenda there. Does she want to donate the mansion as a home for slum dwellers? Does she say, 'We already have a house. What about the people who don't have any?' If she were thinking like that, well, then we'd have something to award."

Ruth hadn't even gotten to what she thought of as the controversial part, and it was already a ping-pong match. The crumb-bedecked lady in the back raised her hand: "Let her address her topic, please. Let the lady speak." She had the heavy Yiddish accent that went with her age, the shapeless figure, the shapeless dress, the green hat, huge and hot looking. She took off the hat and set it in her lap, and her thin white hair did indeed look sweaty. Ruth nodded at her, and Myrna looked to see who had spoken.

"Most of our parents were part of the great wave of immigration from eastern and southern Europe at the turn of the century," she said, making eye contact around the room. "But there was another great wave, in 1914, when Henry Ford put out the call throughout the country . . ."

"The anti-Semite," Alva said, lighting a Kent.

"We know that, Alva," Ruth answered. She looked back at her audience. "The idea was that Ford would pay five dollars a day to anyone who came to work in his new marvel—the River Rouge plant—and hundreds of workers who couldn't earn wages like that anywhere else streamed into the city, including many Negroes from the rural South."

A few women lit cigarettes. Ruth had quit about a year ago, but it still smelled good. "Imagine," she said, "what Detroit must have been like then. Most of us were only babies, or not yet born, but think of these people flowing in, mixing, adjusting to circumstances they knew nothing about. I'm sure my mother had never before seen a dark-skinned person. And most of the Negroes had never lived in a city. Many criticize Ford . . ."—Alva raised her hand at that, the cigarette poised between her fingers—". . . for not having considered where all these people would live, or the tensions that would flare between them in the Tower of Babel he was creating. But somehow in those years, and since, a pattern became established that the Negroes had an easier time settling around the Jewish neighborhoods than they did anywhere else."

"You know what they say in the WASP neighborhoods?" Alva said. "Don't sell to Jews, because they'll sell to Negroes."

"Oh," said Myrna, eyes flashing, "the WASPS wouldn't?"

"Where did you hear that?" asked Mildred Lazar.

"My cleaning lady," answered Alva. "She worked for a family on the southwest side. That's what she heard them say. Don't sell to Jews, because . . ."

"Can she go on?" Mildred asked. She raised her voice above the splinter conversations that had begun, about who would or wouldn't sell to whom, about what they had or hadn't heard that was similar. Mildred tapped with her teaspoon on Ruth's glass until the voices quieted.

Ruth went on. "These feelings and these kinds of comments have a long history in Detroit, as I've been saying. What people say about each other in private, they often wouldn't say in public. Let's be honest. No one's above it. We all have our attitudes."

Myrna squirmed, a challenge taking shape like a gas bubble. Margo, Ruth's manor-dwelling neighbor, moved forward in her seat, perhaps becoming more, or less, intent on getting together now that Ruth had said, "let's be honest." Minnie lifted her coffee cup between trembling fingers and drank. Someone cleared her throat. Ellie nodded. To have someone with slash eyebrows like those nodding in approval seemed like a miracle. Ellie wrote something on a notepad. To have said something that Ellie found worthy of recording seemed miraculous as well.

34

Although, as Ruth admitted to herself, she might have just remembered the items she needed from the grocery, or the amount of cash she needed to bail her son out this time around.

"My topic, as Mildred said, is changing neighborhoods. And my goal is to get us thinking about how we as Jewish women of Detroit see our community and our city, what makes us feel safe and unsafe. This discussion is going on in many homes and businesses. Hudson's built its Northland in 1954, the first major shopping center of its kind, both following and leading suburban development. Also in 1954, the Jewish Center opened a suburban branch, though the main branch is still in the city. Congregation B'nai Moshe moved to the suburbs in 1959, Shaarey Zedek in '62. But Temple Israel is still in Detroit, as is Beth Abraham, and many others. How are these institutional decisions made? What do we as women have to offer to the conversation?" She handed Mildred the timeline she'd prepared, instructing her to take one and pass the pile to the next woman, and so on around the room.

"First, I want to say something about attitudes, as we were discussing before." She waited while the timelines were passed. "Around the time of the 1943 race riots, a group from Wayne's sociology department did a study on race relations and attitudes." She paused again, waiting for the papers to stop shuffling. "The lead researcher trained student assistants and sent them into the Hastings Street neighborhood to do surveys, interviews, and observations. As you can see on the timeline, by then, most of the Jewish community was centered in the Dexter-Davison neighborhood."

Myrna interrupted. The eyes, the sharp tongue. "Whose study was this?"

Ruth shuffled through her note cards, even though she knew she'd neglected to record the man's name. She looked up, lost. She took a sip of water. The cloudiness had settled to the bottom third. Mildred, seated beside her, said, "I'm sure she can get that information to you later. Let's hear the point."

Ruth stared straight ahead, halfway up the wall, afraid to look at Mildred. Because if she did, then Myrna might accuse them, as she'd done with other speakers, of having conspired to censor her, saying that everyone knew her thoughts were not welcome in this group. But Mildred was not the kind of person you had to conspire with if you needed support. Behaving in that way simply made sense to her.

"I'll read a few findings from the Wayne study, just to give a feeling."

35

She looked to her cards again, but it took a few trembling shuffles before she found the right stack. "One," she said, "Jews believe they have an obligation to treat Negroes well because they too have been persecuted, but only 50 percent actually do treat Negroes well."

"What did they mean 'treat them well'?" It was Myrna. "You can't just say 'treat them well' and expect us to know what it means. It could be anything: saying please and thank you, not cheating them in business, not spitting on them. Someone might think he was a hero because he managed to restrain himself from burning a cross on a Negro's front yard, and then the surveyor comes up and says, 'Do you treat them well?' and he says, 'Sure. Of course. Why not?'"

"Most of them don't have front yards." This was Ellie. "I think this is one of Ruth's points, if you'd let her get to it. That the Negro population has to live *somewhere*. They've been systematically barred from neighborhood after neighborhood, partly because people don't 'treat them well' or see them as they would any other home buyer. It's not been an easy road for them."

"You think it's been an easy road for us?" said Minnie Rappaport. Another one with the accent, which gave her away as someone who had been through something unspeakable in the war years. It was troubling, sometimes even annoying, having to think of that pain every time Ruth looked at her.

"No," Ruth said. "It hasn't been an easy road for either group. That's what I was going to mention next." Minnie sometimes asked her for a ride home, because Ruth was one of the few in the group who could carry on a whole conversation in Yiddish. Not today, though, Ruth hoped, avoiding eye contact with her. She needed to swing by Cunningham's, where they had the two-for-one sale on Halloween candy. "Another finding of the study was that because of their mutual persecution, Negroes expect better treatment from Jews than from other whites." Several women made notes. "Also, the researchers found that the greatest amount of Negro-Jewish conflict occurs in the worst economic and social conditions. I guess that shouldn't be surprising."

"'Greatest' compared to what?" Myrna asked. "If the study focused on the Hastings neighborhood, what is the comparative population?"

Ruth looked at her, and Mildred said, "Will you let her get to her point?"

"Well, what *is* the point?" Myrna asked.

Ruth put down her cards. "I'm not sure there really is a point, in the sense you may be looking for one, Myrna." And here, she looked first at Mildred, then back to Myrna. "But I found this interesting, and I thought others would. I think it gives an opportunity to hear people's more private thoughts, and I like the idea of students going into the neighborhood and having the courage to talk to people about the subject of race—something few people anywhere have the courage to do."

"Fine," Myrna said. "But if the terms are so unclear and the methods so muddy, how do we know what anyone really thought?"

Mildred looked around at the women in the room. "Is this something people want to discuss more, the subject of method, or should Ruth go on?"

"Go on," Ellie said. And several others echoed.

"I wanted to read you some quotes from the Hastings neighborhood interviews. First, the Jewish business owners talking about the Negroes. 'They tell all their business out loud—about money that is owed, who's in jail.' 'They have no pride.' 'They curse violently.' 'They only think about night life, and they spend their time and money in the saloons, reeking of alcohol.'"

She sipped from her water glass. "The Jews in the survey also talked about the Negroes' bargaining procedures, what it was like to do business with them: 'They don't feel they are right unless they squabble.'" There, Ruth used a Yiddish accent. "The Jews in the survey expressed extreme fears of Negroes, describing them as 'nocturnal,' saying they had to handle them 'with kid gloves,' that they had a 'chip on their shoulder,' and the only way to avoid race conflict was to compromise."

"What's wrong with compromise?" Myrna cried out. A few women leaned over and whispered to each other. Coffee cups rattled in saucers as knees shifted.

"Did she say there was anything wrong with it?" Mildred asked.

"But if a business owner sets a price on something," one of the younger women said, "that's the price he wants. Why should he have to compromise on the price because he's afraid of the customer?"

"But we have no way of knowing if that's what was meant," Myrna said. "Whether they were talking about price."

"True," said Ruth. "But let's hear from the other side—something most of us don't get to do much." She read from one of her cards: "'The Jews make their money out of us, then live and spend their money in another neighborhood.'"

"*Anyone* who can is going to want to live in a better neighborhood,"

Alva said. She still stood by the kitchen counter. She stubbed out her cigarette.

Ruth nodded and placed that card in the back of the pile. She read from the next one. "The giving of credit was seen as a major factor in Negro-Jewish conflict, with many arguments occurring over bookkeeping, and the Negroes saying that the Jewish merchants cheated them— by selling inferior goods, shortchanging them, short-weighting them by, for example, filling a chicken with stones, laying their arm on the scale." She put down her cards. She looked around the room. "My own father was a *shochet*, working at a place on Hastings, selling chickens to the public. You can imagine how I feel reading this."

"Oh, let's not be sentimental," Myrna said. "What's the point?"

"The point," Ruth said, "is that these are the kinds of suspicions and misunderstandings that existed between the two groups, that probably still exist. And both groups were trying for a better life, but the Jew could cut off his sidelocks, buy decent-fitting clothes. In enough time, he could lose the accent. But the Negroes were stuck with the color of their skin—which for many white people, Jewish and Gentile, broadcast danger, immorality, and so on."

"Does anyone want more cake or coffee?" Alva asked. "There's plenty more. Please don't leave me with all this cake." A few, including that lady with the green hat, said they would take more.

Almost an hour had passed, and Ruth had so much still to cover before 3:00, when everyone had to leave to be home for their kids. And here was Alva, whose only goal in life was to not be left with too much cake. When the room quieted again, Ruth continued. "What I'd like to talk about next is how changing neighborhoods have been addressed in the past—including behavior, I hope you'll agree with me, we don't want to see repeated."

Alva put down her cake plate and opened some windows. Finally. Ruth's nylons felt like laminates.

"I'm sure you all know about the white neighborhood associations of the thirties, forties, and fifties—the kind that tried to 'educate' their members to sell only to a particular type of person and to use only certain real estate agents. And the members had to agree not to 'break' a white block. If a Negro family managed to buy, the association used 'other means of persuasion.'" Ruth used her fingers to make quotation marks around the appropriate words and phrases. "Not violence," she said, "at least not at first. A group of neighbors would approach the family and ask them to move. If they didn't, neighbors were told to 'sit tight and freeze out the undesirables'—meaning they'd tell the grocery stores not to sell to them, the neighbors not to speak to them, and eventually, the hope was that they would move. Of course, it didn't always work that way."

"Are you suggesting that it should have?" Myrna fired.

"No," Ruth said. "Of course not. I'm just reporting what Detroiters have done in the past, in hopes that we can learn from it." She asked Alva for some more water. The old woman in the back row appeared to be nodding off, but she might also have been nodding in agreement. "Sometimes, as you probably know, there was violence and mob action when Negroes tried to or did move into white neighborhoods. Dr. Ossian Sweet in the twenties was one troubling example you probably know about. But there have been others—even on the northwest side, where many of us now live. As I drove in today, to Alva's, a little lost, I admit, I kept coming up against that Birwood wall—something most of us now simply take for granted. We don't even think about why it's there." Snoring came from the direction of the old woman. People turned to look, embarrassed for her, no one certain whether to wake her.

"I didn't know about any of these events before doing the research. But here they are—all in our general neighborhood. On Halloween night, in 1956, a cross was burned on the back lawn of 14201 Appoline. In 1958, a house at 19737 Greenlawn was listed for sale with a Negro real estate dealer; a few days later a stick of dynamite exploded on its porch. In 1959, a widow on Snowden put up her own for-sale sign. A rumor spread among the neighbors that she had sold to a Negro, so a crowd of thirty or so gathered on her front lawn, and one man went to have a 'chat' with her. The next day, a white real estate agent came by, took down her sign and posted his. This is only ten years ago. Less."

Some women stole glances at their wristwatches. They had children coming home from school, roasts to get into the oven, laundry left in dryers, Halloween costumes to assemble. There on Alva's table was the pecan coffee cake, the tempting pyramid of chocolates on its china pedestal. And there in the room were also the personal discomforts: the heat, the folding chairs, the snoring woman. This was always the case, that people rarely had enough time or emotional capacity to take something in fully, that a set of facts like these had to be squeezed between one practical consideration and the next.

39

"But that's outrageous," Ellie said.

"Yes," Ruth agreed. "How many of you have heard this before?" Most shook their heads no. Some whispered to each other. None raised a hand. Alva said she'd heard about it, but Ruth never believed anything Alva said. Myrna questioned Ruth's sources, since Myrna never believed anything that anyone said.

"Imagine," Ruth continued, "if you were a woman on your own who had to sell your house but faced that kind of intimidation." She was already scaling back what she'd have time to report—about the agents and land developers who were now trying to get the whites to move out of the city, sending letters that announced the wonderful new properties available in the suburbs, in Birmingham and Bloomfield, towns that would not previously have sold to Jews. Hiring Negroes to drive through white neighborhoods to scare the residents into selling.

"In one case, the neighborhood association visited a homeowner they heard was considering a sale to Negroes and said—here I'm quoting the homeowner's report—'What you plan to do is, of course, perfectly all right and legal, but we'll find out where you're moving, buy a house next door, and move in the most shiftless and dirty family we can find.'" She looked at the faces of the women in her audience; they were listening. She could see that. "Then there's this quote from the notorious Ruritan Park Civic Association." She shuffled through, looking for it: "'We believe in equal opportunity for all in all phases of life, but we do not believe that there is any shortage of land on which to build homes or any shortage of housing that necessitates our giving up our homes or suffering the depreciation that occurs as soon as the area becomes a mixed neighborhood.'"

"It sounds like the South," Mildred said. "What we hear about the South."

"It sounds worse," said Ellie. "Because here, it's more covert. Here, we think we're more enlightened." She folded her hands on her knees. "That's ridiculous about there being no shortage of land or housing. If no one will sell to you, there's a shortage of housing."

The room was quiet. "During our last few years living on Fairfield," Ruth said, "everyone was talking about the deteriorating school, the rough play of the Negro children, that they carried weapons, that Puritan, the street to the south of us, was a gang hangout, that multiple families were living in the two-family dwellings. People complained that adults drank in the streets and threw empty bottles. I myself never saw any of this. But I admit, it was hard not to be influenced and frightened by the talk. I'm sure many of you had similar experiences. In the end, we did move, but we told ourselves we were doing this because I was having my third child, and that the house on Fairfield would be too small.

"The irony was that shortly after we settled in the new house, a man came to our door, a representative of a new neighborhood group. He had a petition to change the boundaries of the local school district to keep Negro families out." She looked around the room at the faces, trying to get a sense of their response. People were taking notes, some were shaking their heads. Some were eating cake.

"It sounds like it almost doesn't matter where a person goes," Ellie said. "The fears are the same. That 'they' are going to bring the neighborhood down." Ruth had heard a rumor that Ellie and her husband had already bought a lot in one of the northern suburbs, that they were working with an architect.

"It was a test, of course, to see where we stood. We had just moved, our boxes were barely unpacked. I was pregnant with Franny, and here was a man, a representative of at least some of my neighbors, asking us to take a stand on an issue like that."

"What did you do?" asked Selma Schneider. Her voice was ethereal, soothing. She slid open her curtains of heavy hair, so Ruth could see her face for a moment before the silky draperies fell back into place.

"If it was me, I would sign," said Alva. "What's the difference? You sign. You get rid of the man. You go on with your life. You're not asking for trouble. What does he need to know one way or the other what you think?"

"Because it's important to take a stand," Ellie said.

"Yeah," Alva said. "Like Custer. He took a stand." She lit another cigarette.

If Margo Solomon had an opinion, or if she had faced down the same petition, she didn't say.

"Okay," Mildred said. "Let's hear from Ruth."

"We refused to sign, pointing out that we were new to the neighborhood and didn't know enough about the issues. The man tried to persuade us, but Harry, my husband, said no. If Harry hadn't been home, I'm not sure what I would have done."

"Of course you don't sign," said Myrna. "It's not even something that needs discussing."

41

"It certainly does need discussing." Mildred again, the voice of reason. "That's the whole point of this meeting. If people can't discuss, they have no hope of understanding each other."

"My real point," Ruth said, "is that in Detroit, and other cities too, some block clubs want to welcome newcomers. So we have options. Just because it's been a history of intolerance doesn't mean it always has to be that way."

"I don't think it's the skin color," said the pretty young woman in the cowboy boots, the one Mildred had her eye on for leadership. "It's the class differences, the worry that schools will be compromised if people don't have the same values. The schools are the key for most families. They are for me." Her friends nodded.

"The schools are certainly important," Mildred said. She'd been a science teacher in an inner-city school. Ruth knew her stories about how hard it was to get supplies for science projects, how she couldn't even count on the old standards—asking children to collect leaves and acorns in the fall—since the neighborhoods where they lived barely even had trees.

If she were going to make full disclosure, this could have been the time for Ruth to present the statistic on Mumford, the high school where most of these women's teenagers went. Sixty-two percent Negro in 1965. Most of them wouldn't guess that the percentage was that high (Ruth hadn't), since the administration, and the realities of the world, kept the school so segregated—with the white kids, in their college-prep courses, in the northern wing, and most of the Negro kids, in trade and vocational programs, in the southern one.

"The white and the colored aren't meant to live together," said a woman seated in the back row. She had a stubborn bulldog scowl and a stiff helmet of hair that suited her.

"Who says?" Ruth answered. She didn't know this woman. At least she had that to be thankful for.

Mildred stepped in. "It's not whether we're meant or not meant. Most of us simply don't know much about people unlike us. We don't have many opportunities."

"I don't want that opportunity," the woman said. She crossed her arms over her chest, and a few women laughed.

Ruth closed her eyes, like a child trying to manage her agitation by blocking out a monster or a troubling feeling. "Look, we have Mayor Cavanagh as a resource. He's trying to do something about poverty.

He's going for the Model City funds. He's got ideas. These are hopeful signs."

"We're not responsible for the city," the woman barked. "We're responsible for ourselves and our families." She sat beside another woman Ruth didn't know. Maybe these were neighbors of Alva's. Both had the same helmet hairdo, probably the same hairdresser. "Look at what they do to the neighborhoods where they live," the first one continued. "You want that?"

"When too many people live packed together, with not much money, in places they don't own and can never hope to own, relying on someone else to maintain the places, usually a white man who doesn't really care, you can't expect House Beautiful to emerge." Ruth paused. Her heart was beating too hard. "My point is this: Wouldn't a neighborhood have a greater chance of remaining viable if some reasonable number of white homeowners and business owners stay put?"

"Easy for you to talk about staying put, with a guard dog in your house," Alva said.

"Sappho? A guard dog?"

"She's a Doberman," Alva said. "Why else would someone get a dog like that?"

"Look," said Mildred. "What kind of dog a person has? I think you're getting off the topic, Alva."

As if getting off-topic was now the thing to do, Minnie, in her front-row seat, spoke up: "Why don't they try to fit in better?" she asked. "The way they talk . . ."

"They way *who* talks?" asked Ruth. "What about the way *you* talk?"

"Ruth," Mildred said. She made it a multi-syllable word, and Ruth looked straight ahead, at no one, pretending she hadn't been stung by the scolding tone.

Lynn Hochman, the pianist, spoke next. "It's not surprising that people would get emotional here. These aren't new issues for Jews, about trying to read the signs, and knowing when to leave, what you may lose by staying behind. All the way back to Exodus."

Other hands went up. "Good point," Ruth said.

Myrna, who hadn't even raised her hand, spoke first, turning to Lynn, who was sitting behind her and to the right. "Surely you don't expect me to buy that analogy. The socioeconomic paradigms of ancient Egypt and 1960s Detroit have nothing in common."

"Socioeconomic paradigms?" That was Lynn.

43

"Plus, okay," Myrna continued, "even if there is an exodus under-way, the Jews aren't slaves in the land of Detroit. We've got power. Power and money. And Jewish money and Jewish men are driving a lot of this exodus—real estate developers, insurance agents, bankers and mortgage brokers. Let's face it. Some of your own husbands and broth-ers." She looked around the room. "Who do you think has been shap-ing white flight since the fifties?"

Myrna's husband was a librarian in some inner-city branch of the Detroit Public Library, so it surely wasn't him. Ruth's husband owned a wholesale shoe business in a two-story brick building in a rundown neighborhood of Detroit, so it surely wasn't him. Mildred's husband ran a scrap metal business with his brothers, so it surely wasn't them. And Lynn's husband was a oboist, so it probably wasn't him either.

"I don't have a husband," Alva said. Some women laughed, remem-bering the Stone Burlesk incident, but others didn't.

The young woman with the cowboy boots raised her hand. "Well, I don't know about socioeconomic paradigms," she said. She looked at Myrna. "The big concern for my friends and me is that we have young children in the Detroit public schools, and let's face it, we've got lots of reasons to be thinking about moving. Many of you," she looked around the room, "are in a different situation—your children already in col-lege or in their last years of high school." She looked at Ruth now. "This has been a wonderful presentation, Mrs. Levine, and I wish we had more time to hear about your findings and the thinking of people like Mrs. Hochman." She turned to Lynn, to acknowledge her. "But shouldn't we consider the recommendations we want to make to the larger community? How can we go about drafting something practical we can all agree on?"

"Excuse me," Ruth said. She stood, even though it was a tight space, between the sofa and the coffee table. She stood, even though she was the only person besides Alva standing. She stood because she couldn't help it. If she were Avrum Bruchenhartz and this woman in the cowboy boots were a child, Ruth would soon be giving her an airplane ride. "What is your name?" Ruth was maybe fifteen years older than this woman and her friends, this woman who had probably been the high school homecoming queen, privileged and adored all her life, thinking she could put her agenda ahead of everyone else's, with her put-on gratitude and highly polished manners, already shunting them aside

44

and making them feel old by calling them Mrs., expecting that everything should be arranged to meet *her* needs.

"Carol," the woman said. "Carol Sugarman."

She might be related to Sugarman the builder, who used to live in
the big silver-brick house at the curve on Outer Drive, the house that
was all gussied up like a New Orleans bordello. The Sugarman who was
putting up those houses around Greenfield and Ten Mile. This woman
would never have had to carry a lamp on a bus in order to move to a
new house. This woman would ride on a leather seat in a Cadillac while
her father smoked a fat cigar and steered with one finger and told her
about the room with the canopy bed she would have at the new house,
the built-in pool and the playhouse in the yard. "Well, Mrs. Sugarman,
are you saying that because of your age, you have a greater investment
in the outcome than the rest of us?"

"That wasn't what I meant," Carol said. "Though I think each of us
has our own concerns, as you can see by the discussion." She looked
around the room for the support she was accustomed to. "I just want to
make sure we get to the practical side of the issue. Before we all have to
leave." She checked her watch. "It's 2:30 now."

"Look," Alva said. "Who really needs a recommendation? It's inevitable. It's the way it always goes. The people who have the means will
move. Just as they have in the past; you included, Ruth, so we might as
well face it. You think I'd stay in this place if I had a choice?"

"Who says it's inevitable?" the woman in the green hat asked. Her
voice was deep and slow and very Old World. "It doesn't have to be inevitable." She paused. It was a long pause, so Ruth wasn't certain
whether she planned to say more, but the interruption had been so
commanding that no one had the courage to step in and perhaps get in
the way. She breathed deeply, noisily, a snore, a sigh, some combination, and it seemed that she was deciding whether it was worth the
trouble to share her thoughts with this group, to put the words together, to make sense of Ruth's rambling presentation, repair the gash
left by Myrna's comment about the husbands and brothers.

"You ladies know Jane Jacobs?" she asked. "A very smart lady. Probably about your age." She looked at Ruth. "She writes books about
cities." She took a bite of the pecan coffee cake, chewing, swallowing,
everyone watching its passage. "You know what she says? That cities
should be messy places, full of people out on the streets. Like in New

York. Children, shopkeepers, garbage collectors, women with baby carriages, old people on their front porches, all mixed in together. Skin colors. Languages. Ages. It makes a place alive. It makes it safe. People know each other. People talk to each other in cities like that, in lively places that aren't torn up by expressways. People think she's crazy, this Mrs. Jacobs. Maybe a little bit like this lady." She gestured toward Myrna, two rows in front of her. "A challenger." No one responded. She shrugged. "You want to move to the suburbs where people hide in their yards, thinking they saved themselves? Okay. So go. But remember," she said, "keep your suitcases packed for the next move. Because if you're afraid, *that* you can't move away from." She took another bite of cake and folded her arms over her broad chest. "Me? I'm staying."

"But you left Europe," Carol Sugarman said. "And that's why you're alive today."

The woman chewed. "What are you?" the lady said. She looked at her challenger. She let the question hang in the air, until the women began to feel uneasy. "An optimist?" The woman laughed, a good deep laugh with shoulders bouncing. And so did some of the others. Ruth did, despite herself. Mildred, Ellie. They laughed too. You couldn't tell about Selma, with her hair falling in front of her face. You couldn't tell about Margo Solomon.

It was late. People were packing up to leave, looking for car keys, folding handouts, talking to neighbors. Myrna had moved over to the woman in the green hat, and they were talking. Alva was clearing dishes. No time for formulating recommendations. No time for wrapping up, nor for the concluding line Ruth had crafted: "Do not consider your home a *sukkah*," she'd wanted to say. "Make it a permanent dwelling."

Mildred took charge. "Ladies," she said, tapping her teaspoon. "Ladies." The room quieted. "These are difficult topics we've been discussing. Let's all thank Ruth for having the courage to get the discussion going." She demonstrated by clapping, and the women joined her. "Can we revisit this next month? It's important enough, and we were probably unrealistic to think we could finish in one session." A few said yes, but the group was already breaking up; some women were already out the door. Even Minnie Rappaport and the lady with the green hat had arranged for their rides home with Carol Sugarman. Mildred asked Ruth to wait so they could talk, but Ruth, gathering her things too, voice shrunken down to almost nothing, said she'd have to call her tomorrow. She thought about asking Alva whether she could take the leftover Halloween candy, so she wouldn't have to stop at the store, but then she'd have to talk to Alva.

Out in the parking lot, a few women were gathered beside Selma's little white Thunderbird—a Ford no matter what fancy name they called it. When they saw her, they stopped talking. Selma waved. In another section of the parking lot, Carol Sugarman was shuffling her passengers into her Buick.

As Ruth unlocked her Chevy, Margo Solomon appeared beside her. Car doors slammed around them, engines started. Leaves floated down on gentle air currents.

"Great job," Margo said.

"Thanks."

"Really. It's such a divisive topic, with everything that's going on. It took a lot of courage. I agree with Mildred. And it's not an easy group."

"No." The car door was open now. She threw in her purse, her satchel.

"We should get together sometime," said Margo.

"Yeah," Ruth said. When was she going to learn to be like Myrna, and call her bluff? Or Carol Sugarman, and know the charming thing to say? Or even Mildred, and not care about getting invitations to glamorous homes from elegant women who never followed through.

"I'd love to have you over."

Ruth nodded.

"We could have lunch," she said. "Not next week, though. Bill and I will be in New York."

"Oh. Nice."

"I mean it," Margo said. "I'll call you. I'm really impressed with what you did today. That story about when you first moved onto Appoline. How you handled it. I liked that."

"Thanks." It helped to know she had listened, remembered, though it was odd that she didn't mention how or whether she had handled it. As Ruth slammed her car door, she knew the annoyance would burble up again soon. It would happen on the way home. It *did* happen on the way home, when she thought of Alva ("Easy for *you* to talk about staying put, with a guard dog in your house") or that other woman ("I don't *want* that opportunity"). And it happened again when she got home, and Sappho was crazy to be let out, and there was Harry's silly card, still sitting on the table, stirring up her feelings about how life had once been and how it was now ("Boo"). And later still when Harry pulled into the driveway, and she realized she had indeed forgotten to stop for Halloween candy. And even later, during their quick dinner, when she didn't have a chance to even mention the meeting. And especially after that, when Harry went out trick-or-treating with Franny (dressed like a beatnik with her hair hanging down curtain-style the way Selma Schneider wore hers), and Ruth stayed home to give out pennies from the big jar in the front hall, with Sappho closed up in the basement so she wouldn't lunge at the door every time a child came to the porch, and Ilo called, asking when Harry was going to bring Sappho—or whether he still planned to—since he'd asked her that morning. And then she got around to, "You have to be kidding. Didn't your husband tell you what happened at the office today?" And Ilo told the story in her plodding way, and Ruth had to listen without giving her sister-in-law any satisfaction. "He didn't tell you?" she asked again, getting satisfaction from that very point.

No. That was the truth. He hadn't even said boo.

PROJECTS

Everyone had stories about the *schwarze*. It was suddenly like a teach-in. Like the day Harry was out raking, a week or so past Halloween. The big elm on his neighbor's lawn had finally given up its summer wardrobe, and the crunchy brown leaves had accumulated like trash all around Harry's house. He didn't hold it against the neighbors, that their leaves blew onto his lawn and that they weren't out raking. He wouldn't hold it against them, no matter what color the people were. At least this was what he would say if someone asked, which no one would, at least not yet, since on this block, everyone was still basically the same color.

These were still the days in Detroit when a homeowner could burn leaves in the street, when a fire was nothing more than an evocative fall ritual. Children jumped into leaf piles, buried each other, fragments catching in their hair and clothes. The men were the fire tenders, rakes in hand, moving out of range of the smoke as it shifted with the wind. Sometimes, keeping a watchful eye on the smoldering piles, one man walked over to talk with—or at—a neighbor. As he raked his leaves toward the curb, Harry could see them down the street, the small congregations. He knew the topics: How it was at the business. Who'd gotten a new car and with how good a deal. The Tigers' disappointing third-place finish. The Lions playing the Steelers. Who in the neighborhood might be selling, what would happen to the block if they did. Harry didn't go for all that talk. But a man had to rake, and so it was that he was out that day, cleaning up the mess from the neighbor's tree, the sweep and swish of the leaves as he organized them into piles, wearing his heavy gray cardigan, his old khaki pants, and his new brown corduroy cap. And so it was that Marvin Deitch, who lived directly across from the Levines, got talking with him.

"You heard what happened to my Bobby, I suppose."

"Me?" Harry *had* heard. Who hadn't? But when a man wants to tell a story, he's going to tell it, no matter what.

49

"This was just last week," Marvin said, "when he was on his way home from school. Riding his bike. Like kids have done for years. A few days after Halloween. It's not a lot to ask. Right? A boy riding his bike home from school?"

Or a man having a normal day at work. It's not a lot to ask. For days after Harry's window incident, as he had come to think of it, he had felt a clutch and flutter of anxiety as he came in each morning, through the long narrow stretch of the building, through the shoe aisles, his sister trailing behind.

Harry moved around his fire, raking in the leaves on the periphery, getting out of smoke range. It was an encampment out there, all along the street, the men of the houses, the blazes. Marvin moved with him. He had fleshy lips, like his son Bobby.

"It wasn't even dark yet," Marvin said. "My boy knows better than to go around at dark. Not that it's a crime. But these days, you know. It's not like the old days."

"Oh, yeah," said Harry. "The old days, like when the Purple Gang ran Detroit, with machine guns. It was safe after dark back then." The wind shifted, and Harry moved with it. Marvin did too. A person could say practically anything to Marvin, and he didn't seem to hear.

"Bobby cut across the school playground," said Marvin, "coming home from a friend's. He's not a big boy. You know my Bobby. He's actually on the bookish side."

Bookish, Harry thought. Dirty books. Down the street he could see the other men talking: Julius Weiner in front of his double lot, Sam Rabinowitz with the white birch on the front lawn, Morris Feldman, with his little boy Freddie beside him, learning the secrets of manhood. Bill Solomon, who owned the big house, wasn't out. He had a service that came to rake his leaves and transport them away in the back of a truck tucked under a canvas cover.

The smoke rising from the many fires joined somewhere above the block, swirled off above the city, the remnants of the leaves transformed, dispersed. Harry would never tell any of these men what had happened at his store Halloween morning. Imagine the deal they would make of it.

"He had his geometry book with him, my Bobby, his chemistry book, American literature. Imagine," Marvin said. "These are important subjects."

"Okay," Harry said. "My girls take the same subjects. I'm aware of geometry."

"He was minding his business. Carrying a geometry book, for god's sake."

"This part I've got," Harry said.

Marvin waved his hand at Harry, to say, I'll tell it how I want. I'm the one with the story.

"Okay already," Harry said.

"Five boys—five *schwarze*. Came across the playground toward him in a line. Who else would do like that, coming at you? At one boy alone. My Bobby. With a geometry book, for god's sake. Do you know what it takes to learn geometry?"

Besides the thick, sensuous lips, Bobby had black shiny hair, slicked back. A careful part on the side. Much like his father. Bobby was in Joanna's grade. A troublemaker. Horny. Joanna had told Ruth about him, the out-of-control one at the sixth-grade parties. Who backed girls into the furnace room. Who pushed them up against the wall. Soft sweaty hands groping.

"They formed a circle around him, before he knew it, Bobby said. He was looking at all of them. He knew some of them, he said. From school. One boy was bigger than the rest. Bobby hadn't seen that one before."

Harry consolidated the pile of leaves he had on the park lawn. The fire was low and ready to receive a new batch. He wiped his brow with his shirt sleeve. Two kids rode by on bikes, small kids, on the sidewalk. He carried his rake with him, over to his front porch—a cement slab—where he'd left a glass of water. Marvin followed, talking while Harry drank. The glass, a former jelly jar, had bright-colored drawings of umbrellas: orange and green and bright blue. These were the days when people still designed things that had several uses, that weren't simply discarded, to become a problem of waste after their first, brief use. The two men walked back to the curb, and Harry fed leaves from the park lawn into the smoldering pile. The flame rose, awakened.

"So then one of them says to Bobby, 'You got a quarter?' and Bobby says, 'No I don't.' He's always polite, my Bobby. He could have told them to shove it up their *tuchis*."

Old Mrs. Weiner, Julius's tiny, bent-over mother, came out her front door in the long black coat that covered her feet, making her look like

51

an anthill. She sat in her usual place, in the lawn chair on the cement porch. The terror of the block. The one who screamed if anyone put a toe on her lawn.

Julius ignored his mother as he tended his leaves. Some evenings, though, when she came out to sit, he stood on the porch beside her lawn chair, hands in fists on his hips, as if daring anyone to trouble her. He had a tight, shiny-red, high-blood-pressure face, an affliction among these Jewish men. But Julius's face also had a slant-eyed effect, the kind kids got by placing a rubber band on their lids.

"Did he give it to them?" Harry asked.

"Did he give it to them?" Marvin answered. "Five of them against one of him? And you expect him to give it to them? My Bobby's no coward, but five *schwarze,* and you expect him to give it to them?"

"No," Harry said. "I mean the quarter. Did he give them the quarter?"

"Of course not," Marvin said. "You think he's giving into extortion?"

Extortion. Marvin knew a word like extortion? "So what did he do?" Harry asked. His hands held the wooden rake, good solid wood, worn with use.

"He said 'I don't have a quarter.'"

Marvin's wife, Seidel, appeared on the Deitch porch and called to her husband. She was a good-looking woman, slim and shapely, Miami Beach blond, as Ruth described it, but she had a hard edge—mouth tight, eyes skeptical, sharp red fingernails. And she also had the look of someone who would one day pare back to all bone, all ribcage and spine.

"Telephone," Seidel called. "It's your mother."

"Tell her I'll call her back," Marvin shouted. "Tell her I'm busy." She turned and went into the house.

"So they kept saying, all of them joining in now, about giving them a quarter. And Bobby holding onto his bicycle handles, knowing of course that this had nothing to do with quarters but with whether they could get a white kid—a white kid alone—to do what they wanted because then, then, they could do anything they wanted to anyone."

"Uh-huh," Harry said.

"What do you mean?" Marvin said. "You approve of such behavior?"

"No," Harry said. "But it is how the world works." The leaf fire was dwindling, the waiting pile down to almost nothing. Harry moved away to gather the scattered remains.

"The world?" Marvin said. "You tell me that when it's your girls."

"So go on with the story."

"Now one of them grabs Bobby's books, from where they're sitting in the basket of his bike, and he hurls them across the playground, way off. And Bobby's looking around, hoping someone is going to walk by. Maybe one of the neighbors in the houses across from the playground will look out. Someone walking by, someone driving by, even a little kid who would run home and tell his mother. Even the police maybe would be circulating, like they should be."

"Yeah?" Harry said.

"But no one. So my Bobby has to take matters into his own hands. He lowers his head and he pushes through, between two of the boys, like a battering ram. And keeps walking, like a demon. He feels someone knock him on the back of the head as he goes; someone else kicks against his leg, but he knows it was only the side of a hand he felt on his head and only a light kick on the leg. It could have been much worse. A rock, a pipe, a brick. 'Where you going so fast?' one of them calls. 'We're just playin' with you,' shouts another. And someone else, 'Don't forget your school books,' like he's going to go back and get his books. Like he's stupid or something. 'Don't forget your bike,' they called."

"Well, I know he's not stupid," Harry said.

"No, he's not," Marvin answered. "But he couldn't help himself from the anger. Once he got some distance, he turned, and looked back."

Harry could imagine that face—rage and fear and indignation, and pure surprise to be on his feet, alive. Mouth open, thick lip curled down, breathing hard through his nose, like a bull.

"And then those colored all laughed at him. Having a great time. And then Bobby snapped out of it, turned, and walked as fast as he could. When he got to Outer Drive, out of sight of the playground, he ran. He ran all the way home. Came in panting. I saw him. I'd just gotten in from work. 'What happened, Bobby?' I said."

"What happened to the bike?"

"What do you think? They're going to bring it over to the house?"

Joanna was coming up the street now, on her bike, with her friend Gina. They'd been at their dance class at the Jewish Center. Harry waved as Joanna turned into the driveway, and Gina rode on by to her house down the block.

"I tell you, Harry," Marvin said. "You better watch your girls. Me? I wouldn't let them ride their bikes around like that."

The last embers in the leaf pile were blinking out, tended and contained. All those mountains of leaves gone, dispersed into the air. In the spring, a new crop would sprout, starting with the smallest swellings on the twigs in March.

"Listen, Marvin," he said. "We all have to live in the world. There are bad people in it and good. Every color, every religion. The problem is, you can't tell the good ones from the bad just by looking."

"So?" Marv asked. Harry went to his porch, with Marvin following

"Sorry to say, but we were all young once. We all did things we regret." Surrounding a boy, taunting with an ugly word or name, sticking a foot into the aisle at school, scrawling a message on a window—impulsive acts that came from some dark place of confusion and boredom and power-hunger. Perhaps it had after all been Alvin who'd written those words. Perhaps, too, the act was forgivable. "Unfortunately," he said to Marvin, picking up his glass, raising it to his lips, having forgotten it was empty, "we have to give people a chance."

"Okay," Marvin said, "*you* can give them a chance. Give a chance. Take a chance. Not me. Not my Bobby."

"Okay," he said, "I'm sorry about what happened. Tell Bobby he can come over and pick whichever bike he wants from my basement." Ruth said that when someone lost something or someone, the thing to do was give them something else, to fill the void, at least a little. It didn't have to be the same thing they lost. It couldn't be. No loss could be completely undone. But by receiving a little unexpected something, a person could perhaps begin to feel that a benevolence, a generosity, was afoot in the world again. That's why she gave him the brown corduroy cap, the one he wore today, after he'd told her—minus the drugs and the Black Panther literature—what had happened to him at the store, on Halloween.

"You got one as good as the one he lost?" Marv asked.

"I guess you'll have to come and see." Harry took off his hat and wiped his brow. Even with the cool fall air, he had gotten overheated. The exercise, the fire, the conversation. The conversation alone could get a man overheated.

When Harry began his broken-bicycle project, he was with Joanna in the empty lot down the street from their house on Fairfield, the place they lived before they moved to Appoline, and it was a spring day in 1955. The bike was missing a tire, and its frame was rusted and bent, but he lifted it by the handlebar from where it lay in the weeds and looked at the wobbly mess. "Daddy," Joanna said, "why are you picking that up?" He couldn't exactly say. "Why is it here?" she asked. And he couldn't answer that one either. He wasn't wondering how the bike had ended up there in the empty lot, who had left it, or how it had fallen into such disrepair. He wasn't even wondering why the lot was empty—who might own it and what might have gone wrong that nothing had ever been built there. He wasn't thinking of anything besides how abandoned and broken the bike looked.

Although the father and daughter often roamed in that field, they had never before found anything like that bike. Far more typical were the burrs and nettles that stuck to their pant legs. Elms and maples and Queen Anne's lace. Goldenrod, which made Harry's eyes itch like crazy. The lot also had tall grasses that generated the bloom that his girls referred to as softies—the little bottle-brushes that probably held the seeds, that probably were the flowers of the grasses.

In the field, they collected milkweed pods, which held a million secrets, as Joanna described it, and the little blue chicory flowers that grew everywhere along the side of the road, and also right here, in their own empty lot on a city street in the densely packed Automotive Capital of the World.

The truth was that Harry had felt at a special loss that Sunday morning when they found the bike, Joanna asking him, as always, to tell her a story about when he was a little boy. And he could not think of anything to tell her, as usual, nothing that seemed magical or important enough that she would want to know about it. He'd told about the twice-broken fingers of his left hand, many times, the family move to New York, the return to Detroit. The pickup baseball games. He didn't want to tell those again, not now anyway.

Maybe it was because they'd recently learned that Ruth was pregnant, an unexpected turn of events—with Joanna now seven and Lena ten. They hadn't been planning on having another, and little pieces of him were arranging and rearranging themselves inside, as they were more literally inside Ruth, making way for the new baby, thinking about how they would manage, what this would mean for their family, for the girls, whom they hadn't yet told.

So he was casting about, through the empty lot where they had walked so many times, and that no longer held any magic for him, though it seemed to for Joanna, who wanted to go back again and again, imagining that she and Harry were Indians, roaming the plains or the prairie at some time before the city had begun. And it was true that this place he thought of as only "the empty lot" did have some magic, representing some remnant of a past, nestled as it was in a city that otherwise retained little imprint of the woods and prairies it once had been. And there it was, in this empty lot, the bicycle, keeled over, weeds poking up around and through it. Harry couldn't know then that one day, by the turn of the next century, Detroit would be snaggle-toothed with vacant lots, so dense with weeds and high grasses that pheasants, plump exotic birds with long tails and ringed necks and red caps and mottled coats, lived and roamed among them.

On that day in the empty lot, it was no wonder Harry could not think of an amusing story to tell his young daughter. Besides contemplating the new baby, he was wondering whether it was time to follow the trail of so many of their friends and neighbors, on the move north and west once again, hopscotching across the city, one generation over the next, some pioneers already crossing the city line at Eight Mile, into the suburbs. People said that their neighborhood was fraying. For-sale signs were sprouting on front lawns.

Harry had not himself seen signs of this fraying, nor had Ruth, and he said this to the friends and relatives, and even the real estate agents, who told the stories about the trouble that was brewing, the danger and deterioration. For him, moving—even the thought of moving—felt like giving up on something.

Nevertheless, by 1955, the year Harry and Joanna found that first bicycle, he could see that the proportion of Negro to white children was changing at Halley School, where Lena and Joanna went. And it was also true that he and his family could use a bigger house, with the new baby coming.

In 1955, too, the whole city was changing. It had just ended its street-rail service and sold all hundred-plus streetcars to Mexico. And by then, the city fathers had begun construction on a system of expressways over which Detroiters would now move at formerly unimaginable speeds via their own made-in-Detroit automobiles. Progress, they called it, which would benefit the many, while displacing the powerless.

The John Lodge, when done, would run north and west, starting downtown and sweeping all the way to Eight Mile. The Edsel Ford, begun during the war to link Detroit with the Willow Run bomber plant, would cross the city from east to west, bisecting and destroying densely populated neighborhoods, and the Chrysler, only a few years off, would run north and south, paving over Hastings Street, now the neighborhood called Black Bottom.

Considering all the ways Harry's own life was about to change, and all the ways the city was changing, and the speeds at which the city planners intended to move people through and across the city, it was a sweet, almost quaint and reassuring thing for Harry to find a discarded, rusting bicycle in an empty lot.

"We'll take it home and fix it," he said to Joanna. "We'll do it together. This is something I liked when I was a boy. Riding my bike and fixing things."

"Do you know how to do it?" She touched the rusted blue frame with her finger.

"We'll figure it out," he said.

From there, it became a passion. He and Joanna went out together looking for them, at yard sales, along the railroad tracks, in empty lots, in the want ads. And they worked together in the old shed behind the house. When they followed the trend of their friends and family and moved to a new house after all, they had ten bikes to bring with them, and Harry set up a workshop in the basement. As the collection grew, Joanna kept track of all the bikes in a little spiral notebook, listing them by color, size, make, and special characteristics, like drop handlebars or handbrakes, banana seats, air pumps, baskets, training wheels. She made charts with columns, enumerated features. And so it was that by the time Bobby Deitch, surrounded on the school playground, had lost his bike, Harry had plenty of possible replacements for him, hanging from hooks on the ceiling and racks on the walls and squeezed in together under the stairway.

Just as the idea to collect bikes came to him at an uncertain moment in a wooded field near their old house more than ten years earlier, the idea to give all of them away came to him at the dinner table, the smell of leaf smoke still on him—in his hair, his mustache, the fibers of his old gray cardigan—the harangue of Marvin Deitch's voice still in his ears, and the disturbance of the three soaped words still in his heart.

57

He asked Lena to pass the hamburgers, which Ruth had set, fragrant and juicy, in the way of browned meat, on a beige, oval serving platter. Lena passed the platter to her father and returned to chewing a carrot stick. She'd been toying with the idea of vegetarianism.

"Since he asked for the hamburgers," Ruth said, "he'll also want the . . ." She said it like a fill-in-the-blank test, like a teacher weary of working with her remedial students, as if two plus two had thus far been beyond them, but one needed to press on nonetheless, despite the diminishing likelihood of success. "Same with salad," she said. "Someone asks for salad, you also pass the dressing." The teacher was not the only one who was weary of this lesson. The remedial students, too, had heard and resisted it many times.

"If he wants the ketchup, why doesn't he ask for it?" Lena said. "He might not want the ketchup. Not everyone does."

"I want the ketchup," Harry said.

Without looking at Ruth, Lena pushed up the sleeves of her army surplus jacket, picked up the ketchup, and passed it to him. Joanna looked out the window into the night, pretending she hadn't noticed any of this. She leaned back in her wooden chair, hands on the oval table that had served as the gathering place for their meals as long as she could remember. She rested her head back, on the red wallpaper with the repeating pattern of colonial kitchen images—iron stoves and milk churns and metal implements like cherry pitters and pie wheels, kittens curled on oval rugs in front of fireplaces. The wallpaper, some designer's conception of hearth and home, had been there when they moved in, almost ten years ago. Franny pushed canned corn around her plate, hoping to compress it.

The daughters were like three variations on a theme, with sufficient overlap in appearance that often Harry interchanged the names, stumbling through the lineup until he arrived at the right one. All had the black curly hair they'd gotten from Harry, some curlier than others, he'd grant that, but all with the dark eyebrows that were his too, the serious mouths with the full lips and reluctant smiles (his), all with the noses that bumped out just below the bridge (Ruth's) and bulbed softly at the end (Harry's), with variations in width and length, but still, the nose a testimony, right there in the middle of the face, that they were a tight mix of both mother and father. Temperamentally, he thought, they were more like Ruth—quick to anger, to tears, to explosions of all kinds.

58

The three had their differences, of course—Lena with the fair complexion, like Ruth, and the thin boyish body; Joanna more olive, like Harry, browning nicely in the summer sun, and also rounder, with the plumpness, the *fleisch,* that the elders loved to pinch when she had been little; and then Franny, delicate and graceful, everything in proportion, as if on the third try, they'd gotten it right.

"You could call it Table Mind," Lena said to her mother, not in a nice way. "It could be your philosophy. It's kind of Zen." She was studying Eastern religions in school, along with anthropology, along with socialism, communism, and democracy—"all very practical subjects," Harry usually said to Ruth after Lena left the house to go back to her apartment in the decaying neighborhood around Wayne State, usually helmetless, on the backseat of a motorcycle with one of the endless string of dirty-fingernailed boyfriends with black leather motorcycle jackets and unknown pasts and decidedly un-Jewish noses. And Ruth would shush him. "Learning is important," she'd say. "They'll find their way." But Harry was skeptical about how a person could find her way by studying faraway cultures, odd religious practices, and repressive political systems; he was also skeptical about where exactly she would find her way *to.* What his grandfather Wolfe Levinsky, who'd brought them all to this country, like specks on his coattails or seeds in the pack of merchandise on his back, would have to say about anthropology and Zen . . . the blank and incredulous look that might settle on his furious face . . . well, some things were simply beyond the older generation.

"It's a mid-range form of giving," Ruth said. "Giving before one is asked. And it's not Zen. It's Jewish. Maimonides. Twelfth century." The teacher had now moved on, considerably beyond remedial.

"Passing the ketchup is not charitable giving—and it especially isn't charitable if the person doesn't want what's given," Lena said.

"He did want the ketchup," Joanna said. She only spoke up, especially with Lena, when she was absolutely certain of a point. "He said so."

"But only after *she* brought it up," Lena said. "So we'll never know whether he really did want it."

Harry waited for the slow stream of ketchup to reach his hamburger, shaking the bottle, encouraging its progress. It had seemed like such a simple, concrete thing—hamburger and ketchup. Then it came to him, the way ideas do, two or more unrelated preoccupations converging: "You know all those bikes in the basement?" he asked. Oh, they knew. "What if I brought home a truck one night, Bernie's furniture truck, and loaded them up?" he asked. "I could drive them over to Eight Mile, where the projects are, or down by my store, some place where people don't have bikes. And then I could hand them out, just give them away, to whoever came."

Franny had given up on the corn project, the hope that reconfiguring the bright yellow niblets would make them diminish or disappear. She couldn't stand their squishy texture, the way the skin popped between her teeth, the cloudy, milky liquid that seeped out, the little pool that accumulated around them. But she knew that no one at the table would force her to eat it, that it never came to that. If she held out, someone would eventually notice her despair and whisk the plate away.

"It would be like insurance," he said. "If you give someone what they want, they don't have to take it."

Lena now was the one to look skeptical. "To have some white guy drive in and stand on a street corner, giving stuff away? And something valuable, like a bike? Wouldn't you wonder what the trick was?"

"They can wonder," Harry said, "but there's no trick. I think it would be a good thing to do."

Ruth got up from the table. She sat again. It wasn't her kind of thing. When she was growing up, her family always kept a *pishke,* a blue tin box painted with a white Jewish star, for depositing spare change that would then be sent off to some unclear charitable purpose in Israel. But in that family of seven children, where they had little surplus of any kind, she'd always felt that they should keep the spare change for themselves. Her instinct was to hold onto things. "Don't you give enough already?" she asked.

"What do *you* think?" he asked, turning to Joanna, his bicycle-repair partner.

"I don't know," she said. Her standard answer to almost anything these days. It wasn't that she didn't know. It was that she had learned uncertainty, learned to worry that what she thought might not matter, might not be important enough, might be wrong or embarrassing.

Ruth looked pained, or annoyed, with this perennial answer. "How can you not know?" she asked. "You agree. You disagree. You like the idea. You think it's stupid. You like it *and* you think it's stupid. One way or the other, you know *something.*"

Of course, Joanna knew, but she didn't yet know that she knew, so most of what she knew stayed locked inside, in one big misty mass. No one and nothing would be able to pull it out of her until she was ready. Certainly not her mother's annoyance. She shrugged.

"And you, Franny?" Harry asked. Franny, so much younger than the others, found it hard to keep up, wasn't sure what insurance was, and she didn't understand how her mother, so concerned with anticipating what people wanted at the table, didn't anticipate her dislike for canned corn. She shrugged.

"Does anyone want to help me?" Harry asked. He looked around. "Joanna?" She'd lost interest in the bicycle project, in her inventory, the past few years. She didn't like being around Harry nearly as much as she used to; she didn't like the way he walked, the large serious steps, the worried look on his face when he put up the storm windows in the fall, the way he spoke to her friends—"like we're all stupid," she said. Though the truth was, he barely spoke to her friends, since she had made him so self-conscious about what he said.

She had a bite of hamburger in her mouth, so she couldn't speak right away. It was good, the burger, and the time it gave her to sort through the feelings. "I don't know," she said. "Okay. Why not?"

"Anybody else?" Harry asked. Franny looked a little interested now that Joanna was going to do it, but Ruth said, not Franny. Franny was too small. And with that, she cleared the table, looking with disapproval at the pile of corn kernels on Franny's plate.

So there they were, sitting in Bernie's truck, which Harry had loaded by himself that morning, packing them in, bicycle by bicycle, before he woke Joanna. The sleep was still in her eyes, as she sat hunched in the cab beside him, eating the cold toast he'd brought for her, the butter soaked into the golden brown ridges, the golden sun shining on the road. A chill was in the air, but it was warm for November. By noon, it might be warm enough to take off their jackets. For now though, Harry had the heat on, turned up high, and it blew on them, swirling Bernie's dust as they bumped along, the bikes rattling in the back.

"Why does it have to say Formica City all over it?" Joanna asked. Big red letters adorned the driver and passenger doors, the two side panels, and the sliding door on the back.

He could have told her the whole story, of what it took to ask the favor of Bernie, who would barely speak to him after the window incident, of how he had told Bernie he wanted the truck so he could finally clean out the old Bruchenhartz furniture from the basement on Grand

61

River, which prompted Bernie to accuse Harry of planning to move his business, and on and on through the whole awkward and annoying exchange. But he didn't. "It's the only truck I could get," he said.

And after that, they didn't say anything as they headed for the stretch on Eight Mile, not far from their own home, which had once been an army barracks, and was now one of the few places on the northwest side where Negroes lived, represented as a solid black band on the census maps, and recently the focus of the urban renewal movement. The projects. The Levine family had passed by many times, wordlessly, watching the shack-like barracks come down and the new units go up, no explanation requested, and none given. Until today, no Levine had ever actually pulled off the road, into the midst of this settlement.

Along the front, where Harry pulled in, rattling and bumping over the rutted field in the old, battered truck, muffler thunking, bikes bouncing, tires crunching in the gravel, day laborers stood, waiting for someone to need them. Others sat on cinderblocks, flat caps on their heads, legs spread wide, big hands on knees, dusty work boots, lunch pails on the ground beside them. All their eyes turned to the truck, Formica City, looking to see what it might have to do with them, with their quest to bring in a good day's pay. Joanna looked at them, then looked away, down at her hands.

Behind the men were rows of tightly packed one-story houses. They looked like the portables the public schools had added in clusters on their playgrounds, to accommodate all the baby boom children. Too, the rectangular dwellings with their flat roofs reminded Harry of shoe boxes. They had fake wood siding that, although fairly new, already had a look of deterioration—slats askew or missing, water-stained edges. Two cement steps led up to the doors, and each had one small window in the front, to the right of the door.

One man came up to the driver's-side window. He threw his cigarette into the gravel as he did. He was thin, and brown, with a scraggly beard, wiry little black hairs that grew on his chin and cheeks in patches, like the thin patches of grass that dotted the empty fields around the shoebox houses. His brown wool jacket, stained and fraying, hung on him, a few sizes too big, like he was in the process of shrinking while everything around him, the jacket as one indicator, stayed the same.

Harry rolled down his window.

"You moving furniture?" the man asked. The cold morning air came in with the man's voice. Harry turned down the rattling fan on the heater. "I can do just about anything."

Joanna withdrew into her corner of the cab, pressed against the door. She stared ahead, at the little houses, wondering how many people could fit in one. When she'd agreed to come, she'd pictured children. Children and bicycles and joy. This was something different.

"I'm sorry," Harry said. "I'm not looking for workers. Right now." As if not looking for workers was a temporary situation. He might change his mind any minute; something might come up as they sat there in the truck.

Another man came up to the truck. "What's he looking for?" the new man asked. He wore a red scarf, tied like an ascot. He didn't look at Harry, but at his fellow day laborer, as if he were the translator, as if there was no point speaking directly to the foreigner.

"He ain't said yet," the first man said.

He hadn't said because this was not an easy question to answer. The thing was that he wasn't really looking for anything he could say in a way that would make sense to these men, who were looking for something far more tangible and important than what Harry was looking for—at least that's how it seemed to him at the moment. And he couldn't simply say, "I'm looking for children," because that would probably make him sound suspicious. And he couldn't say "insurance," which was how he'd explained this outing to his family, because men like this would know this was not a place that a man like him came looking for insurance, and certainly not in a big old truck with rattling cargo that said Formica City. And he certainly couldn't explain to them what he meant by "insurance," because that would be an insult—like saying, I'm here to bribe you so you won't rob me.

"I've got a truckload of bikes," Harry said. He indicated with his thumb. "To give to the children."

Two more men had come up by now.

"What did he say?" one said.

"Something about bikes," said another. "For the children."

"Bikes?" said the first one, adjusting his cap. "Bikes?" He paused. "What are you? Santa Claus or something?" The other men laughed. "You sure don't look like Santa Claus."

Which made Harry wonder whether this meant that the man knew he was Jewish, whether they could guess, whether it showed on his face. "Nope," Harry said, "not Santa Claus. Just have a lot of bikes and want to give them away where someone might be able to use them."

The longer this went on, the more uncomfortable Joanna became, staring straight ahead through the windshield, pretending she didn't hear anything that was being said. But also, the longer she stared, the more she noticed that the houses weren't all exactly alike, as she had originally thought, that some had special touches. One had curlicue metal railings around the postage-stamp porch and up the steps. And from the railing hung a flower box with marigolds in orange and gold and yellow. That same house had fancy metal numbers to indicate the address, and a wooden mailbox painted bright yellow.

The house next door to that one had a board over the small window, and pieces of siding were missing, revealing tar paper. The address on that one consisted of crude crooked numbers painted on the surface of the house. Another house had a board nailed across the door, but the one next to it had a lawn chair on the front porch—it almost filled the whole space—and pretty curtains with a lacy edge showed through the window.

"You brought your assistant with you?" the man with the red scarf said. "An elf or something?"

"She's my daughter," Harry said.

Seven or eight men had gathered around the truck by now—all on Harry's side. "Well, come on then," the man with the red scarf said. "Show us what you brought."

Harry hesitated. He had envisioned himself surrounded by children, not grown men. But these men didn't seem threatening. Harry was a man, too, not Bobby Deitch. This wasn't the school yard. They were standing near Eight Mile, with lots of traffic passing. And if they stole all his bikes? Well, he had come to give them away, so what would be the difference?

He turned off the engine and got out. He reached behind the seat for the poster Franny had made with stenciled letters that were slightly off center and sloping.

"Dad," Joanna said, "Don't."

But he had already pulled it out. "Bicycle Giveaway. Come get a bike." Below the letters were drawings Franny had made of bikes. All shapes and sizes, including a unicycle, and one of the old-fashioned kind with the huge front wheel. Harry showed the poster to the men, as if it were a credential.

"Nice sign," the man in the brown jacket said. And the others appeared to agree. "You really got a truck full of bikes?"

"Yes, I do," Harry said. He handed the sign to Joanna and walked around to the back of the truck. He opened the padlock and slid the door up. What a racket it made, groaning and clanking up its tracks. He stood aside and the men looked.

"He's got bikes," a man with a black cap said.

"He sure does," said the one with the red scarf.

By then, a few women and children, a few teenaged girls, had gathered. Harry left the back open and went to get Joanna.

"Come on," he said. "It's okay."

She sat plastered against the door. She didn't want to get out. She wanted to go home. She didn't like being there. She didn't like the hard-packed dirt field with the patchy grass, with the broken glass scattered about and glinting in the sun. She didn't like the men talking about Santa Claus and elves. She didn't like the small box-like houses, even if some had curlicues. She didn't like being the girl in the big truck with all the bikes and the father who had a business rather than a cinderblock to sit on while he waited for work. Not that she wanted the alternative, unless the alternative was not having to know about any of this.

"Come on," he said again. She shook her head no. But then she saw a little boy standing behind Harry and watching her. Maybe he was seven or eight, dark and wiry. He wore a striped T-shirt, and his hair was closely shorn, looking like a tight, fuzzy cap. He was eating a piece of toast, but he didn't have a jacket. And she remembered the notebooks she used to keep with the rows and columns and checkmarks, her bike inventory. What was the point in keeping track, in accumulating, in having an inventory, if it hung on hooks, jammed in and increasingly tangled in a basement? Bikes were for riding. And here was a little customer.

She opened her door, slid down from the truck, and walked around the back, staying close to Harry, keeping her eyes to herself, embarrassed that someone might recognize her from school, or that she might recognize them. All the times she'd driven by here, she'd never thought about who might live here, that kids she knew from school might. That they probably did. Where else would they live? They didn't live on her block, nor on the blocks of anyone she knew.

Harry pulled a wooden step stool from the truck, unfolded it, and motioned for Joanna to climb up. He followed her, and together they untangled a small Huffy, one that seemed like it would fit the small boy in the striped shirt, pulling and lifting it out from the rest, moving others out of the way, pedals getting caught in spokes of neighboring bikes, handlebars hitching onto each other. He wheeled it forward. He held it out, over the side of the truck, the small bicycle hanging in the air, in his hands. "Here, son, would you like this one?"

The boy nodded, staring at the bike, finishing the last bite of toast, wiping his fingers on his pants. "Go ahead," Harry said. "It's yours." Harry sat on the edge of the truck, so he could hand the bike to the boy. Other people came closer, to see what it was about, to see if the boy would take it, to see if this was a joke or trick that the white man was playing, if he would grab it back, once the boy reached out, if he would laugh, or insult, call the boy greedy. If he would call the police, later in the day maybe, to give the description of the striped shirt, the shaved head, a boy perhaps seven or eight. The man with the red scarf was there, as was the man in the brown jacket. They watched.

"It's real," Joanna said. "Come on. Take it. Look how many we have." The boy looked.

"Are you going to take it?" Harry asked. He got down from the truck and put the bike on the ground in front of the boy. It was too small to have a kickstand, so Harry lay it on its side. The boy stooped to look at it. He spun the rear tire.

"It's yours," Harry said. "Do you know how to ride?"

The boy nodded, while tracing his finger over the handlebars to the blue and white plastic streamers that hung from them. He held the streamers in his hand, as if he were weighing them.

"Well, good," Harry said. He got back on the truck. He looked around at the crowd that had gathered. At the women, some walking slow and heavy with big loose housedresses and big, heavy sweaters they held wrapped around themselves, and collapsed shoes that flapped off their heels like house slippers, bright-colored cloths tied tight on their heads. At the teenagers with their tight bodies and tight clothes. At the children, all sizes and shapes. At the men who were still waiting for someone to come hire them for the day, distracted from their focus on work by the curious white man and his truck, his bikes, his young assistant. The people stood in a circle, waiting to see what would happen.

The little boy picked up the bike, sat on it, and rode, wobbling at first. All the heads in the crowd turned to follow him, looking back and forth between the boy pedaling, and Harry, on the truck with his back turned, surveying the contents of the truck, disentangling one bike from the next, passing them to his daughter, not even watching the boy as he disappeared between rows of houses.

Harry turned back toward the crowd and saw a little girl, standing near the truck with someone who looked like her older sister. He found a small bike, with a sparkly banana seat and a horn, and he wheeled it forward. He climbed off the truck and asked Joanna to hand him the bike. He placed it on the ground.

"Here's one for you, if you'd like it." He beckoned to the little girl. He squeezed the rubber ball of the horn, to show her how it worked, how it squawked. She startled at the sound, recoiled against her sister's leg. He tipped the bike toward her. She came forward, but her sister grabbed her shoulder, then her hand, and led her away. The little girl looked back over her shoulder, tripping over her feet as her sister kept moving.

"It's okay," Harry said, calling after them. "She can have it if she wants." But they didn't turn back, the sister half-dragging the little girl.

"You can give me one," said a tall skinny girl with long legs and a big wide smile. It was so simple. All you had to do was ask. Her hair was pulled back and twisted into a tight, neat ponytail that stuck out stiff. She might have been about twelve. Harry bet she was a fast runner. Girls like her could usually run pretty fast.

"Okay," Harry said. He left the one with the banana seat lying on the ground and climbed back on the truck to disentangle a purple Schwinn that looked about her size. "Here you go." He handed it down to her. She was tall enough that she could reach up and take it. She got on the seat and pedaled off, with a boy and a girl chasing her, trying to catch the fender. She rode standing up, her head held high, laughing and whooping, like she'd been waiting for this moment all her life, like she was born to ride. The kids chasing after her didn't have a chance, so they gave up, and ran back to the truck, breathless, their jackets off their shoulders and flapping on their arms behind them.

Harry saw another little girl in the crowd—maybe four years old—

younger than the one who'd been dragged off by her sister. Her hair was divided into perfect squares, with her scalp showing through in straight lines, and each section of hair was twisted into a little braid, with a small bright-colored plastic barrette attached. She had a pink jacket tied around her waist, like a long skirt, and she was dancing, dancing like the jacket was the skirt of an evening gown. Her skin was nut brown, and her eyelashes were curled so tight, they made her look even wider eyed than she was.

A very fat lady stood beside her, watching her closely. The lady's legs had ripples and folds, and her feet spilled over the sides of her shoes. Her cotton dress was a big, loose tent, as was her cloth coat. The little girl with the pink jacket and the curly eyelashes threw herself into a wild twirl, and knocked into a little boy beside her who tumbled over and rolled into the legs of a woman who held a baby. "Whoa," said the woman with the baby, who managed to keep her balance but looked crossly at the little boy.

"Tanya," the big grandmother said to the little girl in the pink jacket. She said it fast and loud and in a commanding way, scolding. Her look was stern, and she grabbed the girl by the arm. With that, the girl settled down. But then Harry got off the truck and wheeled the small bicycle with the banana seat over to her, honking the horn as he went. "Here you go, little girl," he said.

She hopped on one foot. She hopped and jumped as if on a pogo stick or a trampoline, as if the packed earth of the field they were in was a big springy mattress. She hopped right over to Harry and the bicycle, and she sang a little song without words but with the sound mmm-mmm, like she was just about to get something delicious, chocolate cake with thick shiny frosting or honey-baked ham with bright red maraschino cherries.

"Tanya," the woman said. She had a deep voice, and it had a sharp edge when she spoke to the little girl. But Tanya was hopping and twirling beside the bike, laughing, so deeply immersed in mischievous abandon that the summons didn't penetrate. "Tanya," the woman said again, a second warning.

"Oh, let her be," Harry said. "She's having fun." He said it like he might say it to his brother-in-law Irv or to Marvin Deitch, a swipe disguised as playful banter, with a sharp undercoat of judgment. With Irv . . . well, they said things like this to each other all the time. Their word

68

volleys had a veneer of affection, but the offenses added up on some invisible scorecard, since they didn't know any other way of talking to each other besides this banter implying that neither of them had feelings. Tanya's grandmother, however, had feelings, and Harry had overstepped the bounds, not considering that anyone might have a reason to deprive this delighted child of anything, not considering that someone might see it as a poor lesson for a child who all her life might face accusations of wanting something-for-nothing.

The people in the crowd put thoughts of bicycles aside for the moment. Even the children turned away from the truck to see what would happen between Harry and the grandmother.

"I can't let her be, Mister," the big woman said. "I got to keep my little girl in line, and I don't think it's up to you to tell me how to raise her."

Harry was still operating primarily in the Irv mode, where conversation was a ball thrown back and forth until someone missed. "I'm not telling you how to raise her," he said. "Just saying to let her enjoy herself." He still held the small bike by the handlebars, so he was bent over in an awkward posture. Joanna stood up on the truck bed, with a broader view than Harry had. Tanya stopped hopping. "You're only young once," he said. As if this were a saying that everyone would recognize and value, as if it were a magical incantation, a solid argument.

"I don't let my girl take things from strangers," she said. The grandmother had Tanya by the hand, and with her now-blank face, it was hard to say what lesson the little girl was absorbing, only that it was a hard one—the magical sparkly banana seat, the red bulb of the horn just within reach. The fact that she would not be allowed to have either. The white man bent over. His frozen smile.

"What do you say to the man?" the grandmother asked. Tanya did not appear to know. From the stillness, she began to jiggle. She began to roll up onto her toes and back onto her heels. She pulled her hand away from her grandmother and began to bounce. The bounce turned into a hop. "Tanya," the grandmother said. She grabbed the girl's hand. The little girl became still, but she kept looking at the bike. "You tell him 'No, thank you.'"

Harry couldn't straighten up and hold the bike at the same time, so he placed it on the ground. Tanya pulled her hand away from her grandmother again. She squatted and squeezed the wonderful red ball of that horn. *Honk*. And *honk* again. Harry laughed and looked at the grandmother, still not understanding, still thinking that *she* would soon get it, that she would soften.

"You don't listen to what I tell you," the grandmother said, "you got to go home and think about it." And her grandmother pulled her away through the quiet crowd of observers.

"No," he called after them. "It's okay. Really. I want her to have the bike."

But the grandmother kept walking, holding Tanya tightly by the hand, and soon they were gone. And gradually the moment became like one of those moments when the teacher has been summoned into the hall to talk to the principal, and the moment becomes two moments, three, four, and then the unraveling begins, the realization that the room belongs to the children. Joanna saw it happening from her perch on the truck.

"Who else?" Harry said. "Who would like this bike?" It lay on the ground, and Harry picked it up again.

"Me!" three boys said at once. They were maybe ten, eleven years old, wearing dungarees and T-shirts, gym shoes, baggy sweatshirts.

"Okay," he said. "Then come on." He handed it to one of the boys, then climbed up on the truck and worked through the inventory, getting Joanna to help him, looking for boys' bikes that would fit the other two.

While his back was turned and he was busy scanning, sorting, untangling, maneuvering bike from bike, the crowd moved in closer, to get a better look, to have a better position if this strange event continued, turned out not to be an illusion or a tease or a ruse.

Joanna saw them, felt them moving in—not disorderly, not at first, but quietly stepping forward, like they were all connected, pulled by a magnetic force, all that metal, all the fenders and handlebars and spokes and chains and crossbars that her father had situated in their midst. The two boys who had spoken up before ("Me!") but who hadn't yet gotten bikes were pressed up against the truck. They waved their arms, jumping, shouting "Me, me," each pushing the other out of the way, afraid Harry would forget who they were ("Me! Me!"), that they were next in line, with the others pushing up behind them. They wanted to be sure he saw their faces and distinguished them from the mass.

And the mass consisted of girls from Joanna's grade school named

70

Nellie and Patricia who played rough during gym, who she avoided on the playground. Boys from Reading Group 2 who stumbled painfully through every sentence, every word, when the class took turns reading aloud. A kid from the row next to her in second grade who had disappeared somewhere in the middle of fourth grade, shortly after he'd started humming loudly during class and writing strange notes to people. She'd gotten one with lots of exclamation marks that said, "Whoa, a Hershey bar in the REM!!!" She'd puzzled over it, with its dirty possibilities, laughed about its craziness with her friends, then left it on the teacher's desk. Soon, the boy was gone, his seat empty. Now, here he was, older but looking equally strange, his eyes too big for their sockets, his mouth hanging open and his tongue the pink of a strawberry lollipop.

"Me, me," the boys shouted. And children behind them shouted too, pressing, jumping above the crowd, as if they were shooting baskets, jumping so they could be seen, heard, noticed.

Being up high, she could see so much. She could see the men who had been waiting for work out front. She could see a woman whose eyes were so deep set as to be almost invisible, and that woman had a pair of glasses pushed up, resting on her hair. Her hair was pulled back tight, and she wore a pair of gold earrings—long ones that caught the sun and shimmered beside the thin line of her jaw. Her head was cocked, taking in the scene, her lips pressed together, and she shook her head, slowly, as if she were speaking to Joanna with her closed lips and the pivot of her head, saying, "What are you fool white folks up to now?" Joanna could see the woman's collar bone, the lines beneath her eyes, as if all the fool white things she had seen were written there in tiny script.

"Joanna," Harry said. "Pull some bikes out. The kids are waiting." So she got to work, as if she wanted to prove to the woman that what they were doing was good, and not a fool thing. She pulled out an old Huffy, the kind with the radio built into the tank. It was rusty, and the radio's battery pack was missing, but it was a good bike. She'd ridden it, and she knew. When she wheeled it toward the crowd, the two boys scrambled over each other to get to it.

"Hey," Harry said. "Slow down. There's enough for everyone." He handed the Huffy down to one of the boys, trying to be slow about it, to control the energy of the crowd with his own pacing, to leave time for the thank yous. What he didn't see was that there weren't enough for everyone and that some bikes were better than others. And also, that he couldn't possibly have a precise match between the bikes on the truck and the sizes and wants of the children.

And then it seemed like the kids in the crowd realized that too, and hands, arms, faces, eyes were everywhere, grabbing. "Me," they shouted. "Give *me* one." Harry and Joanna felt bicycles ripped from their hands—bikes with crossbars, bikes with baskets, one with blocks on the pedals that Harry had concocted.

Joanna backed up and stood behind him, saying dad, dad. She saw the woman with the earrings turn away, saying something to herself, or to the people around her, weaving through the crowd, disappearing into the cluster of little houses. She saw her father trying to keep order. And her voice got louder. "Dad, dad."

"That's a sissy bike," one kid said when he saw the one he'd gotten. It was pink. He knocked it over and used it as a step stool to hoist himself onto the truck.

"Whoa, whoa, whoa," Harry said. And the crowd would whoa for a minute, but then it would be all hands again, grabbing, tugging—not just from Harry, but also from each other—then with the victors riding off in every direction, some bikes with two, even three kids on them, one on the seat, one on the back, one on the handlebars.

"Dad," Joanna said. She had backed far into the truck, and the way she said "dad" was the way she said it at home, when he drove her crazy with his stupid questions and theories about what she should do and how she should do it, his preaching and teaching, about how we get marked every day of our lives and we shouldn't judge anyone until we've walked a mile in their shoes. "Just give them the bikes," she demanded, "and let's go."

She took the handlebars of a boy's Schwinn to wheel it out of the tangle, but when its pedals caught on the pedal of another bike, she yanked, pulling over a cluster of bikes, one knocking against the other, cascading into her. Harry turned to help, but when he did, two boys, around eleven or twelve years old, jumped up on the truck. Several other kids were also hoisting themselves.

"Wait your turn," Harry said. But they weren't waiting. They went right past him, each going for the Schwinn in Joanna's hands.

This wasn't what he had imagined at the table that night when he thought about anticipating a need. This was a need way deeper than he'd anticipated, way beyond ketchup with a hamburger, dressing with a salad. But it wasn't robbery either. Joanna was right. Get out of the way and let them have what he'd come to give.

The man in the red scarf was now beside him, one of the day laborers who had greeted them. He yelled at the kids who were trying to climb up, told them to back off. Then he turned to the two boys on the truck, and told them to get down, but neither of them would let go of the bike they were wrangling over. One boy was bigger and stronger than the other, but the smaller one was tenacious. He had a firm hold on the crossbar, while the bigger kid wouldn't let go of the handlebars. "You got another one of these?" the man asked Harry. "So we don't have to pull a King Solomon?"

"Joanna?" he yelled. "Do we?"

"Not exactly," she said, "but kind of." When it came to something she could see and touch, she did know. "There's a Raleigh." She looked around, saw it, and pointed. "It's a girl's bike, but it's got the three speeds, like the Schwinn."

"We'll take it," said the man. She unraveled it, wheeled it to him, and he placed it before the boys. "One of you take it," he said. Neither of them did. He looked at Joanna. "It's a good bike, right?" And she said, yes, it was. A very good bike. Something else she knew.

"Look," she said, pointing out the features, "it's got an air pump, a speedometer, and this little bag." She swung the kit bag that hung behind the seat. "The Schwinn doesn't have those. Plus the Raleigh's from England." The two kids were listening, like customers in an auto showroom.

"Slow down, young lady," the man said to Joanna. "You're making too good a case."

He was right. Both boys let go of the Schwinn, which the man caught, and they made for the Raleigh.

"Oh no you don't," he said. "You're both winners now, so no complaining." And he pushed the Schwinn to the bigger boy, the Raleigh to the smaller one. "Go now," he said. "Go." And they did, hopping down, Harry and the man handing the bikes to them, watching them pedal away, through the crowd. The crowd turning to watch them go, then turning back to the truck. Kids shouting and jumping and waving their arms. Me. Me.

"How many more you got?" he asked, looking over the stock.

"Eighteen," Joanna said as she finished her count.

"Well, then," the man said. "We'll give out the rest, and then you leave. Okay?"

"Hey, Santa Claus, hand me a bike or five over here," the thin man with the brown fraying coat said. He stood behind the truck, and he had five kids around him, all ages. His hands were reaching, ready to receive. They were big hands, the fingers long, the skin waxy. "Come on now."

So they came on. Joanna, Harry, and the man with the red scarf, separating out the bikes, like undoing Chinese puzzles, wheeling them over and handing them down to the hands that were reaching up.

Finally the truck was empty, and the riders ridden off. Some kids hadn't gotten bikes, and they hung around, hurt, angry, kicking the dirt, kicking the gravel, fists clenched, lips trembling, facing one more injustice among the many. Harry stood by, up on the truck, watching.

"Don't be fussing about losing something you didn't have to begin with," said the man with the brown jacket.

And when all the kids had been shooed away, he turned to Harry, saying, "You see now what you stirred up?" And Harry did see. He pulled out his wallet and handed each man five dollars, thanking them for their help, his voice a tight squawk. And then he and Joanna watched them return to their cinderblock seats by the side of the road. Harry pulled the strap on the back door of the truck, which slid-clunked down along its tracks until it hit bottom and the latch caught.

It was past noon, and the sunny November sky had clouded over to gray. Harry drove along, not knowing how to discuss the awkward, out-of-control parts, the shame and the clumsiness of their morning, so he avoided them, focusing on the positive, saying what a great help Joanna had been, what a natural she was at sales

"Sales?" she said. "That's the best you think I can do?"

"I didn't mean it that way."

She looked out her window, and he couldn't think what else to say, so he didn't say anything. He wasn't ready to go home, to explain the morning to Ruth and Franny, so he drove on, not paying attention, and by the time he was paying attention, he had passed the turnoff to their house, and there they were, way east of where he meant to be, almost at Woodward, almost at the row of cemeteries, among which Ruth's parents were buried. He turned down a side street, and stopped the truck.

He needed to get out. He said something vague to Joanna, that he needed a minute to check, and whether this made any sense to her, she didn't say.

He stood beside the truck, staring at his feet, not even fully aware what he was staring at. His shoes? The ground? When he looked up and saw the two Negro men coming toward him, both dressed in tight pants and tight button-down shirts, unzipped leather jackets, one with a toothpick in his mouth, his hands jammed in his jacket pockets, the other built like a wrestler, he felt the wave through his chest.

He thought of Joanna, sitting in the truck. He thought of the keys dangling in the ignition. He thought of the money in his pocket. He thought of Bobby Deitch on the playground.

No one else was on the street. No cars. No pedestrians. No insurance. Just like with Bobby Deitch. Deserted by his city. Harry looked up at the windows of the two-story brick houses with the broad stone porches. Not one face looking down at him. Not one person stepping out the door to fetch the newspaper or check the day's temperature. Not even a child playing.

The men cut over onto the parkway where Harry stood, the one keeping his hands in his pockets. The men looked at the truck. Harry was afraid to look at them. Like Bobby Deitch, he lowered his head. And when the men were right there, practically foot to foot with him, one of them spoke. "Hey, man," he said. Harry kept his head down, thinking about charging through, like Bobby had, when the man asked him for whatever he was going to ask him for. But Bobby hadn't had Joanna sitting there. All Bobby had to protect was his bike and a geometry book. Harry liked to tell his daughters to give people the benefit of the doubt, meaning don't think the worst. People are people, he liked to say. But right now, on this patch of pavement, on this particular day, with these particular men approaching, and no witnesses, he couldn't quite make himself believe it.

And then the man spoke again. "Nice truck," he said. "Hauling furniture?" But the two didn't wait for an answer. They kept walking, crossing the street, that rhythmic walk, proud in the chest, shoulders back, heads cocked.

BUSINESS

It was a minefield, the business, as was everything else. At least that had been Harry's thought over the past month. But then something had lifted, he thought, or changed, because at the turn onto Grand River that Monday after Thanksgiving, the turn where his foreboding usually peaked, where he could see the line of buildings among which his building stood, where he tried to see the condition of his front window (intact? defaced?), he thought, Okay, maybe not a minefield. There he was at the turn, and he thought, okay, maybe . . . a chess game.

"Here we are," Ilo said, "at the beautiful Riviera." Her standard travelogue line when they made that turn and passed the palazzo-like theater. "Or should I say 'Iviera'?" Because of the moldering *R* at the top. "And there, across the boulevard, the Castle." Based on the names, you might imagine something quite different.

"Do you say that because you think it's funny?"

"Yes."

On the street, it was the usual. Neighborhood men gathered in small clusters, leaning against buildings. Women gathered at the bus stop, many reversing the commute Harry had just made, heading out to clean and cook for white families to the north and west. Merchants pushed back grates on their storefronts. A smoky haze vented through the small chimney of the White Castle. Loose pages of newspaper tumbled down the street, or wrapped themselves around telephone poles and against building fronts, held there by the cold November wind.

Okay, a chess game then. And even if he sometimes blundered, muddled his strategies, failed to anticipate the moves of the other players, or to fully foresee the effect of his own, as with the bicycle giveaway, at least he knew the board, the horizontals and diagonals of his well-worn route from home to office, the aisles and the stairs of his warehouse. At least the geometry of it was predictable.

Maybe it wasn't a chess game. Maybe it was more like a temple, he thought as he opened that same familiar door to that high-ceilinged room with the dry smell of old wood and brick, of boxes and new shoes. It had always been there, threaded into the deepest part of him and, it seemed, it always would be. Like a temple, or what he knew of temples: Part obligation, part refuge. Part tedium, the groan of being forced yet again to go, to be part of the mindless repetition. This place of business was a temple in which he blessed and kissed up to whatever it was in the universe that kept the orders and invoices and customers and receivables coming month after month. In the middle of dark nights, and in the midst of the monotonous commute, Harry often felt gratitude to that something beyond himself and his father for the mysterious momentum that allowed him to provide for his family.

In this temple-warehouse, Harry was the rabbi and the president, all tied up in one. Ilo was his sexton, the administrator, though he didn't admit as much to her. Without her, the shoe warehouse would be more like the bike workshop, the place where he had been king, emperor, and dictator ("Il Duce," Ruth called him), with its smell of oil, its greasy coated rags, the pitted workbench, cobbled together and holding the jumble of nails and screws, of wrenches and hammers that might take a whole afternoon to find.

In this temple-warehouse of shoes, however, due to the sexton, the efficient conduct of business was possible: Order forms and other supplies (pencils, typewriter ribbons, adding machine tape, packing materials) were there when he needed them. Days had regular rhythms: Mornings were the times when most orders came in and were assembled. Afternoons, Harry usually went out to visit customers, check their inventories, and make deliveries. Most deliveries were small enough to fit in the trunk and backseat of Harry's Dodge, sometimes filling the passenger side of the front seat as well. When customers placed big orders, they usually came rattling over through the alley in their trucks to get them. When Harry had to deliver a big order, which didn't happen often, he borrowed Bernie's Formica City truck and drove it himself, as he had for the bike giveaway.

Harry knew the blessing of order, and he especially felt grateful for it that morning, the Monday after Thanksgiving, as the sister and brother walked in, the phone already ringing, loud in the high-ceilinged temple-warehouse.

77

Ilo rushed ahead to catch the ringing phone. Uncharacteristic, the speed, the willingness to take the lead to the front, and that was good because of what he'd been thinking in the car, that gradually the clutch in his stomach, instigated by the window incident and all the rest, had diminished, and maybe it had in her stomach too.

He came up through the hallway, past the boxes, the shelves, turning on the lights, unbuttoning his wool coat, not stopping to hang it up, anxious to find out who would call so early.

"Hallo," she said. "Yes," she said. "Yes." She beckoned him to the desk, holding the phone to her ear with one hand, getting a pencil and paper with the other, writing the word *Hudson's* in blocky letters on the customer line of the order form. How many times had Harry tried to get someone there interested in buying from him? How many calls rebuffed, phone messages not returned, noncommittal responses—the time he'd paid a visit, got in to see an assistant buyer, schmoozed him as best he could, then having forgotten his hat came back to the man's puny office to catch him dropping Harry's business card and samples in the wastebasket beside his desk. Hudson's calling him? You're not small potatoes when Hudson's calls.

Ilo had the order pad and was filling in numbers. Harry stood beside her. "Just a minute," she said into the phone, then covered the speaker with her hand, held it away. "How big an order can we handle?"

"How much do they want? And when?" He still wore his coat; so did she.

"Maybe you better talk to them."

The man on the phone didn't even give his name, and later all Harry could remember of the call was the repeated question "Can you do it?" and the demand, "If you can't, don't waste my time," and the feeling of being sucked into something that he'd wanted for a long time but that now it was here, now that he was filling in the numbers on the form, marking the numbers in the little boxes, it didn't feel right, might not be the best thing for him, might not work out at all, and was not making him feel like a larger potato. "We'll try" wasn't good enough for this man on the phone who didn't even feel the need to identify himself, nor was "let me check." What he wanted was a commitment, but with no give on his end—no time extension, no fall-back positions on the numbers, no two-installment delivery schedule. They weren't even willing to send their truck over to pick up the goods. And when the man hung up, they hadn't even discussed prices.

Ilo sat in her chair, shaking her head. "If it had been me," she said when he hung up, "I would have told him . . ."

"You wouldn't have told him anything different than I did," he answered.

She looked skeptical. "What good are they if they make you feel like nothing?"

But he was already walking through the hall to the big back room, rebuttoning his coat so he could go upstairs to get Curtis. And she was looking over the order forms, recopying numbers, sorting it all out—one sheet for the tennis shoes, one sheet for the men's work boots, one for the oxfords, and one for the baby shoes.

It was a good day. Even though he had to go up to get Curtis, it was a good day. His brother-in-law Irv was wrong. Detroit was *not* kaput. It was *not* time to get out of wholesale shoes, become a lackey in Irv's building company, and join the northern lemming-exodus from the city. Hudson's had called. The Grande Ballroom, a beautiful building, like something from the Arabian nights, had just reopened across the street. A white man had revived it from its stint as a mattress warehouse, and named it Detroit's Original Rock and Roll Palace. And that palace was bringing rich white kids (even if they didn't like to look that way) into the neighborhood every night. That was a good sign.

Of course, he wouldn't say it that way to his Lena, who he hoped wasn't one of the kids flocking to that drug-infested fire trap, though she probably was, since she had been the one to tell him the proper way to pronounce the name. "Gran-dee, Dad," she said, "with the accent on the second syllable."

He was almost at the top of the fire escape, feet on worn wooden steps, hand on banister, coat open to the cold day, the voice of that Hudson's man in his ears ("Can you do it?" "Don't waste my time"), and it occurred to Harry to wonder what Alvin and his friends thought about the Gran-dee—all those white kids coming into their neighborhood with money in their pockets. Who knew what Alvin thought about anything? Not that Alvin would tell him. (*1. I want freedom. 2. I want full employment for my people.*) And not that Harry would ask him, especially

79

since he had managed to not see Alvin since Halloween. And he did not particularly want his luck to change now, which was why he would have preferred Curtis to come down that morning looking for work rather than Harry having to go up. A minefield? A chess game?

Nothing to be done about it. Alvin opened the back door, and the heat of the apartment hit Harry as if he had opened the oven on Thanksgiving to check his turkey, or as if he had found himself on the threshold of a different climate, South Florida maybe, or the Mohave. And more: Alvin was shirtless, long, sinewy arms and chest sculpted in a way that looked like an illustration of the muscle groups in a biology text. Pectorals. Was that what they were called? Tiny little black chest hairs curled against his dark brown skin.

He didn't give Harry anything. No look of welcome. No look of any kind. Just the flat, cold face. No "Can I help you?" or "You want my dad?" or even a simple "Good morning." Just a quick glance to Harry's face and down at his own bare feet. Bare feet! During the winter. Did he think he was at the beach?

When it came down to it, a thank you might actually be in order. Because Harry had gotten him off the hook that day with the police. Because Harry could have caused a lot more trouble. Because, Harry thought, something about the annual end-of-November holiday last Thursday might have triggered a little something in the young man. Surely Alvin had an inkling he'd gotten lucky that Harry was a better person than Bernie or Stan, who would have felt civic pride for having catapulted Alvin and his friends into a departing squad car. Considering all that, plus it was Harry's dime paying for the heat that made it warm enough for Alvin to go shirtless and barefoot on a day when Harry had to finally concede it was wool-coat weather, Alvin could have helped, could have turned and gotten Curtis, which he surely must know was the reason Harry now stood before him.

On the other hand, perhaps it should have occurred to Harry that Alvin might not be prone to sunny, grateful thoughts about his landlord: for one, the missing marijuana (deposited in the trash behind Karp's Drug Store on Seven Mile); for two, the missing phone lines (rolled into a neat coil and stored in the upstairs closet); for three and four, the missing pages of the Black Power writings (folded and stored in a drawer in Harry's dresser), and the bitter humiliation of a skinny white cop holding him up on a public street.

"So, Alvin," Harry boomed. He felt like the Pillsbury dough boy next to Alvin's sleek musculated youth, with a voice like some hairy-nosed, bad-breathed great-uncle who didn't know how to talk to anyone, especially a teenager. "No school today?"

"Just getting ready."

"Well, that's good," Harry said. "That's real good." He had to say something. Repetition was one strategy. Alvin may have nodded in response, but Harry would have needed a seismic detection device to be certain.

"Still enjoying your algebra?" Curtis had mentioned his son's talent for math, for finding X, an unknown quantity, operating on both sides of the equal sign, discovering how one variable related to the other. He knew all the answers in class, the teachers said, but he wouldn't do his homework. "Engineering," Harry had said to Curtis when he'd told him about his son's math abilities. "Or architecture." But Curtis had laughed, a dream beyond comprehension.

"Algebra's a subject I've always liked too." Harry felt like he was trying to talk his way through a roadblock—like talking to the receptionist for the buyer at Hudson's. "Your dad home?" It squeaked out, like the first words you say when you've been alone and it's late in the day and you don't realize how long it's been since you've spoken to another person and you're out of practice.

Alvin didn't answer. He didn't say anything. Yes or no or maybe, or I'll go see or I think he's in the shower or I haven't seen him in days or even *I have no idea,* as his daughters sometimes said when they were annoyed with his questions. Alvin stood there, using the power he had, to withhold, to refuse to make Harry comfortable. Then the gaze slipped away. And they stood together in silence, Alvin looking over his shoulder, as if he thought maybe Curtis would come up behind him, and if he didn't, that was fine too. Harry thinking that the cold from the outside must eventually penetrate the tropical heat of the apartment and force Alvin to respond, just to get the encounter over, just so he could withdraw again, into the warm interior.

But Curtis was apparently not yet on his way, and the cold did not appear to be creating the anticipated push. He could have said, "Look, I'm in a hurry, with a big order." And this was true, but facing Alvin, Harry had other questions and statements colliding and intertwining with the pressure he felt to get to work. And every time he imagined himself saying any of these things, he in turn imagined the answers, and thought, "Why even say it?"

Like "I never said anything about it to your father." As if Alvin wouldn't know if Harry had told Curtis, as if Curtis would keep it a secret, tiptoe around his son, trying not to make waves, the way Harry did with his own daughters.

So why bother saying that, if all Alvin would say in response was something like "You can tell my father if you want." And then Harry, derailed, would have to say something like "I don't want. That's the point."

Or he thought about saying something like "You know I don't really care about any of it—the phone, the marijuana. And I really don't care who wrote those words on the window, even if it was you. Everyone makes mistakes, right?"

But why would he say that? Because he was looking for a confession, in addition to gratitude? Well, neither would be forthcoming, so why bother? For a man who portrayed himself as straightforward with his words, he was being rather labyrinthine. He would have to think twice in the future when he accused his daughters of "making things so complicated." He saw now, a little bit, how complications worked.

Alvin, wearing only a pair of slim pants with a sleek, high waistband, had a toothpick in his mouth (the toothpick, like the man who had scared him on the day of the bicycle giveaway), and he shifted it, rolled it, pulled it in, so only the tip showed.

"Aren't you going to say anything?" Harry wanted to ask. "I'm telling you you're off the hook. I'm not planning to cause any trouble." That was what he wanted to say. And what might this accomplish? Alvin might nod. He might nod several times, seeming to indicate that yes, he already knew all this. None of it was particularly a concern of his, not something he needed to be told. And regardless of Harry, plenty of hooks still clearly hung along the path of his future.

Behind Alvin, Harry heard the sound of the television, a flow of words that was just beyond the range of comprehension. Clearly, they were words, because of the rhythm and the flow, sometimes with music behind them, to indicate suspense, or swelling emotion, resolution, then sometimes with an outburst of canned laughter.

Okay, then, if Harry couldn't say any of those things that he'd already rejected, he could try something patriarchal and coach-like, something along the lines of "You're a clever fellow, Alvin. Why don't you make something of your life?" He could bring up the architecture idea. Harry heard Curtis's low chuckle, in response to something on the television, as the canned laughter kicked in.

What he wanted to say then was something along the lines of "We're all people, Alvin. It doesn't matter what color the skin is, what religion. That's what I tell my daughters." At home, this line never failed to elicit moans and annoyance. After all, as his daughters liked to tell him, he wasn't the one who got his shins battered by those fast, wiry girls with the crooked braids and cracking gum during field hockey at school.

But with all these things he wanted to say, and all the arguments against saying them and all the answers or nonanswers he'd already formulated, all he could do was stand there with his hand open and say, "Look." It was a silent standoff because neither one knew what the other was thinking, and neither one knew how to say what was on his mind, nor even whether he could say what was on his mind—nor what sort of trouble the saying might bring.

So why attribute something hostile or intentionally rebellious to the young man's silence? Why not chalk it up to benign confusion? Why should he regard Alvin's silence as any different from Joanna's when she sat pressed against the side of the truck at the bicycle giveaway? It was one thousand ways different, and one thousand ways the same.

"Ah, look," Harry said finally, "What do the two of us have to say to each other? Not much, right? So how about you go and get your father for me?"

Something softened in the stone face, the tense muscles of the arms, the fists, as if to note that the man before him had said words that made sense, that sounded true, that clicked in somewhere within that bare brown chest, and Harry felt that too, a relief at finding something from all that chaos of thoughts and imagined assertions and sarcastic rejoinders. There was comfort in that, comfort in finding that even in the midst of the greatest discomfort, a person, even Harry, could stumble onto something.

"His back's sore this morning," Alvin said. The old injury that had put him out of work at GM. "Cold mornings, hard for him."

"You think he can work?"

Alvin shrugged, and turned away. Going to find out, Harry guessed.

For all this time he'd stood at the door, waiting for something to happen, anxious to get back to work, he'd been aware of the sounds behind Alvin, coming from the front room of the apartment, at the end of the long narrow hall—the television voices (people with so much to say to each other), the canned TV laughter (people with something to laugh about). Now Harry became aware of other sounds, sounds behind *him*, feet on the fire escape stairs, the tremble of the staircase, the old wood, reinforced here and there to get a few more years out of it. And voices, singing, in time with their footfalls. And then there they were, as he turned, their eyes meeting his, Alvin's two buddies, Wendell and Otis. *We're not boys.*

They halted what sounded like a beautiful song, in mid-word, as if an angry parent or neighbor had yanked the needle arm off the vinyl. And in a morning that for Harry required efficiency, movement, more hours than a day had, everything stalled again. The two friends didn't know what to do any more than Harry did. He blocked their way, just as they and Alvin blocked his. And now Alvin was back, at his shirtless post. And they were all together, the four of them, in that small space, with Harry in the middle.

"Hello, gentlemen," Harry said.

They said hello, then got straight to business. "Hey, man," Wendell said to Alvin, "you're not even ready for school."

And Alvin looked down, as if he had just then realized that he was half-naked, standing there on a cold November day. "Yeah," he said, "I'll go get ready."

And then there was Curtis, the whole reason Harry had come in the first place, also dressed for summer, with a sleeveless undershirt, yellowed and thin with wear and washings. His broad chest, muscle going to seed, pressed against the thin fabric. Curtis took in the scene. "How long did you keep Mr. Levine waiting here?" Wendell and Otis seemed to feel this was Alvin's question to answer, despite its all-encompassing reach. And Alvin seemed to feel an extreme pressure to get ready for school. And Harry really didn't care about the "how long" at this point, as long as it didn't get much longer. Whether minefield or chess game or temple, he went for abrupt, setting out the practicalities: the order, the work, the pressure to complete it. Which everyone present seemed to appreciate.

"Sure, Mr. Levine. I can use the work." He didn't say anything about his back. He didn't say anything about Alvin, apologies or scoldings or anything else. A man who understood priorities, the meaning of business. "Just got to get my shoes and shirt."

84

When Curtis closed the door behind him, Harry looked at his two companions. He would try to remember their faces, the small pockmark, like someone had scooped with a tiny spoon, near the nose on the one, the sparse, youthful mustache on the other, though he couldn't remember which was Wendell and which was Otis, which one had said *We're not boys.* "Excuse me, gentlemen," he said, moving around them in as wide an arc as he could manage in the small space.

When he was back downstairs, he heard them laughing. "Excuse me, gent-le-men," one said. "Excuse me back," said the other. And on and on. "Excuse me," "No, excuse me," and the laughing until he had locked all the locks, taken off his coat, looked at the high-ceilinged temple of a warehouse, and until he heard the clatter of the three going down the stairs, passing in front of the window, the three singing again, words he couldn't make out.

Ilo came from the front office. "What took you so long?" She was the disapproving den mother of the business, actually of all the merchants along their stretch of Grand River—one of the few women around.

"It wasn't long," he answered, brushing past.

"You were gone almost fifteen minutes," she said. "That's long. To walk up a couple flights of stairs and ask one question. I was ready to send the Canadian Mounties." This was her humor.

"It wasn't that long." He took off his suit jacket and hung it on a hanger by the door. He rolled up the sleeves of his white shirt as he walked toward the front with her following. In the office, he leafed through the order forms.

"And if you and the man didn't talk price," she said, "what am I supposed to put on the invoice?"

"If he was too busy to talk price, we'll tell him the price."

"And what price is that?"

So he told her the prices, and she told him back. She had a radio on her desk, tuned to WJR, so some symphonic melody hung in the background as they argued it out, as they settled—higher than Harry had first said, but not as high as Ilo had dared to go (for the pain and suffering, she said).

She bent under her desk to get her tennis shoes. "I'll help pack," she said. She took her cotton housecoat from the hook, to protect her clothes. It was a shapeless flowered thing, like an old bubbah would wear.

"You don't have to." He took the forms and walked past her, out of the front office, toward the metal shelves. She followed.

"I know I don't have to."

He made a noncommittal grunt, an indicator that the comment had been heard but that he was unwilling to acknowledge whether it was valid or relevant. He sorted through the order forms she had reorganized so that Hudson's sprawling wants had become manageable, divisible tasks. "Okay," he said. "You start with the women's tennis shoes." And she went off to pull the sizes.

By the time Curtis knocked at the big metal back door, and waved through the barred window, stacks of white and beige shoe boxes stood on the old wooden packing table, and Ilo was checking off the sizes against the order forms. Harry opened the locks one by one—the deadbolt, the chain lock, the padlock. He had his tie tucked between the buttons of his shirt. Ilo wore her housecoat.

Curtis knew how Harry did things, and he went to the packing table. He picked up an order form. "Hudson's," he said. "Guess you hit the big time." He matched the numbers up against the piles of boxes, working at the opposite end of the table from Ilo.

"As long as they pay their bill, they're the same as any other customer," Harry said.

"Okay, then. You want me to pack?"

Harry gave the nod, so Curtis pulled several cartons from the shelves under the table where they lay flat. He opened one and folded its flaps to form a bottom. He ran the thick brown tape over the wet roller and taped the seams closed. He flipped the carton over, ready to receive its cargo, and assembled the next one. Ilo went back to the tennis shoe aisle, to pull more stock.

"You have a good holiday, Mr. Levine?" Curtis asked.

It could be a trick question. In the prior days and weeks, Harry had wondered what Curtis and Alvin would do for Thanksgiving, but he didn't want to ask, in case the answer was "nothing." And if the answer was "nothing," and Harry was left to imagine a day like any other, the void-filling sound of the television in the background, the two of them eating a can of pork and beans or some other bargain food in their undershirts, Alvin perhaps roaming the deserted neighborhood in the afternoon, cold and snuffling, while everyone else gathered with families in fragrant kitchens, then . . . well, then Harry would feel responsible.

86

So he'd struggled with a stream of questions . . . whether to bring a gift basket (impossible, to make them more beholden?), to slip Curtis a twenty before leaving on Wednesday (embarrassing, and besides, you couldn't create a Thanksgiving, complete with family, for twenty dollars), to leave something anonymously on the back steps (but how would Harry know they'd actually received it, that someone else wouldn't make off with it? and even if they found it, who else would have left it but him, so how could it be anonymous?).

And the final mad idea, whether to invite them to Harry's own home for Thanksgiving. Oh, this would make for a festive evening: the awkward silences, the whispering in the kitchen, the two dark faces standing out as they might on the pages of a children's magazine in which one had to identify what was "wrong" with the picture. Alvin, his eyes downcast, having been forced to come and sit at the oppressor's table, Curtis attempting to bring his good-natured folksy wisdom to the assembly, to make everyone else feel comfortable, while sweat trickled down his spine. Irv's wife, Rhoda, pretending to have a migraine so she could go upstairs to one of the bedrooms, pull down the shades and lie on the bedspread in her smart woolen dress, her high-heeled pump hanging from her left toe.

Ruth said, how did Harry know what Curtis and Alvin did or didn't do? They might have a full, rich community through their church or neighborhood. They might have more people at their table and more food piled on it than Ruth and Harry did. Why was he looking for worries?

"It was okay, I guess," Harry answered. He ticked off numbers on one of the order sheets, checking sizes, as he counted the boxes. "The usual crowd at our house. Ruth's family. Ilo. Good food. Ate too much."

Ilo chimed in from her remote location in the forest of shelves and shoe boxes: "Rhoda caught Sappho licking the onion dip on the appetizer table and practically had to be revived with smelling salts."

The phone rang in the front, and Ilo went to answer.

"Let's hope it's not another big order," she called. The slow times were a worry, but so were the boom times, if he couldn't fill the orders.

"You see the Lions game?" Curtis asked.

"Not in my house."

"You didn't miss much." Curtis kept working, at a good pace. "Lions came out flat in the second half, lost 41-14." He had four cartons assembled, so Harry lowered stacks of shoe boxes into them, making notations on the lid flap as he did, tracking what he put in. He still used the systems his father had set up years ago. Checking, rechecking, so their deliveries would be accurate, so the customers would know exactly what they were getting—ten sixes black, ten sevens black, and so on.

"You and Alvin watch the game?" The four cartons were full, the contents checked. Harry ran the brown tape over the wet roller and sealed them.

"Some," Curtis said. "We go to church on Thanksgiving. New Bethel, over on Linwood and Philadelphia. Give thanks for what we've got: the roof, as they say, the food on the table, good people to share it with. Alvin singing in the choir where Aretha still sometimes comes. I know you can't imagine it, Mr. L., from what you see of him, but the boy is blessed with a voice. The music is a salvation."

"I've heard him," Harry said. The talk between them about Alvin used to be easier—Harry always encouraging, telling Curtis about his boy's potential. Don't worry so much about him, he'd say. Lately, since the Halloween incident, the subject had an extra layer or two.

"*Ev-e-ry day is Thanks-giving,*" Curtis sang, in a low, loving croon as he lowered the last of the boxes on the table into the waiting cartons and joined Harry in checking and sealing them. "After the service, Reverend Franklin invites everyone down to the church basement, and there are the tables, laden—hams and turkeys and cornbread, greens and sweet potatoes and sweet potato pies and Tennessee blackberry cake and pecan pie and macaroni and cheese casseroles. The children's eyes are so big. They play games under the tables, run up and down the halls. Those church ladies make sure everyone's fed properly. Always trying to get me to take a little extra."

Harry finished the notations on the outside of the boxes, sealed a carton, and wrote "invoice enclosed" on the flap. Moved on to the next box.

Curtis got the dolly.

"Your back okay for that?" Harry asked.

"I think." He loaded a carton onto the dolly, picked up another to place on top. It could hold a stack of four.

Ilo returned, telling them that it had been Wiley's on the phone, placing an order for oxfords. They could wait until the end of the week. "Somebody reasonable for a change."

"Good." Harry wheeled the dolly to the back door and slid the cartons off.

88

"You planning to borrow Bernie's truck?" she asked.

"I guess." Maybe he could get her to ask this time. But then she'd tell Bernie the whole *megillah,* showing off about the big order at the same time as she complained about the demands of the Hudson's man ("Who do they think they are?"), how Harry had caved in without even trying to get a better deal, that they hadn't even talked price. Maybe he could send Curtis down to ask. But Bernie might say something like, "About time Harry cleaned all his in-laws' stuff out of the basement," trying to get information about whether Harry really had moved the stuff the last time he'd borrowed the truck, whether he was thinking of moving the business. He might ask Curtis whether he had helped that day, and of course, Curtis wouldn't know what Bernie was talking about.

Was there a name for it on the chessboard? Where each available move had competing advantages and disadvantages? That's not the chessboard, you idiot, he thought. That's life.

Ilo carried stacks of tennis shoe boxes from the shelves, refilling the table Harry and Curtis had just cleared. The morning sun shone in, and the bars on the windows cast diagonal shadows on the packing table, on the cartons, on Harry's arms and back.

Curtis took an order form and moved to the shelves where the men's oxfords were. Police shoes. "Looks like I should go down the basement so we can start filling in. We're running low on stock up here."

Harry couldn't remember whether Curtis had been in the basement lately, and he didn't know what Curtis knew about it. So they had a little tussle about who would go down to the basement, with Harry telling Curtis to stay and finish packing the tennis shoes, but Curtis saying, no, his back was fine. He'd get what they needed from the basement, and he headed off.

A chess game. A temple. Ridiculous. It was his business, a place for selling shoes wholesale. And Harry was the boss. At least that thought went through his mind as he rushed to finish packing the tennis shoes, lowering them into their cartons, asking Ilo if she could make the final accuracy check and seal them so he could go help Curtis. It was time. He would do it. Have the talk he'd been wanting to have. Clear the air about Alvin and the basement.

"Curtis," he called as he walked down the narrow stairs. In the inventory room, the line of bare bulbs cast shadows from the rows of shelves, the stacks of boxes. He couldn't see Curtis right away, in the maze of shelving, the narrow aisles, though he heard the sound of the boxes being pulled, stacked. Slide, thump. Slide, thump, a sound both hollow and full. He sometimes woke at night, thinking he had heard that sound.

In the third aisle from the back wall, Curtis was stacking boxes on the floor. The work boots were heavy; they made the loudest thumps and were the most unwieldy to carry up the stairs.

"Would you look at this?" Curtis held out the order form. Harry wove past the stacks. "Do they want eight size tens, or eighteen?"

"It must be eight. No." The paper his sister had recopied because she was so efficient was supposed to hold all the answers. "I can't tell." He moved closer to one of the lights, but it did not reveal the true answer. "Do we even have eighteen?"

"Doesn't look like it."

Harry took a sheet from Curtis's stack, moved down the aisle and started pulling the twelves. "Well, then we'll give them eight." He was the boss. It was his building. He'd say the things on his mind, and they'd keep working. It would be like having conversations in the car, everyone staring straight ahead. And Curtis would understand. He'd be appreciative.

"I've been meaning to say," Harry said. The slide of the boxes off the shelves, the thump as one of the men placed them in a stack; slide, thump; slide, thump. The pilot light on the boiler kicking in, the clunk of the pipes. Two men, working side by side. "You know that day when the police were here?"

Curtis's slides and thumps slowed, but he continued to work, surrounded by knee-high piles of shoe boxes. "Best say what's on your mind." Curtis pulled a handkerchief from his pocket and wiped his brow, the back of his neck, even though it was chilly in the basement.

"When I came down here," he said, "to find the cleaning things." Harry had pulled all the twelves he needed, and he made a tic mark in the margin. He moved to the thirteens. Curtis took an order sheet from the shelf and moved across the aisle. "I found more than that, but I didn't say."

"Like?" Curtis continued to work, pulling the sizes.

"Papers. Writing. About the Black Panthers." He didn't say the part about Stokely Carmichael. The Jewish landlords. He didn't say the part about "*Stay here and do it.*"

Curtis turned to Harry. "I know about that."

Harry stopped and looked at Curtis, but Curtis wasn't looking at him. "You think young people know how to handle that kind of talk?"

"Alvin is reading. And Alvin is thinking. And Alvin is parroting. They say, 'Don't you ever apologize for any black person who throws a Molotov cocktail,' so he likes to say it. They say, 'Don't you ever call those things riots, because they are rebellions,' so he says it. I've heard it, Mr. Levine. All about the white oppressor." He kept up his work. Harry had stopped somewhere in the midst of this, a box of shoes in his hand. "Just repeating what I've heard. That's what Alvin's doing too. He says, 'Motown is selling *out*.' He says Diana Washington, a girl raised in public housing right here in Detroit, is acting white. 'Wage war on the honky white man,' he says, and I say to Alvin, 'Those are ugly words.'"

"See what I mean," Harry said. "The young people get carried away. They don't understand what they're saying."

"About Motown?" Curtis reached for a stack of sizes on a high shelf, wincing from the reach, the strain. "He just talks that way because of how much he wants to be one of them."

"That's not what I mean. You didn't see the way he kept me waiting at the door this morning, the look on his face." What Harry didn't understand was the effect it had, when a parent heard someone talk about his child. Or he did. But he didn't understand that it would feel the same way to Curtis as it felt to him.

"I think my Alvin understands. He understands that something's got to change. He's looking for a way to change, a hope. That's a good thing."

"But the violence, Curtis. That's not a good thing."

"You've got to understand something, Mr. Levine." Now he stopped his work, to look at Harry. "When Alvin was a baby, just a few days old, my mama took him. Because his own walked out. But his grandma loved him, and she had him all wrapped up, in a yellow blanket and cap she knit for him, with her own hands, and I came in, saw him sleeping in her arms. You know those baby eyelids, with their little soft creases?" Harry nodded. He did know. "The only way the baby's got to hold off the troubles of the great world for a time. He looked like an angel . . . from heaven, I'm saying . . . sleeping there in her arms. And I couldn't help myself, thinking what the future holds for this angel. I'm going to have to teach him a way, I thought. It's my job. To keep at least some of the angel in him, to not let it be beat or stricken out of him because of how people are going to see him. And there I was, crying right there, looking at the baby, and nobody needed to ask me why."

Harry listened. He was afraid to look at Curtis.

"I talk straight to my son. Even now, as big as he is. I sit close to him, don't let him squirm away. 'Look,' I say, 'no one is watching out for you but me. I don't care what your friends say to you. I don't care what you're reading or what you're hearing. I'm the only one you got to turn to, the only one who's going to bail you out. And I hope you never need bailing out. Because bailing out takes money.'"

Harry held two stacks of boxes, six in each stack. His plan had been to carry the boxes to the bottom of the stairs.

"And it's not just you talking about Alvin. Alvin talks about you too, Mr. Levine. He says, 'Why are you friends with that white man?' But I stand up for you. I say, 'That's no white man. That's Harry Levine.'"

Harry leaned against the shelving with his load of heavy boxes. "Thanks, Curtis." And he was thankful even if he wasn't sure what Curtis meant. He wanted to ask. And he also wanted to say, "I'll take it as a compliment," because he felt that it was, but then, because he was embarrassed, he said, "Now, you want to help me carry these over to the steps?"

Curtis bent to gather the boxes. He followed Harry to the stairs. "And don't think I didn't wonder when I saw that writing on your front window." Curtis brought another stack. "Sometimes it gets hard for people to hold the feelings in. My Alvin, he may not be able to make it through, holding the feelings in. Sometimes I think it's mainly talk with him, and I hope so, but you know . . . people who don't feel they have a lot to lose . . . Alvin needs to feel he's got something to lose. Like I said before, the angel part of him. The singing part."

Upstairs was Ilo, the creak of the old wooden floors as she moved back and forth to the packing tables from the shelves that held the women's tennis shoes.

"But those people in Watts," Harry said. "Those people burned down their own homes."

"Like Alvin says, quoting one of his Panthers, 'Can't worship the revolt against mother England, then rail against the uprising of Watts.'"

Harry laughed, a startled laugh. "At least he's learning some history." They stood at the foot of the stairs, boxes piled around them. "Look, we better start carrying these up." So they did, gathered and lifted, ten at a time, two columns of five, balanced against the chest.

Curtis walked behind Harry on the stairs, their feet trudging in rhythm, carrying the boxes, police oxfords, work boots. "Talking about that day on the street . . . If they'd been white, like those hippies over at the Grande, the police never would have treated them that way. Those three would have walked by with no one even looking."

"Maybe. Maybe not. Those hippies get plenty of looks." He thought of Lena, her mass of curls and long skirts, the boyfriends with the beards and stringy hair. They deposited the boxes on the table, and both men began assembling cardboard cartons, folding the flaps, securing the seams with the wet brown tape.

"And those police?" Curtis said. He was short of breath, from the stairs and the load he carried and the talk. "Well, let's just say they don't provide us the kind of service anyone would want. Always making us feel that whatever problem we got, we brought it on ourselves. 'You know anything about the fight over on Clairmount?' Pushing you around like you're nothing. We got a problem around here, we don't call the police. Creates more problems than it solves."

"Can't celebrate the uprising in Watts," Harry said, "and expect the police to love you." He regretted it as soon as he said it, the way it came out. He kept his eyes to himself.

Ilo came in with the last of the tennis shoe order. "We don't have all the sizes." She deposited them on the table.

"Well, we have what we have," Harry said.

Curtis returned to the basement to fetch more oxfords and work boots. Harry built eight-box stacks, paired them into sixteens, counted the piles again—eight, sixteen, thirty-two, sixty-four.

It was mid-afternoon, and they'd worked through the lunch hour, finally acknowledging that they could fill only about 70 percent of the Hudson's order. Ilo went over to the White Castle to get burgers and fries, the kind of greasy meal that made no one feel better in the long run, but in the short, it felt like an indulgence. They ate while they worked, grabbing a bite while they moved around the table, trudged up and down from the basement, assembled boxes, taped seams, lowered armfuls. Alvin passed the window on his way up to the apartment, home from school. Ilo was in the front office, taking a call.

"Mr. L.," Curtis said as he packed another box, "I see you had your daughter here a few weeks ago."

Harry nodded. "Veterans Day." He kept stacking, packing. Lift, bend, lift, bend. Wiping his hands on paper towel between bites of hamburger so the shoe boxes would be clean. "That was Joanna. She gets a day off school, and she probably doesn't even know what a veteran is."

"Like you said, maybe she can learn some history." In the quiet of the big room, it was the two men again. Lift, bend, lower, notate. Repeat. "Well, I'm serious. It's good for her to come down with you. Good for a child to see her daddy working."

"Yeah? Well, she comes down, she helps, but she doesn't understand a thing. 'Every month's a new month, starting from zero,' I tell her. What does she know?"

He pulled the coarse rope from the wheel, wrapped it around a stack of boxes, baby shoes, eight tall, two across, sixteen in all. Tied a double knot, cut it with a knife. He made a rope handle by looping and tying so that he could carry the stack. He expected Curtis to answer, to agree, to say he knew what Harry meant, to be two men working and commiserating about the good-for-nothing youth.

"At least you don't need to worry about my son being spoiled. You've got enough to worry about with those girls of yours. Like I told you downstairs, I keep a close eye on Alvin."

Harry looked up from his work.

"They're good girls," Curtis said. "I can see that. Smart. But maybe a little too smart in the mouth. Smarter than I'd allow." He pulled a length of brown tape over the roller, tore it off on the jagged cutting edge, and sealed the last carton. "Don't mean any offense, of course," he said. "It would be for their own good if they learn a little more civility."

"So you're getting me back? For what I said about Alvin?" Harry didn't even need to ask what Curtis meant. Nor would he want to hear Curtis's rendition. Which would surely include one of the girls scowling out, "How can you *stand* this place?" when they arrived in the morning, loud enough for anyone—obviously including Curtis—to hear. Or "You expect me to do *what?*" when he asked them to bring stock up from the basement or answer the phone or file the orders. Or those times they made him wait when he asked them to do something, and if he reminded them or told them he needed it done right away, they'd say "okay" or "fine," but with that tone—spit out and furious and put-upon. They always did the work in the end, and did it reasonably well, so he preferred to ignore the smart mouths rather than to risk escalation. Especially when others were around. He always hoped that no one else had heard, wondered whether they had.

"Call it what you like," Curtis said. "We're just sharing observations. And one observation is we better get these shoes loaded on the truck, if you're still planning on delivering them today."

The truck.

"Want me to get it?" Curtis asked. "And don't worry. I know how to handle Mr. Formica City. Answer a question with a question—as your people say."

That Curtis. He did know what to do. Got the truck. Got his son down to help with the loading. Drove the truck, weaving his way through the city, then through the alley to Hudson's long loading dock. Kept the truck out of the way while Harry managed the preliminaries with the dock clerks.

"You're making a delivery and you don't know who it's *for*?"

"You heard me," Harry said.

Then the two men—Harry and Curtis—unloaded the cartons. Onto the dock. No help from the Hudson's men, Harry working in his business suit.

"Make 'em sign for it," Curtis said. Which Harry might have forgotten in the rush and blur of feelings. A minefield? Well, no one had been critically wounded. A chess match? Well, not without a clear winner and loser. A temple? What a thought. This place?

FAMILY

To Ruth, a nineteen-year-old girl looking for escape, the quiet of Harry's house was first sanctuary, then tomb. In the early days of courtship, she loved to go there, to be in that orderly place, even if it meant sitting on the sofa, staring at her hands. Some might find the silences awkward, wearing, but for her, at least at first, it was respite. Harry's mother, always in a tidy unwrinkled dress, with stockings and sensible pumps, smelled of lilac talc. Always with her hair done, in perfect white finger waves. This, in contrast with Ruth's own mother, who hastily bound her long hair into a low bun, and whose rumpled housedresses were stained with chicken fat or chicken blood, whose support hose were rolled down to her thick ankles or adorned with thick runs, whose shoes bulged where her bunions pressed against them, and who had cut holes in her house slippers to allow the bunions to protrude.

At Harry's house, the furniture was polished. On the side tables and shelves were small china statues of fancy ladies in lacey gowns seated on garden benches while men tipped top hats to them. Beds were made first thing in the morning, and cushions remained on chairs and sofas rather than becoming forts or shields against flying objects. Walls were smooth and freshly painted rather than spotted with handprints and gouges. The language was English, unaccented, unless you counted the hint of New York they'd picked up from the ten years there, when Joe tried to make a go of a small department store with his brothers in Flushing. At times, at Harry's house, Ruth worried that she smelled like a piece of gefilte fish or the vinegar of a dill pickle amid the lilac calm— the odors of her own home clinging to her clothes, embedded in her pores. And especially during Chanukah, when for the first time she had been invited to dinner, she wondered if she radiated latke odors.

It wouldn't have mattered to Harry if she did, because he was crazy for her, from his first taste in the alley behind her house when, in what seemed to him a miracle—as miraculous as the little bit of oil that allegedly burned in the temple for eight days and eight nights—he'd maneuvered himself from the lonely silence of the Levine living room, where he often stood at the window watching the Bruchenhartz pandemonium across the street, right into the soft pillow of her lips. And he loved latkes, from the first time he tasted them in the Bruchenhartz kitchen—and came home smelling of them himself.

His first invitation to dinner at Ruth's house, and there he stood, spatula in hand, wearing a wool jacket and tie, side by side with Rosa Bruchenhartz, frying the potato pancakes, setting them to drain on brown paper bags, and watching one or another of the Bruchenhartz siblings snatch them before anyone had a chance to sit at the table to eat. That evening at the stove in the Bruchenhartz kitchen, Harry finally saw how one got fed in a place like this, and he himself, finally, snatched a latke from the brown paper, just as Ruth splatted a spoonful of sour cream on its golden surface.

A few nights later, in an evening of high contrast, Ruth learned how a person got fed in a place like Harry's. There, the table was set by the book, the way it looked in the homemaking diagrams at school—forks, knives, and spoons in descending order of use around the plate—perfectly folded and pressed cloth napkins, snowy white linen tablecloth with hand embroidery, un-chipped china with a blue and gold pattern. It was a Friday night, but the table had no shabbos candles. And it was Chanukah, but there was no menorah. To be fair to the Levines, they might not know it was Chanukah, because of the way the holiday changed dates from year to year, wandering around December from early to late. It wasn't a major holiday—not the Jewish Christmas, as some misinformed goys liked to think—so unless a family had one of those little blue Jewish calendars the Bornsteins gave away free at their bookstore on Dexter, or unless they went to shul, how would they know?

At the Levine house, Harry's mother, Eileen, stood and ladled soup from a china tureen—a clear chicken broth, not a speck of anything in it—for each diner, who sat with napkins unfolded in their laps as they waited to receive their portions. Conversation was sparse, directed by Joe, at the head of the table, who spoke primarily to Harry.

"Friedman sure can sling that ball," Joe said. Even he felt ethnic pride at this Jewish hero. Harry shrugged, looked down at the table, played with his fork.

97

"Benny Friedman?" Ruth said. She didn't know anything about Benny Friedman, or even about football, but she'd heard her brothers talk. "Football has never seen a quarterback like him," she said. She had no idea what a quarterback did or was; he could be some malformed fraction of a human for all she knew.

Everyone looked up from the soup, and she looked back, especially at Joe's bulldog face, with the bulbous nose, thinking she could see a subtler interpretation of that nose on Harry. "Benny's mother said she put eighteen cents, for *chai,* into a *tzedakah* box for him every time he played." She spooned some soup. She swallowed. "And did you hear what he said about that, Mr. Levine?" Mr. Levine didn't answer. "Benny said, 'I never questioned whether it was my ability that kept me from getting injured. I let it go that *chai* was working for me.'"

No response. Except the spoons dipping into the bowls. In a way, it was a relief, because she couldn't have carried it much further if Joe had wanted to get into plays or passes or the like.

"*Chai,*" she said, "it means life, or something like that. Like a good-luck charm. And *tzedakah* . . . charity. Giving." It was incredible, she thought, what they didn't know.

Eileen cleared the dishes when they'd finished the "soup course," as she called it. Then, using a tray, she brought in the roasted chicken, mashed potatoes, green beans, and gravy. She placed the chicken in front of Joe, who stood to carve, as they waited. At Ruth's house, by now one of the brothers would have grabbed the drumstick, spilling at least one glass of the sweet homemade wine on the already stained tablecloth, and Avrum Bruchenhartz would be cursing in Yiddish about cabbage heads and eternal states of nausea.

Eileen portioned out the meal, placing a piece of meat, a dollop of potato, a neat pile of beans on the plate in separate sectors. Joe and Harry received the largest servings. Everyone waited their turn. People said please and thank you.

Ruth broke the silence. "My parents send their regards." They hadn't sent anything of the kind, and the thought of them saying anything so goyish as "send our regards" was perfectly absurd. In fact, the parting salvo from her father was something along the lines of "You're going to eat that *traef?*" referring to the unkosher food they imagined the Levines would serve, the shabbos dinner with no blessings. And as she took her dish from Eileen, she did imagine a taint, like a coating of bacteria, and she did wonder about the effect. She'd let it go that *chai* was working for her.

And it had more or less. Because here she was all these years later, another Chanukah. All Ruth and Harry's parents now gone, and despite the arguments that had raged in both homes over what looked to them like a mixed marriage, the two young people had carried on. The business. The traditions. The candles. The blessings. The *yahrzeits,* when Ruth went to the cemetery to say the *kaddish.* The family get-togethers. The potatoes, still being grated into her mother's big wooden bowl. Her mother's latke recipe, written on a sheet of lined paper, pulled from a spiral notebook, in her mother's Old World handwriting, the childlike look of a new alphabet learned well into adulthood. The paper, decorated with multiple food stains, had been folded and unfolded many times—a family heirloom, so many splats of memory recorded on it. "Five potatoes large. Grate them on a grater," her mother had written. "Add egg, a *bissel* flour and salt. If you like, a *bissel* onion, grate it too. Mix."

They were going to Irv's this year, for the Chanukah party. The family had always gathered at Ruth and Harry's, because they had the largest house, but this year, since Irv had moved to West Bloomfield and wanted to show off his massive new split-level, they were going there. Harry had been complaining—in the way he complained, meaning sarcastic swipes about big-macher Irv getting rich off people's fear of Negroes, a vein that would never run dry, and building suburban houses so shoddy that Irv himself would never consider living in one. "He wants me to ooh and aah about that? And to top it off, he wants us to bring our own latkes?"

In addition to latkes, they were bringing their three daughters. And Lena was bringing her new boyfriend, Pete. He had blond hair, frizzed out, and he wore a beard and mustache, a thick one, that was well kept, not scraggly like the ones on some of the boys Lena brought home.

The latkes, fragrant and golden, were piled on a platter, covered in tin foil, and Ruth carried them to the car, placing them at her feet in the front. Harry loaded the presents and other items in the trunk. And they were on their way. Franny was in the back seat, next to Joanna. Next to Joanna was Pete, with Lena on his lap. Harry drove through the night, past the snowy houses and fields, into the developing suburban world, snow mounded along the sides of the roads where the plows had left it, melting snow splatting on the windshield when they went under an overpass.

After several wrong turns and disagreements about which way to go and outbursts of incredulous annoyance over the absence of street signs and street lights to guide them, they seemed to have arrived. It was a barren wasteland where every topographical feature had been plowed under. A few completed houses sat upon this denatured earth. A few skeletal structures indicated that more were on the way. Harry had stopped the car in front of a circular driveway, and the house beyond it with the columns of a fake plantation was Irv's. Spotlights shone on it, as if it were a tourist attraction or a funeral home.

Ruth was lifting the plate of latkes. Lena noted the lawn jockey—a black-faced one with big white teeth, holding a lantern. "God," she said, "it's so embarrassing to be related to someone like this." And then they were getting bags from the trunk—the gifts in one, the applesauce and sour cream in another, the Chanukah song sheets and menorah in yet another, with the scratchy old record of Chanukah songs Ruth had bought when Lena and Joanna were little girls.

Other cars were arrayed in the drive—Irv's Caddy, which, Harry pointed out, he could have left in the garage if he hadn't wanted to be such a showoff; Ted and Helen's Plymouth; Eric and Dorie's Chevy. Ruth was glad to see that Eric and Dorie were there already, meaning their little ones would be too. Having the small children around made it seem like Chanukah—the downside being that it gave Irv another opportunity to gloat about the mini–population boom his daughter was generating—the infant, Reva; a toddler, Amy; and four-year-old Carl.

The family was gathered in the living room. Ted, a little man with stooped posture, held some indeterminate position in Irv's real estate development company. He was Rhoda's brother. Helen, his tiny wife, worked as a school nurse in Southfield. In the car, Ruth had said that they were so petite, they barely existed, but she conceded that Helen actually had something intelligent to say occasionally. And Harry said that he thought Ted had more going on than working for Irv. Investments or something, and that he might be the brains behind Irv's business. Joanna liked them.

The air in the house was heavy with smells of latkes and brisket and roasted chicken. Everyone got up for the obligatory kisses and hugs, like a round robin, moving from one to the other, while the newcomers still wore their coats, while Ruth carried the latke platter, while Harry carried the gifts and Joanna carried the other bags, all of which prevented any seriously meaningful hugs. Pete stood in the background as this ritual unfolded, even Lena abandoning him momentarily, as the greeting dance overrode everything else. Bending low to the smallest children, to baby Reva in Dorie's arms, straightening up for the adults. Harry weighed the question of which was the most awkward phase of these events—the greeting, the departure, or the actual sit-down.

"How do you like my little granddaughter?" Irv asked, as he took the coats, piling them on his arm. He was one of the hawk-beaked Bruchenhartz types, with the bow of the nose reaching almost to the mouth, the crescent-shaped squint eyes, in Irv's case suggesting perhaps a touch of indigestion. "An angel, right? Like her grandpa." Rubbing it in, Ruth thought—three grandchildren already, and her daughters nowhere near settled. Everything about him broadcasted smug self-satisfaction. But Ruth saw through all the overlays, going back, back, back, to the skinny little boy who was too frightened to take the bus to school unless she held his hand the whole way.

Rhoda took the latke platter from Ruth, the bag from Joanna, and whisked them into the kitchen. The menorah was ready, on the dining room table. It was a showy silver one, pretentious. The table was set—with Rhoda's everyday dishes, a fact she apologized for, as if anyone would have noticed or cared. Lena introduced Pete, who with his blond hair and broad muscular frame looked like he was there to install the landscaping rather than sit at the table and eat the Chanukah meal with the family. Ted stepped up to shake Pete's hand—which was more than his sister Rhoda did. And Helen, Ted's wife, stepped up too. They seemed so tiny next to Pete—especially Ted, as if he were a different variety, even species, of man altogether, all the way from his small polished shoes to his thinning wiry hair, next to Pete's six-plus feet of young man, all the way from his scuffed motorcycle boots to his luxuriant blond follicular display.

An awkward hiatus ensued. Ruth had the sense that she and Harry and the girls had been the interrupted topic of conversation. The family milled, waiting to see what would come next, who would come up with a topic or a direction. Ruth said they should light the candles, since it was so late. She looked for her menorah, which Rhoda had taken into the kitchen.

"My sister? Complaining that it's late?" Irv said. He used to be the skinniest one in the family, but those days were over. His cardigan couldn't cover that belly, the pregnant-male body, as Ruth referred to it. "I want to show you the house first."

Ruth agreed to go, and Harry did too. Might as well. It was inevitable. Franny followed because she wanted to be near her parents. Joanna went because she was actually interested in houses, in the modern look of the place, of the large rooms, so new and fresh. She wanted to be able to tell her friends about it—that her aunt and uncle lived in a place like this. Rhoda joined them. She was dressed in smart slacks and a soft, fuzzy sweater in exactly the same color as the pants: eggplant. She had stayed thin. And shapely. She'd been a cheerleader in high school. And she still did calisthenics every day, with the *Jack LaLanne Show*, which she loved to tell everyone about.

On the tour, Irv and Rhoda showed every modern convenience, with narration about vendors and where they got ideas, with trials and tribulations, setbacks and triumphs. Rhoda was particularly proud of the wall socket in each room where she could plug in her vacuum cleaner hoses. "They're constantly sucking," she said. "Feel." She leaned down, to show how to flip the little door up, and holding her hand over the round opening, she demonstrated the suction effect. Ruth, being uncharacteristically compliant, did the same, though she found the image both comical and frightening and would tell and retell this story many times. In the kitchen, they witnessed the little cupboards that were only revealed when you pressed the flat wooden panel in one certain way. Behind one was the Mixmaster, which Rhoda could pull out on a sliding platform. And mix to her heart's delight, Ruth would say later, when she retold the story. The house had skylights, too, which hardly any house had yet. But, Irv explained, the visitors couldn't even begin to appreciate them, because, one, it was night and, two, they were covered with snow. Harry wondered what would happen when the snow melted and whether the seal would hold, but he didn't say.

In the hall, they had closets that appeared big enough to house an elephant. And the master bedroom suite—a new concept at that time—

had its own private bathroom with two sinks, and a whole wall of equally mammoth closets.

Ruth and Harry did their best to seem interested. Ruth, in fact, *was* interested—interested in identifying the flaws, as she was fighting down a form of extreme jealousy, a sense of being left behind. "Just use it in good health," she said. Something she'd learned somewhere along the line from people who didn't know what else to say, who didn't want to say "It's not my taste, and I can't imagine how you could like something like this, but I see you do, so . . . well, use it in good health."

"What do you think, Joanna?" Irv said. "Pretty nifty, eh?"

"Yeah," she said. He was trying to bond with her, with that *nifty,* which was a word that no one used.

Irv was going on about square feet, appreciation, construction mortgages, development variances. Harry nodded. Ruth paid no attention.

Franny looked out the window into the blackness. No street lights. Just the flat earth, stripped of trees and foliage, waiting for more houses to be planted. Row upon row of them lay in the future. And someday, trees again, to replace the ones that had been knocked over and pulled up by the roots.

"It's getting late, Irv," Ruth said. "We should light the candles. And the latkes are going to get soggy."

"That's all you have to say?"

"For now." She turned to leave the huge bedroom, but wasn't sure which way led back to the living room. That's how big the house was. Or how bad her sense of direction was. Rhoda brushed past her. Everyone followed.

Back in the living room, Pete and Lena were canoodling near the front window. When Joanna came in, she sat on the floor with the children, showing them the Hebrew letters on the dreidel, and getting them to repeat them after her. Franny sat on the couch, her dress arranged around her like a perfect flower and her legs the little stem. She felt she was too old to play with Eric and Dorie's children. The adults . . . were okay, but.

Helen and Ted tried to make conversation with her—asking the usual, about school, which was not a good subject, since lately her parents had been arguing about whether to transfer her to a different one, farther west, to one that had more white children. But then Ted remembered that she'd won the science fair at her school last year, and he even remembered the subject: why leaves change color. And he asked her if she'd made any new discoveries lately. She would have answered, but Ruth interrupted.

"Okay, come on already," she said, motioning everyone to the table. Irv's menorah was at one end, and Ruth placed the simple brass one Harry had cleaned that afternoon at the other end. When the family had gathered, she lit the shammos, lifted it from its high, central position, and sang the blessing as she lit the other candles. Rhoda did the same with her fancy silver menorah, but she did not sing. Ruth had one of Irv's grandchildren on either side of her. It was so much easier for her with other people's children. She placed the shammos back in its holder and reeled in the little boy and girl as she sang "Rock of Ages," solo. Then she asked them to pass out the song sheets.

"Can we save the singing for after?" Irv asked. And Rhoda added that all the food would be dried out if they didn't eat soon. Ruth nodded, took the song sheets back from the children, and placed them in their manila envelope, under her purse, on the chair near the front door.

Irv sat at one end of the long table, and Ruth sat at the other. The candles of the menorahs were burning, the flames shifting in response to the family's movements.

Latkes and bowls of sour cream and applesauce passed from hand to hand. Eric brought the chicken. Rhoda carried the brisket. She offered it around to everyone, even though she knew that Lena and Joanna had stopped eating beef. "No?" she said when they declined. "No?"

"Chanukah," Lena said, plunging her fork into a latke. "The miracle was not that a little bit of oil lasted for eight days. The miracle was that the community was willing to imagine the possibility. They were willing to see what would happen."

Ruth nodded. Helen and Ted looked interested. Dorie and Eric were preoccupied with managing their small children, making sure nothing spilled, making sure they all had what they needed.

Irv, chewing, said, "They were making the best of what they had." He took a slice of brisket. "Besides. It's just a story."

"But why diminish it, when you can make it something wonderful?

Something huge?" Lena's reply came out sharper than she might have wished.

"You can't make something into what it isn't," Irv said. He added a dollop of sour cream to his plate and passed the dish to Dorie, who was feeding Reva a bottle, so she had no free hands. He put down the sour cream. He'd once had the thickest, curliest hair in the Bruchenhartz family. Where had it all gone?

"But you can," Lena said, "with imagination." She turned to Pete. He nodded but didn't speak. It wasn't his family. It wasn't his place to contradict his host, a man he barely knew. He focused on the latkes, which were challenge enough. He seemed to be having his doubts about applesauce on fried potatoes.

"Look at all I've got," Irv said. He looked around the big dining room, which opened onto the big living room, the long cloth-covered table, laden with food, the grandchildren, the baby sucking happily on her little bottle, the big portraits on the walls, of him and Rhoda and the children at various stages of life and hair trends and dentition, and the reproductions of Gainsborough's *Blue Boy* and Lawrence's *Pinkie*. "I don't need to imagine it."

"That's such a limited view," Lena said, "It's stultifying, the fear of doing anything different or extraordinary."

"I think this house is pretty extraordinary."

"Ugh," said Lena.

"Now, Lena," Irv said. "Don't go saying things you'll regret."

"Why would I regret saying what I feel?" Lena got up from the table and left the room, her plate still half full. Pete followed, saying "excuse me," and for a few moments the table remained silent while everyone considered how they might move beyond, absorb, and digest. And then Carl and Amy got restless—one of the blessings of children, their role in helping to fill the gaps—and Amy dropped a chicken drumstick on her party dress, a problem that became the focus of several family members, and then Irv asked for more brisket, and then Rhoda got up to replenish the gravy, and Ruth said that she'd have another latke, and then Irv got down to commerce.

"So when are you going to get out of that shoe business?"

"What are you talking about?" Harry had just reached for a latke, one he had fried himself.

"What I'm talking about is, face it, what do you need it for?" He chewed.

Joanna noticed that her father had just taken a latke, so she passed him the sour cream and applesauce.

"What do I need it for?" He cut into the latke. "It's what I do for a living."

"There are other ways to make a living," Irv said. He took a forkful of brisket. No one, Joanna noticed, had anticipated his potential need for the gravy.

Harry looked at Ruth, who was saying something to Joanna. She might not even be listening to this conversation.

"You can come work with me."

He really meant *for* me, Harry thought.

"Make some real money. Live in a house like this." Irv gestured at what he had. "Real estate development is through the roof out here." He reached across the table for the latkes. They were the ones Ruth and Harry had made. He moved one onto his plate, then added a second. "People can't wait to get out of Detroit."

"We like where we live," said Harry.

Franny swirled the sour cream into the applesauce—watching the texture of the two spiral together, the tiny pale yellow grains of the apple brought down to its basic units, with the perfectly smooth, glossy cream.

"You like where you work, too?" said Irv.

In the Levine menorah, the candles were small stubs, with the wax dripping in great cascades from the shammos. Drops of wax dotted the tablecloth.

"Who wants more latkes?" asked Rhoda, holding up the platter with the latkes she had made, small and soggy compared with Ruth and Harry's. Eric said he'd like some—the good son-in-law.

"I'd say things have gone pretty well for us," Harry said. "I've got no complaints." He put his fork down. "Everyone needs shoes. It's a good business."

"Everyone needs houses, too," Irv said. Little Carl got out of his seat and went over to his grandfather. Irv hugged him. "Don't they, sweetheart?" Carl nodded from the tight circle of Irv's hug, and Joanna noticed the tight circle of Irv's wedding band, cutting into his finger like a choker.

"The work isn't half-bad," Ted said, giving Harry a wink. It looked like between him and Helen, they'd eaten maybe one latke. "We've got some interesting people coming out this way. And the area is full of beautiful little lakes. We're creating a community by building these houses." His voice was gentle. The way he said it, it sounded possible. Like something good, as though between the two of them, they could build something noble. Harry couldn't tell whether Ruth was listening. Her face was so . . . blank.

Next to Harry, Franny swung her feet, and the toes of her party shoes knocked into the table leg.

"What's a matter?" Irv said. "You don't like money? We're selling the houses out here for a fortune."

Harry drummed with his fingers on the table. The man was so *crude*.

"And you feel good that people can't get anything for their houses in Detroit?" Harry said.

"That's what happens when you wait too long." Irv chewed.

"So you're making huge profits off the houses, while the buyers are hurting on both ends."

"You better hope I'm making huge profits, or I wouldn't even be doing this, and the Detroit Jews—including you, eventually—wouldn't have anywhere to move." Rhoda left for the kitchen. Dorie took Reva into the living room because she had begun to fuss. Carl followed them. Amy was looking at the chicken stain on her beautiful taffeta dress—still there, even after all those experts had tried to fix it.

"You're helping to pull the plug on Detroit, is what you're doing," Harry said. "You, and the mortgage brokers, the bankers, the insurance *gonifs,* the builders. All of you, luring people to the suburbs, scaring them in the city."

"You can stay and hold the plug. Fine." He called into the living room to Carl. "Sweetheart," he said, "tell Uncle Harry the story of the little boy with the finger in the dike."

"The boy saved his whole country," Ruth said.

Irv picked at a piece of brisket stuck between his teeth. "Anyway, it's not what I hear—that you're so happy with your business."

"Do we need to see the whole excavation?" Rhoda asked, as she came in from the kitchen to clear more plates. She pushed his hand down, and as she did, Joanna realized that Rhoda hadn't ever joined the meal, only alighted briefly at the table, a small forkful of this or that, then up and out to the kitchen, carrying things back and forth.

"Yeah?" Harry asked. "What do you hear about my business?" He regretted saying it, giving Irv an opening.

Ruth got busy, clearing plates with Rhoda, trying to send Irv signals to shut up, but Irv was not good at signals. Eric, the good son-in-law, got up too, to help in the kitchen. Amy toddled off to join her mother and siblings in the living room. That left Irv, facing off with Harry. Franny and Joanna with their hands in their laps. Ted and Helen too.

"Halloween," he said. He motioned with his hand, the way someone did in charades, to encourage the guesser. "Your front window."

Joanna took a bite of latke. Lena and Pete returned to the table and slid back into their seats. Harry had asked Ruth not to tell.

"Are you going to sit there waiting for something worse?"

No one spoke. The dishes and pots rattled in the kitchen. Someone turned on the water spigot. Someone turned it off.

"You didn't tell your girls?" Irv asked.

"Of course I didn't," Harry said. "It didn't mean anything. Why bother them?"

"Someone writes honky Jew boy on your window, and the police come, and it didn't mean anything?"

"Harry," Helen said. "How upsetting."

"It wasn't upsetting," he said. "It was soap. We washed it off. The police came because Ilo got hysterical. We all agreed it was nothing, and they went away."

"*Honky,*" Lena said. "That's a Black Power word."

"I'm talking about the *Jew boy,*" said Irv. "What do I care about the honky? And those tenants." He pushed his plate away. "I'm saying, what do you need it for?"

Harry looked stunned. This, he hadn't expected. "My tenants?" Harry looked for Ruth. Where the hell was she? "What's wrong with my tenants?"

Irv made that constricted-exhale sound between his lips, meant to indicate that he was some combination of amused, incredulous, and stupefied at the stupidity. "Just wait and see. When the whole thing blows, like it did in Watts."

"Just drop it, Irv," Ruth said, coming in from the kitchen. "We're not in a hurry to make any changes."

"Grandpa," said Amy, calling from the livingroom. "When can we have the party?"

"This *is* the party, sweetheart." He looked back at Harry. "Okay," said Irv. "Let's go. Time for the presents." He got up.

"Wait a minute," Harry said, having gathered himself. He stood, as if Avrum Bruchenhartz had come up behind and performed a half-airplane ride, just to get his son-in-law going. "I want to finish this conversation."

"What's to finish?" Irv said. "It's a good thing you've got that dog. Maybe you ought to get a second one. One for the home. One for the office."

"Now that's enough, Irv," said Rhoda. Ruth too interrupted him. "This is not party conversation."

But neither man was ready to let go. Neither one was thinking party thoughts.

"They're decent people. My tenants. I'm not afraid of them."

"That boy is a decent person?"

"What do you know about Alvin?" Harry asked. "You don't know a thing about him. You've never even seen him."

"I've seen plenty like him. There's nothing more to see. They're like animals."

"This is something you say in public? In front of your children?"

"Look, do what you want. I'm reaching out a hand to you. Take it or leave it."

"That's not the kind of hand I want to reach back to," Harry said. He looked around for his family. "Lena." There she was, at the table. "Will you get the coats?"

"Harry," Rhoda said. "Don't go running off."

But then Lena had the coats, and she handed them out. Arms sliding into sleeves, buttons quickly buttoned, feet sliding into boots, eyes kept to themselves.

Irv followed his fleeing guests onto the porch as they walked in a line to their car in the circular drive, Pete in the rear. "You love the *schwarze* so much, you can stay with them."

"I'd rather be with a *schwarze* than a *gonif* like you," said Harry, slamming the car door. And then he was driving through the dark streets, past the earth mounds and the rutted earth surfaces, leaving the suburban future behind.

It wasn't until they were back on Orchard Lake Road, turning onto Maple, and the snow was falling again, in big splats like it had been earlier in the day, that first he, and then Ruth, and then everyone else remembered that they had left the presents in the middle of the floor waiting to be opened, the song sheets sitting on that little chair by the door in their manila envelope, and the menorah and latke platter on the table. The scratchy old Chanukah record too. All of it.

"Annoying," Ruth said, wondering how Irv and Rhoda would orchestrate the rest of the evening, and what it looked like in that living room now. The raising of multiple eyebrows. The shrug of multiple shoulders. The "go figures." The questions from the children (*Where did Aunt Ruthie go? What will we do with all these presents?*). It actually made her laugh, as she enumerated the many conundrums the Levines had left behind in that sterile mansion, with its constantly sucking wall sockets. But they hadn't really left them behind. Those conundrums, you never leave behind. Those conundrums, you can't vacuum away.

What she didn't say, and Harry didn't either, was that maybe it was better, the original Bruchenhartz style of dining—the crispy latkes, hot in your fingers, and off you went.

BOILER

A phone. On a bedside table. The sleeping mind, pierced by the unrelenting sound. Struggling toward the surface, to place the disturbance in the watery, floating space of dreams, to re-grasp the logic of a world imprisoned in laws of time and space. The hand reaching, Harry's hand, without knowing it was, to the source of the sound, bringing the bungled instrument into alignment, scanning the anxious inventory of possibilities.

Lena, in the ragged apartment, coming and going at all hours.

Or Ilo, alone in Joe's old brick house, in her upstairs bedroom, set like a nest or a teepee under the sloped ceiling.

All this, before the voice, the real-world, true explanation was presented.

"Okay," Harry said. Ruth sat up, watching. She pulled the little chain on the bedside lamp. Even its low, gentle light seemed harsh this time of night. 1:10. "Okay," he said. Again and again. He squinted into some point in space that seemed to contain nothing, while Ruth made hand signals, shoulder signals, eye signals, all asking for a clue as to what could be so decisively okay yet merit a middle-of-the-night phone call.

"What?" she asked.

He held his hand over the phone and told her.

It was Curtis. Alvin had been in the basement when he heard a hiss. And then the place had filled with something white that looked like smoke but felt like steam, snaking into the room where Alvin sat. (Maybe thinking, maybe drinking or smoking, reviewing the list of Black Panther wants: *an end to the robbery by the capitalists; decent housing, fit for the shelter of human beings.*)

Better tell his father, Alvin had thought. Which he did. Woke him. Curtis groggy. For him, also the jagged reaching into his sanctuary of sleep, the sense of alarm on coming to the surface. The questions. The answers. The next thought: Better check the basement himself. Fast. So he dressed. Went down. And saw the steam spilling into the hallway—it wasn't smoke, of that he was certain—and heard water, dripping, and the hiss. Closed the basement door, went into the silent, frigid night, down the few sidewalk squares to the twenty-four-hour White Castle, which had a pay phone. That's where Curtis's story left off.

Harry put the phone back to his ear. Remembering Joe's boiler stories—the Chicago church, the Boston school, the Seattle restaurant—doors, walls blowing out, hurling concrete, glass, bricks. Remembering his impatience at Joe's stories, warnings, big-man talk. Harry heard the sizzling of the grill, the clink of spoons in cups, forks on plates in the White Castle, where Curtis held the phone. "Okay, I'll come. I'll be there as soon as I can." Ruth stared at him.

"In the meantime," Harry said into the phone, "can you shut the thing off?" He described the big red button the boiler man said he should install. But he couldn't remember, right then, whether he'd actually gotten around to having the man do it.

Curtis didn't answer, and the rustle of the hamburger joint filled the silence. But then he did: He wasn't sure about going down there, to look for something that might not even exist, push it the wrong way, or push the wrong button. He just wanted to know if he and Alvin needed to get out of the building. Harry said no. He thought it would be okay. Even if the pressure relief valve failed, they had the low-water shutoff. He'd be there as soon as he could.

"You're going?" Ruth asked. It wasn't really a question, since she'd heard him say he was. Or it was a question, but a different one—like, "And you want to be there in case one of these disasters happens?" She'd heard his father's stories too, the kind of thing Joe liked to talk about, warnings about being sloppy.

He threw back the covers, slid his feet into his worn leather slippers, the ones with Sappho's teeth marks. He gave Ruth a look and went down the hall to the bathroom. He was fairly certain about the low-water cutoff and the pressure relief valve, that they were safeguards again fire and explosion. But even so, things go wrong. Mechanical failure. Because of age. Changes in water pressure to the building. Something in a pipe hidden in a wall. Under a floor. A trap. A valve. A seam. Things he'd ignored. Like the clanking and the clunking in the pipes.

He dressed quickly—the worn corduroy pants, the thick flannel shirt—explaining to Ruth that the banging had stopped, several months ago, or maybe it was only that Curtis didn't mention it again. So it became one of those things. Annoying. Puzzling, like Alvin without a shirt on the Monday after Thanksgiving. He should have thought about that, why it was so hot upstairs. But because the pipes hadn't clunked for a while, and because no one said anything, and everyone had their shirts on as far as Harry knew, he turned to something higher on the list of priorities.

"People have these bombs in their homes?" Ruth asked.

He hurried to dress, to leave. "But they have better safeguards. These days they do. It would have to be a whole series of errors, of things gone wrong. Or neglect. To make it blow up." Still, she had the creeps. So did he. What it might mean. What it might cost.

While Harry sat on the bed to tie his shoes, Ruth put on her robe and left the room. And while he was in the front hall, putting on his jacket, she came up from the basement carrying a stack of blankets: the blue-gray one with the geometrical pattern, from that photo on Belle Isle ("Boo"), and a yellow quilt with a tear in the covering. And the silvery green satin one, the feather quilt with the fringe, her romantic pouf, that had been a wedding gift, and that slipped off the bed at least four times a night, until she had finally given up on it, folded it and stored it away. She put all the blankets in a big plastic zipper case and handed them to Harry, for Curtis. In case the heat was going to be off for a while.

It seemed to him a pessimistic gesture, a lack of confidence. At the same time, it was a woman's touch. They were folded so carefully in their plastic case, they looked as though they'd just come from the linens department at J. L. Hudson, something for a trousseau. She could have handed him tourniquets, a first-aid kit. If you wanted to talk about pessimism.

It was then that he decided to take Sappho.

She tugged on her leash the way she always did when the front door opened, her narrow head and snout a bullet ready to shoot through a rifle chamber. He held his toolbox handle in the non-leash hand, the package of blankets under his arm. And there was the face-freezing world, the blast of cold cutting into him, through the thick quilted jacket, the brown corduroy hat with the earflaps pulled down, the scarf tied around his throat, the big black galoshes zipped, with his pants tucked in. Ice crystals beaded on his dark nose hairs and mustache. The diamond world was silent, covered with ice, except for his narrow, shoveled, salted paths.

A man in a city like Detroit, with the whole frozen world to himself. Except for skinny Sappho, in her fur jacket, a short-haired one, her amber markings now grayed to tan, whose nails clicked and slipped on the ice. He threw the blankets in the trunk, placed the toolbox on the floor in the back, and Sappho scrambled in. In the car, Harry scraped the inside of the windshield, clearing a patch until the defroster kicked in.

Once he began driving, Sappho paced, crossing back and forth across his rearview sight lines, likely fantasizing about how she might get back to her own small oval beside the heating vent. She stepped down into the narrow well between the front and back seats, got up again, tried to sit, got thrown off balance when Harry stopped and started.

"Down, girl," he said. He told himself he was immune from danger because he had ownership rights, near Grand River and Joy Road, because he knew his way around, because he had been there day after day, year after year. He wasn't some misguided tourist taking a wrong turn, some drunken businessman on a spree, trying to find his way home, some ignorant white college kid, coming glassy-eyed out of the Grande believing the Age of Aquarius truly was in full bloom. Harry had a purpose, a responsibility, a desire to serve. But lots of people, through all human history, had headed out with good intentions. Think of soldiers. Not all of them came back, no matter the nobility of the cause.

He was trying to explain to himself how he'd let things go with the boiler, despite the signs: Alvin, shirtless; pipes, clanking; annual maintenance, overlooked.

Maintenance meant cleaning the burners, brushing out the flue pipes. Draining off the sludge. Sludge. What a word. It wasn't hard to picture the damage sludge accumulation could do, clogging and rusting. Then, if the holding tank rusted, it wouldn't *hold,* and then the water would seep or spill out of the system, and if the low-water shutoff was clogged, the gas burner would keep burning, and the cast iron would keep heating like a kettle on the stove with no water . . .

His father had shown him how to drain off the dregs, refill the tank, then check the temperature and pressure gauges. He'd shown him the coiled innards of the boiler, the lines of the manifold, the pilot tubing, the thermocouple. He'd said, "Who needs to hire someone?" Joe tried to push Harry to get in there, with his head, his hands, poke around, deal with the fear. ("It's only a machine," he used to say, "you can't hurt it.") This, just after telling about the exploding boilers of Chicago, Boston, Seattle, the doors and floors and walls raining down on the passersby. So when Harry would be slow about it, or tentative, Joe would get impatient, take over. Fine. That had been what Harry wanted anyway.

"You did it to yourself," Harry said. He said it out loud. One of Joe's well-worn expressions, giving debit where debit was due. As when someone complained about being stuffed after a meal. Or woozy the day after staying up late at a party, having a few drinks too many. Or neglecting to do something important.

The route: Appoline, to Outer Drive, east past the big brick houses, set back far on their snow-covered lawns with their graceful garden beds, defined by the shrubs, whose branches glowed in the night, outlined with sleeves of snow. Outer Drive to Livernois, then south. Wide Livernois had the fancy shops, all dark now. The sidewalks, usually dotted with pedestrians and shoppers, were empty. Harry stopped at the light at Seven Mile, a long one. Interminable, especially measured against his ticking urgency. He stared down the red, willing it to turn, tapping his gloved hands on the steering wheel, wondering if he'd dare to defy its command. Sappho seemed to be wondering, too, what miracle had brought the rocking chamber to a standstill. Ah, a red light, she might conclude. A godsend.

Finally, the green. A relief to him, another tumble for Sappho. He passed a drug store with big signs in the windows for antifreeze and sidewalk salt, snow shovels. He passed an auto supply with tires stacked in the windows. Tiny snow pellets bounced on his windshield; the wind whipped them around the car. Only criminals were out this time of night, or people partying, drunk, stoned. Sane, hard-working people were home in bed, resting up for the next day. People out at night were deranged, using the darkness as cover. Excluding him, of course.

He could have insisted that Curtis go down and turn the thing off. He could have said they'd get it fixed in the morning. But he wanted to prove he could come and go in that world, that all the talk about dangerous neighborhoods was hooey. "Fear is for people who are afraid," he might say to Irv. "What's the big deal?"

Livernois to Grand River. He passed dark apartment buildings, aligned right up against the sidewalks; electric and plumbing supply firms, with neglected front windows. He passed warehouses and bars, lots of bars; packaged goods stores on corners, with letters missing from their signs; a few all-night restaurants. Tiny grocery stores. A few big slick cars passed him: El Dorados, Impalas—cruising, the drivers with one hand, one finger, on the steering wheel. But Harry in his Dodge Dart, held tight with both hands, drove the speed limit, while Sappho whined in the back.

He switched on the radio. Static. He turned the little knob up and down the dial. Nothing, or nothing worth listening to, religious stuff, incomprehensible languages, Polish, maybe. He turned it off.

When he stopped at a light, a Town Car pulled up beside him. In the front seat was a tall dark-skinned man, wearing a fedora, and a woman with a big hairdo pressed up close to him. Harry and the man exchanged glances—the quick look through the adjacent bubbles, caught in the act but pretending not. The man in the Town Car revved his engine as they stood at the light, and before it turned green, he sped off, smooth and silent on the high-class Town Car engineering, while Harry's car coughed and stalled. He cranked the key, but in the cold, the car was balky. He pumped the gas pedal. Sappho panted, wheezed. "All right, girl," he said. "All right."

His throat was dry, and his hands hot inside his gloves as he worked the pedal and the key, giving it a rest, then trying again. He unraveled his scarf, unzipped his jacket. He flung his gloves onto the seat beside him, tore off his hat, rolled his window down a crack.

Harry worked with the key and the gas pedal, and an involuntary prayer. "Just let this god-damned car start," he muttered. Which was not perhaps the highest form of prayer, but it seemed to be effective, because the ignition and whatever magic confluence of gas and vapors and sparks and internal combustion that make these things happen suddenly sprang into action.

Left on Grand River. The magnificent Iviera. Then the short jog past Joy. Past the Grande. Even that psychedelic palace was dark. Then into the alley, rocking and slipping in the tracks frozen into the ice, like Harry was on an amusement park ride. His tools clunked in their metal box on the floor, and Sappho stared through the window. When he pulled into the space behind the building, and got out, Curtis started down the wooden stairs to meet him, pulling on his jacket as he came. Alvin stood at the door, watching, with the light from the apartment silhouetting him.

Sappho ignited at the sight of Curtis, as if the primal switch had been thrown. She ran back and forth on the seat, down in the well, paws clawing at the windows. She coughed the barks out from her whole body, an endless string of warnings and insults. Curtis stopped midway down.

What a mistake, bringing nervous Sappho into this. What had he expected her to do? Lie down and have her belly scratched by the friendly neighbors, and then go frolic in the snow with Alvin? Roll in the fluffy drifts while catching snowballs in her teeth? Wrong. First, Alvin was not at all the frolicking type. Second, this neighborhood had no fluffy drifts. What it had of snow was packed-down ice mounds, blackened with car exhaust, dangerous and ugly mixed with broken glass and tinted with substances that one would rather not see. And what it had of neighbors were in bed, trying to sleep so they could face whatever burdens their next day might bring.

Harry rolled down his window. "I'll get her under control," he shouted to Curtis, straining to be heard over Sappho's barking. "Give me a minute."

Curtis would not likely remember the stories Harry had told him in the past, about how Sappho had come to live with them. A gift from an old army friend in Greenwich Village. An animal with mythic associations of savage brutality and Nazi commandants, a strange pet for a Jewish family, but Harry hadn't been able to say no to his friend. And then there she was, the puppy arriving one morning, the spring before Franny was born, having been shipped on an airplane, with her ears and tail bandaged from having been trimmed, nervous and quivering, wounded-looking, wondering what nightmare she'd been caught in.

And even if Curtis did remember Sappho's checkered biography, including the time she'd chewed the dog obedience book from the library (Harry remembered Curtis laughing at that one) and the time she licked the onion dip on Thanksgiving, sending Rhoda off to the bedroom with a migraine, it would hardly seem relevant or true at the moment. Even to Harry, who knew this dog, it was hard to recall how she trembled on her thin legs when she did her business in the yard, how she cried and whined in her sleep with her paws crossed over her head as if during a duck-and-cover drill, and how the family had to rouse her, rubbing her side, saying "Sappho, Sappho. It's okay, girl. You're okay."

Harry turned to Sappho, spoke to her sharply, "Quiet down." But Sappho would not or could not quiet down. She continued her rhythmic hacking, eyes on Curtis, unrelenting, painful in Harry's ears, in the enclosed space of the car.

"Calm down, girl," Harry said. Curtis went back up the stairs and closed the door to his apartment. And gradually, Sappho let Harry calm her, let him run a firm hand down her back, again, again, and gradually the decibels decreased. "Sit, girl," and finally, she sat. She calmed to a low growl segueing into a whine and back to a growl, but with her ears and tail still in the en-guard position, meaning she'd be willing to get going with the barking again at the proper stimulus.

Now, at the top of the wooden stairs that crisscrossed the back of Harry's building, Alvin appeared, throwing the door open, in attack mode himself, leading with his shoulders, hands clenched, jaw set, breath exploding into the cold night. He shouted something down toward Harry and Sappho, and his father came out after him, held his shoulders, but the boy flung his father's hands off. His father caught him from behind again, by the arms.

Harry felt as though he was watching a silent movie, at the drive-in, but without the little sound-box speaker hitched to his window. The sound was all inside his car—the barking. It wasn't hard to imagine the words, though, even without the speaker, Alvin's lines something like "How dare he?" And "If you don't do something about this, I will." And "What does he think he is, bringing that dog?" And Curtis saying, "Get a hold of yourself," and "Don't make me raise my hand to you," and "This is no business of yours," which was not entirely accurate, as Alvin was an inhabitant of the apartment too, where the pipes clanked and clunked. And he had been the one to hear the hiss of the boiler and see the steam. And now it was the ferocious dog in the alley. But accuracy had little to do with such moments. Moments of dark rage when hands, arms, backs, shoulders told the ageless story of father and son.

Alvin stopped on the stairs, chest to chest with his father, Curtis broader than Alvin, both men breathing hard, their breath visible on the cold night air, like cartoon bubbles, standing in for dialogue. Alvin looked at the car, its dome light on, creating another theater or cinema from his vantage point: the barking dog, Harry getting out of the car, using his body as a barricade against Sappho.

"I brought some blankets." Harry motioned toward the trunk, where he'd put the pretty package from Ruth. "We could give them to Alvin. In case it gets cold up there."

Father and son stood on the steps. "He don't need no blankets. He needs to cool down." And then the two stood silently, clouds of breath the only exchange between them, eyes on eyes until Alvin turned and went back up, back into the apartment.

"I've got her on a leash," Harry said, and Curtis descended as Harry coaxed Sappho out of the car ("Come on, girl. Come on"), the leash, a choke chain, wrapped around his gloved hand. Feet scrunched in packed snow. Sappho panted, feet on ice. The security lights bounced and sparkled off the metal collar.

"You don't have to come in, Curtis," Harry said. "You can go back upstairs. Go back to bed. Where sane men belong this time of night."

"As long as you can keep your dog under control, I'll go with you. See how you shut that boiler down."

The owner and his dog exchanged a glance, as if control were something that no one could ever fully guarantee.

Curtis walked slowly down the last few steps, giving Sappho time to adapt to his presence. "I'm not scared of dogs," he said. "They're okay. They're fine with me." Sappho remained calm, as if proving the old maxim that when the person wasn't afraid, the dog knew it. "Doesn't mean I love them, though, or want to kiss and hug them. Like some people do."

"Can't say I feel much different," Harry said. He held tight to the leash, kept it short, and he asked Curtis to please get the toolbox from the back seat. Curtis nodded and kept his eye on the dog as he reached into the car and as Harry nudged his body against Sappho's sleek side to turn her toward the back door.

Then came the door-opening ritual: the three locks, the hand reaching in, turning off the burglar alarm, flipping on the lights, and the two men entered the big back room. Steam. He smelled it right away. Like at the old Jewish *schwitz*, or like entering a laundry, not clean like a laundry, but moist like one.

Harry and Sappho led the way, and Sappho's nails scrambled and slid down the crooked wooden stairs, and the steam rose to meet them from the hard and aging netherworld. Harry didn't say anything, unzipping his jacket, taking off his hat and gloves, stuffing them in his pockets, as he headed more deeply into the *schwitz*. He used a flash-light, afraid to turn on overhead lights, afraid of sparks in case there was gas. Shadows hovered on the ancient cave walls and supports, cutting across the fog, making odd angles for them to pass through. Sappho was all forward motion. Curtis babbled almost, about how his glasses were all steamed up, that he couldn't see a damn thing with them on, nor, it turned out, with them off, apologizing for the disturbance, for calling Harry, re-explaining the need. And as they went, the toolbox knocked on his leg, or clunked against the brick wall when he changed hands.

Harry ignored his talk, focused on the real subjects: pilot lights and pipes and condensation and pressure. Curving metal channels, joined one to the next, moving steam against gravity, up and through, and finally into radiators, those deco dream creatures, that looked as though they might any moment dance away on their skinny curved feet, especially when they clanked at you, cycling on and off, trapping the steam so that it became condensate, then letting it off, like a family member, through vents and conduits. The subject was valves—gas valves and pressure relief valves and vents—small devices for regulating flow, each a mechanical part that could wear, stick, clog. And the subject was how gas mixed with flame, and electricity with water in some way that was safe for humans, that was for some reason not explosive but comfortably warming—not the sweltering, menacing steambath that this basement had become.

"Heel," Harry said. But this meant nothing to Sappho. "Heel, Sappho," he repeated, tugging at her, yanking, without knowing why controlling her was a consideration at all. Down the hall, clouds of smoky steam poured from the boiler room, and water trickled in rivulets into the hall. Sappho whined as she pulled, the little cry that came from deep in her throat when she had a bad dream.

And then, there, in the boiler room, *the culprit*, the hissing, gas-fired, steam-spewing, pressure-containing thing. Its duct-and-pipe arms reached up and out and across in a complex maze. Headers, risers, supply main, the words his father had taught him, enveloped in clouds. A pool of water on the floor.

"You don't have to stay, Curtis," Harry said. He looped Sappho's chain around a support pillar, stood by her and calmed her—"there girl, there"—watched her adapt to the space, to Curtis, who kept his distance, standing across the room, holding his glasses in one hand, the heavy red toolbox in the other—a flash of color in the room.

"You say that again," Curtis answered, "and I'll start to think you don't want me to stay."

"Can you hand me some rags, then?" Harry asked. "From the toolbox. And I've got a bone in there too, for her."

Curtis placed the box on the floor on a dry spot in the hall. He opened it and stared at the jumble of wires and nuts and screws and tiny crumpled paper bags and plastic bags, and coils of rope and balls of string and wads of electric tape. Old pill bottles full of nails, greasy rags, small wrenches, a can of WD-40. "How do you find anything in here?" He lifted the top tray. The tools lay below in another jumble: screwdrivers and hammers and socket wrenches and pliers, and more wire—a thin, multicolored variety, like filament, and a heavy-duty copper variety. Among all this, the flashlight, loose batteries, less-greasy rags, a big old dry soup bone—gnawed at the edges.

Curtis handed Harry the rags, keeping one for himself, which he used to pick up the bone and roll it across the floor toward the dog. "They put the emergency shutoff right *on* the boiler?" Curtis asked. "You sure about that?"

The answer was no. He wasn't sure about it. And who knew what knucklehead had been responsible for placing it there, or why, or whether he himself was the knucklehead who had agreed to it those times he'd opted for the handyman's special rather than the professional boiler repair. Because there it was, the emergency switch, big and round and red, right on the side of the boiler. Standing in a puddle, he put on his gloves and held his rags like an oven mitt. Steam poured from headers, and water leaked from seams and rents. He pushed the red button, and the gas burner died with a collapsing sigh.

Harry turned on the light. He got the push broom, and swept water toward the floor drain. Sappho settled in, an eye on the human action when she could tear herself away from the fascination of the bone. Curtis left the room, but came back carrying an old metal Bruchenhartz lawn chair, green paint chipped off its tubular frame, its flat seat, and its broad seashell back. He sat and took off his glasses as they steamed up again.

Harry set down the broom and picked up the flashlight, pointed the light beam at the boiler, shone it on the expansion tank, batting away the steam, looking for rust, for the leak. If it were small, maybe a welder could patch it. If it were a large one, he'd have to replace the whole tank. Or the whole boiler. He kneeled, on the wet floor, looking for the gauge glass, which was so filthy he couldn't even see the water level.

Curtis watched from his chair, hands braced on the metal armrests. "You know what you're doing there?" he asked.

"What does it look like?"

"Looks like . . . I'm not sure what."

"If you've got something helpful to say, say it. Otherwise . . ." Harry tripped on a wrench as he got up, knocking it across the floor, and the sound startled Sappho, who leapt up, in the full Doberman stance, as if to say you can only push a dog so far. You can only ask so much. But when she saw it was just them, and a wrench skittering across this godforsaken floor, nothing to get all worked up about, she went back to work on her bone.

"There it is, Curtis." Harry motioned to the other man to come and look at the ragged scar in the tank, a few inches long, with the corroded edges, almost lacy, pitted, where something dank and acidic had bubbled up and through. "I'll get someone to come in the morning. Stanley's, over on Madison, does boiler work." He looked at his watch. Almost 3:00. At 6:30, 7:00 he could probably reach someone. They'd done work for him before, were pretty honest, not as bad as some—one of the few willing to come into this neighborhood. He was thinking what it would cost. Whether it would cost a fortune.

"Cold night, for no heat."

Harry's corduroy pants, wet at the knees, touched his skin. He wanted to sit. Just sit.

Curtis shook his head, small slow pivots, like he was showing disapproval to himself. "You know I don't like to complain."

In better circumstance, Harry might have said, "Of course, Curtis. I know that." He stood, flashlight in one hand, wearing his old brown work gloves. With the wet patches, he looked like he wore kneepads. Curtis was silent, his eyes down. "What?" Harry said.

Curtis kept his eye on the dog. "You let something like this happen to your own house?"

Harry wasn't sure. Everyone let things go. Took things for granted.

That machines, everything, would keep working. Just because they mainly always had. But not this time. The water still collected on the floor, draining from the various leaks. The steam was disbursing, leaving a damp cold behind. Curtis sat in the chair, bouncing, the way one could in those old metal lawn chairs. Harry tried to lighten things. "I'd like to have someone to blame besides myself." There was that cousin of his neighbor, who'd worked on the boiler, even though he didn't have a plumber's license. "Maybe I'll still think of someone." There was his father, for saddling him with the business.

"It's no joke," Curtis said. He kicked at a chip in the floor, and his chair bounced more decisively on its metal C-frame. "I feel like I'm talking to my son."

Harry straightened. "Look, just say it. What do you want from me?" It was the same everywhere he went. His best efforts were never enough. Alvin and the police. The bicycles. His daughters. "You think I need this?" He walked over to Curtis. "I could dump this place in a minute." He snapped his fingers, up close in Curtis's face The sound, louder than any finger snap he'd ever snapped, shocked him.

Curtis looked at Harry. He stood. He situated his waistband. "Don't be snapping at my face."

"*Your* face?" Harry said. "This place snaps at my face every day. Your son doing who knows what down here, and I don't say anything. Just clean it up, little by little, sneaking things out the back and into the car, so Ilo can't see—liquor bottles, bags of I'm not saying what." He paced as he carried on, something both coiled and wild about him. "Don't talk to me about your face."

Sappho was on her feet. She pulled at the choke chain, reared back as it caught her by the throat, enraged at her dilemma, being tethered to a pole when something deep inside her demanded that she respond.

"What are you saying about my son?" Curtis asked. "Alvin is my business." If someone had been watching this scene from afar, as Harry had watched Curtis and Alvin earlier, and Alvin had watched Harry and Sappho, the viewer would be able to see the anger and also the thing that held it back—a well-ingrained self-control, instinct overridden by rules, resentment overridden by the scoldings of mothers, and the switches and icy looks of fathers, the need to prove manhood struggling with the need to prove personhood. Backs, shoulders, arms, hands, thumbs, fingers, mouths, shouting, *My* face. *My* son. *My* business.

Sappho, too, barked commands, warnings, orders, dos and don'ts, with her whole body. But the men didn't listen, talking over her, too addled and enmeshed with each other to hear.

"It's *your business* all right. *Your business* to know what your own son is doing." Harry's face was red.

"And *your* business to take care of this place, this building."

The sound of Sappho's voice finally penetrated. "Shut up," Harry shouted at her. "Shut your big mouth." He grabbed her chain and yanked.

"You brought her," Curtis shouted over the din. "No reason to mistreat her. She's just doing what she knows to do."

It was a complicated thing that settled on Harry then, and he looked into Curtis's face, in a way he had never looked before, seeing the lines around his eyes and mouth, the pits in the skin, the real dark-coffee color of it, and the brown eyes minus the glasses, the full human weight of the planes and curves and textures. Seeing the face and breathing deeply, in, out, in, out, was what kept him from saying anything back, was what allowed him to hear what Curtis had just said, and recognize the truth of it, and feel the shame of it. And the looking and the recognizing seemed to soothe Sappho as well, and she too recognized that Curtis knew more than Harry did about all this: dogs and basements and boilers and what it meant to lose and gain control.

Harry unwound Sappho's chain from the support, pushed her with his hip, toward the door, toward the stairs, "Come on, girl," pushing her that way, up the stairs and through the packing room, and out the back door. When the cold hit him in the face, he was so hot that it felt good. He was outdoors, and wasn't even certain how he had gotten there. And also without knowing how, he and Sappho were in the car. His coat was unzipped, all bulky around him, and his hands were bare. And the car was a toboggan in the icy tire-worn ruts of the alley. And he was on his way. They wanted to determine their own destiny, or whatever that first point on the Black Panther program was, let them start with the heat in their own home.

But he couldn't. Couldn't. With Irv, they both knew they would patch it up, some way, even if the way was to pretend the whole thing had never happened. But with Curtis? And Alvin?

Back inside, he looped Sappho's choke chain around the leg of the packing table and returned to the basement, carrying the blankets Ruth had sent. If he could do nothing else, he would wait it out until morning, showing that he would take on the discomfort of his own neglect.

In the furnace room, there was Curtis, sitting in the lawn chair. Waiting for him. With another chipped metal lawn chair, this one daffodil yellow, beside him. He held up a bottle with amber liquid, a pinch bottle, swirled it. "I guess you missed a few things, when you raided Alvin's blind pig." Two Bruchenhartz schnapps glasses sat on the floor. He poured into one and drank from it. "Help us keep warm, while we wait until morning. Like you said, nothing else to be done until then." Harry shifted the blankets to his other arm. "Come on," Curtis said, "sit with me." He nodded at the other chair. "You look like you need a seat."

"I guess I do." Harry sat, more like landed, in the chair, which wobbled under his weight on the wet, uneven floor. He unzipped the plastic casing that held the blankets. A scent of mothballs and lingering perfume drifted out from the silver-gray satin one with the delicate fringe, into the dank cave-like space.

"OOO-wee," Curtis said. "Look at that." Both men laughed. And Curtis went into the other room to fetch a third chair, a rose-pink one, on which he placed the pouf, making sure that none of the corners fell to the floor.

Harry wrapped the torn yellow quilt around his shoulders, and Curtis did the same with the Aztec-patterned picnic blanket. They stared at the boiler as if they were two old Indian chiefs seated around the campfire, long after it had gone out, keeping watch for the whole tribe. The bottle was the peace pipe—the great bonder and destroyer of men.

"Have a drink," Curtis said. He handed him the bottle and the second glass. "Keep you warm. Like I said."

"I'm not a drinker." Harry looked at the liquid in the bottle, swished it, like Curtis had, as if to stir up all the good stuff from the bottom before the pour. He filled his shot glass and drank, got a look on his face like, *swallow it if it kills you.*

To fill the hours until morning, they told each other stories, the kind men tell, about things they've done, and things that have happened, not artful, perhaps, not something Ruth would find interesting, but important to them, something they thought should be remembered, known.

"Used to be the caretaker in a little shul in Memphis," Curtis said. "Don't think I ever told you about that one."

"No," Harry said. "I don't think you did." He didn't look at Curtis, just stared at the big machine in front of them, following the pipes and connections.

"Slept there on Friday nights so I'd be there Saturday morning to get things going. A shabbos goy." Harry turned from the boiler to look at Curtis. "Don't worry. I know what they call it."

Harry turned back. "It's an ugly way to say it."

"I won't disagree," Curtis said.

"I remember one night, a Friday, it was raining, a flood of rain, getting to feel biblical. It had been raining all day, the night before too, steady, drumming for hours, against the windows, against the roof. I got up out of bed to use the bathroom, stepped into a puddle not far from where I slept in the basement, a small room next to the boiler room." He sipped from the schnapps glass. Upstairs, Sappho paced. "Had a big boiler, even bigger than this one. I didn't stay every night. Just on Fridays, to close up the shul after the Friday service, open up and get it ready for the Saturday. You ever get up, step in a puddle? 'Whoa,' I thought. 'Something bad.'" The chair wobbled on the uneven floor when Curtis moved. "But then, too, in a basement, you start worrying about electrical. You know, water and electricity."

"Yeah," said Harry. "I know."

"That dog of yours is okay when she's sleeping. What's that name you call her?"

"Sappho."

"Where's that come from?"

"My wife's idea," Harry said. "Something about the community of women, about sisters. I don't know. I liked the sound of it. I said if the Marx brothers had a sister, that could be her name. None of them thought it was funny." He wobbled in his chair. "So what was the deal at the shul?"

"I went to look around. Found pools forming all over the basement. It was coming up through the cracks in the linoleum, and dripping down the cinderblock walls."

Harry gave some kind of preverbal response along the lines of *keep talking* combined with *I know the feeling*.

"Upstairs, I found water coming through the carpet in the sanctuary. Now that's serious. When it starts getting to the holy parts. They had one of those small pumps, and I got it going in the basement, running it out into the alley." He used his hands, to show the hooking up, the running out. "Then I mopped up the rest. Lucky for everyone, the rain was slowing. I got some fans going. Got some rags and towels to blot the sanctuary floor, and I set up fans there too, to dry the carpet on the bima. Kept it up until morning, blotting, wringing, fanning, mopping. By the time they got there for their worship, they didn't even know anything had happened. Just a little smell of wet carpet."

"So what did they do about it?"

"You can't bother them about business on their shabbos, so the next week, I told the old rabbi, Mermelstein, he got to do something. Once you get water in the basement, you're going to get more, but he never wanted to think about it. 'What am I supposed to do?' he asked me. And I told him. I told him more than once, about patching the cracks, about getting the water to drain away from the building, installing a sump pump, about other ways I knew to help with water, but people, they're not interested in those kinds of problems. They don't want to put their money into it. They got more important things to do. Like praying. 'God don't fill in cracks. He's not in that business,' I wanted to say. But those men would rather look at their books. Your people, they always got their nose in a book."

"Not all of them." Joe? Irv? Books? Hardly. But the noses. They did have the schnozzolas. With the blanket over his shoulders, he got up and got the push broom from the corner, started sweeping down the water again. "Does it look like I have my nose in a book?"

"Well, that's okay because you've got your job to do, taking care of this place. When it was my job, I took care of it." Curtis was sunk down in the chair, his legs flapping open and closed. "I made it as nice as I could for the people who used it. Jewish people. They got their ways, and they like their ways. Special ways of cooking, eating. Got to be just so. Special ways of praying. I remember that. The hat. The shawl."

"You've suddenly got a lot to say about 'my people.'" Harry put the broom back in the corner.

Upstairs, Sappho's long nails clicked and scratched, skittering on the wood floor. She whimpered.

"Your people have their ways too. I could say a lot about that."

Curtis looked up at him. "Plenty to say about all kinds of people."

Harry wasn't used to telling stories, and he didn't understand their twists and turns, the way someone could hear them in a different way than they were meant. He wasn't even certain why this story in particular came to him, but it was his turn, so he told one from the early days of his marriage, when he was at Fort Snelling, a place where soldiers learned everything from operating railroads to speaking Japanese. He didn't mention his own job at the Fort, as he called it, in the medical corps. Instead, he told the story of Parker, their downstairs landlord in the two-flat in St. Paul.

Harry joked that someone knew what they were doing when they named that man Parker because he was so huge and flabby that wherever he was, he seemed parked, immobile, there for the duration—in the worn chair in his living room, which smelled of old socks and aging meats, or on the front steps in the summer, or in the scrubby yard under the apple tree with the rotten, worm-eaten fruit.

"The cheapskate wouldn't turn on the heat until late November, and Ruth was pregnant, always cold and huddled in a blanket. Kinda like we are. Even the same blanket." He held his glass up, indicating Curtis's wrap. "Then there were the raccoons in the attic. We could hear them all night. It drove Ruth crazy." Both men looked up, as they heard Sappho shifting, pacing. "She said it gave her nightmares, like they were crawling all over her. I told her it was no big deal, just ignore it. But Ruth said it *was* a big deal, soon they'd be gnawing through the ceiling. She said I should talk to Parker, which I didn't want to do. It wasn't easy to find a place in those days, near the base, that we could afford."

Curtis looked at him as if he had a question. But Harry went on, saying he didn't like to be a troublemaker—making trouble was trouble in itself; it took time, effort, and he didn't think it was right to ask for too much. The rent was cheap, they were lucky to have a place, he said.

"Ruth, she had other ideas. She went to Parker one afternoon, complaining to him about the heat and the raccoons. And he told her that if she didn't like the raccoons, she should get a broomstick and pound on the ceiling. And Ruth said that was the most ridiculous thing she'd ever heard. And then Parker said just what I thought he'd say: 'Leave if you don't like it. I could rent that place in a minute.' She probably said something foul to him, though she wouldn't admit it to me."

"You know what you're saying?" Curtis asked.

Harry still didn't. "What do you mean?"

"That I shouldn't want the heat to be right in this place, and if I do, I should keep it to myself. And you bring that dog to let me know that's what you mean."

"Curtis." He said it, startled by the misinterpretation, how two pairs of eyes could come up with such unmatched pictures. But he also got a creeping sense of having let things go too far, and of having no excuse. Like he was at the edge of something and he'd ended up there by not paying attention, not anticipating, as he had supposedly learned to do at the dinner table with Ruth. It wasn't the last time he'd feel that way during this night in the basement with Curtis.

"You can bring the dog back down if you want." It was because of her pacing and her whining that sometimes went to pitiful howling. "Girl gets lonely up there by herself."

When he brought her down, she seemed accustomed to the strange circumstances, and once Harry looped her leash around that old, familiar pole, she folded herself down and rested her muzzle on her front legs. Harry went back to his daffodil chair.

"Why are you staying down here with me?" Harry asked. "You know you don't have to."

"One, I asked you to come down here, so I'll sit it out with you. Okay? Two, fellowship and appreciation." With this, he raised his glass and drank a shot. "Three, well, to make sure you're as uncomfortable as I am."

"Okay," Harry said. "Fair enough." Sappho got up, took a turn around her space, circumscribed as it was by the length of her leash. She settled back down, and gnawed, scraped her teeth on the old bone, digging them in, going at it from every angle, licking too, as if she intended to get to the bottom of it, no matter what. "What about Alvin?"

"Separate but equal," Curtis said. "I'm sure it's cold and uncomfortable up there too." He pulled his blanket around his shoulders.

"You think he'd like the pouf?" Harry asked. There it sat on the rose-colored chair. The two men looked at it.

"Alvin? The pouf?"

"It wasn't right, you know," Curtis said, "not telling me about Alvin, what he had going down here." He set the bottle between them.

"I tried. That one day," Harry said. "I didn't know what the right thing was."

"The right thing is to tell the parent. It's their job to deal with the child."

Harry rubbed his eyes, then his whole face, in circular motions, as if massaging it would release the thought in the proper words. "But you're rough with him," he said. "I was afraid what you'd do."

"A parent's got to be strict with his child," Curtis said. "I know your people have a different way. Believe me, I've seen it. When I worked in that shul. How those children talk to their parents. Insult their father one minute, then ask him for a hundred dollars the next. And the father gives it. Doesn't matter how high up in the business world, how many people he's bossing every day. When it came to the children . . ." He picked up the bottle, refilled his glass. "Not their fault if their parents never taught them. Raising a child holds your feet to the fire like nothing else. But once you got them—they didn't ask to be here—you got to show them the way. My Alvin, if he's heading for trouble, I got to rein him in. Somebody knows something about my Alvin, I expect them to tell me."

Harry flushed, adjusted his blanket around him. Sappho got up, paced, then thudded back to the ground. "If your people are so strict with the children," Harry asked, "tell me why they are in so much trouble."

"Did I say anything about 'my people'?" He leaned his head back and closed his eyes. He rested his hands on his big forehead.

Harry had to confess that he hadn't.

"Look. When Alvin was little, he liked to make up stories, to write them down. How he struggled with his letters, erasing until the paper tore through."

This was hard for Harry to picture: Alvin as a little boy, struggling over his paper.

"One time in grade school—second grade maybe it was. And the teacher told them to write a story about anything they wanted. Alvin's story was about a boy who went to visit his grandmother, and that grandmother owned a candy store with a magic jar that could make anything you wanted, as much as you wanted. He even named the candies—Good 'n' Plenty, Snickers, things he always wanted, Milk Duds. Every child's dream, right, all the candy he wants?"

"Like on Halloween."

Curtis drank the amber liquid. The bottle still had plenty left for a whole night of stories. "But no need to worry about your teeth. That was the real magic of the jar. All the candy without the tooth decay, which he wrote as *DK*, just the two letters, you know, because he couldn't spell the whole word." Curtis looked at Harry, and Harry looked back. "Well, he handed in that story, and his teacher, a white lady, asked him to stay after. 'What is this DK?' she said. Like she couldn't figure it out. And then she says, 'Who really wrote that story? You might as well tell the truth.'" He wagged his finger, showing how she must have scolded. He picked up his glass. "Stupid bitch. Who else going to write that story? Me?"

Harry shrugged, because he honestly did not know the answer, thinking of his own girls, their stories about teachers and other troubles at school.

"He came home that day so mad and crying. At first he wouldn't tell me what happened, but then, he finally did. That was cruel, break a little boy's heart like that. If it was you, I know you'd be taking your little girl on your lap, letting her cry it out, then take her out for an ice cream soda. And your wife marching off to the school to let them know how they can and can't treat your child. Not me. I just told him this is how the world is. This is what you've got to face. If you want to write your stories, write your damn stories. Doesn't matter what some old white woman says."

"That's harsh," Harry said. He drank a shot.

"Me or the teacher?"

"Both."

"That's my point." Curtis poured another drink for himself. "Got to be ready. Look at those young people writing the Motown songs. They're writing beautiful stories, set to music. Plenty of nasty old ladies in their lives too." He set the bottle back, a little harder than he meant. "Of course, the Motown stars are not the only talent around. I tell that to my son. They wouldn't sound like much without the Funk Brothers playing behind them. Do they get any credit for what they do? No. But they keep playing their music anyway. Great music. Great musicians. Playing over on Twelfth—at the Chit Chat, Eagle Show Bar, Collingwood. If you've got the talent and the need, you keep on, no matter who pushes you down."

Harry stretched his legs and leaned his head back, as if he were in the dentist's chair, waiting for the order to open, unsure whether he wanted to. He stared at the ceiling for a few beats, studying the piping. "You're what my anthropologist daughter would call an informant." Harry reached for the bottle, then noticed his glass was full. "It's like a teach-in." He raised his glass in the air, made the clinking motion. "*L'chaim*," he said. "We're informing each other, seeing what the other has to teach."

Harry got up from his chair, unsteady but determined, a man with something on his mind, a flashlight in his hand. "I'm gonna show you something," he said, and he left the room, getting a rise from Sappho, but nothing she couldn't handle.

When he came back, he held a small shoe box. From the room where all the remnants were stored. He opened it, and folded back the tissue paper, in the professional shoe-man way he had.

Curtis looked. "Baby shoes?"

"Yup," Harry said. "My own design." And he sat down to tell. About the kind of shoes manufacturers made for babies when Lena was little—rigid things that trapped and bound the feet. Not much better than those skinny boots up in the window. "I'd been thinking about it, and to be honest," he said, "I doubted whether a baby needed shoes at all." He rested the box in his lap.

Curtis reached over and took the box from Harry. He took one of the shoes out of the box—so small and unused. "Not the best argument for a shoe man to make. I wouldn't think."

"Right. So I tried to imagine the least shoelike shoe possible: something wide in the toe, forgiving in the last, open in the ankle. Something that would allow the baby's foot to grow and develop naturally, in a healthy way, while also protecting it."

Curtis nodded.

"I told my father what I'd read, about the dangers of a poor fit, that it could cripple a person for life. And I reminded him that it wasn't much more than a hundred years ago that some cobbler realized he should be making one fit of shoe for the left foot and a different one for the right." Both men looked at their own shoes—right and left shaped in their own way.

"Showing him it was time for another breakthrough."

"Yeah, and talking to him about it until finally, one day, who knows why, he said, 'So go. See what you can make of it.' And so I did."

He left little Lena and pregnant Ruth, and the daily routine, and drove east during the golden fall, in his Chevy Fleetmaster, through flat Ohio, into the mountains of Pennsylvania, headed for the few still-thriving shoe manufacturing plants of New England: Tiara in Dover, New Hampshire; Endicott-Johnson in Binghamton, New York; Brockton Shoe Manufacturing in Massachusetts.

"I even thought of a name for my baby shoe—Dr. Levine's, inscribed into the bottom of each one." Harry took the box back from Curtis and showed him on the bottom, where that name was stamped.

In the plants, he said, he met the workers: the designers and patternmakers; the cobblers, cripplers, and markers. The tack pullers, the tongue pressers, the wrinkle chasers, and Harry's favorite, the sole scrapers. He learned the terminology—the shanks, and the lasts, the box-toes and quarters and saddles and vamps. The heel seats. And in Brockton, he met a patternmaker named Richard Heney who understood what he wanted. Together, the two men sat at Richard's big table, covered with brown paper and cardboard, with pencils and Richard's wooden-handled knife, and they settled on a design.

But when the box from Richard Heney arrived a month later, the tiny shoes nestled inside, Joe said that no one would be interested in buying them. " 'Bedroom slippers?' he said, 'For a baby?' " It was too big a risk, he said. And Harry couldn't convince him otherwise, so the little box ended up in the basement of the warehouse on Jefferson, and from there moved to the basement of Grand River, where it had remained.

He folded the tissue back onto the shoes, one side and then the other. He closed the box, set it down beside him. He looked up at the ceiling. He looked all around the boiler, at where he was. And he told the rest. In the army, working as a clerk in the medical corps, one silver-haired officer, Griffiths was his name, had said that when the war was over, Harry should consider medical school because he seemed to have the aptitude.

The word *aptitude* had come like a gift. And the dream Griffiths planted with that word had grown into a fully formed scene that Harry played and replayed in his imagination as his term of service drew to a close and as he prepared to leave St. Paul. In that scene, Harry would explain his plan to his father—that he would not go back to the wholesale shoe business. That he was finished with the dark old warehouse building on West Jefferson. That his father had a good business, an important business, everyone needed shoes, but Harry had discovered in the service that he had a different calling, a different *aptitude*.

Once back in Detroit, wearing his army uniform, crisp and pressed, his shoes highly polished, he walked into his father's house. The two men sat across from each other at the kitchen table, drinking coffee from the fancy, flowered china cups his mother collected. But before Harry could even launch his imagined scene, his father launched his:

that the business was growing and that he needed help moving to a new location, because the warehouse section around Jefferson was being bulldozed for the big veterans' memorial and the new civic center. That he'd found a new location, a building he was going to buy, in a better neighborhood than they had on West Jefferson.

When Harry didn't respond, Joe sat back in his chair and looked at his son, his bushy eyebrows raised to an uncharacteristically sharp point. He put his cup down. He placed his hands on the table. He hoisted himself up and went to his newspaper, thus bestowing the dreaded Levine silent treatment in which the abandoned victim was left to interpret the void, clear only that the subject was closed.

"The fact was," Harry said, "I had the mortgage payment, and I had Ruth and Lena to support, so . . ."

"And maybe you weren't sure you had what it took? Like the man said, the aptitude?" Curtis poured for both of them.

Harry nodded. He hadn't thought about any of this for so long.

"A father can sit on top of a son too hard. Is that what you're saying? A father can sell his son short?"

"Maybe so, Curtis."

Both men drank, closing their eyes as the whiskey warmed them, and for a while it looked as though they'd fallen asleep.

"Let me ask you something," said Harry. It was getting close to 5:00 A.M. The water still dripped from the boiler. The eyelids were at half-mast, the whites of the eyes shot with red.

"Sure."

"No one knows what to call your people anymore. Negro, black, colored?"

Curtis took a long inhale and looked at the ceiling, as if the answer might be there. "Best thing, call me a person. That's what I like to be called. Or a man."

"But I mean, your race."

"You asked me. I'm telling you. You only need the label when you're talking *about* me. It's the talking *to* me that matters."

"You know what they say about white people?"

"Maybe."

"Say that when white people get wet, especially their hair, they smell like a dog."

134

"I'm wet," Harry said. He moved the blanket, to show his knees, where his pants were wet. "You smell anything?"

"Don't know, as we got a dog over there, confusing the situation." The two men laughed.

"Anyway," Harry said, "white people say that about Negroes too—that they smell bad."

"Yeah, well, Negroes say that white people are dirty, that they got bad hygiene."

"Whites say the same thing about you."

"But how would white people know?" Curtis asked. "Since they never go into a black person's house, while black people got about two hundred years of experience cleaning up after whites."

Harry sipped. He felt like the straight man in a comedy routine, providing the setup for Curtis's punch lines.

"And another thing," Curtis said.

"Yeah?" Harry bounced in his chair, pulled the blanket around his shoulder, arranged it over his legs.

"You know how white ladies are always playing with their hair? Running their fingers through. Swinging it. Like the whole world's in love with them."

Harry had to think about that one. "I'm not sure I know what you mean."

"You don't? Living with all those ladies like you do—wife, daughters."

Harry thought about all the hair crises he'd witnessed over the years, and the changing shapes of his wife's and daughters' heads—ballooning out to stiff bubbles one year, lying in flat curtains that covered their faces the next, the curls tamed into submission—the multiple products in the shower and the medicine cabinet and the drawers and on the counters and shelves. But the swinging? "What do you mean?"

"You notice," Curtis said. "Look around and you'll see what I mean." He stretched his legs. "I was riding on a bus once with Alvin, a few years ago, sitting behind a lady with long shiny hair. And she was swishing and swinging that stuff around, practically in our faces the whole ride. I leaned over to Alvin and said, 'If she does that one more time, I'm going to say something.' And he knew just what I meant—made a little face, to show. 'Disgusting,' I said to him. 'Dirty, too.' Well, fortunately for us, she got off at the next stop, so I didn't have to take it up with her. Filthy habit. Almost like picking your nose."

135

"Oh, come on," Harry said. "You're kidding."

"Not kidding. No I'm not."

"Now you tell me something white people say."

"Nah. I don't want to."

"Why not? We're just having a little chat. A teach-in. Like you said. Informants."

"Nah. No point in causing trouble."

"Come on," Curtis said. "And have another drink. It'll keep you warm." The bottle was down to the halfway mark. Past it.

"Okay," he said. "You asked." Harry drank. "Say I'm driving my car, and I'm stopped at a stop sign. If a group of Negro kids crosses in front of me, they walk as slow as they can, as if I'm not even there. People talk about that."

"Could be challenging you to try something," Curtis said. "How else they got to show their power?"

"Their power? The way they walk in those big groups? They've got power, the power to scare people out of their minds."

"White people been scaring us out of our minds for centuries. Of course we walk in groups. And we loud because we like to be. You're all so buttoned up. Ice men, we call you. I'm afraid to walk alone down your streets too."

And from there, with the whiskey flowing, it degenerated.

"You ever heard Jew canoe—for those big expensive cars your people drive?"

Harry gave him a look. "No."

"You ever hear *porker*, because you won't eat pork?"

"No."

"I know you know kike. That's a bad one."

Harry knew kike. Though no one had ever called him one, to his face, so he didn't know how it would feel.

"They're all just words," Curtis said. "You know what they say . . . sticks and stones one thing; words another."

"Jungle bunny."

"Eagle beak," Curtis said. "People say you're like vultures. That's why you got the beak." He took the bottle back, wiped the top while giving Harry a stern look.

136

Harry sniffed. The nose. Always the nose.

"You ever hear white people talk about Negroes being like apes?" Curtis asked. When Harry didn't say anything, Curtis pressed him. "Come on," he said. "You're among friends."

Harry looked around. Curtis. Sappho. The boiler. "Yeah, okay, I know people who have said it."

"Said what?" Curtis asked.

"Oh, come on. I'm not going to say those things."

"What things?" Curtis asked. "Gorilla? Baboon? Porch monkey?"

"All." Admitting these secrets. The things people said. The things he'd heard. The things he'd let go by. "But not me. I don't talk like that."

"How do you talk?"

"You know how I talk, Curtis. Listen to me." He stood. He got the push broom and moved the water that had pooled since the last go-round, directing it toward the drain. He looked at his watch. 5:30. An hour, hour and a half until he could call the boiler guy. "I've heard 'nigger toes' for Brazil nuts. But I don't say that."

"Ah-hum." Curtis drank. "Sure are tasty, those nigger toes." He tapped his feet on the hard concrete. "And honky, for the Detroit Jews who sit out in their big cars, honking for their Negro girlfriends to come on out."

"Curtis."

Harry stared at the gash in the boiler. "Whites are scared, Curtis." Now he'd switched from a straight man in a comedy routine to a commentator on the 10:00 news. "They're scared of people like Malcolm X, Stokely Carmichael, and H. Rap Brown. They're scared of what those men are stirring up."

And across the table, on the 10:00 news, the counterpoint: "They have a reason to be scared, Mr. Levine, because they know colored people have a right to be angry. They know in their hearts that things can't and won't continue the way they are." The two commentators took a pause for a drink.

"But that anger. People like you and me, we know how to manage it. Other people. The young people. I don't know if they do."

"The anger will go away when the young people start seeing some benefits. Like those Motown singers. They sound angry to you? No.

They're singing about love." Curtis refilled the glasses. "The Panthers are angry. They're not singing about love. But they know what they want. You heard about that ten-point plan?"

"Yup," Harry said. He'd heard about that, folded up in his dresser drawer. *Decent education. Free health care.*

Curtis nodded.

"Do you know what *you* want, Curtis?"

Curtis threw back his head and laughed. "Where shall I start?"

"Want to hear a joke?" Curtis asked.

"Oh, now you're ready for jokes?" Harry sipped.

"Yeah. No. It's a good one. I heard it at Baker's Keyboard Lounge—one of those black and tans. Up in your neighborhood, near Eight Mile. The man told it was James Moody."

"Never heard of him."

"A great tenor sax player." Curtis settled in, like he was remembering the music, like he was making certain he remembered the whole joke. He sipped. "Okay." He began. "A zebra dies, and when he gets to the pearly gates, he says to St. Peter, 'I've got to see God.'

"'Well,' says St. Peter, 'God's pretty busy. Why do you have to see him?'

"'All my life,' the zebra says, 'Something's been bothering me: Am I black with white stripes or white with black stripes? It's driving me crazy.'

"'Hmm,' says St. Peter. 'As I said, God's pretty busy, but if you want to wait, you can ask him when it's your turn.'"

"Oh, I know what you're going to say," Harry said. "That it doesn't make any difference. It's all how you look at it."

Curtis looked disgusted. "And you would call that a joke?" he said. "You need to learn to sit back and listen. Like that dog of yours." Sappho looked up, as if pleased to be acknowledged. "Can I go on now?"

Harry nodded, his glass in his hand.

"So the zebra decides to wait, and after a long while, God summons him. After the formalities, the zebra asks his question: 'Please, God. Tell me, am I black with white stripes or white with black?'

God looks him over and says, 'My son, you are what you are.' And that's that—the zebra gets dismissed."

"Is that the joke?"

138

Curtis gave Harry one of those famously stern Malcolm X looks. "I don't know if you even *deserve* to hear this joke."

"Sorry," he said. "Tell me."

Curtis took a shot of whiskey, bounced a little in his chair, rearranged his blanket around his shoulders, and resumed. "When he gets outside, and back to St. Peter, the zebra's scratching his head, with a puzzled look on his brow.

"'Did you get your answer?' St. Peter asks.

"'I don't know,' says the zebra.

"'Well, what did God say?' asks St. Peter.

"'He said, "You are what you are,"' answers the zebra.

"'Okay. Well, then, you're white,' says St. Peter.

"'How do you know?' asks the zebra.

"'Because if you were black, he would have said, "You is what you is."'"

Harry winced, uncertain, while Curtis laughed until he had to wipe the corner of his eyes with his handkerchief.

"Now, why is that funny?"

"It's honest," said Curtis, sipping from the bottle, flapping his knees. "That there is a difference—a difference of style."

Harry nodded but still wasn't ready to laugh. "I'll tell you one thing. No white man would tell that joke with any Negroes around."

"I'd like to hear a white man pull off that joke," Curtis said. Harry stood, a little unsteady from the whiskey. He'd been listening to the talk almost his whole life, watching the moves. He'd give it a try. "You *is* what you *is*," he said, using his hips and his shoulders and his hands in what he thought might be a decent imitation. "You *is* what you *is*."

"Not bad," said Curtis.

"You ever heard peckerwood?" Curtis asked. "About southern whites?"

"That's a new one on me," Harry said. He was sitting again, his face still flushed from the exertion. It was almost 6:30.

"Peckerwood, peckawood," he said. "You know, like the bird. But pecker. You know what that means. Just a way to speak of someone you don't like. Lots of ways to do that." He stretched his legs out. "I know your people say *schwarze*." His Yiddish pronunciation wasn't the best.

Harry didn't say one way or the other.

"You ever heard this one?" Curtis said. "That because the white man

139

was evolving or whatever in those cold climates, he had to have a small dick to keep from getting frostbite." Curtis laughed hard at that one, slapping his thigh.

"That's the most ridiculous thing I ever heard." Harry put his glass down, hard.

"Getting a little personal?"

"That's just ignorant."

"And the rest of it?"

They were drunk. The words were slurred. The eyes red. The air damp.

Harry floated off, on the cushion of alcohol and fatigue. He pulled the blanket around him. "My wife, Ruth."

"Yeah?"

"When she met Gregory, the man who gave us Sappho." They both looked over at Sappho, sleeping with her paws over her head, like this had finally turned into the most humiliating of all experiences, drunk men in a cold basement trading dick jokes. "She said, 'I am so happy that Harry has a non-Jewish friend. Now I've got a chance to see an uncircumcised penis.'"

They laughed, diffusing laughter, tension-relief laughter that goes deep. Honest, strong. "That's some wife you got." Curtis looked at him. "She ever get the chance?"

"Curtis," he said, as if shocked and offended, and at the same time reaching for the bottle and reaching a little too far and his chair tipping over and knocking into Curtis's chair, and Curtis's chair knocking over too, and even knocking over the chair with the pouf. And then they were laughing and scrambling to get themselves back to separate, vertical spaces, and their legs were in the air, their arms tangled in blankets, and whiskey spilled on the floor mixed in with the boiler water, and the men, clumsy from drink and from cold and from tension and from crazy joking and insults and lack of sleep, took turns saying "you is what you is" and "you are what you are."

And then it was Alvin. "*This* is what you're doing?" And at the same time, it was Sappho, ears and tail erect, barking that angry, unrelenting bark, one bark at a time, percussive, teeth bared, because a stranger had entered the formerly safe little circle. "You, getting drunk with *him*? And me up there, all these hours, not knowing *what* is going on, afraid to come down. Thinking you might be gassed out or electrocuted." Spitting out the words, and pointing fingers in his father's face.

He had the two men's full attention, as they sat on the damp floor, looking up at him. He was dressed in a way Harry had never seen him before, with layers and layers of old, ragged clothing, so he looked bulky and poor rather than tailored and sleek. Old dungarees. A scarf wrapped around and around his neck. A sweatshirt with cuffs that hung by a thread. "And that dog? How *dare* he bring her?" Shouting over Sappho, as she continued her angry harangue, her response to this danger and that danger.

Harry felt sleepy, like he was watching this scene from above, through a membrane.

"Leaving me up there, all this time not knowing? And him? With that dog." Sappho lunged, and lunged again, the choke chain, biting further into her self-control.

Harry looked at Alvin. And he looked at Curtis, who was looking up at his son, like the older man was a child, caught in the act. "I brought her because I was afraid, leaving the house at night. Coming here." Harry was shouting. He had to, to be heard over the din.

"See what I told you," Alvin said. "Listen to what he's saying. What he thinks. This is his place, but he's afraid to come *to* it."

"It's not what I *think*," Harry said. "It's different from thinking."

Alvin kept his eyes on his father, even though the words were for Harry. And he did hurl some impressive expletives, all the pain and anger of what he'd seen, of what he'd heard, of what he'd read over all the years—tired of being seen as stupid and lazy, incapable, as no better than an animal, of all the labels: childish and shiftless and immoral; primitive and excitable and odiferous; incompetent, superstitious, and mentally inferior; apelike and homicidal, and if not that, oversexed and generally criminal. Looking alike and being good for nothing more than janitors and domestics. It was all of that, and no way to even begin to know what to say about it. "Bull*shit*," was what he came up with as a punctuation mark.

"You get a hold of yourself, son," Curtis said.

But Alvin did not get a hold of himself, could not get a hold of himself. He spewed and he spit and he spoke well and with good sense, righteous anger, schooled, familiar with the injustices and the big view of things, the new views, the gloves-off view, the ten points—what he wanted, what he needed. And then the slur, about the Jews in Nazi Germany: "They expect me to care about that? They expect everyone to care about that?"

And Sappho, tugging at her choke chain, and rearing up, could not get control of herself either, and Alvin swung around in his anger. And Curtis grabbed an arm, saying, "That's how it's got to be. The parent's got to control the child." But Alvin pulled himself free, and then Curtis slapped him, full in the face. Hard. "I told you to behave." And Harry stunned, not knowing where to intercede, or how, or whether he should. Sappho, Curtis, Alvin, all out of control.

And all the shouting and ruckus, and suddenly, the ragged cuff of Alvin's sweatshirt caught in Sappho's teeth. And Alvin tugging and Sappho tugging back, up on her hind legs and down, and Alvin screaming with fear and rage, tears streaming down his face, and then blood, trickling from his hand as the cuff ripped off, and Sappho shook her head, holding the cuff in her mouth.

"Get back, girl," Harry said. The words he remembered from the library book. He tried to approach her, speaking firmly, trying to establish control. "No Sappho. No." But she was beyond that, lurching and barking and growling, under the control of something primal and hormonal and essential.

"No way she's going to calm down with all this going on," Curtis said. "We've got to leave her to calm herself." He took his son firmly by the shoulders. He guided him up the stairs, and Harry followed.

They stood in the packing room. A triangle. "I'm so sorry," Harry said. The second, third, maybe fourth time that night. To Alvin. To Curtis. For the boiler. The dog. The bad jokes and stories. He held his hands out, an offering, afraid to look at Alvin, hearing the snuffling, imagining the need for a clean handkerchief, the young man's attempt to compose himself. Sappho had the shots, he explained, for rabies. Harry had the training, from the army. He had a first-aid kit. If Alvin would let him, he told Curtis, he could clean it, bandage it. The wound, he called it.

"No need for that," Curtis said. He looked at the hand and Harry did too, still avoiding the face, the eyes, the wide nose. "Just a scratch. He's got to learn. It's not the first time he bled. Probably not the last." He looked again at the hand. "You see it's just a scratch, right?"

"I'm going to bandage it," Harry said. He'd learned it from the nurses in the army, that you should always treat a wound, even those that weren't serious. Because of the comfort of the human touch. "I insist."

And they squabbled. Tiptoeing around those confessions from the basement teach-in, about who smelled like what and who had big noses and small dicks and big cars. Who was loud and who was pushy, who was buttoned up and who was too indulgent or harsh, and who was afraid and why, and what a young person had to learn to survive and how a parent ought to behave. Alvin stood by, silent, holding his hand to his chest, as if he were saying the pledge, the blood dripping slowly into the torn ragged sleeve of the sweatshirt. In the end, Curtis said yes, okay, so they went into the front office, and Harry had Alvin sit in the desk chair. He found the first-aid kit on the first try, in the bottom drawer of Ilo's desk, and got to work, focusing on the trembling hand, applying pressure with the clean gauze.

"There," he said. "It's not too bad." And he knew he was right, and that the hand would heal quickly, but he lingered over it nonetheless, longer than he needed to, warning that the iodine would sting, hearing the little gasp as he applied it. His brain was still thick from the alcohol, but he remembered what Griffiths, the doctor from Fort Snelling, had told him—that the toughest, meanest ones were sometimes the most afraid. But, he always added, knowing that wouldn't necessarily help you if they wanted to hurl you across the room.

He could feel that Alvin was calming, from the touch, though he didn't speak, and the two didn't look at each other. He remembered another thing Griffiths had taught, that sometimes you just talk, talk about anything, and the sound of the voice can calm the patient, that calming the patient was sometimes the most important part of the job. So Harry talked, about how Sappho had come to him, how small and frightened she was that morning he picked her up at the airport.

"Are you looking at my hand?" he asked. Holding it up, to show his patient the three curled fingers, the ones he'd broken as a boy. And he told about his heedless youth, that when he was young, nothing could hold him back, not even the memory of the pain from those broken fingers. All the while, Curtis stood leaning against the file cabinet, his arms crossed over his chest, and Alvin sat in the chair, his hand resting on the desk.

And then Harry said that he thought it was time to see about getting the boiler repaired. And they all went where they needed to go. Curtis and Alvin went upstairs, and Harry made the call to Stanley's Plumbing and Heating, still hearing Sappho below, barking and crying, and Stanley said he could be out around 8:00. Then Harry called Ruth, to let her know he was going to stay, that everything was more or less all right. She was furious, as Alvin had been, not knowing whether her husband was dead or alive. She'd been about to call the police or the hospitals. And there he was, saying it again. Sorry, he said. Sorry.

"Is that a slur in your voice?" she demanded. "Are you drunk or something?" And he said, yes, they'd drunk some whiskey, to keep warm. And now he was going to the White Castle for some coffee, and could she call Ilo, to tell her he wouldn't be by to pick her up. And he'd call later, when he knew what the damage was. By damage, he meant money, how much it would cost to fix or replace the boiler. And then he said, sorry again. Sorry. Sorry. Sorry.

"Didn't you hear the phone ringing?" she asked. She'd called and called. And he said that honestly, he had not heard. He honestly had not. "I am what I am, I guess," he said. And she said, "What does that mean?" And he said, "Just what it sounds like."

Then Harry went back down, and there were the chairs, still tipped over, and the whiskey bottle and the blankets, including the pouf, in a wet muddle on the floor. And there was Sappho, trembling. "Sit," he said. "Stay." And Sappho did, panting, worried, at what she'd done, at how everything had so gotten out of control.

And he rubbed her head. "It's okay," he said. "It's okay. Don't get so excited. It's okay."

NEIGHBORS

It was a complete surprise. After the multiple promises and come-ons. One day, on the cusp of winter and spring, the phone rang, and there she was. Margo Solomon, inviting Ruth to lunch—a *luncheon,* in Margo's words, more important because of the two syllables—with a few of her friends. So what if Ruth *was* most likely a last-minute add-on, to fill in for someone who had cancelled? She would go anyway. Yes, she would love to. And it was her birthday, no less, though she didn't mention this to Margo.

In her best coat and shoes, on her way down the block at the appointed hour, she saw Seidel Deitch, the across-the-street neighbor whose eyes missed nothing. Seidel waved from her car, and Ruth felt the all-seeing Deitch eyes follow her as she walked up Margo's porch steps, as she lifted the brass knocker on Margo's front door, as she entered Margo's home.

Ach. She was overdressed, if that was the right word. Misdressed might be more like it, compared with Margo, who wore a flowing floor-length gown, a deep blue, with gold embroidered bands around the key-hole neckline and cuffs. Beside Margo, Ruth felt like a toad in the brown wool coat she had dearly loved just moments ago, and as she handed it to Carrie, the Negro maid in a white dress with a black apron, she suddenly remembered that she had worn the exact same matronly skirt and sweater to the Changing Neighborhoods meeting in the fall.

"That's beautiful," Ruth said, about Margo's blue gown. Everything else was beautiful too—the sculptures and the carvings and the big abstract paintings on the walls—a couple of Warhol's Marilyn panels, the bright rugs, the elaborate shelving units with the detailed moldings, the palms and purple velvet chairs. She'd been in the house before, but only at the big annual parties, when the house was full of people and the furniture was pushed back to make room for the café tables.

"Isn't it?" She held out the skirt, to show its breadth. "To go with the Morocco theme." She turned, to show the back. "We were just there."

"Oh."

"Didn't I tell you that it was a Moroccan theme?"

And then the doorbell rang, and the other women arrived. Both had been at the Changing Neighborhoods meeting. Lynn Hochman, the pianist, had come from the tennis club, with the healthy flush of exertion still in her cheeks. Porcelain complexion, sporty hairdo. A nubby sweater, slim pants. She stepped out of a pair of high-heeled pumps that looked like something Marilyn Monroe herself would have worn. The other, Selma Schneider, wore dark glasses and a black leather coat. Very smart. Very put together with her heavy dark hair. Big eyes revealed once the glasses came off. Carefully bohemian makeup. Way out of Ruth's league. It would just be the four of them.

Margo laughed, realizing she hadn't told *anyone* it was a Moroccan theme. No matter. She had caftans for each of them, that she'd brought back from the trip. And she showed them to the bedrooms, one for each, where they could change. The large room where Ruth was installed had a bed with lots of toss pillows, a silky bedcover, and an elaborate headboard-canopy combination—the room of one of Margo's daughters who was off at boarding school or college. The gown lay on the bed: deep green with pale-green embroidered bands around the neck and sleeves, around the hem. She slipped off her shoes, and stepped onto the thick white carpet. She looked at the gown, afraid it would pull across the shoulders and chest, where she was broad, that she'd have to come out and tell them it didn't fit. She was afraid she would perspire in it, leave a sour smell. She held it up. Okay. She didn't seem to have a choice. Okay. It was a bit tight under the arms. Too long. But okay. She could manage. It was beautiful.

When they all came out, each admired the others, a little shy and flushed, and Margo offered them a selection of sequined slippers with pointed toes. She led them to the back room, lined with windows, looking out over the yard. Cloths in deep reds and purples were draped from the ceiling, to look like a sultan's tent. A square table was set with china and crystal, and with bright-colored cloth napkins. Candles of many widths and heights glowed on the tables and shelves.

When they sat, Carrie brought a platter of lamb and chicken, with grapes and almonds and chickpeas, nestled in a bed of couscous, a tiny grain, perfect little balls. On a matching platter, sliced oranges were accented with radish and purple onion. The women served themselves, and Margo poured red wine into long-stemmed glasses. They talked.

They told about their recent ventures: Selma told about new acquisitions in the African collection of Detroit's Art Institute. She held the stem of her wineglass. She wore a ring with a deep red stone. She was on the board, she said, and she'd just come from a private showing. She described a wooden helmet mask with the horns of an antelope, the jaws of a crocodile, the tusks of a warthog. Ruth struggled to imagine this but could only think of Mrs. Rappaport, the lady who had lived with her mother, after her father had died.

"Africa!" Margo said, and she told about the Moroccan market where she'd bought the caftans and slippers, the warren of spicy smells and sights. She told about the hotels where they'd stayed, converted castles, marble and onyx, palm groves and gardens, the lace work of rose-colored stones.

And Lynn told about her current reading: Katherine Anne Porter's collection, which had just won the Pulitzer. The stories, she said, were magnificent. "María Concepción," she recited, "walked carefully, keeping to the middle of the white dusty road, where the maguey thorns and the treacherous curved spines of organ cactus had not gathered so profusely." She put her fork down. She folded her hands on her lap, on the cloth napkin, she swept her hair back behind her ears. "How's that for establishing place and mood?"

"A narrow place," Ruth said. She sipped from the long-stemmed wine glass. She ate a radish, the crunchy bite of it mixed with the juice of the orange.

The women looked at her. Waiting. Surprised. Heads tilted. As if she had just appeared, a genie from a magic lamp.

"*Mitzrayim*—a refuge, an enslaver, the birth canal of a people." She became embarrassed, the way they looked at her. "That's what the line made me think of." She'd gotten carried away. The wine. The gowns. The slippers. "But I haven't read the story."

"*Mitzrayim?*" Margo said. She had a piece of lamb on her fork. She ate the European way, the knife in her left hand, the fork poised near her mouth, backwards.

"The Hebrew word for *Egypt*. It also means *a narrow place*," Ruth said. Almost as if she were apologizing for knowing this small arcane fact. "A place of constraints. It's a funny coincidence. Maybe you know this already? About the name Detroit?" It was the early 1700s, she explained. Still apologizing. She'd learned it from her daughter's civics book. Antoine Cadillac? The city's French founder? She said it with the question marks, as if she were unsure, sweating a little into Margo's beautiful caftan. Telling how the noble explorer had emerged from his canoe, climbed to a bluff overlooking the river, and declared the place good, defensible, and named the site *le Détroit,* the Strait, a narrow place. Between Lake St. Clair and Lake Erie.

"Now *that's* interesting," Lynn said. They all drank.

"She has a dog named Sappho too," Margo said, about Ruth, as if it were an additional credential, beyond what they'd just heard. They drank more wine, more than Ruth was used to. And she said more than she meant to, especially when Margo invited her to tell about herself.

"If I hadn't had children," she said, "I might have become a rabbi." She drank the rest of the wine in her glass. "The first woman rabbi." This was not something she had ever before said out loud.

"Ah," Selma said. "Delusional on several fronts."

Margo mentioned the Changing Neighborhoods meeting, said it had ended with so much still to discuss, and the others agreed, though none mentioned the promised follow-up, where they would formulate their recommendation to the patriarchs. And no Council woman likely ever would. Ruth flushed. They had all given up—maybe on her, maybe on their alleged yearning to wrest decision making from their husbands. Well, she wasn't going to be the one to push herself on them, even if she retained a bitter annoyance at their convenient memory lapses.

"Tell us more about your research," Margo said.

Research. That was safe. Or at least safer. So she told about Mamie Clark, the famous Negro psychologist, and her experiments in the forties with children's self-image. That when given a choice, Negro children, as young as three years old, opted for white dolls over dark-skinned ones.

Margo offered more food. Each took a little. Ruth took less than she wanted. She became aware of her unmanicured nails. She thought about Harry, his business. Margo's husband was in real estate—hotels, luxury shopping malls, casinos and resorts. Deals in Miami. Las Vegas. Way, way beyond Irv, who built cookie-cutter houses in the suburbs.

"She knows Yiddish," Margo said. Their houses had been cleansed of all of that, they told her. And, they agreed, they felt something missing. They had the high-holiday dinners, but no one gave much thought, really, to what it was about. They were out of temple before noon on both Rosh Hashanah and Yom Kippur. They didn't fast or tap their fists against their chests during the confessional, though they'd seen it done. The seders were short, all in English.

"No Yizkor?" Ruth asked. They didn't know what she meant, the memorial section of the Yom Kippur service. They wanted her to tell them, about it all.

"There's a lot to tell," she said. "You can't expect to learn it in one sitting."

Margo rang her small brass bell, and Lynn said, "Margo, that's so embarrassing."

"It doesn't mean anything. Carrie knows that. It's just so she doesn't have to stand listening by the door." She rang it again, a high, lovely sound. "It's pretty. Don't you think?" Carrie came in with a tray and collected the dirty dishes and the platters of leftovers. She came back with a tray of honey-drenched desserts and left them on the table. Next, she brought a tall contraption, with a bowl at the top, like a candleholder, and a glass base with a bulge above it. A narrow brass stem extended from the bulge, and from the stem, a long narrow hose. Margo nodded, and showed her where to place it, on a brass table near the couches. Carrie returned to the kitchen.

Margo pulled a small glass vial from her pocket, uncorked it, and emptied the chunky contents into the bowl at the top of the contraption, where the candle might have gone had it been a candleholder. The other women kicked off their slippers, walking with bare feet from the lunch table and reclining on the deep leather couches. Ruth followed. The couches were so commodious that the women could stretch out, heads resting on big red and purple cushions, made from a wool that looked coarse but was soft. Margo fetched a box of matches from the table and lit the dark brown substance.

"I picked this up in Morocco," Margo said. "A narghile. A hookah. Bill thought I was crazy, but I love the idea." She picked up the hose, inhaled deeply, and the water in the glass base bubbled. She held the hose in her hand as she held the smoke in her lungs and closed her eyes. She exhaled and opened her eyes. "Never pass the water pipe directly to another person," she said. "Always put it down and let the next person pick it up." She placed the hose, with its horn-colored mouthpiece, like the mouthpiece on one of Harry's pipes, on the brass table. "Selma?" she said, beckoning with her hand. And Selma reached out from her place on the couch.

"Have you smoked?" Margo asked, looking at Ruth.

"Lucky Strikes. For years." She still got the urge. The oral craving. She sometimes felt like chewing through a door frame. "Oh," she said. "I'm sorry." Quickly aware of her error.

"It's hashish," Margo said.

And then it was her turn to pick up the mouthpiece. The flavor was both sweetish and earthy. She held it in her lungs until her eyes watered and until Lynn tapped her on the shoulder, to remind her to place the mouthpiece on the tray. And so it went, around the circle, with laughing and conversation. Once Ruth had a few "tokes," as Margo called them, she found herself wishing that Harry and the girls would take care of themselves, and she could have the whole evening to herself because even though it was her birthday, she knew she'd still end up taking care of them, worrying about choosing a place for dinner that *they* would like, saying the right thing when they gave her their gifts, making sure each of them got sufficient attention.

"Be careful what you wish," Selma said, not necessarily to her, at least she didn't think so, not sure, really, whether Selma had said that at all. But Selma was tapping her on the shoulder, to signal that it was her turn next, to pick up the mouthpiece. She felt that her face was frozen in a smile or some combination of smile and frown, and she focused on the design of the pillow fabric, every thread, tight in its place. "It's so beautiful," she said.

"What is?" asked Margo.

"Everything," said Ruth. She took her turn, then placed the mouthpiece on the brass table. "The windows. This room. The light. You could never leave this house, could you?"

Margo smiled, then inhaled from the hookah and leaned back.

"It's my birthday today," Ruth said.

The women sat up. "It is?" It seemed that they all said it at once, as if rehearsed.

"We'll have to give you gifts, then," Margo said. And they did. Lynn took off her gold earrings and clipped them on Ruth's ears. Selma went to her purse and found a small red leather pouch with a zipper. She went to the table, wrapped it in a cloth napkin, and handed it to Ruth. A manicure set. Margo removed one of her necklaces. "Tuareg pendants," she said, putting the chain with the two engraved silver pieces around Ruth's neck. They looked like creatures from outer space. "They're crosses, made to dispel evil to the four corners of the earth."

"I can't take these things." She felt like a pirate, like Robin Hood, as though she'd ambushed them on the high seas or in the forest and made them hand over their valuables. She couldn't tell if it was real, if they meant her to accept the gifts.

"Oh, forget it," Margo said.

"Really," Selma said, "it's our pleasure."

Ruth looked from face to face, still trying to understand whether it was a joke on her. And then she remembered her daughters. "Excuse me," she said. "I need to get home." She got up from the couch, woozy from the wine and the hashish, stumbling a little on her long skirt. She couldn't remember where she'd left her clothes. It was a trick. She was trapped. They were taunting her. Carrie had listened at the door, despite the bell, and would be waiting to tell her what she thought of her big ideas, her research, her Mamie Clark, what kinds of dolls Negro children preferred.

"Here," Margo said. "It's this way." She smiled, but Ruth couldn't tell what she meant by "it." "Don't look so worried," Margo said. She led her down a hall. "You'll be home in time. You're right down the street." Margo opened a door, gestured. And inside was the room decked out for a princess, and her clothes, folded neatly where she had left them, her purse, with everything in it (she checked the wallet). She changed. Came out of the room, feeling somber beside them in their long lovely gowns, like the three Graces. They walked her to the door, each kissing her and saying happy birthday as she walked into the cold day, and into the view up and down the block. Reality. Margo's house with its big windows and graceful stonework. And, for contrast, the two lines of fake colonials—Ruth's with the moss-green shutters, and the Deitch house across the street with the powder blue ones.

Ruth turned up her own front walk—the silver pendants around her neck, the gold earrings clipped to her lobes, and the little red manicure kit tucked silently in her purse. Detroit was a wonderful place. Her neighborhood was wonderful. Look at the kind of people who lived here!

The exuberant flush wore off that very night, during her Chinese birthday dinner at Lotus Gardens on Seven Mile. The food in its pedestal

151

serving dishes looked crude and gloppy after Margo's dazzling table. Ruth's head carried an unpleasantly empty rattle in the wake of the afternoon's buzz. And the two foreign cuisines clashed along her narrow inner passages. Moreover, Pesach was coming in just a few weeks, and the subject of who would go to whose house for the first seder had to be broached. She broached it, starting with the facts: Harry and Irv not talking since the Chanukah party ("If you could call it a party," Lena said). The phone conversations that had been going on behind the two men's backs, with Ruth having gotten it to a place where Rhoda didn't dare say anything about not wanting to drive all the way into the city.

Franny rested her cheek on the table, preparing for another impenetrable conversation, but it landed in a small puddle of sauce from the lemon chicken, so she got busy with her napkin and her water glass, and the cleaning-off project, while Joanna wondered why anyone would mind another look at the amenities of Irv and Rhoda's new house. Plus when Uncle Irv led, which he surely would if it was his house, the seders were usually shorter. He wasn't a stickler for all the twists and turns; he was happy just sticking to the script.

"Why can't we go to *their* house?" Joanna said.

"Because then we'd have to watch him act like some kind of Moses," Lena said, "because he already made the Exodus."

Harry got a sour look, which was not so much about who would host as about the ordeal in general, the next round with Irv, which was inevitable, but which he'd thus far avoided, and which was all mixed up with his ongoing tug-of-war between embarrassment and self-righteousness over the hurried exodus from the Chanukah party.

Ruth rifled in her purse, looking for her lipstick, but found the little manicure set, which gave her the extra push she needed to play the birthday card. "Look. It's my birthday. I want to do this. Just go along." And he said okay, fine. They'd host the seder at their house, Irv and his whole brood. The subject was closed.

Then came the fortune cookies. And the almond cookies. The scoop of vanilla ice cream with the pink birthday candle. The secret wish (*just don't let anything change*). The candle blown out. The singing. The presents. A book of poetry by e. e. cummings from Lena. From Joanna and Franny, a four-bottle set of Faberge cologne—Tigris, Woodhue, Flambeau, and Aphrodisia—each with a twist-off cap tied to its theme. And a blouse from Harry.

Harry paid for dinner. He left a couple folded bills on the table for a tip. They drove Lena back to her apartment, Harry shaking his head about that neighborhood where she lived, the broken lock on the security door, but not asking yet again why the landlord still hadn't fixed it, because he knew she'd only get mad at him for saying it, and then they went home.

Home. The morning after the seder didn't start out any different from any other. Even though the seder marked the night, they say, that is inherently different from any other: Different because of what they ate (the bitter, the salty), how they sat (leaning, leisurely), how they conducted their meal (ritualistically, with the extended prelude of blessings and storytelling and questioning and dipping).

A morning of small domestic tasks that can swallow up hours. Restoring order to the house—the chairs back to the basement, the special serving dishes to the upper shelves, the extra wine glasses back into their boxes. Attending to the stain in the rug where Irv had spilled his last glass of wine. Vacuuming the matzo crumbs. Doing laundry. Working on the tablecloth. Then it was lunchtime. Ruth went to the kitchen. She took a hard-boiled egg. She tapped it on the counter. She peeled. She put it on a paper plate.

Meaningless tasks. Adding up to nothing except making everything un-different. And then she found the Afikomen. The missing piece of the middle matzo, needed to complete the seder. It lay in the pocket of her blue cotton apron with the cartoonish flower print. An ingenious hiding place.

Ruth had been the one to suggest that four-year-old Carl, Irv's grandson, hide it, to assuage the small fit he had mounted when he learned that Franny would be the one to ask the four questions about why the night was different. But when the seder was wrapping up, and no one could find the middle matzo, he clammed up. Regardless of the adults' bribing, cajoling, impatient demanding, and sweet-talking, he refused to reveal the hiding place. And the family dispersed without reclaiming the broken piece. A first in their history.

"Now that's different," Harry had said, trying to make a joke of it. But Ruth hadn't laughed. She felt unfinished, as if the Israelites were frozen somewhere in the path through the Red Sea, the walls of water held back to permit their exit from the narrow place, but for how long?

The perfect egg on her plate. The margarine, its waxy yellow on the bumpy surface of the flatbread. The salt shaker, one Harry's mother had always kept on her table: cut glass with a silver top. She would remember that—the salt landing on the buttered surface, silent, almost invisible to the eye, but not to the taste buds. Her first bite into the Afikomen, discovered in the apron pocket, imagining that the Israelites might now complete their crossing before the water spell was broken.

And then the roar of an engine and the gasp and squeal of the brakes. The matzo in her mouth. The cold she'd caught from Franny, that had blossomed as she was making the final preparations for last night's seder, so the tears of the salt water and the wateriness in her own eyes, the nasal zing of the horseradish and her already raw nasal passages, all merged.

It was the drone of engine-idling that brought Ruth to the front window, still holding the Afikomen, and there it was, the moving van, parked down the block. Big, strong men, moving men, got out of the cab. One carried the paperwork in his hands. They stood on the curb, in conference.

In those days, a moving van was not a welcome sight. Not the kind of event, like once upon a time, that brought the children running, to sit near the curb and watch the strong men carry refrigerators, bureaus and beds, couches, pianos even, huge items riding on their backs. What kind of men could carry weight like that? The women watched the sleek muscles, the big hands, the strong legs in workmen's pants, the forearms with veins you could trace all the way into the hands.

As Ruth watched, the men finished their paperwork and their conferring, and they opened the doors to the big truck, the big hinges squealing. One man walked up the front walk to the Solomons. And so it began.

The Israelites became strangers in the land of Egypt because the world had changed around them; any person could become a stranger by staying put.

One by one, the moving men entered the big stone-faced house, pushing dollies. And after a while, they emerged, solo, or in pairs, carrying the goods, or pushing the dollies piled with cartons, going back in for more, stopping now and then to drink from a big thermos or to arrange the furniture and boxes in the big van: Sofas and bed frames wrapped in large green quilted cloths; boxes labeled "living room" or "kitchen." Boxes labeled "books" or "records." "Stereo." That's how it worked. Ruth had moved. She knew. All the household possessions, organized into categories by room, by function. "Work bench." "Baby clothes." "Pots and pans." So this was it. Finally. The first family on Ruth's block to leave. And not just any family. It was the Solomons.

The moving van. Big doors, wide enough for sofas and bureaus and appliances. And big wide ramps that the moving men strode on with their enormous loads: "master bedroom," "rumpus room."

In the old days, when a moving van pulled up, it was like a holiday, like the circus coming to town. It could have been prancing ponies with feather crowns, descending from the ramps. Or a line of elephants, trunks swaying like some ungodly extensor hand. Clowns doing cartwheels down the ramp, riding on funny scooters. It might as well have been. You'd think it was. Peanuts. Popcorn. Cotton candy. If the ice cream man pulled up, the children would beg, and the mothers would concede. And the tinkly tape loop of Mr. Softee music played as background to the thud of the moving men's work boots up and down the ramps, or the simple bells of the Good Humor man in his immaculate white suit, his immaculate white truck, to remind you of the creamy frozen treats stored in the freezer with the big metal handle.

As soon as the "old" people and their possessions were gone, yet another moving truck could pull up, and the mystery would be revealed. It could be anyone coming, and in those days, anyone coming was a good thing: new best friends for the children; a kindred spirit for the mother, someone to trade stories with, advice about child raising, about problems, even recipes, housekeeping. New gossip. Looking out to see what kinds of things they had: fine furniture, thrilling toys, artwork, lamps, bed frames, headboards. So this was it, Ruth thought. This was really it.

You tried to guess who was moving in, by what they brought: the size of the bikes, or if there was a crib, a high chair, a play pen. A piano. A ping-pong table. The preview of coming attractions.

Someone on the block found out first, who they were, where they came from, then passed the information along, down the street, over the back fence, or out on the front lawns.

"They came from New York." Or from Chicago or Baltimore. Here for a job transfer. Or to live closer to family. Or from another part of

Detroit, farther south, or west, for a bigger house, or the better school. All kinds of reasons people came, people moved, changed houses, in the big game of musical chairs that life was.

But now, too many for-sale signs lined the streets of this neighborhood. And the women peered out the windows still, but now with trepidation. The men, as always, the decision makers.

These days, the people who left tried to explain their reasons, tried to slip out with little fanfare. Some, Ruth had heard, paid higher rates so the movers would come at night. In the morning, the house was deserted. But even after dark, anyone could hear the rumble of the truck, the squeal of the big truck doors being unlatched and thrown open. The heavy footsteps up and down the ramps to the truck bed. Men shouting at each other—"lift up a little on the left" or "slow down" or "watch out."

It was the Solomons whose house was being emptied. The beautiful red-stone Georgian. And Ruth had not known a thing about it. She left the front window. The Afikomen had disappeared again. But this time because she had eaten it. In the kitchen, she took a piece of gefilte fish and covered it with horseradish.

Gone. Without posting a for-sale sign, and despite the fact that only a few weeks ago she'd been a guest in that house. Only a few months ago, all the neighbors had been at the Solomons' annual winter cocktail party, with champagne and a table with bowls of caviar, so full that the glossy little eggs spilled out onto the ornate silver trays. And now they were gone, to a new, larger, even more tasteful home in the suburbs—probably Birmingham—where not so long ago, a Jew could never hope to buy. In retrospect, that lavish winter party, the Moroccan luncheon, were simple buy offs, or kiss offs, as in "See you, suckers."

On the phone, it was the all-seeing Seidel Deitch. And the heat of the horseradish still searing the back of Ruth's eyeballs.

"Had you heard?" Seidel asked. Not even hello.

"Heard what?"

"That they were moving?"

"Did you?" The old tradition. Answer a question with a question.

"Well, I'd heard rumors," she said. "People were talking." Ruth didn't say anything. You didn't need to say much with a Deitch. "What did you expect, after all? Ours was one of the few *intact* blocks. You don't need to be a genius to guess who would go first." Ruth looked out the back window, at the forsythia, starting to open. They'd be a blaze of yellow in a few days.

"Uh-hmm."

"And right after the party," Seidel said. "Carrying on like we were one big family. Can you imagine? You know what Marvin said?"

"You already talked to him?"

"Of course." Phones were tethered to kitchen walls in those days, so Seidel was probably looking out her back window too, meaning that neither woman could watch the action in front. "He said it's Marvin Gaye who's moving in."

Ruth paced, wrapped the squiggly cord around her finger, around her arm. Her gefilte fish lay waiting on the counter, the red horserad-ish bleeding into the crevasses of the fish, soaking into the white paper surface of the plate. Sappho rushed in to have a look, then went back to her post at the front window, where she continued to lecture the movers.

"At least that's what Marvin says."

"Marvin who?" Ruth said. Marvin this, Marvin that.

"Moving onto our block. You don't have to act so surprised. It's not like no one knew this was coming."

"Isn't he at work?"

"I don't know where he is," she answered. "How would I know that?"

"I thought you just talked to him." The cold made her feel like Alice in Wonderland, everything too big or too small.

"Down the block, the moving van. That's what I'm talking about." She paused. "Do you have a cold or something?"

"Yes." She let the hoarseness in her voice show, for maximum effect.

"I hate a spring cold," Seidel said. "You need anything?"

"No," Ruth said.

"I've got some soup from last night."

"I've got some too." If Harry were home, he'd say it was nice that Seidel had offered, but to Ruth, it wasn't nice or considerate or any-thing like that. It was a way to get into the house for more gossip, and then Ruth would never get rid of her. Harry didn't understand any-thing about how all this worked. "What were you saying about Marvin?"

"Look, if you don't know," Seidel said. "Marvin Gaye. He's a singer, from Motown."

"Oh."

"Colored, Ruth." She whispered it, as though there were someone else to hear. "But famous." Seidel said. "And not just in Detroit. He's probably a rich man. Though you know how they spend their money."

"Well, I guess we'll have two Marvins now."

"You sure you don't want any soup?"

"Yes." It would be fine with Ruth if they hung up now. But she hesitated, a moment too long, not sure how to initiate her sign-off.

"I know you liked her."

"What?" The moving men calling to each other outside. Sappho barking. The yellow promise of the forsythia. The lingering wah-wah of the horseradish.

"Margo. I know you really liked her."

That's why she was in such a hurry to tell about Marvin Gaye. Because she'd seen Ruth that day, going to the Solomons. Well, that was enough. *Dayenu.* "I've got to go, Seidel," she said. "I'm hanging up."

Abrupt, okay, she knew. Rude, okay, she knew. She finished her lunch, standing at the counter. Then she opened the drawer next to the sink—re-rolled the ball of string, gathered the shabbos candles in a bundle and put them in a bag, sorted through the instruction booklets, takeout menus, coupons, some that had expired years ago, discarded those, put the others in neat piles, gathered the Green Stamps, found one of Franny's drawings crumpled in the back, of a girl with straight yellow hair and a kite, a perfect little shiksa. And she was thinking all the while of that day, going to the Solomons, and Seidel watching

A narrow place? They must have thought she was an idiot. And she'd gone home that day, her birthday, thinking of herself as the queen of Sheba or something. Floating into her house as if on a cloud of rose petals. She ate the last bite of fish. Into the trash went the paper plate, smash.

She'd told friends, bragged really, about Margo, the Moroccan luncheon (minus the hashish), and the invitation into Margo's private study at the last neighborhood cocktail party. "I know you'll understand what I'm doing," Margo had said to her, closing the door to the study and opening her sketchbook, with the charcoal drawings of Carrie: the face, the details of eyes and hair, lips. The one of Carrie's large hands, with the long fingers and big knuckles. The intimacy revealed in the drawings. Margo's turquoise outfit, silk scarves and a shawl and silver bangles. And then Bill Solomon, knocking at the door, angry that

Margo had distanced herself from the party. "Would you come out here?" he said. "We've got a house full of people." And they had come out, Margo winking at Ruth, over her shoulder, as she left to greet her other guests.

Maybe it was the husband, she thought. Bill. What kind of name was that for a Jew? Maybe he was the one who made the rules, who said that Margo couldn't tell anyone about the move.

"If he was like Frank Sinatra, I'm sure I would have heard of him." Ruth reached into the matzo box and broke off a piece. She handed the box to Franny. Each of them hovered over a steaming bowl of chicken soup and matzo balls, left over from last night. The soup soothed Ruth's cold, the steam in her face, the rich broth.

Harry hadn't heard of him either. "And if he were like Frank Sinatra," Harry said, "he wouldn't be moving onto *our* block."

It was Joanna who'd made the comparison, incredulous that no one at this table had heard of Marvin Gaye. Franny ate dutifully. The soup. Her favorite. The matzo balls, like clouds, so soft and warm in the mouth. Today, after school, she had gone to Renee's to work on their science project—building an incubator for chicken eggs—and Renee had told her the secret. Her family was moving. As soon as school was out. It was the first thing Franny told Ruth when she came home, walking up the porch steps backward, watching the movers close the big doors to the van. And it was the first thing Ruth told Harry when he got home, whispered it to him in the bedroom as he changed out of his work clothes.

Ruth removed the soup bowls and brought the other leftovers: roasted chicken and potatoes, matzo stuffing, gravy, peas that were dull green and very, very mushy.

"Are you trying to say this is a bad thing, to have him move onto our block?" Joanna took a chicken leg.

No, they certainly didn't want it to be a bad thing.

"Are you going to go introduce yourself, like you always have with new neighbors?"

"I suppose we will," Harry said.

"Of course we will." Ruth motioned to Harry to pass the gravy. "When he moves in. Whenever that is."

"He's practically royalty," Joanna said.

"Does he have kids?" Franny asked.

"I don't know." Ruth picked up a chicken wing and bit into the thin bones. "Do you know, Joanna?"

"I think he's divorced or something. He was married to Barry Gordy's sister."

"What songs did he sing?" Franny asked. Today, she had the peas to contend with. It was one disturbing pile of vegetables after another.

"You wouldn't know them."

"Maybe I do."

"Joanna, why don't you just tell her."

" 'How Sweet It Is.' " She said the name with a grudge, as if it pained her, as if such ignorance could not be corrected, so why bother. Then, despite the grudge, the music got into her, and she sang the first few bars of "Ain't That Peculiar," trying for that mellow Marvin Gaye voice and phrasing, layered with church and do-wop and jazz that had been prodded into R&B once he got to Detroit. "You know 'Hitch Hike'?" Franny didn't know any of them. "Great songs. He's handsome." Now he had the beard, as he was growing into a more serious poet and artist. But before he grew the beard, you could see the long, square chin that underscored his perfect straight mouth. And even with the beard, there was the perfect, fine line of his nose, opening to the wide, flat flare of his nostrils, like an arrowhead. He looked like a fox.

Ruth got a can of Manischewitz chocolate macaroons—the only dessert they had this time of year. Neither daughter was interested, so they left the table, while Ruth and Harry sat, sinking their teeth into the dense little mounds.

"Where did the Solomons go?" Harry asked.

"How do I know?" she answered, not in a nice way.

"I thought you might."

"Well, I don't."

With her at least, Harry knew when to stop.

There were things they said to each other and others they didn't say as they sat in the kitchen, speaking in low voices, so Franny and Joanna couldn't hear, working to understand what it meant, how they felt. She said nothing about Margo, and neither did Harry. He said nothing about Renee's family moving, and neither did Ruth. He didn't talk about his reaction to the photo he'd seen in the newspaper last week, of the new principal who would take over at Franny's school in the fall.

The dark skin, the shiny processed hair. He had gotten a feeling around the borders of outrage when he saw it. "What the . . . ?" Then he had stopped himself, when he felt the guilt of the unguarded response. But when Ruth mentioned it in the kitchen over the Pesach macaroons, he said, "Well, I think it's a good thing." Which closed the question of whether it was or it wasn't, and whatever Ruth's initial unguarded reactions might have been.

"It's not good for anyone to be in the minority," Ruth ventured. But as soon as she said it, she realized that this thought only came out now—never before, all the years when the Negro children were the minority in Lena's and Joanna's classes.

"But those weren't your children," Harry said, "so of course you're not going to worry about them the way you do your own."

"True," she said. But still, something about it was false: that she was mainly thinking about Margo. Whether she would try to find her. What she would say if they ran into each other—at the museum, in the touted African art collection with the warthog mask, or at the Jewish Center book fair, where they'd seen each other in the past. Margo wouldn't dare show up at a Council meeting again.

"She won't have any friends," Harry said. "That's not right for a child." What he didn't say or even notice: the assumption that having Negro friends wasn't an option.

Ruth noticed, and she moved to her perennial pursuit: reorganizing. Drawers and cabinets. The refrigerator. She transferred leftovers into better-fitting containers, folded kitchen towels so their corners lined up. The girls were upstairs now, in their rooms. "You know what she asked me?"

"What?"

"She wanted to know whether the Negro children know they are Negro."

Harry laughed a laugh of surprise. "What did you say?"

"I think what she really meant was, 'Do they know all the bad ways people see them?' And if they didn't, she wanted to be very careful not to be the one to break the news."

"So what did you say?"

"I said I thought they knew, and it was kind of sad. After all, they were just children. They hadn't done anything wrong. They were just born the way they were born."

Alvin in the yellow baby blanket. You is what you is, Harry thought. He was tempted, a little, to tell the joke, but then she might ask where he had heard it, and then it might open up the whole subject of that night in the basement with Curtis and the whiskey and everything she still didn't know: Alvin's anger, his wound. How crazy it had been, all those hours with Curtis. That the two men could say all those things. But then the feelings of danger, of thin ice, of lost control, that had fractured the night until he didn't know what to make of it.

She moved to another cupboard, where she kept the seasonings. She opened jars, sniffed, complained that they were all dried out, that all she had was oregano and bay leaves. Salt and pepper. Cinnamon. Dried parsley. Why didn't they have a more interesting array? Why were they so mainstream in their tastes?

"That's not the point, is it? That's not what we're talking about."

"Who cares what we're talking about." She got the step stool. She took plates from the shelves and stacked them on the counter.

"What are you doing?" He sat at the table. He didn't know whether this was something he should help with.

"I want to wash down the shelves," she said. "They're driving me crazy."

"Now?"

"Yes, now. Can you take these?" she asked. And Harry got up, took the dishes from her as she handed them down. He placed them on the counters until there was no more room, and then he piled them on the kitchen table. Ruth climbed down and got a bucket of warm soapy water and a sponge. She climbed back up on the stool, and washed the shelves one by one as he looked at her muscular calves. He kissed the right one. "Harry," she said. "What are you doing?"

He couldn't think of anything else to do. He couldn't think of how to explain, so instead he nibbled.

"You want me to fall?"

And he said no, he didn't. "I want you to come to bed. It's late."

"I know," she said. "I'll be in as soon as I'm done." She was sure it was the husband. Bill. Bill Solomon with his real estate empire. Wanting to live in Birmingham, where the rich people lived. He hadn't liked the friendship with Ruth.

There was a man who passed Ruth and Harry's house every weekday, with his business suit and his briefcase and his long strides. You could set your watch by him: 7:30 in the morning, outgoing; 6:00 in the

162

evening, incoming. Day after day, the stride always the same, long and swift. To catch the bus at Seven Mile and Meyers in the morning and to return home in the evening. You could tell the weather by him, as he dressed for the seasons and whatever inclemencies the Midwest tossed his way. The only man in the neighborhood who took the bus. He whistled when he passed, waved to the children. They called him the bus man.

"Some kind of a nut," Marv Deitch said. He and Harry were out doing yard work on a Sunday afternoon after the Solomon house had been emptied. When Marvin Gaye was scheduled to appear was still a mystery. And some wondered whether the rumor was true, that Marvin Gaye was the person moving in. The bus man had just gone by, on a bicycle this time, a Sunday spin, which was what had prompted Marv to cross the street for a powwow with Harry. "A bicycle now?" Marv said. "What's the matter with that guy?"

"Maybe he knows something we don't." Harry wiped his forehead with his sleeve and let go of the lawn mower handles. He had a cold, the one Ruth had passed along, and it made him feel more miserable than usual in Marv's presence. His eyes watering, his nose in the faucet stage. When others were around, he had to keep up with the drips. The inside of his mouth felt rubbery and raw, and his brain felt swollen, impaired. He pulled the handkerchief from his back pocket.

"A man's car is his castle," Marv said. "Who has time for the bus? It must take him all day, with the stopping and starting."

That whiskey-soaked night by the boiler, Curtis had told Harry a story, about a friend who drove a city bus. The friend said that some white people were so stupid, they'd spite themselves and let the bus go by, regardless of weather, rather than ride with a black driver. Curtis said his friend had taken to opening the door, seeing the people hesitate, and saying, "You better ride with me because the driver coming next is even blacker than I am." Sure, go tell Marv a story like that. "The way they pump cars out in this town . . . it can't go on forever," Harry said.

"Who's talking forever?"

"Marv, Marv," Harry said. "Look how this city has changed. These used to be empty fields, farmland. Before that, wilderness. Now all we've got are these little patches of grass."

"You want more grass to mow?" Marv asked. "That's what you're complaining about?" He turned as if to speak to an audience, extending his arms to them. "More grass. That's what he's worried about. That we don't have enough grass to cut." Harry shook his head. Marv turned back to Harry.

"Give the man some credit for taking the bus," Harry said. "He's a pioneer. He's trying to do something different."

"He's doing something different all right."

"Did you ever talk to him?" Harry said. "He's got ideas. About public transportation. About cities and suburbs. About what Detroit has done to itself—slicing neighborhoods up with highways, writing the blueprint for its own destruction. Give him credit for thinking."

"You love him so much? Why don't you move in with him?"

"I didn't say I love him so much. I said to give the man some credit. He's got ideas."

"He's a nut," Marv said. "Did you ever see his house? With some kind of a windmill in his backyard?"

It did look a little odd, the way it stood on the man's lawn, towering over his house, but Harry wasn't going to give in to Marv. "Like I said, maybe he knows something we don't."

"And I know something he doesn't—that having a windmill in the yard isn't doing anything for the property values."

Harry didn't answer. He wiped his nose with his big handkerchief.

"You don't care about the value of your home?" Marv said.

"Of course I care. But they want us to care too much, to the point of panic."

"And who is this 'they'?"

"Bankers, mortgage brokers, builders, real estate agents," Harry said. "Anyone who's getting rich from it. My brother-in-law. He's part of it."

Seidel came out on the front porch, as usual, calling her husband. Thank goodness for her, or Marv would be out here talking Harry all the way to China, or whatever that Yiddish expression was. Marv waved her off. "You want to be the last white face on the block?" Marv said. "You and Mr. Windmill?"

Harry had to turn away.

"I'm just trying to talk to you about these things." Marv moved around so that he and Harry were face to face. "Look, I'm not willing to sit it out if it's at my own expense."

Harry's eyes watered, and his nose dripped. His small front yard was patchy, as it always was in the spring, when everything green was coming back to life. He knew he should replace the lawn, lay some sod. The house could use a paint job too. Maybe this would be the year. There was still the boiler on Grand River to consider. Stanley the boiler man had patched it together, enough to get it through the past winter. He wasn't making any promises about the next one.

"It's not the skin color," Marv said. "It's the lifestyle, the class of people. They're not our kind."

"What are you saying?"

"I'm saying we found a place we like. So we can get out before the summer. Everyone wants to get out before summer. People are talking."

"Get out?"

Marv gave him a look. "You know what I'm talking about." Marv's daughter came out now, to get him, the skinny little girl with the freckled face. She could have been a schoolmate for Franny, but Marv and Seidel had transferred her to Vernor, farther west, after winter break. "Okay," Marv said, "I'm coming."

Usually Harry felt happier when Marv's family came to drag him home. Now, he was tempted to say, wait, so they could argue some more—like "What class of people are you talking about when you don't even know who the people are?" and "I know what class of people I'm talking about, and you do too," and back and forth like that until Marv revealed whether he'd yet sold his house and who the buyer was. Harry looked at his house, to see whether Ruth was at the window. He looked for Franny. Not there. Sappho was, though, in the front window. She didn't bark at Marv anymore. She knew him. She knew all the neighbors. But she had her head cocked, a look on her face. So? She might be saying. So? Are you the only one who's not part of everyone? You and Mr. Windmill?

And then the limousine pulled up, in front of the former-Solomon house. The driver's door opened, and a Negro man got out—dressed in full chauffeur livery. A long gray coat, double breasted, with a red collar. A flat wool cap. Gloves. He walked around the long, black car, opened the back door on the sidewalk side and reached in. When he stood again, he held a large box. It was as wide as his chest and almost tall enough to fill the span from his waist to his chin. But this was no cardboard moving box. It was dark, substantial—mahogany or some such, highly polished.

The man did not take the box into the former-Solomon house. Instead, he walked with it toward the far end of the block, crossed to Marv's side of the street, then approached the corner house, where the Blumensteins lived. He climbed the porch steps. He rang the bell and waited. The door opened. The man in the chauffeur uniform indicated the front of the box, as if he were introducing the box to Al Blumenstein, who had stepped out onto the porch. Again, the man indicated the front of the box, and this time Al Blumenstein reached out to it, and Harry could see that he slid open a drawer on the front as the man in the chauffeur livery supported the box from the bottom and the sides. Al lifted something flat and white out of the box; he turned it over in his hands a few times. The two men nodded at each other, and Al slid the drawer closed and went back into his house. The man in the chauffeur uniform turned, descended, and walked on to the next house, where the Letvins lived. And this ritual was repeated, Carl Letvin coming to the door, Carl Letvin sliding open the drawer, Carl Letvin removing something white and flat, turning it, closing the drawer, then going back into his house. And so on.

Harry and Marv Deitch watched as the man continued, up the porch steps, down the porch steps of each house, working his way up the block toward the Deitch house. At two houses—the Pearls' and the Rosenthals'—no one answered, and Harry wondered, just in passing, whether that meant that no one was home, or whether it meant that the occupant wasn't comfortable or willing to open the door to a colored man. And at those houses, the man opened the drawer himself (not so easy, as he had to reach around, while still supporting the box), pulled out one of the flat white objects and placed it in the mailbox or mail slot as suited to each house.

"What's he doing, Daddy?" Marv's daughter kept asking. "Who is that man?" She poked her father in the leg, to get his attention. "Is that Marvin Gaye?" "Is that the man who has the same name as you?" "Is he going to sing?" "What's in his box?" "Is he coming to our house too?" "What are those white things?"

They were all the same questions the two men had, but Marvin Deitch either wasn't listening or didn't care to answer, or some combination, because the little girl kept coming up with new variations on her questions, and he kept not answering until Harry finally said, "Would you please answer your daughter?" And then it was as if Marvin woke up and said, "What?" just as Marv's house became the next in line

166

for the man's visit, and he took his daughter's hand and went running across street.

"Sir," he shouted. "Mister." Waving and pointing to his chest and then to his house, to indicate that he was the one who lived in that house, and whatever secret was stored in that drawer should be given to him. Marv exchanged a few words with the man, the daughter talking the whole while, reaching up to put her hands on the wooden box, the man with the box, motioning "no, no," with his gloved index finger, and the girl pulling her hand back to twist it in the corner of her skirt. When they were all three on Marv's porch, the man motioned to the drawer. Marv opened it, and then he did as all the other neighbors had done: slid out a large white item—an envelope, Harry could now see— turned it over to look at its front and back, closed the drawer, and went into his house, leaving Harry alone on the street, noticing only now that Sappho, still at the front window, had moved into barking mode.

The man left the Deitch porch and continued his house-to-house journey, finally getting to the last house on that side of the block, where the Shapiros lived. He crossed and worked his way back down toward Harry, who tried not to watch, feeling a nervous suspense. Whether the man would come to him too, whether he would pass him by. His heart pounded. He didn't know what to do with himself. Where to look. How to keep busy. Whether to stay out in front or go into the house. Whether to get back to the lawn mowing. Whether his hands were too dirty to touch the beautiful box, whether the man would scold as he had scolded Marv's daughter. He pulled his damp handkerchief out of his pocket and wiped his hands.

And then the man was there, beside him. "Is this your home?" he asked. His voice was deep, the pronunciation precise and formal.

Harry said that yes, it was. He looked at it, as if making sure. Yes, it was. Sappho barked, as usual, her snout pressed to the window. The man did not even seem to notice. "Please, then," and he indicated the box, the drawer, as Harry had seen him do at all the other homes, except that with Harry, he did not go up to the porch. Harry reached out, but the man stopped him.

"Do you have a cold, sir?" he asked.

"Yes."

"Well, then, allow me." The man pulled the small brass knob, and the drawer slid easily open. "We don't want to be passing that cold to everyone else on the block." And Harry agreed that he did not, wondering now whether the gloves were functional in addition to decorative.

In the drawer, on top, was a white envelope, of a very fine-quality heavy paper. "The Levines," in quotation marks, was written in a fancy calligraphic style, with a crown at a rakish angle atop the *L* and twirls coming off the *s*. The dot on the *i* looked like an accent mark, in motion.

The man nodded his head, for encouragement, and as soon as Harry removed the envelope, the man closed the drawer and walked on toward the next house. Harry went into his own house, pushing Sappho away as she came to greet him, walking down the hall to the kitchen, calling out for Ruth, Sappho's nails clattering after him, Harry turning the envelope over to admire the gold sealing-wax closure, embossed with an MG.

It was a party. And Marvin Gaye was hosting. An evening in May, Memorial weekend. Cocktail attire. Regrets only. And a phone number. It would be worth calling, just to see who would answer. But Marv said, no way was he going. He was on the phone to Harry, not five minutes after Harry got into the house with his own invitation. No way was he going to be bribed, he said, to make it seem like one big happy neighborhood. What was the man thinking, he asked, that people would really attend?

Over the next days and weeks, others joined in, in a similar vein. The Shapiros. The Blumensteins. The Feldmans. Julius Weiner. "He wants me to bring my mother? She has cocktail attire?" Joanna was all for it. She'd started playing the music, loud, now that the weather was warm and the windows open, so the neighbors could hear. Franny, too, was excited about a chance to wear her party dress and shoes. And the invitation didn't say "no children," so she assumed she was included.

"Are you kidding?" Lena asked, on the phone. "Why wouldn't you go?" Ruth and Harry could not think of any particular reason, especially when asked in that way.

At work, Harry thought about mentioning it to Curtis. And every time he saw Alvin pass by the front window or climb the back stairs, he had an urge to run out and tell him. But he felt awkward about going up to him, saying it, so he ended up not mentioning it to either Curtis or Alvin. He didn't even tell them that Marvin Gaye was moving onto his block.

Ilo knew about it—the new neighbor, the party. She had three colored families on her block by now. "Very nice people," she said. "Why complain about it?" And as for the party, she had an answer for that too: "You went when the Solomons invited you, so what's the difference?"

The squabbling and debating went forward on the block, and most likely, inside the homes and kitchens. And one day the moving van pulled up, and gradually, the moving men filled up the house. No one had actually seen Marvin Gaye, and a number of neighbors said they hoped they never would.

But when the night of the party came. Oh well. And the limousines pulled up. Oh well. And someone on Mr. Gaye's staff rolled a red carpet down his front sidewalk. Oh my. And women stepped out of limos in grand gowns, like the ones the Supremes wore on their album covers and TV appearances, complex and sparkly, with fish tails and halters, and fringe and feathers. Ruffles upon ruffles and tight-fitted waistlines. And men got out wearing tuxedos with satin lapels. Carrying top hats that they then placed on their heads. Patent leather shoes. And canes.

"I don't think I can go," Ruth said. She stood in her bra and slip, watching the procession from the upstairs front window, as did probably every other person on the block.

Franny and Joanna were dressed and waiting downstairs. Harry had on his usual work outfit—the dark suit with the thin, knit tie. The white shirt. His Timex. "Why not?" he asked. His shoes were polished. Cordovans. "Don't be so . . ."

"What?" Narrow, she thought. If she only had that blue dress. The one she'd put on layaway for her niece's wedding. With the chiffon skirt and the picture-frame neckline. If she had that beautiful green caftan she'd worn at Margo's Moroccan luncheon. Then, she'd feel she could fit in, at least a little. She could go.

"Come on," Harry said. "Get dressed."

But she couldn't figure out what she would get dressed *in*. And she stood looking into her closet until Harry said, "Would you look at that?" So she went to the window in time to see Marv and Seidel, dressed to the nines, or perhaps it was the tens, crossing the street and strolling on the red carpet up to Marvin Gaye's new front door.

RIOT/REBELLION

Alvin had a new jacket—a showy affair—purple satin, with red letters arcing across the back, from broad shoulder to broad shoulder: Sheikh.

"What's that mean, *sheikh*?" Curtis asked him. He'd not seen the jacket before.

"That's what my friends call me." He'd bought it with the money he made, cleaning up at the Grande, after all the white hippies left. Sweeping the big wooden dance floor, and picking up their bottles and cups and cans along the streets and sidewalks where they parked. Mr. Gibb, the man who owned the place, paid him, said the outside work was as important as the inside, so the neighbors wouldn't complain about the mess the kids left. He wore the jacket that night, even though it was hot—Detroit July hot, meaning thick-hot, sweltering-hot.

"'Cause of what?"

He didn't answer. He didn't want his father to know how people saw him. He wanted to keep it to himself, not risk having it be torn down or built up too much, having his father talk about it to someone else, leastwise Levine. "You know what they calling my son?" Curtis might say while they were shuffling shoes together down there.

"'Cause that's what they like to call me." Saturday night. July. And he didn't want his father to ask too many questions about where he was going. Because it was all up in the air. And the street a magnet.

"Not to that skanky old neighborhood?" Curtis said. Meaning where they'd lived before they moved over here, to Mr. Levine's building. Which Curtis had considered an upgrade, better for his son.

"They got Carter Collins, playing at the Grande."

And for some reason, Curtis left it at that, and a simple, "You be careful now, you hear? Don't do anything stupid, you hear? You know enough not to do anything stupid?" Even though everything was up in the air these days and the talk thick and the street a magnet, for good and for bad and for stupid and for smart. Maybe he left it at that because he had his own business on his mind that night, maybe that lady who sometimes came over to visit when he thought Alvin was asleep.

So maybe Curtis had secrets from Alvin, and Alvin had secrets from his father too. Things they thought they were hiding, which they were not necessarily doing. Alvin's memories of his mother. Or what he thought might be memories of his mother, of a lotion smell, of a rocking feel. Of a face, or a shape of a face, an outline. Sometimes he tried to snatch at it, for a voice, maybe, or a word. But he had no way to know what he was making up and what was real, and he sure as hell wasn't going to tell anybody about any of that. Or about the anger at his father for having disappeared her from their lives—no pictures, no stories, telling Alvin to "leave off" whenever he asked his father about her.

And he wasn't going to tell anyone what Levine had said to him one day down in that warehouse of his: "I heard about a fellow just like you who worked in auto sales, ended up doing so well, he got his own dealership." When he hadn't said anything back, which he rarely did, Levine took it further, thinking he was a missionary or something, bringing the natives along, guiding a ghetto boy's life. "How about a job at Sears? That's a good company. You can get a decent commission in a place like that."

He didn't know what Levine meant by *a fellow just like you,* and he didn't plan to work at any Sears. Plus what happened to those other things Levine used to say—about architect and engineer? Levine was scaling back on him. But he didn't need Levine to scale him up or down. He knew what he had, enough to lift him up, him and his father, and Otis and Wendell, and even his mother, wherever she was. He knew that once she heard, she'd come back, reeled in by the sparkling delight of it—not for the money, not to take advantage, but to bask, appreciate, have enough luxury, surplus even.

What he'd like to say to Levine was, "Tell me what happened to my dope. Worrying about the criminal Negro when you're stealing with both hands." Levine always saying, "Alvin, you're so quiet. It makes me uncomfortable." Alvin wanted to say, "You want to know about uncomfortable? Come on and take lessons from me and my brothers."

Outside, with his friends, Alvin was loud and showy. He knew Harry saw him, heard him. He wanted Levine to see him and hear him, to see how sleek and slick he was, how in his world. "You the one in the prison,

Levine." That's what he wanted to say. "Who's the one behind all the locks and bars?"

He had long, almost Asian eyes, pulled up at the outer corners. Those eyes, and the skin around them, telling a story about what he'd seen, what he'd lived. What he wanted but couldn't say. What he wanted and could barely believe he could ever have. The sheikh.

The thick July air had a tremble, and he merged with the tremble and the heat, feeling good. Out with his friends. Out with them, he could strut, sing. He could tell his dreams. They made fun of him, but they listened. The sheikh: because they admired his way of talking that had truth to it.

"Not a bad thing to feel small. An ant is small, but it's a survivor. Just going its way, keeping up with what it has to do." They were on their way out. Saturday night. Not to the Grande, as he had told his father. But to a party in his old neighborhood, for two brothers just back from Vietnam, over on Twelfth and Clairmount. "We're just being patriotic," Alvin might have said, if his father had pinned him down. They could catch a bus up Joy. Maybe walk instead.

"You saying I'm like an ant?" Otis challenged.

"I'm saying we're all a little bit like ants—a path that no one else can tell where it's going, but we just keep going along, carrying our burden, much bigger than we are. Come to a crack in the sidewalk, you go down, come up the other way. No one knows why. Just keep doing it."

"Hey, man," Otis said. "That's some fancy talking. I like it." He bent his knees and shuffled off, doing an ant imitation.

"It's a plot, man, to get rid of us," said Alvin. "I heard them talking about it—how all the front-line fighting is the Negroes. Ship us out right away when we finish school. Clear out the ghettos. That's the reason for the war."

"You gonna go?" asked Wendell.

"What choice do I have? Don't have the muscle of Ali."

"I hear they've got some real good weed over there. Pretty women, too." Otis walked a few steps behind his friends, down the alley.

"Yeah," said Alvin. "A real vacation. See the world." He threw a rock down the alley. "Don't be talking so stupid. It's a serious situation over there. People like us getting killed every day, shipped back in body bags, half their head missing." He threw another rock from the handful he had. "Of course, half your head is missing already, so you might not even notice."

"Sheikh, sheikh," Wendell said.

Alvin told a crazy story, from when he was working at Levine's, last Tuesday, in the afternoon. Up in the packing room. By himself. Putting together some orders, sealing the damn boxes. "Cat get your tongue?" Levine's sister had said to him. She said it twice.

He didn't know what she meant. All he could work out of it was the "cat," which he thought she might be meaning something about the jungle. No white lady in her right mind talks to someone like him about the jungle. Or maybe she *was* crazy, crazy from working in that office too long, crazy from not having any dreams come true. Too crazy to know that a white lady was supposed to be afraid of a black kid who was almost a man. Crazy enough to be talking about cats, by which maybe she meant *cats*, men who know how to live and move, playing a rhythm in their minds all the time. But how would she know about that?

And no lady talks to a black man about tongues without something in particular on her mind. And there they were in the store, Levine in the basement and her talking about who had his tongue? He tried to concentrate on his work. He hadn't even been willing to say "No, ma'am," not knowing whether that would make things worse.

"Weird, man," Wendell said. "You better watch out for those people."

"Yeah, brother," Alvin said, hand on hip in a flirtatious way, "watch out, or some cat's gonna get *your* tongue too."

A lot of traffic on Joy Road that night. A lot of people heading toward Clairmount, toward Twelfth. Walking, riding. Past Dexter. Faces in the neon, moist. Past Wildemere. Past Genessee. Everything pulling toward that one place, Joy ending at Linwood, jog over to Clairmount. "Hey, man, your father always so strict with you?" Otis asked.

"No, man," said Alvin. "It's no big deal. He's so busy bowing to the man downstairs, he don't even notice what I do." Past La Salle. Past Fourteenth.

And the three disappeared. Into that hot July night, into the crowds on the sidewalks, the night-heat trembling. A magnet. The street. The crowds.

It was an old story.

> The people. The heat. The edge. The line. Where party meets
> rowdy, and exuberance trumps control.
> The crowd. The street. The curb. The whisper. The hisses. The
> shouts.
> Where crowd becomes mob. Where prickly becomes rage.
> The people. The sweat. The rumors. The shouts.
> The police. The stance. The badge. The gun.
> The people. The heat. The tremble. The rage.
> The handcuffs. The stick. The badge. The stance.
> The crowds. The police. The crowds. The police.
> The question of power. When you stand up and when you stand
> down.
> The finger. The fist. The whisper, the shouts.
> The heat. A hand. An arm. The push/push back.
> The shouts. The crash. The glass. The crowds. The nightsticks.
> The flame.

Sunday morning. Ruth arranging the makings of a Jewish brunch: bagels and cream cheese, sliced tomatoes and cucumbers, creamed herring, purple onion. Coffee. Harry sat at the table, schvitzing, the freshness of the recent shower gone, wishing he didn't have to even rest his arms against his body. Ruth placed a cucumber peel on his forehead and one on hers. She'd read about that in a magazine. A summertime refresher.

The *Detroit Free Press* on the table, and on the front page, a story about Mayor Cavanagh's vision: a Model City. His struggle to get the federal funds for housing, jobs, job training. The difficulties, when everything was going to Vietnam.

Joanna had slept over at a friend's house—Sharon, who lived on Kentucky with her mother, a widow. Franny was out in front, with an egg and a spatula because Harry had said, "It's hot enough to fry an egg on the sidewalk," and she wanted to see if it was.

And then Julius Weiner from down the street knocked at their front door, his shiny red face peering through the screen. And brunch all laid out, and Ruth and Harry going to the door, pulling the cucumber peel off their faces, as if caught in the midst of some tribal ritual. Without even saying hello, he asked for a rag or a paper towel so he could clean the egg off his shoe, pointing to the place on the sidewalk where

Franny sat, spatula in hand, with some combination of startled and frightened on her face. Ruth got a rag, and while he wiped, Julius told why he'd come—what he'd heard this morning, from men with property, businesses in the old neighborhoods, where Harry had his.

The mayor, he said, was trying to keep it hushed up, thinking it would blow over. And maybe it would. Julius told about gunshots, the crowds, the pushing, the police, the rocks, the windows, and about it starting at Twelfth and Clairmount. And Ruth was saying, "What? What started?" And Julius told what he knew, which wasn't much more than he'd already said.

Then the three stood and stared, the breakfast on the table, Harry thinking about the Black Panther ten-point program—what they wanted.

an immediate end to police brutality and murder of black people
an immediate end to all wars of aggression

They wanted these things immediately?

And after Julius left, the rumors and phone calls picked up. What this one and that one had heard. And then finally, late afternoon, the first television reports. Bill Bonds on WXYZ. Channel 7.

Ruth and Harry watched flames and black clouds fill the skies of Detroit. Looters slammed garbage cans into store windows, ran through streets with armfuls of clothes, pushed shopping carts with loaves of bread and bottles of liquor, kitchen chairs, stereos, sides of beef. Not only Negroes.

Harry watched for landmarks, storefronts, intersections, faces. He knew those places, knew the broad swath, the sad scary slash highlighted in the TV maps. It had started at 2:00, 3:00 A.M. in that one spot, they said, the shading on the maps changing, the dark arrows, stretching and pointing, eventually reaching to Grand River.

The police were surrounding the areas, to contain the arsonists, looters, snipers—so many specialized titles for previously invisible Detroiters. Newscasters used domestic images—pots boiling over and pressure cookers. Officials placed blame, pointed fingers, analyzed causes. Federal to state to local and back up again, like the arrows on the maps that showed where the fires were burning, where the streets had been blocked off.

"Causes, schmauses," Harry said. "You could feel this thing coming a mile away."

"You saw it coming?" Ruth said.

And finally, there was Mayor Cavanagh, whose televised face barely concealed his sorrow, the explosion of his Model City dream. Perhaps if he'd listened to his wife, refused to move to the governor's mansion. There, in the furrow between his brows, was the disbelief that all the years of schmoozing and negotiating, starting back with his Irish Catholic kinsman JFK, had come to this. There, in the weight sitting on his back and thick neck, were the dashed hopes of reviving the crumbling pockets of the city for the good of all. And then there, beside him, was the silver-haired, immaculate Governor Romney with the ski-jump nose. The two men, the sober faces, hiding their own fears, their own regrets—to have this occur on their watch. They announced the curfews, the restrictions on sales of gasoline and alcohol—the two politicians banning the two incendiaries. And they asked Detroiters to stay home until the situation was under control.

"Oh, yeah," Harry scoffed. "The rioters are going to stay home because you say? They're sitting and watching you on television?"

And then there were the streets again, the chaos, the crowds, the people.

"Yeah, I was here when it started," Alvin said to a reporter, speaking into the microphone, like he'd been waiting for someone to ask. "To celebrate our own," he said, pointing with his thumbs to his chest. "The guys who made it through Nam. That's something to see."

"Ruth," Harry called, getting up from his chair, "come in here. It's Alvin on the TV." But Ruth wasn't in the kitchen. She was outside talking to neighbors.

The newscaster nodded, brought the microphone back to his own mouth, said, "Tell us what you saw." Behind him a crowd had gathered. Children ran circles around each other, waved to the camera, like they were at the State Fair.

Harry could see the sweat beading on Alvin's forehead, dribbles running over his cheekbones. "People were out on the streets. And in the house." It was the people, the party, the music, the heat.

The newscaster brought the microphone back to his own mouth. "This young man is talking about the Economy Printing Shop, across from the United Community League for Civic Action, on Twelfth near

Clairmount." The camera shifted, panned, to show the street signs, the buildings. "When the owner lost his job in the auto plant, he started using the building as a 'blind pig,' as we call it in Detroit—an unlicensed bar." He and Alvin, reporting to the nation. Telling the story.

Franny came in and sat on the arm of his chair. Together they watched. "That's Alvin," Harry said. "I think. My tenant. Curtis's son."

"What drew all these people to the blind pig?" the newscaster asked.

"People like to give their money to one of their own. Where they're welcome. And it was the brothers. Home from Nam." Alvin was well-dressed. Rayon shirt, satin-looking jacket, the clothes bearing up well in the heat. But this was not the Alvin Harry was used to. This Alvin was talkative. The perfect informant. "Too many people there to even jam in the door," he said, "but that was okay, because it was peoples, and it was close. It was rocking." The music, the street, the women in their summer clothes. "Three A.M., and you'd think it was the middle of the day."

"When did you realize there was trouble?" the newscaster asked, using the practiced back and forth of the microphone, from me to you to me, his brow furrowed, earnest. Franny shifted in her place on the arm of the chair. She was eating a peach, one Harry had picked up at Eastern Market. It smelled good, ambrosial. The juice trickled down her arm, and she licked it.

"How we knew, were the lights, that flash of the police lights. And there they were, the police cruisers pulling up, nosing into the crowds, and cops getting out, pushing people. Shoving. They were shoving, like we were nothing, something you could shove out of your way."

Someone in the crowd behind Alvin shouted, "Pasty-faced peckerwoods." Harry knew the word, compliments of the boiler-night teach-in.

Alvin turned to see who had shouted. He laughed, then turned back to the microphone. "One cop had a sledgehammer, making his way to the front, and bam, right through the plate-glass door of that party. 'Hey, man, what's wrong with you, man?' someone shouted. 'Just a party, you damn pigs.' Then people were shouting, and the police were trying to arrest everyone, pushing and dragging them into their wagons, hauling women by the arms, twisted back behind them."

"Getting as much of a feel as they could on the way," said a young man, pushing up to the microphone, and the newscaster looked like he might end the interview, but then decided not to.

"You're saying the police broke the window?"

"That's what it looked like to me." And others behind him said yeah.

People were all up and down the street, crowding in behind Alvin and the newscaster, including those two friends of his, Wendell and Otis, trying to get their faces on camera, trying to get their say. A woman from the crowd shouted, "That was a patriotic gathering." And people laughed and nodded, said that yes, it was. "My country 'tis of thee," someone shouted. And it was still joking there on the TV screen for a heartbeat or two, shouts of laughter, and music blaring, and Harry thinking, *A comedy routine? In the middle of a riot?* And Franny laughing, a forced laugh, like kids do, to be part of it, and then there was a boom, and a flame shot up in the background on the TV screen.

Harry wasn't sure what he was seeing. The TV camera jumping up and down. Someone shouting "Let my people go." And Harry thinking that sometimes a feeling rises to the level of biblical. He was trying to see it that way, and that biblical strikes a chord—even in the heart and soul of the sweatiest, sweet-wine drunkenest.

Harry thought he must be dreaming this scene as the TV camera stabilized and followed Alvin, keeping him in its eye, as he ran down the street as part of the crowd, and the newscaster with the microphone followed too. Franny was watching. They were staring. Alvin ran, people running, shouting, throwing whatever they could pick up—sticks, stones, balled-up newspaper, whatever lay in the street, some laughing with the exhilaration of Pamplona, or of the streets belonging to the people, or of community and ownership and unfettered we-ness, of youthful joy of moving one's body through the street with no traffic and all your friends and no one to stop you.

It was like Halloween, with plenty of treats, way beyond candy, but you wouldn't want the little kids to see because it was all the things you cautioned them against: grabbing rather than asking, failing to say please and thank you, being careless, neglecting to respect their elders. But there was Franny, and she was seeing it, leaning up against her daddy's arm, which was making him even hotter than he already was, and she said, "Daddy?" and he said "Shhh. Let's see what happens."

Groups split off from groups that could be running away from the police or toward some other destination. Someone would become a leader one minute, people following him, and then that leader became a follower, saw someone else running and throwing, in a way that drew him. Women, too, wove in and out, some in high-heeled shoes, tight dresses showing sweat circles under the arms. Men in flashy suits and ties, some stumbling, people running past them, not stopping to see, to check if they were okay. Windows splintered, and people pounded on police cars, smashed windshields.

An old man stood on a street corner, shouting, "Please, calm yourselves. Calm yourself, son. Calm yourself, daughter. Look what you're doing to your own neighborhood. Where are you going to go when all this gets plowed under?" The man waved a towel, forgetting that waving a towel meant "I surrender."

The man with the towel grabbed Alvin as he passed, grabbed him by the arm, hooked him through his hooked elbow, like it looked when a person is trying to get through a door but his shirt tail gets caught on something. "Slow down, son," he said. "What good are you doing, acting like a fool?" His smooth dark face was sweating in the thick fog of heat, and little spurts of spit shot out with his words. "What would your mother say if she could see you out here now? Fine young man like yourself, just heading for trouble."

But Alvin's mother wouldn't say anything because she wasn't anywhere he knew of where she could say anything. And Alvin was some combination of angry and offended and humiliated by the ham-handed questions of that old man. What was he supposed to say? So he slipped out of the man's grasp. He looked around, breathing hard, looking confused about which way to go, and hot, so hot, his shirt stuck to his back, but he would not take off his jacket.

"Sheikh?" the man said when Alvin turned away and moved off. "What is that supposed to mean?" But Alvin wasn't answering. He was panting, and when he got far enough from the man to feel safe, he stopped, bent over, his hands resting on his knees, getting knocked right and left, people running past, people throwing things. A young boy stood on the sidewalk, close to a brick apartment building, shouting up to an open window, where a woman had stuck her head out. "Tell them to come," he shouted. "Finkelstein's Dry Goods is open for business, and everything is free." And the woman pulled her head back in. People stopped when they heard the boy shout. There was so much commotion, sirens in the background, gunshots, breaking glass. Alvin couldn't tell where the sounds were coming from, where the danger lay.

"What's he sayin' about Finkelstein's?"

"How does he know about that?"

"Go see for yourself."

And then the crowd moved again, and Alvin figured they were moving over to Finkelstein's to take it apart. He heard them saying about the old Jew, how he won't cut them any deals, even if their grandmother doesn't even have a chair to sit on, make her put it on layaway, probably hoping she'll never be able to pay it off.

"Go get mom," Harry said to Franny. "She's got to see this." He nudged her off him, partly because of the heat and partly because he didn't know whether she should be seeing any more of this, and partly because he was afraid he'd have to try to explain it to her, and partly because he felt he needed an adult witness there with him. "Go ahead," he said, angrier and more impatient now. She went reluctantly, her eyes still on the set as she left the room.

A young boy, skinny, held three bottles of pop close to his chest. He said, "You can get all the pop you want over at Brown's Drug Store." And someone else said, "Where's that?"

But the little boy was gone, slipped through the crowd. And someone else shouted that Brown's Drug Store had gone up in flames, and that people had gotten trapped inside. And someone else shouted that it was a rumor. And Alvin wondered whether it *was* a rumor, and what part of it was, and whether rumors got the crowds going, or the crowds got the rumors going. Then, someone threw a rock through a window, and Alvin could see that whether you could get all the pop you wanted, or whether the place had burned to the ground didn't matter, because whether or not it was a rumor, once you got there, you could make it true, whatever it was.

More and more people joined the crowd. He looked around for Wendell and Otis. He pressed himself against the side of a building, trying to get out of the flow, catch his breath, keep from getting stampeded. And while he stood there, three men went by carrying car mufflers. And Alvin ran, and so did the crowd, but in all directions, and he had to make decisions every minute, whether to keep running or back down against a wall to get out of the flow. Turn right? Turn left?

"You've got to see this," Harry said as Ruth walked into the room with Franny. "You won't believe it," he said. "I'm watching the riots on television, and I think I see Alvin. He was being interviewed. You wouldn't believe it."

"What?" she said. "What?"

But the image on the screen had switched from live footage to commentators, talking numbers: the number of fires, the number of arrests, the number of blocks affected, the number of police officers on patrol, the number of people injured.

"Numbers," Harry said. "Can you believe those numbers?"

Ruth was like a fly trapped between a screen and a storm. She paced the house from front to back and side to side, then went out to check with the neighbors, who gathered and debated near the curb. There were Marv and Seidel Deitch, Julius Weiner, Al Blumenstein, wives, children. The shades were drawn at the Gaye residence.

"Oh, this is nice. Very nice," Marv said. "We're within rioting distance from the so-called housing on Eight Mile." His moving date was still a couple weeks off. "What's to stop them?" The others looked up the street to the north. They'd never thought of themselves exactly this way before, as living near a border, marked only by a street, a wall. Their homes were envelopes. The windows they'd admired and Windexed were thin pieces of glass. And screens? A knife slit, and you could be finished.

So this was it. Until now, everyone had agreed to accept things the way they were. But now the spell—it must have been a spell—had broken.

Marv said that Cavanagh had always been too soft on the coloreds. And *that Edwards,* the police chief, he'd been a criminal himself. Cozying up with the civil rights crowd, marching with King. What did he expect, giving the message that they could get away with anything they wanted?

"You were willing to go along with it before," Seidel said, "when you thought he was a friend of the Jews, bringing Strichartz in."

"Strichartz," Marv said. "This is supposed to mean something?"

"Who's Strichartz?" someone asked.

"A Jewish law professor," Seidel said. "A big man with Cavanagh."

"He should have cleared out those slums—like they did with Hastings Street. Plow it under. You can't police those kinds of rats' nests." That was Al Blumenstein, a real mensch.

Ruth wanted to say, "Yeah. Clean them out like they did the Warsaw

181

Ghetto," or "You should know. You lived in one of those rats' nests your-self, on Hastings." But she didn't. Maybe if Harry was with her. Instead, she came up with something more moderate: "They thought they had the answers. Nobody has the answers."

The three men said well, okay, fine with the answers. They had their own answers: guns (a Jew with a gun? she thought), they could protect their homes if they had to, and Ruth wondered whether Harry did too, hidden in his closet, whether he'd tell if he did, whether he'd even know how to use it. She couldn't picture that.

The hum and buzz of nerves. The stomach clutch. The heartburn. The sweaty sleep. Every sound, the smallest creak or pop. A jolt.

They finally got Lena on the phone. Harry, downstairs. Ruth, on the upstairs extension. They'd called a dozen times.

"I'm fine," Lena said. Her tone, flat.

He'd like to give her head a knock. He took a deep breath. So. Okay. She was fine. "I just wanted to know where you were, that you were safe. Is that so strange from a father to a daughter in a war zone?"

"I was at work," she said.

"Work? No one is at work."

"Saturday night," she said, "before it started." She didn't sound like herself. So flat. The challenge, gone.

"But this is Sunday night."

"Do you want to hear?" she asked. Her annoyance with him was a stimulant that brought some zing back to her voice.

So she told.

She had the late shift at Top of the Flame—the restaurant crown on the Consolidated Gas Building, downtown, near the river. Pete had got-ten their friend Craig, from a gig at the Red Roach on Plum Street. And it was two or three in the morning by the time they got there to pick her up, and they'd already heard rumors. That the Detroit rebellion was starting—an uprising that would shake the country's leaders as no other had. That was what they told her when she got into the car, still wearing her apron, and carrying her black waitress shoes, dangling them by the laces. She hadn't even had time to complain about the cranky customer who had accused her of ignoring his table, who stiffed her on the tip because she didn't know what they fed the lobsters.

"We could see flames over the buildings. And we heard sirens, but that was nothing new." And Pete had made a crack, which she repeated, about the rich diners at the Top of the Flame: one flame for the rich and one for the poor, that the ones at the top would be coming down soon to the flames of the poor.

These kids. The things they said. "It's a volatile situation," Harry said. "It's not a joke."

"Democracy was an experiment," Lena said. "That's what they taught us in school." And then she went on, spouting some view of this uprising as justified, expected. "You don't live around here," she said, "so you don't know. What it's like to live an authentic life."

He could have said something here, about how she'd benefited from the experiment that democracy was. "Why don't you and your friends come stay over here, until it settles?"

"We're going to Craig's parents' cottage," Lena said. Ruth and Harry knew the place—up north of the city, on Cass Lake, beyond where the suburbs were sprouting. Probably a good place to be. Harry could have said something about authentic lives, that *authentic* people didn't usually have lake houses to escape to.

"Well, I'm glad the boys are with you," Ruth said. She'd take it that *chai* was working for them.

"That's the first time I've heard you say anything like that," Lena answered.

So maybe despite the tone, Lena was scared. Otherwise she might have said something challenging like, "You don't need to tell me what is or isn't a joke" or "They're not boys."

On Monday, Ruth and Harry danced around each other, not used to being in the house together all day, Harry home on a weekday, no errands or outings. Sometimes they alit in the same room to share a piece of news. Ruth made phone calls, the panicked inventory of friends and family, as she regretted now, even more than usual, that she'd given up smoking. She'd been in touch with Joanna, over at her friend's house, to tell her that Harry would come pick her up today.

By now, they'd heard some sketchy news that the crowds and looters and fires had spread somewhere near the Riviera and the Grande.

"We don't know for sure," he said when Ruth gave him a look. "No reason to talk about it." It was maddening that with all the news, none of it zeroed in on the particular block of interest to him.

The TV news showed a shot of Livernois, the fancy street of shops that divided Harry's neighborhood from Sherwood Forest and Palmer

Woods—where the rich kids lived, as Joanna liked to say. Livernois was deserted except for police cars and barricades. The TV camera panned past Alexander's, the dress store with its front window boarded up. Harry knew about Alexander's from Ruth—about Greta, the stunning shop owner, with the perfect complexion and the Austrian accent. About her outrageous price tags. And of course about the royal blue cocktail dress, a layer of chiffon over a layer of satin, that Ruth had not yet gotten out of layaway at the time of Marvin Gaye's party. "Like two dresses," Harry had commented when Ruth brought it home—to see what he thought about her getting it for their niece's wedding. "And for that price, it should be."

Harry called to Ruth to get off the phone and come look at the TV, which she did, sinking into a chair next to Harry's, expelling a sinkingly deep sigh. She didn't say anything about the blue dress, of course. But she said something about Greta, the losses in Europe, now here. And then she kept an eye on the TV while she told Harry what the neighbors were saying, the stories she'd heard. The Letvins had a brother-in-law, Morris, who lived a few blocks from Livernois. When Morris heard about the riots, he grabbed a rifle and ran out to patrol the block. "A Jew with a rifle?" Ruth said. Another neighbor had heard of fires burning to the south, across from Lou's Deli, not far from Ilo's house, but Ilo was okay, Ruth said. She'd just talked with her. She hadn't seen any fires near her house.

But then the TV camera shifted from Livernois to somewhere else, deep into the city. And talk about fires. There was a wall of flame around a building skeleton, a stream from a fire hose. "What are they using?" Harry asked. "A squirt gun." It was true. It didn't look up to the task. A toothpick to spear a monster.

Another thing on his mind as he drove to get Joanna: whether it could come to defending his home and family, whether he'd have to be a man in that way.

Turning onto Outer Drive, he found a path to a reassuring argument: that his neighborhood was safer than the juicy targets in Sherwood Forest and Palmer Woods. Far more to be gained by storming those houses, crashing through those picture windows. Even a wild-eyed drunken rioter could see that. On the other hand, the people who were the juicier targets also had the bigger cushions, the lake houses to escape to. They worked in big office buildings, hospitals. Few of them, he ventured, had so much tied up in a small brick building in the path of the fire-breathing dragon.

He pulled up in front of Joanna's friend's house, fetched his daughter, and left quickly, avoiding conversation with Sharon's mother about the whole . . . situation. He didn't have room to hear the worries and vulnerabilities that she, a widow, might be feeling, without a man in the house. And then, in the car beside him, coming home, Joanna got to talking, about the black girls—that's what she called them—at school, how she'd learned to work around them, not get them riled up, keep her distance on the field hockey court. She rested her face in her hands. And there Harry sat, his hands on the wheel, wearing his thin white T-shirt, driving her home, feeling small. Harry exhaled, some deflation beyond words. He'd been the hero of her life for so long. Well . . . there had been that day with the bicycles . . . a preview of his ineptitude, his inability to anticipate.

The neighbors watched as he drove up the street. They called to him when he pulled into his driveway, Marco Polo returned with the Mongol princess. Marv motioned to Harry when he got out of the car, but Harry kept on going, into the house. Joanna went in too.

Monday's *Detroit Free Press* was full of riot photos and stories. Harry sat in the den and read about Sunday: Some things he already knew, from television. Some he didn't, like the confusion over police orders, the soft touch that Cavanagh had ordered, to contain the troubled area but avoid antagonizing the residents. Just like Joanna said. Work around them.

He read about a Molotov cocktail, thrown through the window of a shoe store (not his) and a reporter who got hit in the head by a rock when he went to investigate. Then, just past noon, the shoe store fire contained, other fires burst out, and the looting picked up—lots of people looting, both Negro and white.

By 4:30 on Sunday, the fire department had sent out an emergency code, calling all their staff to duty, something they had never done before, and the fire company on Twelfth called for police protection, but no police were available.

"A fire fighter?" Harry said, "Needing police protection? He's trying to save their homes. He's trying to save their neighborhoods."

"I guess they don't want them saved," Ruth said.

By Sunday evening, Romney had ordered in state troopers and National Guard and declared a 9:00 P.M. curfew. By midnight, more than six hundred had been arrested.

"Six hundred?" Harry said. "Where do they put them all?"

One photo showed a furniture store—you couldn't see the name, and the caption didn't mention the street. It was a big store with huge front windows, all of them broken, but the door was intact. "Ha!" Harry said. "Probably double locked!" A man stood in front of the door, in a light-colored T-shirt and dark pants, his hands behind his back, holding each other. The man bent slightly forward, as if reading the store hours, which were printed clearly on the door. To his right, three men hoisted objects through the window to three men outside, while another one kept watch. Refrigerators, stoves, washing machines. Three of the men wore straw hats with small brims, kind of dapper; another, the watchman, wore a flat cap. Their shirts were untucked, which gave them a casual, well-dressed summery look. And to the right of all this, half in and half out of the photo, another figure, his face at a three-quarter angle so Harry couldn't quite tell, but there was something familiar about the way his hand fell, cupped at the side, the angle of the shoulder, the cut of the jacket and the pants . . . Alvin? Harry held the photo close, but the closer he looked, the more the photo dissolved into an unknowable pattern of black and white dots.

Where was the man whose store it was? Where did he sit while the world chewed over the meaning of the newspaper image? All the order established over all those years, categories of appliances, each in its row, edge to edge, corner to corner. Categories of merchandise: bedroom, living room, dining room, all arranged, displayed. All the paperwork that tracked and recorded the movement of each item, thrown into bonfires, crackling and curling, blowing away, into the wind, the sky. What happened to everything? People, papers, shards of glass.

The rage, the need, the greed, on display for everyone to see. The locks, like taunts. The delusion that you could keep people out. He had the keys to his business, on his dresser, on a ring with his house keys, his car keys—keys to all the padlocks and deadbolts and so on and so forth—but what did a key mean, a lock, in the midst of all this? A front door or wall with nothing behind it. Or not even a front wall, just a pile of bricks. A scattering of water-soaked shoe boxes in the gutter, a piece of tissue paper flapping in a puddle, a shoe lace. He kept tracing back, to that Halloween day; beyond. All the signs overlooked.

"It's like with the boiler," he said. "We expect everything to keep running just because it *has*."

"You think you're so powerful?" Ruth said. "That what you did or didn't do about the boiler could cause this?"

"What we do counts, and what we don't do counts. And what we want."

"You mean like washers and dryers." They were looking at that crazy newspaper photo of the furniture store, with the locked door and the merchandise going literally out the window.

"That," he said, "but other things too." He got up. "I'm going to show you something." He went to his dresser, to get the Black Panthers' ten-point plan. He showed her.

We want freedom for all black and oppressed people now held in U.S. federal, state, county, city and military prisons and jails. We want trials by a jury of peers for all persons charged with so-called crimes under the laws of this country.

We want land, bread, housing, education, clothing, justice, peace and people's community control of modern technology.

You couldn't really argue with that. It was supposed to be part of the deal.

"Where did this come from?" she asked.

He forgot he hadn't told her about what he found in the basement that day last fall. The already beading beads of sweat ratcheted up a notch. He tried the imperfect-memory technique. "I told you about finding it that day."

"No, you didn't."

"Yes, I did. You forgot."

"I wouldn't forget something like that."

In another photo, an Edison lineman was up on a pole, repairing a damaged power line, while his military escort, two men (so young! babies!), stood guard, machine guns raised, watching for snipers. And in the photo, standing in a doorway down the street, watching, hand resting on the doorframe, hip cocked, again he couldn't quite tell, the focus was off, but the physique, the posture. Was it Alvin?

And then he looked up at the TV, a constant feed and reference from WXYZ, the only station with reporters on the street. One of them was trying to stop people, get them to speak into the microphone, holding it out, asking questions, saying "excuse me," asking what had brought them here, what they thought of it, why, why, why. And one of the people on the screen was Alvin. Or it looked like Alvin. But this time, Alvin didn't stop, tired of being the informant for the whole world.

On Linwood near Twelfth, Alvin passed a shoe repair shop where the door stood open, and in front of the dry cleaning store next to it, a small man stood—he couldn't have been more than five feet tall, nor more than a hundred pounds—and he swung a saber, trying to hold off a crowd. Some in the crowd taunted him, thrusting an arm or a leg, then pulling it back, to show they were faster than he was. Some shouted "No!" and "Stop!"—whether to the man with the saber or to his tormentors was not clear. Others cheered, but again, it wasn't clear what they were cheering. The saber hit a young boy's shoulder, and blood spurted, a few drops on Alvin's shirt, and the spurt, the contact, shocked the man long enough that another young man grabbed him from behind, threw him down, and battered him with a thick rod or a pipe or a table leg. Alvin couldn't tell what it was, and he couldn't tell whether he wanted to look or whether he didn't want to. Someone else grabbed the object from the beater's hand, and ran off down the street with a small crowd following, leaving the small man crumpled on the sidewalk.

And Alvin disappeared into the crowd, trying to make his way back to Joy, looking for his friends, getting snagged in a crowd now and then, getting turned around, getting hot, holding onto that satin jacket, keeping it on despite the heat, the sheikh trying to find his way.

At 8:00 that night, a press conference: Governor Romney, Mayor Cavanagh, and Cyrus Vance, the secretary of state. Vance said he hoped that by Tuesday, people could return to work. He announced that federal troops were arriving at Selfridge Air Force Base, but he hoped—and he knew the president hoped this too—that they wouldn't be needed.

"Like an insurance policy," Harry said. Late into the night, past Harry's usual bedtime, he sat in front of the TV. He couldn't turn it off, or look away for long, afraid he'd miss something. He clung to the news feed. And at 11:00, the three officials came on again, another press conference, saying that "the situation" had not calmed, as they had hoped, and so they were moving the troops into the city from Selfridge. And at 11:30, the cameras switched to Washington, and it was LBJ. He had that basset-hound look, like he still wasn't sure how he'd managed to get himself into all these messes that, powerful as he was, seemed beyond him to control. He slid his glasses off and put them on again, saying that he took this action with the greatest regret—"and only because of the clear, unmistakable, and undisputed evidence that Governor Romney of Michigan and the local officials in Detroit have been unable to bring the situation under control."

Harry looked at Ruth. Their president meant to be comforting, Harry supposed, that he was sending in professionals, but it was really quite alarming, if Detroit couldn't handle its own mess. If the president didn't even dignify the mayor by mentioning his name.

LBJ called the situation in Detroit "extraordinary," saying that law and order had broken down and that pillage, looting, murder, and arson had nothing to do with civil rights. "We will not tolerate lawlessness," he said. "We will not endure violence. It matters not by whom it is done or under what slogan or banner. It will not be tolerated."

"Except in Vietnam," Harry said.

And when the president signed off to his fellow Americans, a camera brought Harry and Ruth the images of troops in full battle dress moving into the city, toward the fairgrounds. And after that, though Harry kept looking, he didn't see Alvin anymore.

On Tuesday, Franny finished building her solar oven, based on a diagram she'd seen in a library book, and she perfected the technique to the point that she could make excellent s'mores. She brought the gizmo out to the front sidewalk, and melted chocolate and marshmallow onto graham crackers for all the neighbors.

At first, no one could believe it was possible—a cardboard box, lined with aluminum foil, balled up newspaper for insulation, a plastic bag over the open panel in the box top. And that was it. It made her feel good, everyone coming to check it out, bringing what they had in their cupboards. Could it melt cheese? Warm a can of soup?

It was a welcome diversion, like the parlor games people trot out during a week at the cottage with bad weather. Games like "What was the strangest job you ever had?" or "What would you wish for if you could have anything?" or "What was your earliest memory?" On Harry's block, while the riots raged and the plumes of smoke hung in the air, the magic of the solar cooker became a small hiatus in a stretch of anxious boredom. No one was going anywhere. No errands. No work. No entertainment. No day camp. Just everyone together, face to face and day after day.

"Who knows?" Marv said, biting into the gooey graham cracker sandwich. "Pretty soon, we all might need something like this cooker." He motioned around him, to indicate the city. "The end of civilization. The end of the power supply. Survival of the fittest." He didn't look at Franny when he said all this. He didn't mention Mr. Windmill. He just pontificated, half comedian, half maniac. They were like people afloat, bobbing in a lifeboat, adequately supplied for the time, but still scanning the horizon for the rescuers, and hoping they got there before the invaders.

It was all the threads coming together. But instead of a tapestry, it was a big horrible tangle, with ends sticking out every which way.

"People can only be pushed down so long," Ruth said. "It's the young ones, the ones who have nothing to lose. We should have been looking at the young people. That's what Cavanagh should have been doing."

"The young ones are the worst," Al Blumenstein said. He was a big, bulging guy, with big hands, paws almost, that made a cigarette look small, like a matchstick. He brought the cigarette to his lips, inhaled deeply, exhaled with exasperation. His wife, beside him, smoked too. Winstons. Being around the cigarette smoke made Ruth edgy, made her need something to chew on, rawhide or something, made her even more impatient than usual with these people, their conversation.

Al had a business on Chicago and Twelfth, only blocks from Clairmount. A furniture store that sold cheap dinette sets, bedroom suites. Like Bernie's place, only worse. Everything all jammed in and piled on top of everything else. "They call them *suits*," he said, making fun of his customers even now, when his place was probably either empty or in flames. Making fun of the accent, how gullible they were, how they wanted things they couldn't afford. He made it possible for them: *creative financing*, he called it. Layaway. He let them make the payments, neither salesman nor customer knowing whether they'd ever be able to claim the goods.

"That's disgraceful," Ruth said.

"Look," he answered, "I'm trying to make a living and also find a way customers can get what they want." He went for the cigarette again. "Is that so bad?"

When it got dark, and Ruth went in, she told Harry the talk. Someone said people had cut through the fences at Kiddieland, and the colored children had flooded in—that they were climbing all over the rides, tearing the place apart.

"Well, of course," Harry said. "All those years they've been looking in at it, and never once able to go there themselves."

Someone said there had been rioting at Northland—the suburban shopping dream. "It was like a community center," she said, "for the teenagers." And for the women, a place to spend a day, buying or browsing, a cup of coffee, the fountains and the floral displays.

"Not anymore," Harry said. "Those were the days, my friend."

She got up. Puttered in the kitchen. In the drawers and closets upstairs. Harry stayed in front of the TV, reading the paper. Then he too riffled through the drawers, and he found a deck of cards. He laid out a game of solitaire, trying through the horizontals and verticals of chance to soothe himself—to keep going as long as he had options. To immerse himself in this game of risk, caution, concentration, memory. A lot to ask of a little stack of slippery cardboard rectangles.

Tuesday night, Cyrus Vance, still in Detroit, suggested that plants, businesses, and offices reopen. But in Harry's neighborhood, the men, gathered around the solar cooker, debated whether they felt ready or willing. The news came out about the National Guard—how ill prepared they were. Some had never been in a city before; some had never before been around Negroes. Many didn't know how to handle the machine guns they were given, and they used them too freely, firing on apartment buildings—in response to anything, a match struck to light a cigarette, someone moving too quickly past a window. And then the barrage of bullets. A four-year-old girl had been killed this way.

"What about the arguments between the police and the guardsmen?" Al Blumenstein said. "And what I heard about gun battles on Twelfth Street?"

"And LBJ's paratroopers?" Julius Weiner added. "Many are just back from Vietnam, and they're wrangling with the Guard too."

"About what?" Marv asked.

"Tactics," Julius said. "Everyone has his own tactics."

Marv bent down and took a marshmallow. "Doesn't sound too safe to me."

Harry read and heard more numbers: 617 fire alarms on Monday. M48 tanks and 50-caliber machine guns. "M48s?" Harry said. "Those were for Europe, to use against the Russians. Those are for Vietnam." He argued into the air, while the others were outside. He read that helicopters were whirring over the city to spot snipers. He heard the thrumming of the helicopters himself, an unnatural sound. And he read that sniper fire had spread into the neighborhood around the General Motors Building on West Grand Boulevard—the architectural monument to the auto industry. "How do they know the difference between a sniper and an official shooter?" he asked, rising out of his seat with the sheer alarm of it, the newspaper trailing behind him. He went into the kitchen, looking for someone to talk to. He tried for a joke about chickens coming home to roost—that General Motors had developed and built those tanks. Why shouldn't they have a few on their doorstep?

Lena called from the cottage at Cass Lake, that odd, flat sound still in her voice. She and her friends had decided to stay a few more days. She read to Ruth and Harry from a bulletin someone had brought to the cottage. It was called "Detroit Rebellion."

"For two days the way wealth flowed in the city has been reversed on a grand scale. Impoverished folk liberated basic foodstuffs from grocery stores where they'd been cheated for years, and less-needy residents could be seen rolling sofas out of exclusive stores like Charles Furniture on Olympia Street. The owner of a music shop reported losing every electric guitar, amplifier, and jazz album in the place—but the classical records were left untouched."

Harry went to the front window, looked out into the dark night, to see whether the orderly rows of homes with the neat front lawns were still there. They were. Which made it particularly difficult to imagine what they told him on the news—that twelve square miles of his city were burning.

"Too bad Alvin doesn't have his bootleg phone anymore, or I could call."

"What are you talking about?"

192

"I told you about it," he said. "That he'd hooked up a phone in the basement on my line."

"You didn't tell me that."

"Yes, I did." He was tempted to return to his chair, pick up the paper, to end the conversation that way. "Anyway," he said, "what does it matter now? He had a phone. I disconnected it. He doesn't have it anymore. Phone. No phone." A telephone? All he could imagine was a melted blob among the smoldering ruins. He went back to his green chair, staring straight ahead at the TV screen, chin sunk into his chest, sweat accumulating in the crevices of his neck, soaking into the upholstery, and everything moist, even the cards he laid out in front of him on the TV table, and the neighborhood so quiet, so very quiet.

TV and newspaper reporters hid behind trees and cars, trying to get their stories. The Wednesday *Detroit News* described a "restless truce," a "bloody battlefield," tanks thundering through the streets and heavy machine guns clattering. "It was as though the Viet Cong had infiltrated the riot-blackened streets," they said.

"Explain that to me," Harry said to the printed page, still carrying on his internal debate about when he should return to work. "Is it more *restless*? Or more *truce*?"

An assault on a police command post at Herman Kiefer Hospital; a blaze at Grand River and Fourteenth, with snipers firing at firefighters. Damage estimates at $200 million. Price gouging at grocery stores. Paratroopers clashing with National Guards. Arrests topping three thousand. And the paper reported that "efforts to restore law and order were taking effect."

To Harry, they didn't sound like they were taking effect.

And the worst: eleven deaths since noon on Tuesday, including three young colored men in a shoot-out at the Algiers Motel on Woodward and Virginia Park. Three young men? Harry told Ruth about the Algiers.

"There's no way to know who the three men were, so why talk about it?" When he tried to give his reasons, she said, "You think Alvin and his friends are the only three in the city?"

Having no response, Harry finally went out to the front lawn, where the neighbors were discussing the shootings.

"What were they doing there?" Julius Weiner demanded.

"More snipers," Marv said.

"You've got no proof of that," Harry said. "Maybe they were just seeking shelter."

"Shelter. Sure. Why don't they go home for shelter?"

"Have you seen the pictures?" Harry asked. "A lot of people don't have homes anymore."

"And whose fault is that?"

"You don't even know if those three men had guns. Where's the proof?"

"I don't need proof."

"Well, I do," Harry said, retreating to his house and his own company.

By Thursday, the solar oven, like all other novelties, had lost its luster. Most shook their heads when they saw Franny coming with her cardboard box, queasy at the thought of more melted marshmallow. Those in the lifeboats had lost the exhilarated feeling of having made it this far, and the question of "what next?" cast its sobering spell.

But then Seidel came out of the house, saying that Mayor Cavanagh had just made the announcement. He was asking, inviting—begging? Marvin conjectured—that people return to their normal routines. The curfews were being lifted, as were the gas restrictions. The bayonets were being sheathed, and the army and National Guard were removing the ammunition from their guns. By Friday morning, the federal troops would be gone.

"Normal routines," Marv said. He licked melted marshmallow off his finger, one of the few who still had the stomach for the solar creations. "Oh yeah. Normal." Ruth heard Marv repeating this word, as if it were a joke he'd thought up all on his own. And she heard Seidel saying, "Enough already with the normal," all the way as they disappeared into their house and the screen door slammed behind them.

But Ruth stayed out on the sidewalk, watching as her neighbors dispersed, into their own homes and living rooms to hear the latest announcements for themselves. She paced, not sure where she wanted to be, inside or out, not sure whether any of the neighbors had noticed—and if not, why not—that Harry's car was not in the driveway, not sure whether to tell anyone that Harry wasn't home, and that she didn't know where he was.

RELEASE

It was sometime in the thirties, so many years ago that he wasn't even sure he remembered it accurately: mid-morning, in the fall, a day between Rosh Hashanah and Yom Kippur, one of the Days of Awe. He remembered that, or thought he did, even though his family didn't observe the holidays in any traditional way. Joe did close the business, but the family didn't go to shul, and sometimes Joe went down to the office to work anyway, though he didn't answer the phone. An odd mix of this and that, a connection with the heritage but hardly kosher, hardly rising to the level of Awe.

That fall, the one he thought he remembered, Harry was only a year out of high school, so he still had the imprinted rhythm, that this was the season when school started. But *he* wasn't starting school, or anything new. He wasn't carrying any clean, empty notebooks, ready to be filled with new learning and possibilities.

Instead, he carried a load of shoe boxes up the narrow basement stairs, two stacks of six, twelve in all. This was when the store was still on Jefferson, and he stopped midway. He didn't say anything to anyone. He turned, walked back down the stairs, and left the two stacks on the floor at the bottom. For a moment, he had considered returning them to their places on the shelves, sorting them, dutiful, orderly, obedient. But for whom?

He was nineteen at the time, and handsome even in his own eyes. And he was thinking of Ruth on that beautiful fall day. That she might be on the bus, on her way down to Wayne, to her college classes. To study subjects like literature and psychology. History and political science. He was thinking of that afternoon they'd spent on Belle Isle. On the Aztec picnic blanket. And his friend Harold Marcus had caught the picture of them, called out to them *Boo*, alarming them out of their immersion in each other. That had been a day of awe, and this would be one too.

Joe was in the front office, on the phone with a customer. And Marsha, their secretary at the time because Ilo was still in high school, was writing small numbers in columns in the ledger book. Harry did not stop in to say goodbye. He opened the back door, felt the cool-warm air of fall swirling up a rush of alley cinder, and he stepped out. He left the back door open wide on its hinges, a big dark yawning space for anyone to see. An entryway the sun never reached.

It wasn't that hard, really, to put one foot in front of the other—he'd been doing that since he was a toddler—past the discarded crates and boxes behind National Dry Goods, Brody Hosiery, Cohen Slippers, J. C. Goss, which manufactured flags. The brick buildings rose around him in parallel lines along the thin corridor, like a chute, a clear path, narrow, dark, with the damp dust of history nestled in the cobbles.

The alley was a friend, a straightaway, a chute. And when he came to the end of the alley, it was just a short walk to the Detroit River, across which Windsor, Ontario, stood. Another country in view, connected to Detroit by the magnificent Ambassador Bridge, the world's longest suspension bridge, not even five years old—and none of this far from the spot where two centuries earlier, Antoine Cadillac had disembarked and claimed the narrow place *le Détroit,* for his French king.

Harry sat on the grass by the river, where a few other people, idle on a fall day, also sat. Who were these people who had nothing better—or worse—to do on a fall afternoon than sit on the grass and watch the river? A ship inched along, carrying parts or materials to the Rouge plant, or hauling completed cars away, that would end up in Pittsburgh or Buffalo, Boston or New York. It blasted its horn, calling out a greeting to those who sat along the river. Its black smoke trailed behind it.

"Quite a sight."

Harry turned to see a man, looking at him, his voice as deep and dark as shoe polish. Harry had been marginally aware of the man, who sat in the grass a few feet off.

"What?" Harry asked.

"The ships, coming, going. That's power."

Harry laughed, a small explosion of surprise, in the throat.

"You know who owns that ship?" the man asked. It didn't occur to Harry to think that way—of a particular human being who owned something as huge and powerful as that ship. He saw it more as a fact of life. An enormous presence that made modern life possible, that linked one huge business concern with another, that moved massive quantities of raw materials and finished goods from coast to coast, that made Detroit possible. But a human being, sitting at the top of that chain? The man who owned that ship, whomever he might be, would not be sitting on the bank of the Detroit River on a fall morning. He'd be building an empire somewhere, or barking out orders, or standing on a balcony looking down on men assembling engines.

"No, I don't," Harry said. "But it's somebody with means."

"That's true enough," the man said. "Someone we can't even imagine. Two arms. Two legs. Probably. We know that much."

"Unless that man was in the war," Harry said. He was getting engaged despite himself.

"Amen." The man rearranged his hat on his head, his eyes still on the passing ship, the plume of smoke. "But there is a difference between him and us. Would you agree with that?"

Although Harry did agree, he was reluctant to put himself too much, so to speak, in the same boat as this man, who seemed to be latching onto him. Everyone was different from everyone else, and plenty of differences likely separated this man from someone like Harry, whose father owned a business. If he turned, he would be able to see it, the building his father owned. Joe might be standing out on the sidewalk now looking for him. Or inside, puzzling over the open door, the missing son, the stacks of shoe boxes abandoned at the bottom of the basement stairs.

Harry nodded, but he said nothing. He was starting to consider an exit strategy. "Well," he might say, "have to be getting back to work." To show that he did have work, unlike this man. But if he did then get up and walk back toward the business, which was not where he wanted to go, the man might follow him, or even if he didn't, he would see where Harry went and might show up some other time, looking for something, a handout, a job, a place to live. And if Harry didn't walk back toward the business, which direction would he walk? And surely, the man would recognize that he was directionless.

"Of course, there's lots of kinds of men in the world. All different. Like me from you," the man said. "You probably got a nice little setup somewhere, a business your father started or your grandfather, come over from the old country, built it up from nothing." Harry flushed because the man seemed to know, recognized his Jewish face, recognized the story, the trajectory, nothing unique about it. The man looked amused. "My people. They've got a different story. A different old country. Nothing to be ashamed of. We just born into what we born into. We do our best with what God gave us." The ship had passed from view now, the smoke trail a smudge of gray on the blue sky, but another one was appearing, afloat, going in the opposite direction.

It was approaching noon, the time they usually took their lunch break at Levine's, eating the food his mother had packed for them, hard-boiled eggs, a farmer's salad, which was cottage cheese mixed up with chopped vegetables: cucumber, tomato, green pepper, radish, scallions. Crackers, and fruit—apples, or oranges, sometimes bananas. Harry felt the hunger, but it was more a reflex than real hunger.

"You want to see something you've prob'ly never seen before?" the man asked. "Talk about all different kinds of men."

Harry wasn't sure he did, but he wasn't sure he didn't.

"You ever work in an auto factory?" the man asked.

"No," Harry said.

"How about your daddy?"

"For a short time," Harry said. "A Buick parts plant. But."

"Oh, I know," the man said, "your people not much for the factories. But you've got to see this. You've just got to." The man was dressed in a loose shirt and loose pants. He wore scuffed shoes. He seemed dangerous and trustworthy at the same time, dangerous because Harry didn't know him, because he'd been so forward to start up a conversation that way, because he was luring Harry somewhere.

"You coming?" the man asked. Harry noticed that the man's nails were long, too long for a man, and very smooth, like horn, like the shoehorn Harry's father kept on his dresser, or like some kind of polished stone. Alabaster. Amber. The hardened nectar of the earth. Okay. Why not?

They walked along the riverfront, until they came to Woodward, where they turned, passing Hudson's and the other fine stores that lined the avenue.

"You know where I'm taking you?"

"No."

"You worried?"

"A little."

"Then why did you come?"

"I'm not sure." He looked at the man. It was hard to tell his age, but he was probably older than Harry, maybe about as old as Joe. His skin seemed thick, like a hide, and pitted. Harry felt ashamed at his thought—a hide, like a mule had, or some other beast of burden, leading him away.

"You don't even know my name," the man said.

"You don't know mine either."

The man reached out his hand, to shake, and Harry looked at the open palm, a lighter brown than the rest of his skin, but with dark lines etched across it, a deep life story. "Name's Root," the man said. "That's what most people call me." Harry shook the hand, dry and smooth and big and easy.

They neared the Wayne State campus, and Harry wondered whether he would see his Ruth, and if he did, what he would say about why he was here and why he was with this man and what she would think. He watched the students, walking with their books.

"Why aren't you in school like these kids?"

"My dad needed help in the business."

"He don't need your help today?" The man began the climb up the broad steps of the Detroit Institute of Art, passed the large statue of a preoccupied man, deep in thought.

"Probably he does," Harry said.

"Probably." They were almost at the top. Harry had often admired those tall broad steps, the ascent, like a temple.

"You been here before?" the man asked.

Harry was ashamed to say that he hadn't. His parents weren't much for art, but Ruth had talked about the paintings that were going up, right now. "I think a couple times when I was a kid."

"You're not a kid anymore?"

They walked through the heavy doors, and compared with the bright light of this fall day, the large room they entered was dark, and Harry stalled as his eyes adjusted. Harry's companion waved to a woman at the desk near the door, and she waved back. They passed into another room, high-ceilinged, one of the highest ceilings Harry had ever seen. It was an enclosed courtyard, with a rectangular pool in the middle. Scaffolds lined the walls, all the way to the ceiling, with walkways at various levels.

Sitting on a bench in one corner, with a paintbrush, was a fat man, in overalls. Black curly hair and bulging eyes, like frog eyes. Others worked around the man, carrying things, moving things, looking at large sheets of paper hanging on the walls or lying on the floor. Up on the scaffold was a woman, pacing. Her heels drummed on the wooden platform. She looked like someone out of a fairy tale, or a bible story, thin with black hair pulled back, tight, and braids wrapped around her head like a crown. She wore a long white dress. He could see the dress through the scaffold—a bright shawl wrapped around her shoulders. The full white skirt flowing as she paced, and all her attention was focused on the man with the paintbrush.

"That man's named Diego Rivera," Root said. And as if on cue, the fat man looked up at Root, and he nodded at him. "He's from Mexico, and Edsel Ford brought him here, to paint this whole room." Parts of wall were already filled with images, though some were only sketches, outlines that looked like machine parts and huge hands reaching and grasping. The men on the walls lifted car parts, soldering, drilling, all crowded in together, like a dance.

Root said he worked here, preparing the walls for Mr. Diego, with all the layers—sand, mixed with plaster, smoothed in the final coat to a surface like marble—and that Mr. Diego was very particular about how it was done. If the wall was too wet when he was ready to work, the colors wouldn't hold. And if it was too dry. "Forget it," Root said. Diego had to paint in sections, so the wall would be just right. "And he can only do the colors in daylight," Root said. "So he sketches at night, starting around midnight." The lady, he said, looking up at her, and Harry followed his gaze, she just watched. Sometimes she came over and stood close to Diego as he worked. And sometimes, Mr. Diego stopped for a moment, went to her, and hugged her. All the men talked about it, the way she dressed, the way she watched, the way the two spoke to each other, in their language, like some kind of music, with syncopation, drumbeats and rat-ta-ta-tat, and the sound of the lady's heels on the scaffolding.

Root pointed way up to the top of the room, the sections with the women of the four races like part of the earth. He liked those, he said, though he wasn't sure what people were going to think about them being naked. Mr. Diego was particular about that too, about making it natural. In one small round section, he'd painted a fetus in the womb. "But look," Root said, "how he made the womb like part of the earth, showing how the earth contains all life, and how a woman was like the earth. It all blends in together. It makes sense if you let yourself feel it."

It wasn't only a celebration, this painting. The faces of some of the workers were going to be green, Root said, as if they were being poisoned. And he pointed to the sketches of the weapons, another product of these factories. He pointed out the weary looks on the faces of the workers in the small panels along the bottom, carrying in their lunch pails at the beginning of the day, and even wearier when they were leaving at night. He described what it was supposed to do, giving you the feeling of being enveloped and surrounded by huge, banging machines, squeezed in with all these other men, and having only one small job to do, over and over again.

"Mr. Diego keeps working. He doesn't answer to anyone, he says. The pictures come from inside him, he says, like the baby from the earth. Once it's formed, it's got to come out. That's what he says."

Most people Harry knew worked in family businesses, scrap metal, auto parts. Or they had learned the trades—plumbing, construction. A few from Europe had skills like tailoring or shoe repair. Some young men his age planned to become doctors or lawyers. But who knew there were options like these, like what Mr. Diego did, or even Root? Who knew that an auto plant could be the subject for art?

"It's really something," Harry said. He kept saying that, as if being something was the ultimate.

The courtyard was like a factory itself, with all the workers and the scaffold. And it was something like the assembly line, too, like Root said. Each person worked on one small part of the job at a time, even Diego. Root wanted Harry to stay longer, to meet some of the other men who were working with him, preparing the walls, moving equipment, but Harry said no, he'd better go. The two men shook hands, and Harry left, descended the broad steps in the sunlight, again passing the big bronze statue of that man, bent over himself, working to figure it all out. Harry stepped onto a streetcar going downtown and got back to Levine Wholesale Shoes in the late afternoon. When he came up the alley, he saw that his father's car was gone, and when he went inside, no one was there.

A note sat on his desk, folded over into small pieces, in Joe's hand. "Harry, if you ever come back, call home. Mother collapsed, and we're taking her to the hospital."

Later, when he told Ruth about it, he tried to explain what he'd felt: that he'd been allowed to enter a world, then been snatched out before he'd had a chance, like being woken from one of those dreams you can't bear to part with.

"But you were the one who decided to leave the museum," she said.

He wanted to take credit for that, for having an inkling that something was wrong and that he needed to get back. "But it was so . . ."

"Did you think that what happened to your mother was your punishment . . . for going off like that?"

"Punishment?" he answered. "No, of course not." Though it had been punishment. Watching his mother, Eileen, in the months after she collapsed. A woman who'd always been so proper, every hair in place, always with her stockings on. For her to be trapped like that in bed. He tried to reassure her that it was fine, that she shouldn't feel ashamed of how she looked.

He'd wanted to be the one who could save her life. To be that powerful. So he sat beside her bed, hour after hour, in deep concentration, trying to find the place in her brain that was eating away at her (it was brain cancer, after all), and to coax it out, tease it out, gently, imagining that then he could wipe it away with a soft cloth, the way a parent cleans a baby, blotting up the mess, disposing of it. But it hadn't worked. Nor had the light machine he ordered from the man in Indiana, with its red and yellow bulbs that flashed in unpredictable patterns while he made her hold the metal handles on the sides.

"Punishment?" he said to Ruth. He got up, as if ejected from the sofa cushion. What he didn't say was that he'd felt cheated because he hadn't been allowed to hold onto that giddy feeling from that day in the museum, of having heard a call (*put down the shoes; go to the river*) and of having listened.

And here he was again, slipping out. It was Thursday, and he couldn't take it anymore. The sitting around at home, wondering. No word from Curtis. Only the papers and the TV and the gossip. The ignorant talk of the neighbors. He'd fixed every damn thing in the house. He must have cut the grass three times.

So he got up early, and once again, all these years later, he slipped out. The streets were practically empty. Like a stage set. A city full of people, all hidden away, except for the ones on television, the ones causing the problems. From here, in this quiet, it was hard to believe it was true, what the papers said, what the TV showed. But you had to believe them, like you had to believe a doctor who told you he detected something. Clogging in the arteries, something malignant growing in the brain.

Every day of the riots—Sunday, Monday, Tuesday, Wednesday—Ruth's eyes had been on him, wondering whether he would go back, wanting him to go back, not wanting him to go. Tuesday, theoretically, it had been safe enough. At least according to Cyrus Vance, the out-of-towner who traveled through the burning city in an armored car surrounded by soldiers.

At Seven Mile and Livernois, a tank blocked the intersection, and a soldier in combat gear came to Harry's car, motioned him to roll down the window. This was something new, something he had never before seen in his city.

"No cars allowed on this stretch of Livernois, sir." This boy, you could barely call him a man, was too young for the heavy weapon. Sweat beaded on his forehead, and anyone could see that he would rather be home with a cool drink and a girlfriend than decked out like that, telling a man more than twice his age what to do.

"But I have to . . ."

Two more guards came to join the first, and Harry thought about doing something irrational, stepping on it, something un-Harry-like, squeezing past the tank, running over the curb if he had to, like they did in the car-chase movies. But he knew the neighborhood well enough that he could find a way around. So he gestured to the baby-faced men and made a U-turn, acting the part of a compliant citizen, cooperating with the powers, letting them do their job, putting his own needs aside in the interests of the larger good.

He drove what seemed to him a convincing distance, then turned off onto a side street of well-kept brick and stone houses. He pulled into an alley and wound his way through, gravel crunching beneath his tires, pink hollyhocks poking out from spaces between garages, rusty fences covered with morning-glory vines.

In an alley behind a boxy little orthodox shul, a man motioned to him, the way a police officer does, directing traffic. But this man was not like the National Guard. This man was tall and thin, brown skinned and stooped, wearing glasses and a gray hat that had a high crown, like a train conductor's hat. He wore a red and blue plaid flannel shirt, tucked in. Funny, Harry thought. A flannel shirt on such a hot day. The man guided him to a parking spot behind the synagogue.

Harry had often seen people walking to and from this shul for Sabbath—the men in their wide-brimmed black hats and the long quilted coats that looked like satin bathrobes—their wives in long skirts following behind, and then the children. Always so many children. Whenever Ruth, riding in a car on Shabbos, saw them—and felt that they might see her—she wanted to duck. Ruth's parents had been like that, fruitful and devout. But once Ruth had gotten serious about Harry, she pulled away from her family traditions, or noose, as Harry liked to call it.

"All that's left of her old ways," Harry liked to say, explaining her instinct to duck, "is the guilt." But that was not true. Remnants, like dust that accumulates in pocket seams, lay in tiny, ancient chambers of the heart. Even in Harry's—a man who wasn't aware he had pockets.

The man with the conductor's hat came to the driver's side window, as if he had been expecting Harry, and Harry opened the door.

"Just in time," the man said. "They need one more for the minyan." His face looked familiar, as did his long fingers with the smooth, curved nails. The man waited for Harry to get out. "It can't have been easy to get over here," the man in the hat said. He held the door open for Harry. "The others, they live down the street."

"How did *you* get here?" Harry asked as he followed the man through the back door of the shul, up the brown linoleum steps. It was cool inside—the cool of a place made of linoleum and cinderblock, closed up against the summer heat. And the cool made him shiver in his short-sleeved T-shirt, damp with sweat.

"Me?" the man in the conductor's hat said. "I've been here since Friday. Can't get home for a while, I guess." Just before he opened the sanctuary door, the man handed Harry a yarmulke, and Harry put it on his head.

The room had tan walls of painted cinderblock, bathed in a cool green light from high, tinted windows, with a balcony for the women, and with the white satin-curtained holy ark on a raised wooden platform in the middle of the main floor. Harry had been in shuls, of course, temples, synagogues—people called them different names— though mainly for weddings and bar mitzvahs, where he could almost feel comfortable, lost in the crowd. But this room had no crowd to get lost in. Only the group of bearded men, dressed in black pants and white shirts, wearing skullcaps, wrapping black leather straps around their arms and heads, and now looking at him.

Harry knew enough to recognize what they were doing with the straps—donning their tefillin—though he'd never before seen anyone put them on. Before now, he'd only ever seen them from a distance, or in pictures. And he himself felt he'd stepped onto the set of the wrong moving picture, or simply slipped through some membrane into a different world. The man with the conductor's hat backed away, let the door close behind him, and one of the worshippers came up to Harry, his tefillin already in place.

The man carried another set of tefillin, dark coils in his open palms, and offered them to Harry, who shook his head no. It seemed a sacrilege for Harry to wear them—not that he would know how to put them on—and he felt a panic of shame. But the man said he would show Harry. "Okay," Harry said. What choice did he have?

So the man began. First, he pantomimed the reverent kiss, and Harry complied, lifting and kissing the two little boxes that were attached to the leather straps, then placing them back in the man's hands. Then, the man, mumbling softly to himself, like praying, made a noose above Harry's elbow with the long leather strap, and placed the little leather box, two or three inches in width and height, on the inner side of Harry's left arm. The box looked like a small wooden house, and Harry at least knew that the prayer was stored in there.

After the man tightened the knots, he wound the leather strap around and around Harry's arm, spiraling down toward his hand. Harry stood awkwardly with his arms out from his body, as if he were being fitted for a suit by a tailor. Then the man left the straps hanging from his arm and motioned for Harry to lower his head. The man was short, shorter than Harry, and he had to reach to place the second little wooden box in the middle of Harry's forehead, above his hairline.

Harry closed his eyes while the man worked, the way he did when he sat in the barber's or dentist's chair. He could feel the leather straps being looped around the back of his head, knotted, and left hanging down the back of his neck. When he straightened, and opened his eyes, he felt as if he had a horn growing out of his head, or as if he wore a little clown hat at a jaunty angle. And the man who was outfitting him had one too, as if they were members of the same tribe or the same traveling circus.

Under normal circumstances, he would have felt silly, perhaps been tempted to make a joke. But these were clearly not normal circumstances, and he felt cared for, groomed. And although he felt anxious, about doing something wrong, for the first time since he'd heard the news of the riots, he wasn't fretting about his business, his building, his inventory, his Alvin.

The man nodded encouragingly at Harry, as a tailor or a barber might, once he was pleased with his work, and he went back to Harry's arm, winding the hand strap three times around Harry's middle finger, one of his three crooked fingers, the ones he had broken when he was a boy, and the man seemed to note this fact, working carefully as if afraid to hurt him, and he said something in a kind voice that Harry could not understand. The man touched Harry's arms, as if to tell him to relax them, which Harry did, and he felt the little box high up on the inside of his arm, pressed into his side. Finally, the man draped a prayer shawl over Harry's shoulders and moved away to get Harry a prayer book and to find his own, stored in a blue velvet bag.

Then the other men, who Harry now saw had been waiting for him, pulled their prayer shawls up on their heads, and Harry did the same. But the man who had been helping him hurried back over to Harry, to arrange the prayer shawl so it would not touch the wooden box but rest on Harry's head behind it.

The men opened their books and began to read and chant—mumbling and rocking, occasionally bending at the knee and bowing forward, in the way Harry remembered from the times he'd gone with Ruth. Harry knew the smell of the musty pages in the old black book with the frayed cloth bindings. And he knew the look of the dancing Hebrew letters, though he couldn't read them. The rhythms of the chanting voices were familiar, too, beyond any familiarity he could describe, as had been the face of the man in the conductor's hat who'd brought him here. Occasionally, one voice rose above the others, an outburst of sorrow or passion perhaps.

Although he didn't know the prayers, he began to whisper to himself. At first, he wasn't saying words, just something like budda-budda-budda-budda, so he'd look like he was participating, helping these men give their prayers the proper weight. But soon words formed: He hoped the best for his city, for Curtis, for Greta and her dress shop. For Alvin, who he hoped was safe at home by now. He sent a blessing to tragic-faced Mayor Cavanagh, whom LBJ hadn't even deigned to mention. He moved in and out of words. And he wished—a wish not a prayer—that the trouble would pass over, rifts would be mended, lives would find purpose, and sweet normalcy would be restored.

He admired the spiral of the leather strap on his arm, like a sacred vein. He felt the steady pressure of the prayer box against his side, like a reminder to his heart. He held the book with both hands, feeling the worn cover, feeling the tight strap around his finger, supporting the book. He let the prayer shawl fall forward around his face and shoulders, and he withdrew into it, a private tent.

The men in the shul chanted, in the smoldering city. They bent their knees and swayed, turning the pages of their prayer books. They bowed their heads. Harry, too, bowed his head, budda-budda-budda-budda, a blessing on this one, on that one, on all he might have been, and all he was. A blessing for his mother, who had been so proper and so sick. And a blessing for Joe, who had struggled across an ocean to build a life for his family. A blessing for all three daughters, each still safe.

And then there was Ruth. How she scolded and soothed him, stroked his shoulder when he woke from a bad dream, as if she was rubbing in a salve. How he annoyed her; how he steadied her. How he'd spied on her from his front window across the street, how he'd finally made his way over to her front porch. How he'd managed to have her invited to dinner, where she'd pretended to know about Benny Friedman, the quarterback who evaded injury because *chai* was working for him, as it must have been also for Harry.

A blessing on the Belmont Hotel, where they had gone shortly after that first dinner. Her idea that they should take the suitcase with them, filled with shoes, to give it weight, to make them look like legitimate travelers, the kind of people who spent the night. How he carried it up the stairs and down the hall to the room, number 2B. She'd laughed at that.

He'd always remember. It had a lumpy-looking bed and a narrow window covered by a flimsy white curtain with a few hooks missing. He'd set the suitcase down inside the door, and they stood close, not touching. Then she took the lead, nudging him with her forehead, nudge, nudge, into his chest, into his breastbone, which covered and protected his heart, nudging him, nudge, nudge, toward the bed. It had a cream-colored chenille bedspread, with a cigarette burn. And she guided him toward it. Nudge, nudge, until the backs of his legs were pressed against the bed, and the nudging finally nudged him over backwards, and he grabbed her and she collapsed on top of him, the whole strong, solid weight of her. That was joy.

She was eager, and sure of herself—far surer than he was. And he didn't want to know how or why she was. Where she might have learned what she seemed to know—the eagerness with which she slid her hands into his shirt and under it, how she went at him, fingers, nails, hands, how she let her thigh slip between his legs and press, press as if she enjoyed the feeling of the pressure, of what she felt. That was joy. She was biting him on his neck and laughing, then rising up and holding his arms down and looking at him—as if she were looking far into their future and seeing all the ways they could know each other and help each other and be the means of escape for each other, that she could take away the silence and the loneliness and the dull sameness of his days, and he could erase the mania, the disorder and sheer crowded chaos of hers.

Her cheeks were broad and her chin narrow, like a heart, and her brows were thick and dark, and her nose large and honest and Jewish. Her dress was sheer, a summer dress, with tiny buttons all up the front. "Borrowed" from her sister's closet, and her sister would kill her if she knew. She'd told him this, as soon as she'd met him on the dark sidewalk in front of her house, holding the skirt out and asking if he liked it. But now she seemed heedless, sisters and buttons be damned. All those tiny pearl buttons pressing into his chest, with her chest behind them.

She rolled over, sat up, unbuttoning the tiny buttons, impatient with the little loops, tugging without looking at what she was doing, violating the basic rule of hand-eye coordination that Joe had repeatedly lectured about—that you had to LOOK to see what you were doing—so that Harry didn't know what was riling and arousing him more, the lace of the slip that had been revealed, her carelessness, the suggestion of what was to come, or some intuition of the tantalizing incompatibilities stretching out into their future.

"Good god, Ruthie," he said, as if coming up for air following a long deep plunge. "That dress. And all those buttons." But she laughed, and lifted the hem of the dress, pulling it up over her head. And she was still laughing as she found herself trapped inside, and he was trying to help her get untrapped, and then they both heard the rip of the cloth and the buttons bouncing across the floor.

"Forget it," she said as she freed herself from the cloth entrapment and saw his worried face. And then they sat next to each other on the side of the squeaky bed, she in her white nylon full slip and he with his shirt unbuttoned. He took off her shoes and kissed each of her toes, sucked on them, wondering at first how he knew what he wanted, then abandoning the question as he kissed up her legs, skipped over, for now, the dark thicket, nuzzled his face into her soft belly, inhaling and submerging, up her soft, inviting body, to her breasts and shoulders, her face, until he didn't know if he was backwards or forwards, upside down or inside out, and she didn't either. That was joy.

At 9:30, he snapped back into the Harry he'd always been, for no one can escape forever, and he became concerned about the time. He worried about her facing her parents. He worried about answering to his own if he came home too late. "We need to leave," he said. And she said okay. She held her dress closed at the top, where the buttons had torn off, while he kneeled on the floor to look for the missing ones, even fingering through the dust balls under the bed until he found the last one. Then, carrying the suitcase, he pulled the door of 2B closed behind them and listened to the lock catch.

Oy, he thought. If these pious men only knew what he'd been thinking. As he took in his surroundings, as he saw where he'd ended up *this time,* he began to understand that if his business was burning, right then, he would manage.

All these years, he thought, the business had been good *to* him and his family. But now, he saw, it wasn't good *for* him. What kind of person might he be if he worked elsewhere, in a bright, modern office building, with meetings, colleagues—he loved the sound of that word—who stopped in to talk about movies and politics? What if he hadn't had the burden of a broken boiler in the middle of the night? Albatross, shackles, prison, dungeon. A man must be made for something more than this.

He knew then that he did want it to burn. And he imagined his whole lousy shoe box of shoes burning with ugly black smoke—even the old-fashioned boots in the window, even the Dr. Levine baby shoes in the basement—dispersed into molecules that could never be reconfigured. Deep within the privacy of his tallis tent, he saw that the horror that had seized the city could release him. It could open his life, push him out, tell him go, be, do.

Then he felt the nudge on his arm, and it was the small man who had prepared him for the minyan. The others had stopped praying, and they were unwinding and kissing their tefillin and prayer boxes, like amulets. And then with the man's help once again, he undid himself, untying and unwinding the tight straps. He joined the others, too, as they shuffled out of the sanctuary, he in his short-sleeved T-shirt among the men in white shirts and dark pants, dark hats with big brims, down the long cool hallway, out into the daylight—the suffocating humidity hitting him full on, still feeling the imprint of the straps on his arm and head, the imprint of the prayer boxes.

RETURN

She was waiting there for him. Standing at the screen door. A cotton skirt and sleeveless blouse. Her short hair pushed back behind her ears. The damp film on her skin, the heat. She, in one of those moments when she didn't know whether to kiss or kill, in one of those moments when the fine distinctions between *schlemiel* and *shlimazl* and *shmegegge* and *shmendrick* became irrelevant. He, like Mr. Magoo, floating in unscathed, oblivious to the mayhem and collapse he had evaded. He'd almost forgotten why he'd gone in the first place, that he hadn't told her. He, coming up the walk with the memory of her at the Biltmore, the buttons on the dress skittering into the corners of the room, his Ruth, and the sense that he had gone out and found something true.

"Where have you *been?*" She, with the acidic anxiety in the back of her throat, feeling anything but Biltmore Hotel heedless.

Marv Deitch emerged from his front door, onto his front porch, as if he'd been waiting at his window, watching with hands on hips. He came down his stairs, and crossed the street, because eventually Marvin had noticed the absence of Harry's car in the driveway. And the word had spread, that Ruth didn't know where he'd gone, and now he was back, and everyone would want to know. Ruth pulled Harry into the house, and she closed the door behind them, cutting Marvin off at the pass, much as she'd cut off his wife that day on the phone when the moving van pulled up. With some people, she said, that's all they understood.

"Where have you *been?*"

Harry explained, the best he could. What he'd set out to do, which enraged her, and where he'd ended up, which caused the distinctions between amazed, astounded, and astonished to become irrelevant. "You?" she said. "You?" Wondering what her father would say if he knew, wondering what *his* father would say.

"It was peaceful," he said. "They needed me." The best he could do, leaving out the part about *him*, what he'd discovered about wants and needs. That he knew he'd go back, to see what had become of his shoe business. But no matter what, he couldn't do it anymore. He left that part out because then she would ask the inevitable, because everyone would: *What are you going to do instead?*

And then it was Sun*day*. And then it was Sun*night*. And Harry decided. This was it. He would go.

"Take Irv with you," Ruth said, "or one of the neighbors."

"Irv?" He looked at her like she was crazy.

And they sat, staring at their hands, at the wall, out the window, still plenty of light in the sky, even at night, in the summer. The girls walked in and out of the frame, restless with all the staying home, the uncertainty, the free-floating anxiety. Sappho circled the yard, collapsed, gnawed at itchy places on her side. She barked. She came in and settled by the heating vent—even in this interminable heat wave, her home and hearth, her little place in the world.

They cleared the dinner dishes. They watched TV—the return to regular programming, a gauge of encroaching normalcy. At 8:00, the peculiar hand-wringing personality of Ed Sullivan. At 9:00, the warmly familial *Bonanza*. And at 10:00, the amusing, disquieting *Candid Camera*, catching people in the act, teasing out their foolishness. And then it was setting up the fans in the bedrooms, an exhaust system Harry had devised to draw in whatever coolness lurked in the dark of night. All these attempts at achieving that normal Sunday-night feeling, edgy and unpleasant though it normally was—regret that the weekend was gone, arranging one's mind and body for the reentry, the plunge, feeling the small clutch. Then the attempt at sleep. Imagining. Trying not to imagine. Trying not to sweat. Sweating.

Monday morning, and he got up at 6:00, his regular time. He dressed for business—his gray suit, a white shirt, and his narrow navy-blue tie. An odd choice, maybe, on a day like this. Maybe he was thinking about his last outing. And that he didn't want to be caught underdressed twice.

He sat at the kitchen table. Ruth stood by the sink. "So," she said. "Are you going to say anything?"

He adjusted a place mat, moved crumbs around with his fingertip.

"It's not like I can keep sitting around here." Some men had gone back to work already, days ago. It all depended on the neighborhood.

"No one said you should." They sounded like children arguing.

"If Curtis was there, he'll have taken care of things."

"How could he be there if the place burned?"

"He couldn't. Okay? It's something we can't know. We just don't know." He was sweating in his suit. He took off the jacket. He unbuttoned the top button of his shirt. He loosened the tie. She had no idea how it felt, that collar around the throat, reinforced by the tie. She wouldn't last a minute in a rig like that.

Ruth stood in front of the window, and behind her he could see the dark trunk of the elm that shaded the house in the afternoons. In the drainer by the sink were the dishes from last night's dinner. In the bedrooms upstairs, their two youngest daughters. In the cottage on Cass Lake, Lena and her friends were preparing to return to their apartment. "We were stupid," she said, "not to listen to Irv. And the others. Not to move on. Before this."

"On top of all my worries, you want me to feel bad about this?" *This* being the kind of procrastination in which people avoid things they don't want to imagine or dwell on—an escape plan from the house in case of fire, legal documents that say where the children go if the parents die, a plan for contacting your tenant in case the city explodes. Sappho got up to pace and pant. Ruth filled the water bowl and gave her a drink. "Plenty of people didn't listen to Irv. A whole city of people didn't listen to him. Smart people. Rich people. Talented people. Well-educated people. The Hudsons, the Fishers, the Fords. They've got big investments in this city, and they're going to protect them. They're not pulling up stakes."

"Yeah, the Fords." She read to him from the newspaper, the quote from Henry, the son, who now ran the place. "'This country may turn out to be the laughing stock of the world because of situations such as we've had in Detroit. I don't think there is much point in trying to sell the world on emulating our system and way of life if we can't even put our own house in order.'"

"But he's not pulling up stakes."

"Not yet." She followed him to the door as he put on his jacket. She had a dish towel over her shoulder. Sappho came too. Franny was awake and watching from the front window upstairs as her parents walked to the car. Sappho watched from the front window downstairs, smearing it with her snout, wet from the drink she'd had in the kitchen. Ruth kissed Harry, a quick one, on the cheek, then a better one on the lips, arms resting on his chest, hands on his shoulder, and she told him to call as soon as he could. "Not like that nonsense on the night with the boiler," she said.

The traffic on Outer Drive was light. The sun was low, peeking through the thick summer greenery. A gentle breeze stirred the leaves, but the humidity wasn't kidding, and the sun was on its way up. By noon, the steering wheel would be too hot to touch.

When Harry got to Livernois, he found the barricades removed. Two National Guardsmen with rifles stood in front of Alexander's Dress Shop. The rising sun reflected off the glass shards under their feet. He'd seen the images on the television again and again, the camera panning through shops, stopping, zeroing in on broken windows, bare shelves. Now he was seeing it in person, but it didn't seem any more real than it had then.

The traffic picked up, as others joined him in the return to routine. Harry loosened his grip on the steering wheel, relaxed into the seat. He wiped his brow with his white handkerchief, rolled the window down a notch. He got a whiff of something charred, acrid, burning rubber, burning everything.

He passed a stretch of buildings, no more than smoldering ruins, cloaked in the hazy summer light. Like Dresden, he thought, like photos he'd seen of Europe after the war. Okay, he told himself. He could live with this. He could get over it, if this was what he found when he got to his own building.

What he couldn't get over was that so little time had passed. Only a week. And yet, he could barely remember what had been here before. How unobservant he had been! In the uncountable times he'd driven past, he hadn't realized that any of this mattered.

He turned onto Grand River, littered with rags, bricks, and bottles. Past the Riviera, standing. And beyond, a whole stretch of charred buildings lay in ruins—Bernie's place, Stan's. But there was the silly crenellated top of the White Castle. Standing. And there was his building. Standing too. Intact. Even his big front window: Unbroken. And something white, splashed on it, something he could not make out from the car.

He parked beyond the bus stop, in a stretch where the street looked clear of debris, respecting the bus stop, even though he wasn't sure whether buses were running yet. They've got to be running, he thought, if the city is going to return to normal. He took a breath, two, after he turned off the engine. Not certain why, perhaps just to have something in his hand, he took a screwdriver from the glove compartment. Glass crunched beneath his feet as he walked toward his store. "You know the feeling," he later told Ruth, "that people are watching but you don't know where from?"

As he got closer, he could read the thick splash-dash letters on the window, paint drips frozen in descending paths: "Soul brother." And he thought of so many things at once: the Passover blood on the doorposts of Jews in ancient Egypt, and a joke his cousin Arnie had once made— that he should call his store Sole Brother. And, of course, the window message he'd found on Halloween. And what Curtis had said about him to Alvin. "That's no white man."

And then there was Curtis, coming out to meet him. And Harry didn't know what to do with the screwdriver when he reached to take Curtis's hand, transferring it from hand to hand, unable to remember which hand one shook with. But Curtis did not reach back with either hand, so Harry put both hands down. He tried to say something about the screwdriver, that he thought maybe he'd need it to open the door, and realized that he didn't know what he was saying and that whatever it was, Curtis wasn't really listening.

There they were.

"I worried about you, Curtis," Harry said. "You and Alvin. It was hard not knowing what was going on. I tried to imagine." But then Harry felt ashamed of saying that anything had been hard for him compared with Curtis. And the two men squinted in the hot July sun, which flashed off the lenses of Curtis's glasses. It was true that Harry hadn't known who to worry about more—himself or Curtis. It was also true that he kept looking at the building, solid, preserved. He kept looking at the window. There were the arcing green letters. There were the old-fashioned shoes.

"I can't believe it."

Curtis nodded, a small continuous nod, as if Harry's disbelief really did pretty much sum it all up.

"You're okay?" Harry asked. "And Alvin? Is he . . . ?"

"Lost track of him, for one thing," Curtis said. "For a piece."

"I hope . . ."

"There were whites out there looting, too," Curtis said. "I saw it. Right here on Grand River."

Harry nodded, that same rhythmic, bobble-headed nod, almost like the men in the shul. "That wasn't what I meant. What I meant was did you find him? Did he come home?"

"Oh, yes, he came home."

"I'm glad to hear he's okay."

Curtis looked around. They both did. "*Okay* is a funny word right now. Once the lid goes off like that." He shook his head now, the nodding phase over. Shook it again, as if there was something he had to keep saying no to.

Harry asked him if he wanted to come in and sit down. But Curtis said no. He'd stay out here for now. And Harry could see that whatever narrow bridge had connected the two men before was in a delicate state. So they stood, out on the street, Harry asking Curtis to tell about what had happened to him, during all this.

Okay, he said. He could tell. He'd been at home, asleep, he said. Just tucked up in his bed. And Harry imagined him dreaming of something sweet, of a woman maybe, another one of those dreams you don't want to be torn out of for anything, and when you are, there seems no greater injustice. And then there were the sirens, Curtis said, the shouting. The sound of glass breaking, not being sure whether he dreamed the sound, or the sound entered the dream. "And that was it for dreaming," he said, "for enticement of the royal kind."

They both looked at the building, tipping their heads back, so they could see to the top, the straight lines and the corners, the rows of brick, one atop the other, a modest, solid structure.

"It seems so strange," Harry said. "My building. One of the few standing."

Curtis nodded. They kept looking at it. Harry couldn't stop looking at it.

Curtis told how hot it was that night. Hot and thick as the day, and about the folks in the street. About calling for Alvin but getting no answer, then finding his son's bedroom empty. He ran his hand over his head, pulled his handkerchief out, wiped his neck, his forehead. Cars passed the spot where the two men stood, a few, skirting the garbage that lay in the street.

He told about getting dressed, going down to the street. "'Cause by then I could tell I wasn't dreaming those sirens. And the flames, I could see, from somewhere not too far away. And neighborhood folks don't gather on Grand River in the middle of the night unless they have something to gather about. Unless it was those hippies over at the Grande. And these were not any hippies out on the street." He looked at the blackened ruins, telling about the people in the street, what they were saying: about people going crazy, down at Twelfth and Clairmount, about guns and snipers, about whether it was coming over this way. "And I didn't know where my own son was."

"It was like that on my block too," Harry said. "People talking. Saying what they heard, what they knew." And then again, he felt ashamed, for comparing, as if the two experiences had anything in common, except for that stretch when Harry didn't know where Lena was.

"Men who lived in the apartment buildings around the corner were saying that if any fires started around here, they'd go door to door, checking on neighbors, warning them. Then, Monday or so, the looting started. And the fires along here." He spoke as if he were not sure himself whether he had this straight, whether telling it was making it more real, or less.

"I joined with the men, and someone said we should go up on their roof with blankets and water, to protect the buildings from the sparks. It was a shower of cinders coming from the fires, raining down everywhere. That was Monday—I'm sure it was Monday—just after midnight," Curtis said. "Alvin still was not back. And some of the others didn't know where their sons were either, but we said we had to do it, so six of us men climbed up the back fire escape of one of the buildings, over on Martindale, up to the roof, and from there, we could see the fires. What a sight it was," Curtis said. "Almost beautiful, if something so awful can be beautiful." One gentleman, named Dempsey, brought along his shotgun. Which gave Curtis a bad feeling, but he wasn't about to say.

"Now I'm going to tell you something, I don't know what you're going to think," Curtis said.

Harry didn't know either, what he would think, nervous, suddenly, that Curtis was about to tell him something he might not want to hear, something Dempsey and the men had said about him, or about what they wanted to do to his building. Harry and Curtis moved in small, nervous gestures, pivots, to fill time and space, hands on hips, hands folded across chests, Harry with the screwdriver continually getting in the way, both trying to think what they could or should say. How much. Where trust lay.

"An elderly neighbor, Mr. Bartholomew, had been watching his television, and he heard the Guardsmen warning citizens to stay inside and keep out of sight. So he decided to come up to the roof to tell us. But about the same time he came, we saw Guardsmen rushing up the fire escape to the roof of the building next door. The one in the lead yelled something about snipers. 'Go back down to your apartments,' he shouted. But another one coming up behind seemed to think *we* were snipers, and he ordered us to lie down flat on the roof. Some pointed guns our way. And of course, Dempsey had that shotgun, but he kept it pointed down, and he never fired any shots when I was there.

" 'Get down,' this one Guardsman kept saying, and pointing with his gun to our roof. 'Get down.' Which we were in no mood to do. Lie down in the hot tar of the roof, when our whole reason for being there was to do a service to our neighborhood? But they shouted at us again. Others joined in with that first one. 'Put down your gun,' they shouted to Dempsey. Which he did not want to do. I said, 'Let's not be fools. Let's do what the first one said, and go on down off the roof.' And Bartholomew agreed, the old man who came to get us in the first place. People listened to him, and we started down the fire escape. We were about seven men then, I think, and Bartholomew was first, and I was behind him, and Dempsey was toward the back. 'I'm going down,' Dempsey said, to the Guardsmen, 'but I'm not leaving the shotgun for some fool to pick up, can do some real damage.' "

Harry interrupted. "Well, you can see how the Guardsman could think . . ." But the way Curtis looked at him, Harry could see that Curtis did *not* see, nor did he *want* to see how the Guardsman could think.

"They *shot* him, Mr. Levine. They shot, and it hit Mr. Bartholomew. When we were between the second- and third-floor landings, and he fell to the landing below, all of us reaching, trying to catch him, and the National Guardsmen were yelling, and running down the fire escape of the next building, and Dempsey shouting back 'now look what you done.' And someone opened a door at the second-floor landing, so we went into the building, carrying Mr. Bartholomew." Curtis went back to the head shaking, like he was telling himself, no, it couldn't have been.

"What happened to Mr. Bartholomew?" Harry asked.

"Bullet hit his shoulder. Lady over on Otsego knows how to fix it, someone said. Someone went to get her. We didn't have any way to get him to the hospital, so it was a good thing we got someone who knows how to help."

And now it was Harry, shaking his head, picturing the men, the lady over on Otsego, wrapping a shoulder with bandages in someone's apartment, blood seeping through, here in his city, while on his block they'd been wringing their hands while making smores in the solar cooker.

"After that I went back home, sneaking down the street pressed against the buildings, staying in the shadows. These Guard were all over the place, maybe looking for us, half crazy with their own fear. You don't want to get caught in that. They say that even Roger Wilkins— Roger Wilkins, assistant attorney general for the president of this country—was down here in this neighborhood. Right here on the corner of Grand River and Joy." He pointed up the street, and Harry looked too. "The man was stopped by a state police, pulled out of his own car and surrounded, by white men with guns, and standing there hands up, thinking he was going to be shot dead right there in the street."

Now Curtis turned and looked in the other direction on Grand River, and Harry turned too. "From my window, I watched up and down the street, the people pouring in. Taking what they could. Little kids, with a bottle of pop, arms full of candy. Fires everywhere. Not in your building though, as you can see."

As he could see. The Riviera. The White Castle. The Grande. And him. "Who wrote it?" he asked, gesturing at the window.

"My Alvin. He found the paint in the basement."

"Ah," Harry said.

"When you have something long enough," Curtis said, "you come to feel it is your own. You come to grasp onto it, depend on it."

Harry understood.

"It's not much," Curtis said, "but it's our home, Mr. Levine." And then Curtis said that it didn't look too good around there, and Harry agreed that, no, it did not. And then Curtis asked what was Harry planning to do with the building. And Harry told him he didn't know, because he really didn't. How could anyone know anything now? And then Harry said he needed to go in to look around, and Curtis said okay. Harry put the screwdriver down on the sidewalk and unlocked the door, looking again at the message splashed in white across the window. It cast a shadow over the old-fashioned shoes, standing in their silent semicircle on the wooden table, just as Ilo had left them.

He closed the door behind him, sat at his desk, and stared at the walls, the file cabinets, the locked safe. Everything, exactly as he had left it. He got up, pushed back his chair, walked through the building, up one aisle and down the next, weaving his way between the gray shelving that reached to the ceiling. And there they all were—all the shoes in their boxes. Stacked by size, brand, color. Everything, in their straight and sturdy rows. His inventory, his albatross. Sevens, seven-and-a-halfs, eights, eight-and-a-halfs, nines. The sizes stamped on the boxes. It was like dreaming. So many waking dreams lately.

If he walked slowly and quietly, he could almost convince himself that it was a day like any other, all those countless days, same suit and tie, same shelves, same aisles, same tall ceiling and barred windows, same bare light bulbs, same reels of rope, same long wooden packing table. He pulled out a box, opened it. The tennis shoes still nestled in there, facing each other, heel to toe, the way twins nestled in the womb. Complete collapse, rubble all around him, but his place and each shoe, intact.

He went to the front, to his desk, to the safe. He opened it, fingers on the metal wheel with its tiny notches. He pulled out the bank records, the ledger books, the deed to the building. He gathered the order forms from Ilo's desk. He took out the checkbooks, the savings pass book, the savings bonds. The certificates from the Bethlehem Steel stock, with all their elaborate curlicues and flourishes, making a piece of paper seem like something very grand. The box of silver dollars from the forties that Joe had collected. The five crisp hundreds that Harry kept in his safe rather than under his mattress—always good to have access to some cash. The life insurance policies (Fidelity; National Life and Accident), the homeowner's policy (Fidelity again), the policy on the Grand River building (American Casualty). The car titles. The two gold rings Joe had left to Harry. The diamond earrings that had belonged to his mother. Rolls of pennies in a shoe box.

He pulled the adding machine to him, and he punched in figures, pulled the handle, punched in more figures, added, subtracted, seeing what he owned, what he owed, what others owed him. The tape got longer and longer, the adding machine digested, chuckling, saying yes sir, no sir, and again and again and again, the figures in red and black ink aligned on the tape. When he had accounted for everything, he let go of the adding machine handle, and it snapped to its resting position. But he still didn't know what any of it meant, not even the final number on the tape. He placed everything back in the safe, twirled the handle to lock it, and left the building, through the front door, locking it behind him, looking at his front window. And then Mr. Soul Brother made a U-turn across the whole width of Grand River, something no one could have ever done in the traffic of the old days (the old days! that was only last week!), something he would not have ever thought to do before, even if it had been possible. And he drove, all the way back, up Livernois, past the old neighborhoods, past the dark ruins and the broken glass, then once again along the lovely sweep of Outer Drive, heading west, and then up the driveway to his home.

Ruth tried to make life seem normal. She cooked his favorite summer foods—blintzes with sour cream and blueberries, farmer's salad (the way his mother used to make it), bagels and smoked fish, cold borscht with sour cream and chopped scallions. He ate. But he didn't want to talk. "Just leave me to think," he said. Or once, "It's hard to let go." This, Ruth understood. Or another time, "You can let go of it, but it won't necessarily let go of you." And this, Ruth grasped completely, even without knowing everything that had happened to him in the shul.

Everyone, it seemed, was trying to figure it out: Mayor Cavanagh, his panel of Hudsons and Fords and Fishers, all doing their soul searching, trying to understand what had gone wrong. Even LBJ had it on his agenda, assembling a task force, the Kerner Commission.

Harry made phone calls. To his customers, most with businesses that had been ruined, a total loss. Some were planning to winter in Florida while they figured out what to do next, while they waited for the insurance settlements. He called Hudson's, where the phone rang and rang. He called other wholesalers, to see if they could use his inventory.

"Forget about the god-damned inventory," Irv said over the phone. "Call your insurance agent."

So he called the insurance agent. It was an old story. The woman on the phone with the weary voice, as if she knew what the caller was going to say before he even said it. The routinized list of questions that didn't even give him a chance to explain his situation. The weary reminder that "everyone has a situation," that the agent had a procedure, a *packet* they sent out, that this was the way it was handled.

The insurance agent: the smiling man who sent calendars at the end of every year so the insured could feel secure that every day would follow the next, as would the months, all laid out in neat rows on colorful pages, in the way they always had as long as anyone could remember, guaranteed. September following August, and Tuesday following Monday, as the routine had always gone.

And the man who sent this parade of calendars? The smiling insurance agent who raised the premiums on a semiannual basis for as long as Harry could remember? Now, he was unavailable. If Harry ever got that *putz* on the phone, he'd say, "Calendars? This is a meaningful form of communication?"

As Harry had suspected, it took no more than a moment to review the insurance *packet,* once it arrived. He didn't even fill it out, as it was immediately clear that he had no "quantifiable loss," no police or fire report to attach, no photos of gaping holes in walls, of inventory strewn in streets. No smoldering ruins for the insurance examiner to survey, shaking his head, making notes.

"Only you, Harry," Ruth said. "How is it that all the business owners we know are coming out of this with something?"

"And all you've got left is me," he said. "You should have stuck with Bernie." That Bernie, who had the nerve to ask Ruth out, all those years ago on Highland, even though he was younger than she was.

"Maybe so," she said. "I'd be in the lap of luxury now." That Bernie, who knew how to dance, ballroom, like the whole room was choreographed around him.

"Yeah," he said, "but it's a skinny lap."

Still, he left at the regular time. He came back at the regular time. Like Mr. Windmill, you could set the clock by him.

But Ilo refused to return to the office. "You're crazy to keep going there," she said. "Do you think that sign on the window is some magic shield? Do you think it means that everyone loves you so much?" Just because *he* was crazy enough to keep going, it didn't mean *she* had to be.

Sitting in his office, he toted up his assets, again and again, coming up with different answers, depending on how he figured it but never being sure whether the news was good. Sometimes he wandered the aisles, or sat in his office chair, tapping a pencil on his desk blotter. Once, he sat at the top of the narrow basement stairs, looking down into the darkness. He considered washing the white letters off his front window. He knew he had the supplies in the basement, rags, a wooden stepladder, razor blades in case he needed to scrape. But he never quite felt that he could do it—stand on the street, engaged in a task like that.

He walked through the basement. He sat in Alvin's lounge. He perused the Bruchenhartz memorabilia. He found the slats for the roof of the sukkah, some dried leaves still intertwined, strings dangling where the playful decorations had once hung.

Alvin came and went, always with the two friends, always the same awkwardness and silence when his eyes met Harry's, when their paths crossed. Sometimes the singing, the beautiful voice on the back stairs. If Harry had all the time in the world, he doubted he and Alvin could ever find a way to talk, to see each other as *people*. They nodded. Sometimes Harry thought he saw Alvin peeking through the back window, watching him. He'd see the fine profile out of the corner of his eye, but then he would turn, and see nothing.

Alvin left papers on the coffee table in his lounge, and Harry found them, picked them up as if they had a note clipped to them from a colleague saying, "Please read." So he did read the messages, even though he felt like a strange combination of a snoop and an underling, following orders, following a trail of crumbs through the woods to understanding. He read pages that Alvin clipped from magazines and newspapers, underlining what he thought was key text—the "wild youngster" theory of ghetto rioting, which called the recent events in Detroit "youthful rampages," blaming the young person's "excitable nature," "rebelliousness," and "failure to recognize the need for social regulation." And there was the "frustration-aggression theory," which explained the July events by saying that "individuals whose basic desires are thwarted are likely to experience intense frustration and react with aggression." There was also the "relative deprivation theory," which stated that "the greater the discrepancy between what men sought and what seemed attainable, the greater the anger." And the final theory in

Alvin's pile, the "riot ideology theory," a view that rioting was a legitimate and productive form of protest, a "way of making demands on the
authority structure."

So? Harry said to the papers.

One day, Harry found Alvin's draft notice in the pile: Order to Report for Armed Forces Physical Exam. October 31, 1967. 7:58 A.M.

Halloween? This is a day to order someone in?

"What are you doing down there every day, Harry?" Ruth asked one
night when he got home.

"Taking care of things," he said. "Putting things in order."

"Don't even think of torching it," she said.

That did get a chuckle out of him. "Well, why don't *you* do it?" he
asked. "Or get one of Irv's slick-haired friends."

But torching time was over; the streets had so recently been full of
torchers, more than the fire department could keep up with, and the
flames had passed him by, as if his building had been encircled in one
of those silver bubbles he often imagined around his girls when they
were away from him, the magical spell he had devised for protecting
them.

He tried for a joke. "Well, maybe the building's still the same," he
said, "but at least they changed the sign."

"What are you talking about?" she asked.

And he remembered he hadn't ever told her the whole story of the
honky Jew boy window and where it had led. "I told you about that."

"No you didn't."

And the shoes. All those shoes. He sold them off in huge lots—a load
up to Bay City and Flint, a load over to Grand Rapids, another to Ben-
ton Harbor. For almost nothing. The wholesalers came with their
trucks, pulled up in the alley behind the building; sometimes Curtis
helped with the loading.

The world was like that. Letting people accumulate, tote up the
numbers, then wiping the slate clean in one blinding swipe. "Before
their very eyes," "before they knew it," "before they could say Jack
Robinson." Poof.

He sat at his desk and looked at the old pieces of furniture: Ilo's
high bookkeeper's desk and the stool she used to sit on. His old oak
desk with the reluctant drawers, warped and balky even once the

swelling heat and humidity of summer passed. The big iron safe. His rolling wooden desk chair. A few wastebaskets, the adding machines, the desk lamps. In the window, the wooden table with the old-fashioned shoes, and the empty built-in glass display cases.

He took home the old-fashioned shoes. One last call to the Bruchenhartz siblings to see whether anyone wanted anything, and if not, it would all go to Curtis. Or out in the alley. Curtis could have the building. Or the city would buy it for a dollar, a symbolic thing, so they could raze it. As he went about his days, as he went about the cleanup, the settling, the sifting, he still could catch a whiff of what he'd found in the sanctuary that hot July day, the tight strap around his arm, the flat square of the small leather box pressing into his forehead.

THINKER

1987

"Tell about working nights at the Coca-Cola plant," Joanna said. It was July, and they sat in the suburban home Harry and Ruth had moved to after the riots. Joanna and Lena were beside Harry at the kitchen table, which was arrayed with bowls of blueberries and peaches, chunks of cool watermelon. Ilo and her husband were there, and the cousins, in from New York and California for Franny's wedding.

"Your mother hated it," Harry replied. He still had the mustache, though it was gray now. "She'd be up half the night worrying. 'A Jew at a Coca-Cola plant?' she'd say." Ruth was gone five years now—her death, all in one day, a heart attack, as sudden and shocking as the way she had conducted much of her life. And the girls were scattered, doing work he could never have imagined—Lena on the East Coast, not far from the old shoe manufacturing towns he'd visited all those years ago, an editor for the *Concord Monitor;* Joanna on the West Coast, an archivist at the Bancroft Library in Berkeley; and Franny in the middle, in Madison, working on her master's in chemistry, now home to be married.

Ilo spooned blueberries into a small china bowl and said, "He would have been better off if the building had burned."

"You don't know that," Harry said, annoyed with her for acting as if she were the first person to ever have this thought.

"Tell about the next job, then, at that appliance store," Lena said, "where you came back from vacation and found a younger man sitting at your desk."

"Oh that," Harry said, leaning back. "That's life. Always testing. Always teasing."

And everyone got quiet, with all the history and feelings on the table among the summer fruits, until Lena said, "Tell about Curtis and Alvin. Their lawn care business, that they still come out here to cut the grass."

"Tell what, Lena?" he asked, getting up from the table. "You just told it."

There was plenty to tell, though he rarely did, still carrying the feeling that few really cared or listened: About his drives into the city, all the memories, all the history. About his visits to the Art Institute, now open only three days a week because of budget cuts. About his consultations with Rodin's *Thinker,* that introspective muscular figure, who'd sat there in front of the museum all these years, shoulders folded in, everything curling toward the center, so much thinking to do, trying to figure it out along with all the rest of them.

About the silver crosses he'd found in Ruth's jewelry box. Crosses? For a Jew? He'd not seen them before, so he'd taken them to the museum and asked in the gift shop. And the clerk, a small woman with sensible shoes and a little knot of hair on top of her head, said they looked African, which they were indeed. Tuareg, for dispersing evil into the four corners of the world. The clerk found some pictures in a book and showed him. "Where would she have gotten something like that?" he asked. But the clerk shook her head. "That I can't help you with."

And then his real destination: the airy courtyard with the Rivera frescoes, a bright jewel hidden in the struggling city. About the spring day when a school group streamed in, the children milling around him in the big room, talking to each other, their voices echoing in the large space, the tour guide explaining about the assembly-line process, pointing out the particulars as he moved around the room. He was a man around Harry's age, and he told the group how the assembly line had changed the manufacturing process, breaking things up into little pieces, so the workers felt alienated, cut off from the big picture.

"Once upon a time," the tour guide said, "a person made a whole product, from start to finish. A shoe, for example: one person did the cutting, the stitching, the hammering. That same person made the upper, the tongue, the heel." *And the sole,* Harry wanted to say. "One person. The whole thing. But look," he said, "look what's going on in these pictures." And the children looked, their heads back to see the whole thing, the men crammed in together, each working on his one task. The tour guide made an observation, though the children were unlikely to see the irony—that the artist, Diego Rivera, had been a communist. "A man like that," he said, "being hired to honor the factories of the Ford family."

The children were small, maybe seven or eight, all of them black (or African American, which some of them preferred to be called in those days), and one said, "Why do those people have green faces?" and another said, "Why is that baby inside the earth?" and another said, "Oo-wee, those ladies don't have any clothes on," looking at their bare breasts of different shapes and sizes.

Harry wanted to tell what he knew about it, how he knew, that he'd been here that day, when Diego Rivera had been here to paint it. What it took to prepare the walls, to make them as smooth as marble, how the artist had sketched through the night so he could paint in daylight, so he could get the colors right. How his woman had paced on the wooden scaffolding, watching, waiting. How all kinds of people had helped to make this painting, people whose names they would never know. But he kept quiet, stayed at the margins of the room, thinking maybe he would stay and talk to the tour guide after the children left. Maybe he could come down and volunteer at the museum. Maybe he could learn to be a tour guide. But later, when he mentioned it to someone, Ilo, one of the men he ran into at the Jewish Center, someone he knew at the grocery store, they said he was crazy for thinking such things. "Drive down there? It's like a war zone," people said. The murder city.

Sometimes, he didn't tell anyone about this, he drove around the old neighborhoods. Where Hastings Street used to be, now replaced by the Chrysler freeway, I-75, not far east of Woodward. And he went into the old Dexter-Davison neighborhood, driving past the brick houses where he and Ruth used to live across from each other, where the whole block could hear her family screaming at each other in the summer when the windows were open. It had been stunning, the din that came from that house with its airplane rides and knuckle punches.

Ghosts. Sometimes, when he drove through the streets, he'd see a pile of rubbish in front of a house, or in front of one of the two- and four-family flats: sofas, chairs, dressers, bags and boxes trailing unidentifiable contents, rain-soaked and filthy. In some places, side-walks had been removed and never replaced. Children clambered over rubble. Some homes had been abandoned, neglected. Others had col-lapsed and the rubble trucked away, so there were empty lots, like the one on Fairfield—where he and Joanna had found the first broken bi-cycle. But that was different. Back then, their empty lot had been a space waiting to be filled.

On the Grand River and Joy Road stretch, his old building still stood with the front intact, minus the window, and with the roof and back caved in. That front, with nothing behind it, was like the fronts of the suburban homes they'd gone to look at, when all that construction had been underway. But, again, the two fronts were different, as the one marked a beginning, while the other, something concluded.

Once they'd made the decision and the down payment, he and Ruth and Franny used to drive out on Sundays and watch their own front and all the rest of the new house go up. One day, in the fall, around Halloween, when the stairway had been installed, they climbed it together. They looked out the windowless window frames at the empty lot across the street where a basement was now being dug, and a steam shovel and backhoe stood in the middle of the muddy, treeless field, not an autumn color to be seen anywhere, in the place where the tree-filled lot with the guppy pond had been only a few months before.

While Ruth and Franny stayed upstairs, Harry went down. He stood on the bare, rutted ground that would soon be a sidewalk and front lawn, and he took a photo of them looking out through the window frame, the peak of the roof sketched in with lumber but the whole open to the sky. He still had that photo. Somewhere. Ruth would have known where to find it.

The fabulous Riviera (or Iviera, as Ilo liked to say) still stood on the corner of Grand River and Joy, with its four-story vertical marquee. Now it was abandoned, its fabulous arched windows broken, trees growing through the roof, doors chained. Who knew what had become of its innards—the grand lobby with the marble staircase, its auditorium that looked like an Italian courtyard? The Grande was there, too, also abandoned. And further up Grand River was an empty lot where the Olympia Stadium used to be, the place where Joanna and her friends had screamingly watched the Beatles perform, and he saw three seats, discarded in the weed-strewn lot, a tire propped up against the end one and other tires lying in the weeds around them. At this, he stopped the car and leaned his head against the steering wheel, his eyes closed.

Downtown, Woolworth's had closed, as had Hudson's. Stroh's Brewhouse and Uniroyal were closed, but part of the Uniroyal façade still stood, another empty stage prop, its wires and steel beams exposed through its empty window frames.

Everywhere he looked, he saw various stages of repair and decay. The world was served up as a spectrum from marvelous to ravaged, with an infinite number of way stops and combinations. People's bodies, a building, roads, a house, cars, even car parts (mufflers, radiators, tires), items in his own refrigerator (a piece of apple pie left too long, a hunk of cheese), tree stumps, relationships. You couldn't say that anything was just one way (decaying or rebuilding, on the upswing or the down, dying or surviving). It all depended on the moment, and on where you looked. It was a matter of proportion. He'd see a detail on the crown of a building, marvelous, left over from its glory days in the twenties, while at street level, a sloppy hand-painted sign or heavy metal grate, even barbed wire, covered its face. Or something could look beautiful on the outside—a woman, a tree—and inside, there was sickness, something growing that was also destroying. This was what he had come to understand about the world.

"Don't go," Lena said. She passed the watermelon to Joanna. She took a napkin from the napkin holder. She passed the peaches. She got up to coax Harry back to his seat at the table. "Tell about that day in the shul."

"Oh, that," Harry said. He wasn't sure how to tell it. He sometimes made a joke of it, painting himself as the pious fool, stumbling out into the heat with a stupid grin "like I didn't know what hit me."

And sometimes before, when he told someone about it, his listener stopped him in mid-sentence: "Didn't you tell Ruth about the shul?"

"Yes, of course I told her." And, he explained, she had listened, amazed that someone as goyish as him had stumbled into an orthodox sanctuary in the midst of a burning city.

What he didn't tell—oh, he'd told Ruth, but no one else—was that he'd wondered whether the building being saved had anything to do with that morning in the sanctuary, the prayer scrolls pressed into his heart and his mind, perhaps detecting some truer truth, some secret, beyond the one he thought he'd discovered. But Ruth had said no, probably not; that wasn't how it worked. They weren't stethoscopes. Still, he'd never forgotten that feeling, of being expected, led, and readied, everything implicit, everything emerging from some mysterious somewhere, him being simply who he was, and no questions asked.